DRESSED TO KILL

DRESSED TO KILL

Emma Lou Fetta

COACHWHIP PUBLICATIONS

Greenville, Ohio

Dressed to Kill, by Emma Lou Fetta
© 2014 Coachwhip Publications
Introduction © 2014 Curtis Evans. First appeared in *CADS* 67 (March 2014).
No claim made on public domain material.

Dressed to Kill first published 1941.

ISBN 1-61646-234-5
ISBN-13 978-1-61646-234-5

Cover Image: Woman in White © M-Image Photography

CoachwhipBooks.com

CONTENTS

INTRODUCTION

Emma Lou Fetta
High School Yearbook Photo

KILLER FASHIONS
THE DETECTIVE NOVELS OF EMMA LOU FETTA
CURTIS EVANS

I. MANNERS AND MURDERS IN THE
GOLDEN AGE OF DETECTIVE FICTION

IF ONE IS ASKED to think of Golden Age detective novels set in the fashion design world, English Crime Queen Margery Allingham's *The Fashion in Shrouds* (1938) surely comes to mind, but likely very few people have heard of American author Emma Lou Fetta's *Murder in Style* (1939), a detective novel set in the New York fashion industry that followed on the haute couture heels of Allingham's *Shrouds* by just one year. Nor is it probable that mystery fans will be familiar with Fetta's two subsequent detective novels, *Murder on the Face of It* (1940) and *Dressed to Kill* (1941). Yet the sophisticated mysteries of Emma Lou Fetta, like those of Margery Allingham, are noteworthy in that they clearly reflect the development within the crime fiction genre of the "novel of manners" style, in which authors place at least as much emphasis on the study of social customs and values as the matter of *whodunit*.[1]

This signal development in mystery writing was apparent to observers at the time, at least in regard to English detective fiction. In a 1939 article in the *Saturday Review of Literature*, "The Golden Age of English Detection," Marxist writer (and later Labour politician) John Strachey, after writing dismissively of the modern

---

[1] Another Golden Age (or near Golden Age) English fashion world detective novel that comes to mind is Christianna Brand's debut mystery, *Death in High Heels* (1941).

English novel, turned with relief to detective fiction. He concluded that in the hands of the best English crime writers, detective fiction was taking the place of the mainstream English novel: "Here suddenly we come to a field of literature—if you can call it that— which is genuinely flourishing. Here are a dozen or so authors at work, turning out books which you find that your friends have read and are eager to discuss. . . . I have myself little doubt that some of these detective novels are far better jobs, on any account, than are nine tenths of the more pretentious and ambitious highbrow novels."[2]

The detective novels that Strachey lauded in "The Golden Age of English Detection" were not those which placed primary emphasis on murder puzzles, but rather those which he believed displayed literary merits comparable to what he had once found in mainstream fiction. For example, Strachey took disdainful notice of traditionalist mystery author Freeman Wills Crofts, a former railway engineer, for what Strachey saw as Crofts' "bleak attention to the mechanics of the detective story" and "ostentatious refusal to have anything to do with literary frivols." The crime writers whom Strachey came not to bury but to praise in his essay were Margery Allingham, Michael Innes and Nicholas Blake. Of Allingham's *The Fashion in Shrouds* specifically, Strachey avowed that the novel, while not "her best as a detective story," was a fine piece of literary workmanship, with "really good social observation of a certain set which exists within the English plutocracy." Heinemann, the English publisher of *Shrouds*, struck a similar note in its blurb for the book, trumpeting that Allingham had produced "a convincingly realistic novel of modern times" and "a powerful modern novel which has something to say about the world in which we live."[3]

Traditionalist puzzle fans carped about mystery fiction more concerned with love interest and literary quotations than clue analysis, but mystery critics and reviewers for the most part were

---

[2] John Strachey, "The Golden Age of English Detection," *Saturday Review of Literature* 19 (7 January 1939): 12-13.

[3] Strachey, "Golden Age," 13.

enchanted by the manners school of detective fiction. Today such writing largely is seen by critics outside the community of detective fiction aficionados as the demesne of a handful of English "Crime Queens" (Allingham, Dorothy L. Sayers, and Ngaio Marsh), plus a few male courtiers like Innes and Blake. American detective fiction often is assumed to have contrastingly consisted mostly of tough, masculine tales by hard-boiled writers like Raymond Chandler. For example, in Lucy Worsley's regrettably superficial *A Very British Murder: The Story of a National Obsession* (the companion volume to the 2013 British television series), Worsley, a historian and BBC presenter, pronounces that "by complete contrast to the suave British sleuth, his American counterpart was tough." She then goes on to treat Chandler's hard-boiled P.I. Phillip Marlowe as representative of all American sleuthdom.[4] Of course, readers (if not necessarily BBC presenters) know that American Golden Age mystery was in fact a "gorgeous mosaic," with different types of detectives, including not only hard-nosed private investigators and no-nonsense cops but flippant gentlemen-about-town, prying spinsters and clever couples.

In the three detective novels that she published from 1939 (the year John Strachey's "The Golden Age of English Detection" appeared) to 1941, *Murder in Style*, *Murder on the Face of It*, and *Dressed to Kill*, Emma Lou Fetta introduced two bright new sleuths to American readers, fashion designer Susan Yates and assistant district attorney Lyle Curtis, and established herself briefly as a more-than-capable exponent of the manners movement in detective fiction, joining not only the British Crime Queens Allingham, Sayers, and Marsh but such American writers as Mary Roberts Rinehart, Mignon Eberhart, and Leslie Ford, who shared with the British Crime Queens a penchant for keen social observation in wealthy and sophisticated environments.

Fetta's debut novel, *Murder in Style*, was praised as "the first mystery story in the fashion business" (the reviewer either meant

---

[4] Lucy Worsley, *A Very British Murder: The Story of a National Obsession* (London: BBC Books, 2013), 279.

first *American* mystery story or must have been unfamiliar with Allingham's *Shrouds*) while her second, *Murder on the Face of It*, was lauded for its "smart, sophisticated New York background reminiscent of that of the play *The Women*" (Clare Booth Luce's hit 1936 comedy of manners about Manhattan socialites that was adapted into a classic film in 1939). When Fetta's third novel, *Dressed to Kill*, was published, the author was pronounced to have "joined the ranks of feminine mystery story writers who know what feminine readers like." Fetta's mysteries, it was declared, "had even more appeal for the ladies than the works of Leslie Ford and Mignon Eberhart."[5]

In a notice in the "Book Nook" of the *West Palm Beach Post*, a reviewer of Fetta's *Murder on the Face of It* summarized the unique feminine appeal of the author's crime tales:

> Emma Lou Fetta's mysteries are inevitably designed to appeal much more to feminine readers than to men. Here is the type of detective stories most women dote on: plenty of atmosphere and subplots, not too gory, all giving the impression of being a story with a mystery, rather than a mystery story. It is all generously flavored with much feminine froth—fashions, love affairs, intrigue. The mystery is finally solved by a knowledge of fashion designing."[6]

Shorn of some characteristic period sexism ("feminine froth"), there is much of truth in this judgment, I think, particularly the idea that Fetta's tales give the impression of being stories with mysteries, rather than pure mystery puzzles bereft of those qualities that Willard Huntingdon Wright (the traditionalist mystery writer S. S. Van Dine) dogmatically dismissed as "literary dallying" and "atmospheric preoccupations." The appearance of Emma

---

[5] *Milwaukee Journal*, 10 September 1939, 12; *West Palm Beach Post*, 16 June 1940, 2, 15 June 1941, 3.

[6] *West Palm Beach Post*, 16 June 1940, 2.

Lou Fetta's stylish detective novels between 1939 and 1941 indicates that the move in mystery fiction during the late Golden Age away from the "humdrum," puzzle-focused, traditional tale toward the manners mystery was not a phenomenon confined within the bounds of England.

II. EMMA LOU FETTA, FASHION AND FEMINISM

EMMA LOU FETTA was well-placed to write mysteries set within the New York fashion world, for when she published her first detective novel in 1939, she had been the "press chairman" of the Fashion Group, a New York body of female fashion professionals that promoted both the fashion business and the women who made careers from that business, since the group's founding in 1930.[7] At the time she joined the Fashion Group, Fetta also worked with the Rayon Institute of America. She published the book *Molecules to Modes: Sources and Uses of Rayon* in 1929 and during the late 1920s and 1930s wrote about fashion matters in a nationally syndicated column. Her professional life commenced in the early 1920s, when she started working as a journalist for the *Indianapolis Star* and the *Cincinnati Enquirer,* contributing stories on a myriad of subjects, including overseas news (she traveled extensively in Europe after the First World War, reporting on social conditions in England, France, Germany, and Italy).

Emma Louise Fetta was born in 1898 in the town of Richmond, Indiana, the daughter of Robert Henry and Ellena (Fulghum) Fetta. Robert Fetta, the son of a market gardener who in 1846 had migrated with his family to the United States from Germany at the age of three, was a mechanic and entrepreneur who patented a mechanism for use in steam boilers and founded the Fetta Water Softener Company. Ellena (Fulghum) Fetta was the daughter of Jesse Parker Fulghum, who was, like his son-in-law, a talented mechanic. Fulghum is said to have "taken out about forty patents, having

---

[7] The Fashion Group is still existence today. See its website at www.fgi.org. As in the case of England's Detection Club, the founding members-to-be of the Fashion Group began meeting informally at meals in 1928, forming an official organization two years later.

secured more patents on agricultural implements than any other man in the west."[8]

In 1917, Emma Lou Fetta graduated from Richmond High School, where she was a member, appropriately enough, of the writers' club, as well as the staff of the *Pierian* (the school yearbook), the dramatic society, and the school orchestra. Her yearbook photo reveals an attractive, intelligent and earnest-looking young woman. After graduation she took voice lessons in Rio de Janeiro, but her father suffered serious financial reverses, filing for bankruptcy in 1922.

With her parents no longer comfortably circumstanced, Fetta pursued a career in journalism and made a substantial success of herself. By 1928 she had moved to New York, where she worked with the Fashion Group and maintained her syndicated column. She also married advertising executive George Walling Minster of New York and Wilton, Connecticut, with whom she had a daughter. In New York, she kept as her professional name Emma Lou Fetta, though at home in Wilton she was known as Mrs. Walling Minster.[9]

In a 1929 newspaper article Fetta addressed a subject that clearly was of great importance to her: the rise of the professional woman in the United States. "The interests of [American] womankind are broadening," Fetta approvingly announced:

> It is no uncommon thing to find [at a New York woman's club meeting or party] an eminently successful woman lawyer, a well-known woman artist or sculptor, a celebrated actress, a prominent woman politician, a distinguished orchestra leader, a woman editor, a woman detective, a scientific woman

8 For information on the Fulgham family see *Biographical and Genealogical History of Wayne, Fayette, Union and Franklin Counties, Indiana*, Vol. I (Chicago: Lewis, 1899). On the Fettas, see *History of Wayne County, Indiana*, Vol. II (Chicago: Inter-State, 1884).

9 *Indianapolis Star*, 6 January 1922, 9; *New York Times*, 12 July 1935. Robert H. Fetta died in 1935 at the Wilton home of his daughter and son-in-law. At the time of his death he designed furniture.

farmer, women from advertising and publicity fields,
a woman broker or banker, women from manufac-
turing fields (all manner of these), and, of course,
doctors, scientists and experts in such work as tex-
tiles, cookery, employment, gardening, interior
decoration, office management or the like—or rather
the unlike!

Furthermore, she added with a fine feminist flourish, "the modern
woman specialist is not content to stop short at being simply efficient in one line or another, but . . . unlike the proverbial 'tired
businessman' who seeks relaxation in trivial interests . . . must
have her collateral important interests." Fetta specifically praised a
woman newspaper editor who had authored a children's book inspiring, "through the fairy story medium, an interest in cookery."[10]

Fetta's interest in promoting careers for women is evident in
her work with the Fashion Group, but also, most pertinently to
this article, in her detective fiction. Clearly Fetta wanted to enter-
tain with her mysteries, but it appears that she also wanted to
appealingly portray for her readers the world of women professionals. Moreover, not only do her books present readers with
extremely capable career women, they also offer a woman, fashion
designer Susan Yates, who is one-half—and the better half at that—
of a talented sleuthing team. Fetta's books succeed on dual levels,
providing interesting murder problems to solve while also offering fascinating glimpses of the lives of New York career women at
the close of the thirties and dawn of the forties. Although it is this
latter aspect of her books that prompted contemporary mystery
reviewers to brand them primarily feminine fare, in fact male reviewers enjoyed them too. For example, the influential Judge Lynch
(William C. Weber) of the *Saturday Review* rendered the verdicts
"excellent" on *Murder in Style*, "ultra-stylish number" on *Murder*

---

[10] (Huntingdon) *Daily News*, 10 July 1929, 4. Ironically, in the 1930s a
publisher's line of detective fiction was promoted as part of the "Tired
Businessman's Library."

on the Face of It and "slithery" (yes, it is meant as a compliment) on *Dressed to Kill*.[11]

III. Emma Lou Fetta and Detective Fiction

When commenting on the comparative skills of Emma Lou Fetta's series sleuths, Susan Yates and Lyle Curtis, a character in Fetta's second mystery novel, *Murder on the Face of It*, gives us what seems the author's own credo concerning her view of the relationship between men and women in the professional world: Women are just as capable as men, but should work with men, rather than try to supplant them. The character elaborates this philosophy as follows:

> "It seems to me it's about time you and Lyle decided you make a pretty good sleuthing team. Why don't you stop passing bouquets back and forth after every victory? Everyone who thinks women can't really do anything will say Lyle did it all anyway, and those who are so keen about women's rights that they forget men have any will say he never could have pulled it off without you. My personal opinion is a smart man and a smart woman can beat a single-sex approach any time."[12]

Susan Yates and Lyle Curtis first meet, appropriately enough, in Fetta's debut mystery, *Murder in Style*, in which death strikes during a meeting of the Tomorrow Club, an organization obviously based on the Fashion Group. As one of the members of the Tomorrow Club, Susan Yates is conveniently on hand when a sister member drops dead from poison at a luncheon round table (the set-up somewhat resembles Agatha Christie's 1945 detective novel, *Sparkling Cyanide*). Naturally the clever and curious Miss Yates soon turns amateur sleuth.

---

11 *Saturday Review*, 12 August 1939, 20, 51 June 1940, 20, 24 May 1941, 20. "Highly seasoned yarn of evil in Manhattan luxury professions," was how the Judge aptly summed up Fetta's *Dressed to Kill*.

12 Emma Lou Fetta, *Murder on the Face of It* (New York: Doubleday, Doran, 1940), 279.

The dead woman, Nancy Pierce ("a very vivid blonde") is one of those classic detective fiction murderees who seems to live for giving everyone she knows ample motives to compass her imminent death. Those with reason to wish Nancy Pierce ill include other Tomorrow Club members (besides Susan Yates herself, Lucinda Mason, Caroline Semmer, Vivian Peabody, Hortense Culbertson, "five delightfully dressed women...famous in America wherever fashions were worn"); Tom Benchley, the Club's newly-hired public relations man; Howard Pierce, Nancy's lawyer spouse; Linwood Semmer, a society doctor; and Ethan Van Weck and Colonel Stanley Gamberson, a husband and a fiancée, respectively, with whom naughty Nancy may have been canoodling. Then there is the ripe redheaded receptionist Ruby Holt, waiter Mike, and bartender Lucien—just what do they know about these high hats that they are not telling?

Susan Yates has reason not to like the envious and nasty-minded Nancy Pierce, who has been poisonously gossiping about her all around town:

> "I always say Susan Yates has the *most* interesting views, messing around with all those odd people, and anarchists and all. It's a wonder to me you do manage to keep best families and leading capitalists' wives. I mean, I don't suppose there'd be much money in making clothes for nihilists and people on relief."
>
> Susan counted three, holding her breath, and then she said calmly:
>
> "Nancy, I'm not an anarchist, nor a nihilist, nor a Lesbian. Please, for the love of heaven, don't go round telling people so."[13]

---

[13] Emma Lou Fetta, *Murder in Style* (New York: Doubleday, Doran, 1939),15. Earlier Yates complains to Tom Benchley, "Nancy apparently made up some fantastic tale about all my clients being queer. Got my nice dowager suspicious I'd begin making trousers for her any minute. Delicate thing to straighten out." Fetta, *Style*, 9.

Like the other women in the Tomorrow Club, Yates could not stand Pierce, but she cannot agree with others that Pierce's death was self-inflicted. "Women like Nancy drive others to suicide," she tartly observes at one point. "They don't commit it themselves." Soon she is looking into the suspicious circumstances of Pierce's death, along with her old friend Tom Benchley and a new man in her life, assistant district attorney Lyle Curtis. "A well-tailored man in his early thirties, who had level gray eyes and a pleasant, warm voice," Yates thinks when observing Curtis. "Behind the surface effects of good clothes and a cheerful manner," she senses that he has "quick muscles and a flexible, straight-thinking mind."[14]

As seen through the eyes of the waiter Mike, Yates has many commendable qualities herself: "Miss Susan Yates was Mike's favorite customer. Mike liked the way her brown eyes were set so nice and level in her face. She was a real lady. A famous designer, too. Made clothes for all the swells. Take the suit she had on now. No ordinary stuff. Green it was, the color of pine trees. Nice hat. The last word, of course, but not crazy like some."[15] It is the level-headed and keen-minded Yates who, with Curtis' help, ultimately solves the Tomorrow Club murder puzzle, though not before a second victim, this one unoffending, dies by another's hand.

Murder in Style is an impressive first mystery outing, with interesting and amusing characters and an intriguing, fairly-clued poisoning problem with good mechanics in its carrying out and emotional resonance in its solution. In Fetta's second detective novel, *Murder on the Face of It*, the setting and characters continue to hold reader interest, while the plot is impressively complex, comparing well with the magnificent convolutions of such puzzle masters as Christie and Crofts. In this tale Susan Yates is returning from France to New York (and Lyle Curtis) aboard the *SS Island of England*, on the eve of the German invasion of Poland. On board with her are two friends from *Murder in Style* (in an unusual twist, the pair, who were murder suspects in the first

14 Ibid., 47, 78.

15 Ibid. 2.

novel, again become murder suspects in the second one). During the voyage, Alma Peters, "empress of the American cosmetic industry," is found dead in her cabin, seemingly of a self-inflicted gunshot wound. Yates naturally is dubious, but officialdom accepts this suicide theory, given that the cosmetics empress seemingly had ample reason to do away with herself, as she was facing prosecution in New York for recently uncovered defalcations from her own company.

After Yates arrives in New York the mystery plot treads water somewhat, though empathetic readers will enjoy following the complications in the love lives of Yates and Curtis and reacquainting themselves with several other characters from the first novel, including the appealing Ruby Holt, who now works for Yates. When one of the passengers from Yates' voyage aboard *Island of England* is found slain in the apartment of another passenger from that voyage, however, a murder investigation finally kicks into high gear. Though Curtis plays an important role in the sleuthing, it is again Yates who hits on the complete solution of a complex series of crimes (in a pleasing touch the fashion sketches that are instrumental in Yates' deductions are included in the text).

Fetta's final mystery, *Dressed to Kill*, takes readers into the advertising business (the field of Fetta's husband), although this is not done with the same depth of Fetta's treatment of the fashion industry in her first two novels. The book opens in fine classical form with a skiing weekend house party of New York professionals at a New Hampshire country estate (complete with a proper butler, Baggs, and a comical cook, Mrs. Bumpet) owned by Lawrence Stratfield, dilettante artist and man-of-wealth. Stratfield's guests are Oliver Penbroke, president of the Oliver Penbroke Advertising Agency; Peter Sutton and David Barron, of the rival Sutton & Barron's Advertising Agency; Sutton's lovely and willful twenty-one year old daughter, Joan; handsome young Hinkle Conway, Joan's romantic interest and a copy-writer in Sutton & Barron's; Hazel Manchester, a "beauty-and-charm columnist"; and, last but not least, the novel's murderee, the beautiful and scheming Prunella Parton, another Sutton & Barron's copy-writer

(Prunella's half-sister, newspaper journalist Carol Parton, also crashes the party).

Prunella survives an explosion that wrecks her bedroom suite, only to be bludgeoned to death in the New Hampshire–New York Express Pullman car in which the house party host and guests were returning to New York (plans of both the New Hampshire country house and the NHNY Pullman car are provided). Lyle Curtis is brought into the case, the train having reached New York City when Prunella's body is discovered. No fool he, Curtis immediately seeks out the expert assistance of Susan Yates, poor Prunella having been found dressed in a most unfashionable combination of long woolen underwear and a dazzling red evening gown.

In *Dressed to Kill*, Emma Lou Fetta has fashioned another entertaining mystery with an impressively complex plot. There are some creative clues and an exciting finish (though somewhat disappointingly Yates tumbles to the identity of the culprit through a convenient coincidence). Throughout the novel Yates and Curtis are openly talking of marriage. I will let future readers find out for themselves just how the author leaves things between her two sleuths in her final published detective novel.

Unlike Margery Allingham's *The Fashion in Shrouds*, the mysteries of Emma Lou Fetta offer an unambiguously positive portrayal of the working world of women on the eve of the Second World War. Lyle Curtis is a man at ease with Susan Yates' professional and amateur sleuthing success and Yates does not see marriage as a blessed escape from career stresses, since she juggles detecting and designing alike with aplomb. As Yates, contemplating her scheme to ensnare a murderer in *Dressed to Kill*, thinks at one point, "she was used to taking chances. She had taken one chance or another every day of her life since she had put a pair of shears into a fifty-dollar-a-yard material to cut her first custom-made gown. She took a chance by being a businesswoman."[16] One might say that Susan Yates (and Emma Lou Fetta) dressed for success.

[16] Emma Lou Fetta, *Dressed to Kill* (New York: Doubleday, Doran, 1941), 258.

DRESSED TO KILL

CHAPTER ONE

ON SATURDAY AFTERNOON distant sleigh bells sounded sharp but lovely in the New Hampshire hills. The brightly sophisticated voices on Lawrence Stratfield's ski slopes vibrated tenuously as if born of the wind itself. All day snow clouds had been massing in the sky, but the storm had not yet broken. The sun was now about to set.

A little extravagantly turned out for her lack of skill on skis, or perhaps to offset that deficiency, Prunella Parton in virgin-white pants and jacket, a scarlet cap crowning her hair, climbed slowly up a short slope. To the man at the top she remarked:

"Those sleigh bells could be an arctic Pan piping for us, darling."

With ironic eyes David Barron studied her faintly oval-shaped ones before he said: "Can it be Miss Parton is feeling sentimental? You astonish me, Prunella."

Abandoning her seductive expression quite as she might have thrust a mask away from her face, Prunella leveled a speculative look at him. She made no immediate retort but laughed. It was an objective laugh, perfectly timed, exquisitely keyed. It might have done very nicely for an operatic aria.

Barron murmured: "The program to which you are listening is electrically transcribed." Then he laughed, and rather unpleasantly. "You do it beautifully, my dear. Very beautifully. A pity you didn't study singing."

"To improve my technique as an advertising-copy writer?"

"I meant to imply it might have made a singer of you."

"If I had it would. Surely, David, you are aware by now that I accomplish what I set out to do."

"Meaning specifically at this moment?"

"Meaning that if a certain vice-president of a certain advertising agency is reasonable I may be very kind to him. I believe in equity."

"In what?" David Barron's laugh was again scornful, but there was the faintest scallop of uneasiness around its edges. "Equity!" he repeated. "Try to postpone dying, my dear, until humor on tombstones has become fashionable—that is, if you fancy this extraordinary self-description as an epitaph."

A few yards away, apparently intent on adjusting his ski harness, Oliver Penbroke, president of the Oliver Penbroke Advertising Agency, bent lower, pinning both his ears backward in concentrated eavesdropping. He finished with the ski, chuckled softly to himself, rose and rested for a moment on his sticks, observing from a corner of his eye his competitor, David Barron, and Sutton & Barron's ace copy writer, Miss Prunella Parton. Then he gave his undivided attention to the slope.

Below, he could see his host, Lawrence Stratfield, looking up. Stratfield was one of those ugly men women find fascinating. Penbroke decided he better go down once more. Peter Sutton being so damn good at his age made it obligatory. And better put everything he had into the spirit of co-ordination. It wouldn't do to have Stratfield think him a dud at anything, not with matters at their present watch-spring point of delicate adjustment, not if it killed him to accomplish the contrary. But a shrewdly estimated descent could usually land you on your feet in life, and he, Oliver Penbroke, liked to land on his feet at all times and under all circumstances. He set himself for the descent and a few seconds later reached his host in fair style, rather pleased with himself.

Faithfully representing her profession of beauty-and-charm columnist, Hazel Manchester at Stratfield's side took her eyes from the pair at the top of the slide and said: "Very pretty, Mr. Penbroke."

Oliver Penbroke watched the course of her returning glance and once more chuckled to himself.

Their host was looking at the western sun. "Night," he said, "often drops with the devil's very own haste up here." Raising his unexpectedly high voice until it sounded like static on the sharp air, he shouted up to Miss Parton and David Barron: "Sunset. Time to go in!"

They waved that they understood, and Stratfield turned his attention to the lower slope and run where two men and a girl were outlined against the pale passion of the setting sun. They looked about the size of carved figures on a Bavarian roadside shrine. He hallooed his message down to them, then observed to Miss Manchester and the bulky Penbroke that Miss Joan Sutton had better look to her skiing style with pretty serious intent if she was going to keep up with such a talented father and a young swain as good as Conway.

Miss Manchester murmured: "But she's not at all bad."

"And not so good," Stratfield disagreed. "These youngsters today seem to think it's more sporting not to be good at sports. They're too damn lazy to exert themselves. They want to know what's the use of playing this or that game as well as some palooka."

"Oh," insisted Miss Manchester, but without too much emphasis, "I thought Joan Sutton awfully energetic, and she's only twenty-one." She smiled brightly at her host. "Anyway, Mr. Stratfield, you've got a perfectly beautiful situation here."

Encompassing the horizon with expressive hands, she proceeded to enlarge on this theme, pointing out that the country was marvelous, the snow magnificent and that she had never had a lovelier afternoon. Her tone was the proper one for a thoroughly ecstatic guest, but as she spoke her dark eyes traveled again to the pair who were now coming down the upper slope.

A moment later Miss Manchester's expression turned discreetly pleased. Prunella Parton had landed in an undignified crumple before them. Really she would have thought her much too clever even to put skis on if she couldn't do better than that. But doubtless Prunella was counting on having her impressive moments this evening, looking utterly lovely under the candlelight and dealing with slippery conversation instead of a ski slope.

Hastily Miss Manchester pulled herself together. It was sense-less to allow jealousy to unnerve her. She'd never be able to carry out her intentions if that happened. It was imperative to concentrate on the job at hand. Turning brightly to Lawrence Stratfield, she engaged him in bubbling conversation as they headed down the slope to Swiss Village Lodge, his unique New Hampshire house. But also Hazel Manchester watched Stratfield's ugly, sensual face and its carefully controlled expressions.

HALF AN HOUR later the group had been shaken apart once more. Along the upper hall of Stratfield's costly adventure into the realm of rustic simplicity closed doors stood guard. From behind their barriers came the faint sounds of well-bred people tubbing and moving about on the business of dressing.

With muffled footsteps and utmost dignity an elderly man servant appeared and disappeared. As silently, but because of awe, a rosy-faced country girl, elevated to the role of lady's maid for the evening, tapped at the ladies' doors, entered and closed them behind her with breathless care. Save for these servitor intrusions eight people remained for a time alone with their consciences.

First to come down to the great studio room on the main floor was young Hinkle Conway clad in dinner clothes and a dark expression. He went to the huge picture window which overlooked the valley and pressed a well-formed but rather too sensitive nose against it, presenting a life-size and far from puny picture of a young man with worries beyond his years. Although his broad shoulders and narrow waist bore witness to the fact that he was no child he looked, nevertheless, a brooding blond Viking yet untested by maturity but already fearing he shouldn't relish it.

The sun had set, but its afterglow lingered as if hopeful of guiding a night inclined on this occasion, and despite Stratfield's prophecy, to waywardness. White clouds of snow touched with rose and the deeper shadows of hyacinth lay over the hills which towered into mountains to the north, over the road winding up from the railroad junction and over the frozen river the course of which could only have been guessed if Hinkle Conway had been inclined to ponder the question. The valley's pulverized carpet missed the afterglow. Night had arrived down there and was slowly mounting the slopes. The sound of distant sleigh bells which had earlier reminded Prunella Parton's sharp copy-writing mind of a piping Pan of the arctic came faintly from the darkness below, becoming no more than a tinkling, mocking murmur in the pastel world above, fading suddenly into nothingness.

Conway shrugged his wide shoulders impatiently.

Immediately outside the window a hemlock caressed the pane with icy fingers. Like brittle crystals ice lay on it and on the pines beyond. But Conway was thinking neither of their beauty nor at the moment of the scene at all. He was thinking of two women. They kept getting tangled in his turbulent reverie, the one seeming so soft but, actually, fiercely determined, the other cruelly, shrewdly seductive.

Then suddenly he did see the ice crystals, and they instantly reminded him all over again of the second woman. Prunella Parton was far from brittle if by "brittle" one meant fragile and easily broken but, just the same, she was like exquisitely spun ice. And ice could kill. A legend from Solon, the Athenian, which he had read somewhere sprang for no apparent reason into his mind: the story of a man who had come out of a tavern one night and been deprived of his life on its very doorstep. An icicle falling from above had stabbed him neatly in the head. It had left no telltale weapon. Prunella Parton left no incriminating weapons about. She kept her arsenal on the tip of her tongue, in the sinuous quality of her beautiful body, locked behind the deeply lashed lids of her narrow eyes.

Conway played with these thoughts. After all, words were his business. He, too, was an advertising-copy writer. A good one. That had been the beginning of it all. Prunella Parton had discovered this his first day at Sutton & Barron, Inc. From the heights of her five years of experience her interest in his career had seemed natural. She could afford to be generous with advice. What he knew now was that she had never intended for him to shine one unnecessary moment. She would stoop to anything to prevent it. She was to do all the sparkling.

Accordingly, she had wrapped the black wings of pretended friendliness about him. Her pretext had even broadened shortly into an expression of attachment even more personal. He had been flattered. Damn it, he had been shattered. He had worshiped her.

Prunella herself, through boredom, no doubt, had unveiled the truth first. Joan Sutton had forced him to see it. But despite Joan's blond prettiness, despite her extraordinary energy Prunella was still in his blood. A cliché. And a rotten one. But fact.

Now Prunella stood in the way of his marrying Joan in more ways than one. Of course, she could hint things to the old man who would certainly not approve of a son-in-law who had had an affair with his ace copy writer. The old man was a Puritan all right. The bright wits at the advertising agency had adopted the French phrase for Sutton & Barron's atmospheric precedent: "Pas de scandale ici!" At least no scandal was allowed at Sutton & Barron which Peter Sutton could get wind of.

Of course, it was extraordinary the things David Barron got away with. Conway admitted he didn't like Barron. He didn't know exactly why. Because Barron was now in love with Prunella? Maybe. He shrugged. It was a foul world. Screwy. Better to have no looks at all and be dumber than hell. Then you might go happily on relief and escape all the frictions of ambition. That was the nuts too. You couldn't bury your emotions by such a program.

Outside snow was beginning to fall like a flat white window shade repeatedly unrolled. Behind its curtain the pink of the sunset's afterglow had disappeared, the hyacinth had deepened and darkened. The hills, the distant mountains, the valley were caught in a purple net the shade of coffin linings. Conway tried to shrug again, and it was more like a shiver, an angry shiver, the half-determined, half-self-disgusted reaction of a young man in the throes of vacillation.

Aloud he muttered, "Indecision's the most hellish thing in the world." He raised his arms, stretched and yawned. Skiing all afternoon made you dog tired. Why the devil hadn't it relaxed his tension? Wasn't that why people exercised?—to make their nerves and muscles function in better harmony? Or because it was fun?

Anyway, he was glad he wasn't a dud. No competition from Prunella on skis. She was awful. Poorer than either of the other girls, much poorer than Joan and not nearly as determined as the Manchester woman who had seemed bent on breaking her own neck if necessary to prove her sportsmanship. What was her first name? Hazel. A beauty columnist or something. Wrote for newspapers. Actually strong legged and pretty well balanced on skis though completely inexperienced.

Funny Joan wasn't better—with her dad so expert even in his sixties. It didn't fit in with old man Sutton's looks or disposition for him to be so good on skis—like finding a poodle a damn good conversationalist. But Joan looked cute whatever she did.

With profound agony he wished Prunella Parton didn't exist at all. If she were only a bad memory he could probably give Joan everything she wanted. In any case, he wanted to marry Joan. He would never want to *marry* Prunella. People didn't want to marry the Prunellas of this world—that is, nobody but rich old men wishing to make younger men envious of their possessions, wanting people to exclaim:

"Oh, see what a beauty, what a seductive beauty, that man owns."

Hinkle Conway felt suddenly a little ill. His stomach rumbled, and he decided he was hungry. Skiing made you hungry. He stretched again and wondered why the others didn't come down. There had been a lot of fuss about an early dinner hour and early sleep so they could be on the slide again first thing in the morning. He glared at the white shade of the falling snow. The wind was coming up, and the crystallized hemlock bough brushed with new persistence against the window.

"Damn her," he exclaimed, "if she just didn't exist everything would be all right."

OLIVER PENBROKE, acknowledging to himself that, after all, he was president and owner of the Oliver Penbroke Advertising Agency, outstanding competitor to Sutton & Barron, Inc., stood shaving before the bowl in his bathroom. His shaking hand brought to his attention the fact that he was suffering from a hang-over. He waggled a styptic stick over the cut on his chin, splashed shaving lotion onto his red face and returned to his bedroom where Lawrence Stratfield's butler had laid out his dinner clothes with precise orderliness.

"What I need," Penbroke remarked to the room at large, "is a drink."

He hurriedly finished dressing and, moving with catlike grace despite his bulk, walked to the door, opened it, went out, shut it and proceeded to the broad stairs. There he paused and listened to the subdued sounds of the house. A shower bath was running behind one closed door. A girl was humming moodily—or so it seemed to him—behind another. There was silence behind the door of his host's room at the head of the stairs on the left. But even if he were first down there must be a decanter or something in the lounge.

Having descended three quarters of the steps, he saw young Conway standing before the big window in the studio-lounge. The dispirited way in which the young man stood suggested not only dejection but positive irritation. Well, perhaps this was a piece of luck after all. Perhaps something of value could be squeezed out of the boy.

Penbroke knew that for the past half-hour he had been doubting his wisdom in having followed both a tip and a hunch in getting himself invited to this week end in New Hampshire. Now he wasn't so sure it hadn't been a good idea after all. He'd be able to carry on all right if Stratfield had plenty of liquor in the house. And Stratfield had seemed delighted to have him. Really exceptionally delighted. That probably meant that he wasn't turning all his allegiance to Sutton & Barron on the Kork-Petulla account.

The trouble was Prunella Parton. It was more than likely that Stratfield was inclined to give *her* plenty of allegiance. And advertising accounts had been lost before on emotional counts. Penbroke stood still at the foot of the stairs and quietly shook himself.

What he needed was a drink. He wasn't going to lose the Kork-Petulla business and the agency commission on a million dollars a year. Not he. Not Oliver Penbroke! Sutton & Barron could behave like a couple of thieves if they wanted to. It wouldn't work. And Prunella Parton could be a—well—she could be what she was for the moment.

At this moment young Conway gave vent to his violent exclamation directed straight at the big window. "Damn her," he said, "if she just didn't exist everything would be all right."

Oliver Penbroke absorbed this with both ears, then turned softly about on his panther feet, remounted a dozen steps, turned and called out jovially:

"Just you and me down so far?"

Conway spun around, his expression an obvious question mark as to whether Penbroke had heard his words. The other's face was so bland and innocent that Conway relaxed. He grinned more with relief than welcome.

"Nobody else yet," he replied, and grinned again less nervously. Watching Penbroke descend the stairs, he thought once more that the whole week end was screwy. Why had Stratfield invited the officers of two competitive advertising agencies to the same house party? Especially why when a battle concerning a million-dollar account was raging? Did he just like to see men knocking their heads together, emotionally speaking?

Penbroke came up and threw himself into a big chair facing the window and the ice-dipped hemlock bough. "Socrates," he remarked dryly, "drank tea made from hemlock. Always meant to look it up further. If it's our variety of flora Stratfield's got enough poison on his doorstep to take care of a Hitler campaign. By the way, Conway, they tell me you wrote that Bellcamp soup campaign for your shop. I liked it. If you could find me a non-hemlock drink anywhere around here I might even break down and offer you a job at my place on the strength of it."

Conway looked at him sharply and saw only the affable countenance of a big red-faced man. Despite a natural suspicion of the head of another agency speaking this way at this particular moment he felt flattered.

"Well, thank you, sir," he said, grinning again. "I'll see what I can do about the drink possibilities. Looks like a liquorette over there." He crossed the room and raised the lid of a console which turned out to be a phonograph. A second trial produced a radio also of modern design, and they both laughed. "I'll get hold of the butler," said the young man, and disappeared.

Going in search of Baggs, Stratfield's ancient servant, he thought, "But it's funny Penbroke saying a thing like that. He can't think I have any personal stand-in with the Kork-Petulla outfit." It was true that Sutton & Barron already had the oil company's face-cream account, but Penbroke had all the rest of their business, and all the rest of it must be worth at least one hundred and fifty thousand dollars a year in commissions. Penbroke must have a fair stand-in himself, certainly vastly more than a second-line copy writer in a competitive agency.

Maybe Penbroke thought he was a confidant of Prunella's, that he would know just what she had been up to in introducing Sutton and Barron to Lawrence Stratfield who was supposed to be a heavy stockholder in Kork-Petulla, who sat on their board and advised on the art end of their advertising.

Stratfield had struck him as a pretty terrible painter but he was known as a man who knew all there was to know about art trends. And, of course, Prunella had planned to use him as an influence for Sutton & Barron, Inc. Stratfield was an old friend of hers.

Outside the butler's pantry door Conway stopped dead. Perhaps Penbroke *had* heard what he had been muttering to himself. But he hadn't mentioned Prunella's name. Just the same, the grapevine telegraph system in the advertising business was efficient. More than likely Penbroke knew all about the way Prunella had played hot and cold with him.

If Penbroke knew what Prunella had been up to he obviously had reasons for not liking her much better than he did. Conway frowned. It certainly would not endear him to a future father-in-law to pull out of his firm and go over to his most hated competitor at this of all moments.

SIMON BAGGS was addressing an audience of one. The audience consisted of a large saffron-faced woman who was weeping noisily and dabbing at her eyes with the corner of her cook's apron.

"Mrs. Bumpet," commanded Baggs in a cracked old voice, "I'm not saying that it may not be I am in agreement with you, but what I am saying is that with a dinner for eight to cook it is unwarranted to start crying and talking about the smell of death."

Again Conway stopped dead. Neither speaker nor audience had as yet heard him enter the pantry.

With another noisy sob the cook said: "But, Simon Baggs, I'm tellin' you I ain't one to smell death a-comin' and be wrong. I can hear the wings too."

"That," disapproved Baggs, "is foolishness, Mrs. Bumpet. I give you credit, being a cook, for a good nose. Hearing wings is something else again—" Then the butler saw Conway and ended his brief oration in midair. "Mr. Conway! Can I help you, sir?"

"There's a gentleman in the lounge pining for a drink. I wouldn't say no to one myself."

With surprising speed for his years the old butler moved into action. Libations would be brought at once, he promised. The cook, muting her sobs, turned back to her kitchen. Conway retraced his steps to the hall and encountered their host descending the stairs with a loose, big-boned gait.

"Well, well," Mr. Stratfield cried in his rather surprisingly high voice. "You've beaten me down, young man?"

Conway explained about Penbroke's request for a drink and what he'd been doing about it.

"Splendid, splendid," approved Stratfield. "It is our sovereign right as gentlemen to get a little ahead, so to speak, of the ladies. Let us proceed to do so." They went into the lounge together and were greeted by a jovial shout from Penbroke. From that moment on Penbroke kept acting, Conway thought, like a man who has cut himself a slice of someone else's cake and is determined to enjoy it no matter the consequences. Conversation switched about a bit and then centered on Conway himself and his skill as a skier.

"You know your stuff, young man," insisted Stratfield. "It's a pleasure to watch you. Glad to have you up here any time. Do you play golf too? That's our summer sport here."

Conway shook his head.

"You do, Penbroke?" Stratfield turned to the elder man.

"I go round."

"In the low eighties, I've heard. Don't be so damn modest."

Looking from man to man, the thought persisted in Conway's head that something was up he couldn't lay a finger on. It was as if they were all talking automatically while thinking of quite different things.

Then Baggs came in from the dining room wheeling a portable bar. Stratfield instructed him to put it near the fireplace and went over to mix their highballs.

The ensuing conversation between the butler and his employer was clearly audible to both the men left at the window.

"I'm sorry, Mr. Stratfield," piped Baggs, "for the delay. Just after Mr. Conway requested highballs Mr. Sutton rang for some assistance with his tie, sir."

Stratfield chuckled thinly. "All right, Baggs. I'll mix the drinks. You needn't officiate in here until the ladies come down."

The butler hesitated. "Mr. Stratfield," he began again, "there's a bit of trouble in the kitchen. Cook claims she smells death around. It puts her off her cooking."

Stratfield emitted a high, explosive laugh. "Smells death? What rot! Tell her to smell the chickens cooking and to make certain we get brown gravy, not that sickening white mess she sometimes fancies."

"Yes, Mr. Stratfield, but it does put her off," piped Baggs, and closed the door firmly behind him with the air of one determined to do his utmost in protecting them from the cook's olfactory findings.

Stratfield returned his attention to the drinks, and Conway asked Penbroke: "Can I bring yours over, sir?"

The big man leaped to his feet with singular grace and clapped Conway on the back. "No, you young pup. I can still walk even if I can't ski the way you can." Together, with Penbroke's arm casually around the younger man's shoulder, they walked over to their host.

Stratfield pointed to the filled glasses and raised his own. "To the missing ladies—and Sutton and Barron."

"I'll take the ladies," boomed Penbroke, and filled the room with a rocking laugh. "The missing gentlemen are my competitors. Never drink to competitors—misguided notion. The best man doesn't always win in this worst of all worlds. Lot of silly talk our fathers and grandfathers engaged in. Didn't believe it themselves, of course." He laughed again resoundingly.

Stratfield laughed also, a high laugh, squeaky like his speaking voice and a seeming contradiction of his big bones and ugly, top-sergeant sort of face, as contradictory as finding a great Dane possessed of Pekingese qualities. "To the ladies, by all means, and no business until Monday," he said. "This is a week end devoted to pleasure, nothing but pleasure." He seemed to like to repeat any phrase which caught his fancy.

"Really? Is that a rule of the house?" boomed Penbroke. "I was just about to do a bit of proselytizing with our young friend here. Thought I might like to steal him from Gentlemen Sutton and Barron. Liked a soup campaign he wrote."

Conway thought he ought to say something and said: "I'll certainly keep it in mind, sir, providing you do and providing I ever get the gate from my outfit." He knew it sounded smug and a little precious, but what else could he say?

Stratfield turned his sharp eyes on the young man. "You won't get the gate," he observed, "if you marry into the firm."

Conway knew Stratfield had telephoned Joan to ask her to come for the week end with her father. She had made no bones about her desire to have him included when Stratfield had suggested it but she had asked him not to tell her father she had had anything to do with it. He didn't seem to be exactly guarding the secret now of how things stood between them. However, Joan had no right to expect people she didn't even know to keep her secrets. She had a way, all right, of expecting her word to be law.

While this was flashing through Conway's mind Penbroke saved him the necessity of answering Stratfield by exclaiming: "Oh, so that's the way the wind blows, is it? Then I'd have a little difficulty in stealing this young man as a soup expert, eh?"

"You never know, sir," said Conway, looking uncomfortable and feeling, as he admitted to himself, an ass.

Doubling over in a laugh, Stratfield managed to look exactly like a jackknife half closed. Despite his bigness he tended to appear thin, and Penbroke's bulk accentuated this. He undoubled and moved expressively the only beautiful things about him, his hands. They were a painter's hands certainly, or a pianist's or a surgeon's.

"I apologize if I've let a cat out of a bag," he said, diminishing his laugh to a chuckle. "Maybe we ought to have another drink." He drained his glass and reached for theirs.

While he made the drinks he chuckled once or twice, again looking sidewise at Conway as if the little episode were exceedingly funny. Conway did not agree. He felt annoyed.

CHAPTER TWO

PETER SUTTON, his snow-white hair damp from the shower he had taken, had explained to Simon Baggs that it was inexcusable for a man of his years to be incapable of tying his own bow tie but that it was like skiing. One had to learn young. If one did not then one never did. He had given a brief, humorless laugh revealing no inner amusement and began to polish his eyeglasses.

Peter Sutton essayed humor because he felt it one of the elements wisely introduced now and again into communications with fellow beings. That was what he told them at the agency. Never introduce humor into an ad for the pleasure of doing so. Use it solely to make other people buying-conscious. He was also fond of pointing out that business was not a "game." It was a "process of making money."

Simon Baggs, with intuitive understanding, had done what he had sensed was expected of him. He had not laughed but had said sedately:

"Very true, sir. Thank you, sir," and retired, leaving Peter Sutton alone with his reflection in the mirror.

The president of Sutton & Barron put on his glasses and surveyed himself for a long moment. He had been sorry to take off his ski clothes. It was something at his age to be better at a sport than the average man half as old. But, then, he had evidently been a natural skier. Even as a boy and a novice on winter holidays in Switzerland he had shown great promise. And he had had the best teachers in the world.

But thinking of Switzerland was unfortunate. It revived acutely the memory he had been trying to forget for nearly thirty years. Nineteen-eleven it had been. Seeing that boy fall. Hearing his wild, smothered cry for help, the flat slap of his body hitting the snow. No, he couldn't actually have heard the fall. It had been soundless. But it would have been absurdly dangerous to have gone to his rescue. They both would have been lost; nothing would have been gained. They had been quite alone, too, he and the other young man whose name he had then not even known.

No matter the bitterness of knowing his name years later. That was fate. An evil fate. Yes, one had to believe in fate. His whole life proved it. And it would not have made the other matter right even if he had saved the then nameless young man. The other disgrace had already been accomplished.

Peter Sutton turned to the window but found no solace in the purple snow-curtained night. Snow! Snow! How ironic that in it he excelled at a sport.

How quickly the other boy had sunk from sight those years ago. Almost instantly the deep drift had swallowed him up. Sometimes he, Peter Sutton, still woke in a cold sweat at night from the dream which had haunted him all these years. It was a stark white dream, always white. Sometimes there was a tombstone bearing the legend: "Here Lies Peter Sutton, Coward." Ridiculous, of course. Fine skiers couldn't be cowards. And yet he was. There were things in life he couldn't face. He could ski because the dangers of it came suddenly. One did not have time to think. One acted in self-preservation. Facing ridicule, enduring criticism were quite different. He could not possibly have let anyone know he had stood there, not fifty yards away, watching a young man buried alive, drowned in snow. That was why when he had discovered his own courage lacking he had not gone for help from the others further down the mountains. They would have asked:

"But why come back to us? Why didn't you do something? He may be dead by now. Are you sure you can find the spot again?" Why? Why? Looking at him as if he were a coward—because he was a coward. No, he hadn't gone for help. He had run away and later, hiding out on a safer level until it was quite dark, he had returned to the inn with a story of his heroism.

Not that *he* had called it that, but even the pretty girl, who was engaged to the missing boy, and her mother had told him with tears in their eyes of their gratitude. Still, with the indelible imprint of the drift which had swallowed the other boy in his mind, he had been able to tell a convincing story. He was late, he had said, because he had missed that chap, "what's-his-name." Hadn't seen him but had fancied he'd heard someone call out. He had looked and looked and stayed out, as everyone agreed, until it had been extremely dangerous. Everyone had extolled him while pitying the other young American.

In a state of self-exasperation with which he was fully familiar Peter Sutton glared at the purple night. The same hemlock beckoning at the picture window below in the lounge was scratching with another icy finger at his bedroom window. It was an irritating sound. He turned his back. Why apologize to himself for himself? He was a success. He was president of one of the world's greatest advertising agencies. They carried millions of dollars' worth of billing. They were known for brilliant art work, for brilliant copy.

This thought led nowhere—or rather, it led directly and devilishly to Prunella Parton. A queer, frightened look crept into Peter Sutton's eyes. Fate was certainly the greatest playwright. Far more subtle and insidious than man. What playwright would have thought to bring Prunella Parton into his office that bright spring morning five years ago? She had preceded herself with a brief note saying who her father and mother were. He had been unable to refuse to see her.

She had come in with a scheming look on her beautiful memory-prodding face, and when she had finished speaking he had known that he would be a coward again. He couldn't undergo what she offered as an alternative. After so many years of living with himself he knew before he did it what he would do. He couldn't face scandal. He couldn't face critical, amused glances in other men's eyes. Better to be blackmailed. That was what it amounted to. Yes, and it was all he had had the courage to do. Beyond it was a blank wall which his Narcissan nature could not climb. He knew he could manage to live with his conscience, but not in a world which did not highly regard him.

There were footsteps outside his door and a quick tap on it. Peter Sutton started, composed himself and called: "Who is it? Come!"

The door opened, and a girl in her early twenties, lovely in yards of yellow chiffon, came into the room laughing. Mr. Sutton regarded his daughter from behind his sparkling eyeglasses.

"Dad," she said, "how am I doing?" and pirouetted for him to admire her frock.

"You look like a Narcissus," Peter Sutton replied without in the least meaning to imply that she was a chip off the old block. But it was true, and he thought of it after speaking. Joan, his lovely little Joan, was entirely and utterly in love with herself. Many Echos would probably have to fade before her demands for self-projection. That young pup in his copy department! How did he hope to manage a girl like Joan? He wasn't at all the chap for Joan. Besides, there had been Conway's affair with the Parton woman. Under the circumstances Peter Sutton had been unable to say anything, to do anything, to appear to know anything. His hands had been tied as securely as if with steel bands. As long as he lived, as long as Prunella Parton lived, she would hold the whip. He wrenched his thoughts outward, listening to what his daughter was saying. Good God, she was talking about that whippersnapper Conway. Why the devil had Lawrence Stratfield invited him?

"What did you say, Joan?"

"I said I wished you'd be awfully nice to Hinkle Conway this week end. And, really, Dad, he has simply scads of talent. I've tried to tell you a million times that that Prunella Parton holds him back, keeps him from showing the stuff he's got, and you let David Barron push her forward all the time. How can Hinkle prove himself?" Deep in Joan Sutton's eyes hovered a look of sharply distilled hatred. Peter Sutton saw it and was afraid.

"You don't understand these things. Must I remind you that in experience you are still a child and really not in a position to run my business?" He tried to sound jovial, even a little capricious. It didn't come off, of course.

Like a scarf which she could retrieve in a moment, Joan dropped the subject, pirouetted once more and laughed.

"What is she laughing at?" thought Sutton. Joan was deep and she had a capacity for hating. He wished she didn't have. There was no hate equal to blood hate. He looked at her sharply, but the anger in her eyes had vanished. She was playing up to him now, consciously trying to make him forget whatever it was he was thinking. It was a trick, he had noticed, that women had. Perhaps they were no better than men at reading people's minds but they guessed with such uncanny skill. They were fiendishly good guessers. Clever ones like Joan always seemed to know the diplomatic time to induce a man to change his thoughts. Joan had been good at it when she was actually a mere child. When she was twelve or thirteen. He had thought it was because she had no mother, because everything had to be projected against himself as the single parent, but it was more than that; she displayed a premature astuteness about men in general when it pleased her to exhibit it. Probably it was just the female in her, a woman's self-satisfaction in being able to lure a man from one mood to another. Women fundamentally were no good. They were a bad lot. They had caused him enough trouble. But he shouldn't be classifying his own daughter in this degrading way. His blood did flow in her veins. But, then, so did her mother's.

Joan's father walked toward the door and held it open. "Shall we go down? Stratfield is having dinner early so we can be in bed seasonably and on the slide in the morning right after sunrise."

On the stairs Peter Sutton said: "I want you to learn to ski better, Joan. Next year I shall get you the best instructor in the country." It did not occur to him that one reason for his daughter's self-absorption was the fact that she had always been told she must have the best of everything, with the obvious inference that nothing was too good for her and few things good enough.

HAZEL MANCHESTER, in black velvet, looking like a dark, tall young woman plucked from the Middle Ages, had been dressed for half an hour. She had watched the sun set and watched the afterglow. She was bitterly unhappy, but the beauty of the evening and the plan forming in her head had given her a kind of solace. She had heard the sleigh bells, too, and they were still tingling in her ears. She turned from the window, looked around the big bedroom which her host had allotted her and thought that if she were going to accomplish what she had come to do she must rid herself of her present mood. There was such a lot to think of. It was of utmost importance, first of all, really to attract Lawrence Stratfield. He was vulnerable. Driving up in the sleigh from the station she had felt his body sliding closer to hers with every turn. Perhaps he simply thought she had interesting bones he'd like to paint, but she thought that though he fancied himself as a painter he was more interested in ladies as women than as models. With a little luck she'd get somewhere. It was an ideal time for the whole plan. David had known her so long he would never guess she was up to anything. It was both a liability and a virtue to have known a man all your life. He was rarely likely to see you as the seductive wench you flattered yourself you were but, on the other hand, he did not see your tricks of trade. He thought of you still as a youngster, a little girl who hadn't known anything, whose naïveté had been a fact and not a principle. Long acquaintance created a number of pleasantly blind spots. What she had to do with David Barron was to uncover some and keep others securely intact. It wouldn't be easy. At least, it had not been to date. But she had never had a campaign before, a complete program. And, after all, Prunella Parton wasn't indestructible.

Miss Manchester walked over to her mirror and surveyed herself critically. "Not bad. And why in hell should anyone expect life to be easy or nice?"

DAVID BARRON, vice-president of Sutton & Barron, Inc., was remarking to himself in the big bedroom to the right of the stairs that it was to be hoped everything would go smoothly. For one thing, the old man could never stand a scandal, and situations that went unnoticed in a business office sometimes had a way of standing out at a house party. Besides, Prunella was scarcely a shrinking violet. He had never known a girl so cocksure of herself. He frowned and admitted that the acquisitive instinct was strong and stark in both of them. But in any case he did not mean to lose. He laughed an unpleasant laugh. His Iagolike expression darkened thoughtfully. Then he heard voices outside his door, Joan Sutton's and her father's.

"I better go down," he told himself. "She'll be certain to take longer dressing than anyone else, and it won't do for me to be late too." Hurriedly he hunched his shoulders into his dinner coat and opened the hall door.

PRUNELLA PARTON smiled at her reflection in a full-length mirror in her dressing room. Stratfield had given her quite a pleasant little suite: a big bedroom, ample and well-equipped dressing room and her own bath, down a short corridor not connected with the outside hall. She wondered if the other women, the glandularly upset little hellcat of a Joan Sutton and moon-eyed Hazel Manchester, privately eating her heart out for David Barron, had been taken care of as well. Probably not. She had Lawrence Stratfield pretty well under thumb. What man couldn't she have with but a little trying? Life on the whole was singularly easy. Just take what you want and use the means at hand—or think up some. It was as simple as that.

Proceeding to the hall door, Prunella opened it first just enough to see out. It was instinctive with her never to throw a door wide.

Hazel Manchester was in the hall, about to descend the stairs.

Prunella shut her door and waited. It would be absurd to dissipate the effect of a grand entrance by sharing it with Miss Manchester.

CHAPTER THREE

PRUNELLA WAS STILL not down, but the others were strewn about the big lounge. Baggs was emptying ash trays. He paused at the picture window to straighten one of its side drapes and heard Joan Sutton saying to young Conway:

"It's ridiculous for Father not to know that David Barron has known Mr. Stratfield all the time. There's no sense in letting Prunella Parton get away with the credit of having engineered all this Kork-Petulla business."

Conway scowled. "Agency employees who know their place don't go around reading vice-presidents' mail. We can't tell your father."

Baggs moved away from the window.

Stratfield's voice rang out: "Ah, Prunella!"

Every eye in the room centered on the bottom step of the wide stairs. In exceedingly low-cut red velvet, Miss Parton stood there, the toe of one flame-colored slipper faintly visible, a short white hand resting lightly on the banister.

"Am I really the last?" she cried. "I simply *had* to watch the sunset afterglow. It was too divine!"

Stratfield went to escort her into the room, lending an arm for the grand entrance.

Joan whispered to Conway: "Should I curtsy or just hiss?"

Having delivered his last guest to the center of the scene, Stratfield turned to David Barron. Oliver Penbroke helped himself to another drink, looked across at Joan and Conway and started toward them but on the way became suddenly obsessed by interest in a magazine lying on a table behind Stratfield and Barron.

"He's too big a boy for that," said Joan. "He's eavesdropping."

"I hear our host plays a marvelous game of golf," muttered Conway, seeing the golden golf ball Stratfield held in his hand.

Joan wanted to know if he played with gold balls, and did Conway suppose he had managed to order a special heaven to be set aside for him too? Her eyes also were on the shining ball in Stratfield's hand.

"Must have been somebody's idea of a trophy," said Conway.

Turning the pages of the magazine, Penbroke heard Stratfield saying that his golf game wasn't half what it had been.

Barron took the gold ball, weighed it experimentally in one hand and handed it back. "Feels worth its weight," he said, and as Stratfield turned to replace his trophy in an open-faced cabinet Barron remarked: "My secretary was telling me yesterday that months ago, long before Miss Parton brought us together, I had a letter from you. For the life of me I can't remember what it was about."

Stratfield said: "From me? I don't think so."

At this moment Baggs announced dinner.

DINNER WAS A SUCCESS. Stratfield sat at the head of his table and maneuvered conversation with an invisible baton, providing each of his guests with a full measure of verbal orchestration. Even Peter Sutton's dignified countenance reflected a benign state of mind when they returned to the lounge. But then a peculiar restlessness descended upon them. It was perhaps Stratfield's fault, for he suddenly abandoned them to their own pursuits. He followed Hazel Manchester to the grand piano and engaged her in a low-voiced conversation as her slim fingers swept softly over the keys. David Barron began prowling about the room. Joan Sutton grabbed the stool before the fire which Prunella Parton had shown every intention of taking, and Penbroke threw himself into a big chair. Conway sprawled on a couch, glaring moodily down the pages of a book. Peter Sutton spoke for a few moments with his daughter, then turned to Penbroke.

Prunella Parton said to Joan: "You'll roast."

"Do you mind?" inquired Miss Sutton negligently, staring into the flames.

"Certainly not, my dear. It's your skin."

Joan made no further retort. Youthful and decorative in her floating yellow gown, she graced the stool like a fire nymph strayed from the flames themselves. The latter caught and held high lights in her hair.

Prunella shrugged and turned to listen to Sutton and Penbroke. Penbroke was saying:

"I hold with Sacha Guitry that most women think too much and reflect too little."

"Perhaps," purred Prunella, "they know better than men the futility of reflecting upon the unimportant."

Penbroke emitted a fat chuckle. "But you will agree with Guitry that the stupidest woman in the world who makes a man do what she wants is considered by other women a superior being?"

"If she circulates an adequate report of her success," admitted Miss Parton indolently. "But stupid people, Mr. Penbroke, want so little. They can always get that much from other stupid people. If you want more than a little you must deal with persons of wit and intelligence."

Joan Sutton interrupted. "Let's play murder," she called to Stratfield.

Immediately everyone demurred. "That dreadful game!" exclaimed Miss Parton. "With everyone crawling around on the floor and someone getting hit with the poker."

Hotly Joan said: "It's fun."

"Why not compromise with maturity?" called Stratfield from the piano. "Get them all to confess to their past sins."

Looking suddenly childlike, Joan giggled. "That's a smooth idea. You start, Mr. Stratfield."

"I should be boiled in oil for having no flowers for you ladies this week end. The florist didn't send them from North Conway. There's a blizzard raging down in the valley, Baggs tells me."

Conway dropped his book and wanted to know why they didn't confess to murders they'd like to commit.

"An enchanting idea," murmured Miss Parton. "Tell us about yours."

Cheerfully, Conway complied. "Certain competitive copy writers," he said, and hiccoughed.

"What a dangerous person to have around our agency," Prunella purred, and Peter Sutton looked as if they were all talking a foreign tongue. "What about you, Davey?" asked Prunella.

Barron stopped prowling around and said: "Cads."

"Too general," complained their host. "I think I could kill anyone who was being unkind to small children or very old people."

"Sweet," said Prunella.

Hazel Manchester struck a harsh chord. "I don't like people who grab things for the sheer pleasure of grabbing."

Prunella laughed. "You're all too amusing. But I can't play this game, because I don't believe in murder. Of course, I believe in self-preservation."

"Of course," observed Joan in a flat tone. "But couldn't you want to champion anyone but yourself?"

Prunella looked at the girl in flowing yellow and smiled disarmingly. "Have you missionary leanings, dear?"

Peter Sutton said he thought they were all talking rather foolishly.

"Blackmailers," proposed Oliver Penbroke, "are nice subjects for murder."

Again, as if they were all puppets propelled by some superior force in the room, general conversation ceased. Hinkle Conway got up from the couch and began to talk to Joan. Miss Manchester started an old Hungarian love song.

Penbroke said to Peter Sutton:

"I hear you golf, too," and they embarked on a golfers' post-mortem.

It might very well have been the opening of the first act of a drawing-room comedy. Then Stratfield rose and pulled the curtain down. "If no one wants a nightcap," he said, "I suggest bed for us all."

CHAPTER FOUR

PERSISTENT THROUGH the evening, the wind rose sharply after midnight. The hemlock bough, nagging at the picture window in the lounge and at Peter Sutton's west window, increased the tempo of its insistence. Somewhere in Lawrence Stratfield's rambling house a shutter banged irritably.

Baggs, the butler, stood at the top of the front stairs and decided that the banging was much less audible there. The loose shutter must be, as he had suspected, in the suite at the east end of the hall. He had traversed its full length to prove this point.

Reflected faintly on the paneling of the walls was one dim light near the front stairs. Another dimly illuminated the stairway leading to the servants' quarters on the third floor. This was almost directly opposite the suite door.

Baggs stood ruminating that he had put Miss Barton in the suite because Mr. Stratfield had said she was an old friend of his and very fastidious. The suite had its own dressing room and the biggest bath in the house, the latter being a two-year-old addition not actually over the kitchen, as the suite bedroom was, but over the driveway portico. It was reached from the bedroom by a short private corridor. The dressing room was on the other side of the bedroom. So the banging shutter wouldn't be in the bath. He wouldn't be able to hear it so plainly if it was, Baggs reasoned. It must be in the bedroom, though it might be down in the kitchen. But he doubted that. He hesitated. He didn't like to admit it, even to himself, but Mrs. Bumpet's claim of smelling death was deterring him from further investigation.

Standing considering the matter, another thought replaced shutters and death. One thing he and Mr. Stratfield's Filipino valet were able to agree about was the suite. They both felt Mr. Stratfield would use it if he ever married. Lately José, the Filipino, was left in New York when they came only for the week end to New Hampshire, but in the summer they had often spoken of the suite as a future bridal one. It was the Filipino's only sentimental thought regarding his employer. They had never been able to convince Mrs. Bumpet. She held that nowadays when gentlemen married they kept their own bedrooms like as how they did in Europe. Secretly, Baggs was a little put out with himself for agreeing with José about anything. José was a communist. And, having once been a married man, Baggs had more right to sentimental opinions. Also, bride or no bride, it was his own opinion that Mr. Stratfield ought to use the suite himself even now. It was the most elegant part of the second floor despite the bedroom being over the kitchen. But his employer preferred the sunny, thoroughly masculine room at the left of the front stairs. Baggs could hear faint sounds of snoring from its interior now and decided it was fortunate Mr. Stratfield had not been annoyed by the banging shutter. It was a marvel, though, that the young lady, Miss Parton, could sleep with such a wretched racket. But young people were like that.

Baggs started down the hall, still indecisive about what to do regarding the shutter. It had been a long, wearing day, what with seven guests, cook smelling death and him having to send the local maid home through the blizzard after dinner because Mrs. Bumpet had got her scared daffy with her talk. Walking slowly, he turned this and another thought over in his mind. If Miss Parton was sleeping through the racket it would be unwarranted of him to rap on her door and wake her, entirely unwarranted. He switched again to Mrs. Bumpet. It was entirely unwarranted of *her* to have got that foolish country girl so upset. Probably the girl wouldn't be worth her salt tomorrow, shying at closets and shut doors, thinking death was a kind of spook equipped by Mrs. Bumpet with giant black wings. But, as a matter of fact, everybody seemed upset this week end. They'd been talking murder in the lounge. Also, he'd had to tell Mr. Stratfield about the conversation Miss Joan Sutton

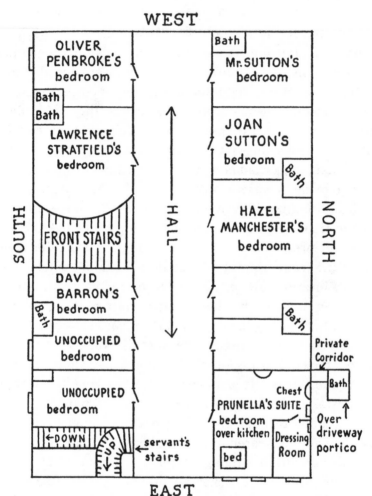

WEST

OLIVER PENBROKE'S bedroom

Bath

Mr. SUTTON'S bedroom

Bath
Bath

LAWRENCE STRATFIELD'S bedroom

JOAN SUTTON'S bedroom

Bath

SOUTH

HALL

FRONT STAIRS

HAZEL MANCHESTER'S bedroom

NORTH

DAVID BARRON'S bedroom

Bath

Bath

UNOCCUPIED bedroom

Private Corridor

UNOCCUPIED bedroom

Chest

Bath

PRUNELLA'S SUITE
bedroom over kitchen

←DOWN

UP

servant's stairs

Dressing Room

Over driveway portico

bed

EAST
SECOND FLOOR LAWRENCE STRATFIELD'S
NEW HAMPSHIRE HOUSE

and Mr. Conway had been having before dinner—about what: something about Mr. Barron knowing Mr. Stratfield better than Miss Parton did. Miss Sutton thought he ought to let her tell her father about it. Mr. Stratfield had said it was nonsense, that young people these days were always imagining things. Mr. Barron was a new friend and could perfectly well be put in the small bedroom at the right of the stairs. Baggs paused there now and cocked an ancient ear. From the silence, Mr. Barron seemed to be putting up nicely with the bed, though the butler felt it inferior to the one in the unoccupied bedroom next the suite. Perhaps Mr. Stratfield had thought it wasn't proper to put an unmarried lady and a single gentleman right next to each other—though he hadn't said so. He'd just said there was no necessity to make a fuss over Mr. Barron and he hadn't inquired where Baggs was putting Miss Parton.

Baggs proceeded on down the hall at his aged pace. He'd been glad to hear Miss Parton saying she didn't hold with murder. Probably a clear conscience was the reason she could sleep with a shutter banging right at her ear.

Baggs took four more tremulous steps and then, as he later conservatively estimated, lost ten years of his life.

The two sounds responsible for this came within a split second of one another, but the old butler was perfectly certain the pounding on the front door came first. Otherwise he would not have heard it at all, because it was immediately followed by something he could best characterize as the last trump of the angel Gabriel. In a flash he reasoned that it couldn't be the oilstove in the kitchen. Tonight he had checked it with special care because Mrs. Bumpet, when smelling visions, was not necessarily to be depended upon. However, despite her upset condition she had turned it out and banked the range. There should therefore be no cause for an explosion. It was unwarranted. Baggs felt very firm about that and equally shattered over the sounds flailing his ears. A second more he wasted wondering if he had become bereft of his senses.

As if to reassure him the explosive detonation was followed by noises which seemed to be a combination of falling plaster and a scuttling of human beings behind the closed doors.

Baggs stretched his ancient eyes down the hall. The door leading to the bedroom of the suite was open, crazily open, drunkenly
leaning on its hinges. There came another blast from below, and
both the light over his head and the one in the servants' stairway
blinked out. Doors were opening up and down the hall. His
employer's voice called imperiously from behind him on the other
side of the front stairway.

"What the devil is happening?"

A series of pops, bangs and splintering, cracking sounds pre-
vented Baggs from answering at once. Guests were crowding
around him, all talking at once. The pounding on the front door
had stopped. An odor of oil was heavy in the air.

Closer to Baggs's ear, Mr. Stratfield again demanded an explanation. In a quaking voice he explained his presence in the hall
and his opinion that the trouble was in the kitchen.

Someone lit a match, and Stratfield's voice said: "We better be
careful with matches. That odor of oil is pretty sharp. Baggs thinks
it is in the kitchen. I'll get an electric torch from my room."

A moment later the beam of a flashlight sent a pale, sharp streak
into the hall, illuminating unreally a collection of anxious faces.
Stratfield trained the beam past the stairway, down the corridor
where it picked up the crazily hanging door of the guest-room suite.

"Baggs," he demanded, "did you check that oilstove? I distinctly
remember telling you to every night."

"I did, Mr. Stratfield. I checked very carefully."

"We're all here but Prunella Parton," someone said.

"'Where did you put Miss Parton, Baggs?" cried the host.

In the tone of an uncomfortable hangman Baggs said: "In the
suite, and the bed's right over the kitchen. The dear Lord help the
young lady."

Stratfield said: "Damn the inefficiency of servants."

While Baggs was wailingly repeating that he had indeed checked
the oilstove Stratfield pushed past him, focusing his flashlight down
the hall. Penbroke, young Conway, Mr. Sutton and David Barron
followed. Mr. Sutton wore slippers but had not concealed his long,
old-fashioned nightgown. The other men were in pajamas; Miss

Manchester and Joan Sutton shivered in elaborately sheer night-gowns. Baggs, bringing up the rear in an ancient dressing gown, was the only one of the lot equipped for the most informal public view.

As the men advanced Hazel Manchester and Joan Sutton were left behind in the black hall.

"What a horrible thing to happen!" It was Miss Manchester's concerned voice.

"I was sound asleep," explained Joan through the darkness. "Am I hearing things, or is somebody pounding on the front door?"

Miss Manchester admitted it sounded like it. Neither one moved.

Miss Manchester murmured something about perhaps it was the fire department. Joan pooh-poohed this, pointing out that Swiss Village sported exactly nine houses.

"But it's past midnight—at least, I'm sure it must be," insisted Miss Manchester. "And no one would be calling in the middle of a blizzard."

"Well, you go down if you like," advised Miss Sutton pertly. "I'm not. That stairway reminds me of a nightmare I used to have. Can you see what the men are doing? Goodness, that odor of oil is strong."

Miss Manchester said it looked to her as if Mr. Stratfield and Mr. Barron had gone into the suite.

"Mr. Stratfield *would* give Prunella a whole suite," commented Joan truculently.

"It was evidently the butler's idea. Mr. Stratfield didn't know who was in there. What if Prunella's been blown up!"

"Well, what if she has?"

"Oh."

"I didn't like her, did you?"

"But you can't want people blown up in the middle of the night."

"Good as any time. Look, Mr. Stratfield's coming out. Let's go up there."

They groped down the hall. Lawrence Stratfield was demanding of his butler what the devil the racket was at the front door.

"Someone knocking, sir, I think," Baggs said unnecessarily.

"Has anyone got another flashlight?" asked Stratfield. Peter Sutton called out that there was one in his luggage and for Joan to get it.

"Go with Miss Sutton, Baggs, and then find out who, for the love of God, has decided to pay us a call at this hour of the night." Stratfield's tone was definitely hysterical.

After Joan and Baggs had disappeared into the blackness Hazel stuck her dark head around the suite door. Stratfield's flashlight played on a gaping hole and struck a pastel wall beyond, reflecting a faint glow over as chaotic a room as she had ever seen. Furniture was pitched about in utter confusion. In front of the opposite door a heavy chest was toppled drunkenly on its side.

Joan reappeared. "Have they found Prunella?" she asked.

"I guess not. There's a hole where the bed evidently was. It looks as if the whole floor might give way."

Joan peered over her shoulder. "Grim," she admitted, "but better than a slow death."

Miss Manchester said: "Prunella must be down in the hole."

"Look!" cried Joan, "they're getting the bed up. *What* a mess!"

At this moment there was a clatter of hurried footsteps on the front stairs, accompanied by voices. Peter Sutton's flashlight, waveringly held by Baggs, illuminated two young men and a girl in a tweed coat and a tweed hat.

From inside the suite Oliver Penbroke shrilled: "If she's down in that hole she's dead."

"Who's dead?" demanded the girl in the tweed coat, coming briskly up to Joan and Hazel. Her voice placed her definitely south of the Mason and Dixon line. She gave an impression of exaggerated nervous energy. Although she wasn't particularly pretty she looked interesting but also as if a moment's repose would be unknown to her. One of the newly arrived young men had produced a packet of matches and was lighting them one after another. They could manage to see each other fairly well now. "Where's Prunella?" further demanded the girl in tweeds of Hazel and Joan. "Lord, what a blitzkrieg! Oh, I forgot to say, I'm Carol Parton, Prune's sister."

She shrugged toward the two men. "We're all from the New York *Globe*."

Joan and Hazel explained that something had exploded in the kitchen. Prunella Parton was missing.

"How like Prune to manage to be right over an explosion!" exclaimed Carol Parton, peering with intense curiosity into the shattered bedroom.

Joan Sutton called out to Stratfield that Miss Parton's sister had arrived. Their host was helping Barron, Conway and Penbroke to pull twisted bedsprings up from the hole in the floor. He looked up, blinking into the beam of the flashlight Peter Sutton held.

"Miss Parton's sister?" he repeated vaguely. They laid the springs on a solid piece of the floor. Conway came over to the hall. "Oh, then it was you at the front door? This is dreadful. Dreadful. A terrible shock. Terrible. You must have heard the sounds of the explosion—" His voice trailed off, and he turned back abruptly to join the informally clad rescue party.

The other men were bringing up from the direction of the kitchen a mangled mass which might once have been part of a mattress.

"Turn the beam right down in here," someone asked Peter Sutton. He shifted the play of the flashlight.

David Barron cried: "My God! She's not there!" A general horror-struck murmur followed.

"Was she," asked one of the men with Carol Parton, "supposed to be in bed?"

"The rest of us were," snapped Joan Sutton.

Carol Parton held a wrist toward Baggs's flashlight and inspected her watch. "It would be on the early side for Prunella," she said energetically.

"Where else could she be?" persisted Joan.

"My goodness, yes, where else?" repeated Miss Manchester. Her eyes were on David Barron's back, bent over the hole in the floor.

The missing guest's sister spoke. "As a rule Prunella would be taking a reducing bath and dozing in her tub about this time of night."

The men in the bedroom turned and stared at her. For a moment no one said anything. In this momentary silence they all distinctly heard a moan.

David Barron wheeled sharply and cried: "It's coming from behind that door over there where the chest's fallen. Is that the bathroom, Stratfield?"

"The bathroom corridor. The bathroom's not over the kitchen. Thank God, she may have been saved!"

A hoarse gasp behind her at this moment made Joan Sutton turn. In the side glow of the butler's torch she could make out the red and frightened face of a big old woman in a long-sleeved nightgown.

"I knew it. I knew it," wailed the old woman. "The smell of death was plain as the nose on my face all evening."

Joan turned back to the room. Moving cautiously across the sagging floor, the men began to tug at the solid mahogany chest. It was a heavy pilastered affair and unwieldy, but in less than a minute they had it upright and began pushing it away from the door. When they got the door open their flashlights picked up a short hall papered in a gay figurine pattern. On the floor, lying on her face, was Prunella Parton. She was entirely nude, and her skin was glistening with moisture.

The two men who had arrived with Carol Parton sounded impolitely impressed, considering the circumstances. The red-faced woman behind Joan started to moan like a gigantic puppy.

Carol was bending over her sister. "She's only fainted," she announced in a tone of having predicted it. "Somebody, please give me a light to the bath. She must have had a robe or something in there." Disappearing down the brief corridor, she reappeared almost at once bearing a satin negligee. She draped it awkwardly over her sister. "Where'll we take her? I guess she'll come to in a minute."

"There's an empty room across the hall," said Stratfield helplessly. He led the way. Barron followed, carrying the satin-draped Prunella. Carol Parton followed him, and Baggs brought up the rear, bearing Peter Sutton's flashlight. "I think," Stratfield called over his shoulder, "it's safe to light candles now, and there should be at least one in every bedroom. Mrs. Bumpet, you come with me."

The red-faced cook moaned something about "the poor young lady" and obeyed. The others stood indecisively in the hall.

Presently two candles were burning in the bedroom opposite, then Barron, Baggs and Stratfield emerged. Baggs brought some more candles. The hall began flashing with dots of light.

Stratfield, looking completely rattled, said: "Baggs, go down and telephone the doctor. He has a sleigh and should be able to get over here. I'll see if I can get down in the cellar and find out what's wrong with the electric system."

One of the young men from the *Globe* said there was no use trying to use the phone. They had attempted it. The line was dead because of the storm. He made some more explanations: "We were trying to drive to North Conway to cover a ski match and were taking turns at the wheel. Carol was driving as we came through your village. The car skidded and damn near demolished itself. Some people we woke up said maybe we could borrow a car with chains at your place. Then Carol remembered that you must be the Mr. Stratfield her sister was visiting. We got a kid with a sleigh to bring us up here. Couldn't bribe him to go to North Conway."

Stratfield had paused at the head of the servants' stairs to listen to the newspaperman's explanation. "You are more than welcome to a car but you can't possibly think of driving through tonight," he said. "We'll get you off as early as need be in the morning." With that he disappeared down the stairs, calling back that if Prunella needed the doctor he would take a sleigh and drive for him.

Penbroke hurried after his host, calling, "I've got a layman's knowledge of electricity. Perhaps I can help."

Those left in the hall began general introductions of themselves, and one of the reporters asked Hinkle Conway if North Conway was named after his family.

Conway shook his head. "Matter of coincidence. Born in Ohio."

Then the cook came out of the opposite bedroom and announced that "the poor young lady" had come to. She was going to fetch her some tea if she could find any way to boil water. Answering her tone of lamentation, the hall bulb and the one on the servants' stairs flickered on.

PRUNELLA PARTON did not participate in the skiing the next day, and the other members of the house party went to the slope nearer ten o'clock than sunrise. Carol Parton and her male companions had gone off in a securely chained car in time to make the skiing match at North Conway.

Prunella's breakfast and luncheon were sent up to her on trays, but she joined the others for dinner, wearing ski pants, a sweater and the expression of a pleased survivor. But she said she couldn't stop feeling chilly.

"Nerves," diagnosed Miss Manchester.

"Shock," added Joan Sutton.

Everyone tried to sound sympathetic, but some way or other the atmosphere remained tense.

The investigation of the kitchen made by Stratfield and Penbroke the night before and by all the men that morning had not borne much fruit by way of explaining the cause of the disaster. The kitchen had proved to be a shambles. His own telephone still out of commission, Stratfield had sent Simon Baggs to the village at noon with instructions to phone the company which had supplied the oil burner. Sunday or no Sunday, he said, he was going to have a man sent over to explain matters. But Baggs had been unable to get an answer to his long-distance call. Stratfield had sent him back a second time with a hotly termed telegram, but, of course, being Sunday, no oil-burner expert arrived. Stratfield was in a fuming mood, expressing suspicion of all persons connected with the stove company and of their deliberate intent to blow up his house.

After dinner he offered Prunella the services of the maid to pack her luggage, but Miss Parton said she had packed a little at a time during the afternoon and had only her toilet articles to lock.

They had coffee with brandy in the lounge and scattered immediately afterward to their various bedrooms to prepare for the trip to the station.

On reaching the guest room in which she had been revived the night before, Prunella went first to the dressing table and stared long and intently at her reflection in the oval mirror and then she walked slowly to the little kidney-shaped escritoire in the corner and, selecting a sheet of note paper bearing the engraved heading of "Swiss Village Lodge," she took up a pen and began to write rapidly. She had finished her letter, had read it through twice and had written the first line on the envelope when there was a tap at her door. She went on hurriedly with the address before calling: "Come!"

Oliver Penbroke walked softly into the room. Miss Parton was licking the flap of the envelope. As he closed the door she looked over her shoulder and said:

"Well, what do you want?"

Penbroke stood with his back to the door, regarding her steadily. At length he said: "I don't know the whole story yet but I shall make it my business to. I have a long memory, Prunella Parton. I can remember way back to things that happened in 1925 and before. I can guess pretty good too. You'd be surprised how well I can guess. Maybe I've guessed exactly why you hate your sister Carol so much, why it amuses you to try to lure the Kork-Petulla business away from my shop. Well, maybe you won't. Maybe not." He laughed his fat jolly laugh.

"Get out!" Prunella's voice was low pitched and very angry. "Go on, get out!"

"In a moment I will. I want to leave a little advertising slogan with you, a cheerful thought for the day. I coined it myself. It's not copyrighted. It's—" But whatever Oliver Penbroke had been about to say was not said. A soft rap on the door tensed his big frame. The voice outside came faintly through to them.

"Could I come in?" It was Mrs. Bumpet.

Penbroke took a sharp inventory of the room and abruptly disappeared into the closet on the right. Prunella glared after him. Her eyes were furious, but she went calmly over and opened the hall door.

Mrs. Bumpet came apologetically into the room. "I was just wanting to see, as Mr. Stratfield told me to, if there was anything I could do."

Miss Parton dropped the envelope she had been addressing into her handbag and snapped the clasp. "Yes, Mrs. Bumpet," she said, "there's something very special I want you to do. Take me down to your kitchen and show me exactly how you make that perfectly divine salad dressing we had at dinner." Carrying her handbag tightly under her arm, Prunella eased the big woman out the door and closed it sharply behind her.

Oliver Penbroke came out of the closet, went to the door and listened, one large ear pressed against it. Then his eyes moved thoughtfully over the room, inspecting each of the five carefully packed open suitcases. Prunella's flame-colored evening gown and a fur capelet were in one, extra sweaters in another. One held a quantity of filmy underwear. In the fourth was a town suit. The fifth was a shoe box.

ON THE OTHER SIDE of Lawrence Stratfield's broad upper hall two men stood at a window talking. David Barron was chain smoking. His expression was agitated. Peter Sutton's face was as nearly as possible the work of a sculptor determined to show a man's physical qualities but to hide all vestige of his character.

"Miss Parton," said Mr. Sutton, "has expressed a particular interest in making this California trip. She did a good job for us with the fruit growers when she went out before. Didn't she, David?"

"Yes but I disapprove of her going at this particular time. I feel it would be an extremely bad mistake. We don't want to press those people."

"I'm sorry," said Mr. Sutton, "but I have told her she may make the trip."

For so apparently trivial an office matter, David Barron's face was a study in narrow-eyed intensity as he stalked from the room.

CHAPTER FIVE

IT WAS SNOWING on Monday morning in New York. A wind as hard bitten as a scandal monger's tongue was blowing. Fat white mounds were steadily growing on the eighteenth-floor window sills of Susan Yates's apartment. Someone was using a shovel on the terrace, a floor below. This unusual sound awoke Susan at eight o'clock. She opened one eye and quickly closed it.

Susan had spent all day Sunday at her salon finishing plans for her spring presentation. It was more than a week away. From now on she would need only to keep her eye on major matters. She felt due a respite. Both as America's premier designer of women's fashions and as a young woman who had a date for the theater that night she decided to take five minutes' more sleep.

In her sleep-drenched head as she dozed off again was scarcely the thought that she would spend her respite in and out of the district attorney's office. Lyle Curtis, chief assistant D. A., was handsome, delightful and a coming man, but Susan preferred seeing him away from his chaotically busy office. Although she had stumbled over two or three corpses in the course of her eventful career they were scarcely her specialty. She slept on peacefully.

At eight-thirty Susan was still asleep. When the phone began ringing she kept her lids screwed tightly shut. Sleep was delicious, telephones a nuisance. Whoever it was should call back at a more civilized hour.

The bell continued raucously. Finally Susan weakened, raised herself to one elbow and, reaching for the receiver, said:

"Hello"—rather childishly.

The steady voice at the other end of the wire inquired: "For the love of Mike, what were you doing? Sleeping?"

Susan remarked that it would seem a normal expectancy, and would it be too rude to ask if the assistant D. A. had lost his mind? It couldn't be more than five o'clock in the morning.

It was, she was informed, exactly thirty-two minutes past eight. Curtis said he had put the call in at eight-thirty. Two minutes had passed into eternity. And how did she expect to be at Susan Yates, Inc., by nine o'clock?

"I don't," said Miss Yates with asperity. "Can't the head of the firm get in late one morning? Don't tell me they've passed a law about it? As a matter of fact, I've overslept. I gave Lillian the night off. I'm too used to her waking me. What do you want?"

"I want you to come over to Grand Central Station. Under it, to be precise."

"How absurd. Why on earth should I do that?"

"I need your professional advice."

"I don't advise gentlemen on their clothes problems."

"Don't talk so much. Listen. We have a corpse with a fashion angle."

"A what?"

"You heard me. Fashion angle. Please, for the love of the Bill of Rights, throw on something and beat it over here. I have a strong suspicion the police are barking up a nutmeg tree. They've got suicide on their minds."

Susan became abruptly wide awake. If the police were talking suicide and Lyle Curtis didn't agree it was a clear case of murder.

"Where do I come?" she asked, putting one foot out of bed.

"Portal 39, upper level of the station. Sergeant Withers will be there to escort you to the Pullman where we're putting a jigsaw puzzle together upside down, in my opinion. Hurry, Susan, will you?"

"Be there in two minutes," and Susan rang off. This was a slightly optimistic promise. She had to dress from the skin out and was more than twenty blocks away from Grand Central. While getting out of her nightgown she phoned the doorman to have a taxi waiting. Without bothering about such niceties as a girdle or stockings, she leaped into a pair of pumps which demanded no hands to pull or tie, dropped undergarments and a street dress over her head, grabbed a hat, a coat and a beauty kit. In the taxi she did her complexion and combed her hair. Eight minutes later she stepped out at Grand Central, a picture of modish self-possession. Throwing the taxi driver a dollar bill, she hastened to Portal 39 where Sergeant Withers stood waiting. In times past he had both tailed and guarded Miss Yates. She greeted him warmly, but the sergeant's expression was grim.

"Mr. Curtis is going to shoot me if I don't get you over the third rails safely."

"Third rails?" gasped Susan.

"The Pullman's on a siding. Kinda hard to get at. No platforms." He led the way, and a now less-composed Susan followed.

They walked the length of a long platform and then, with the sergeant very much in attendance, began to cut across country in a fantastic world of third rails and signal towers, reaching at last a trim sided Pullman. Its shades were drawn and, from its outward appearance, it was abandoned by human occupants. Its name, Susan noted, was Briar Rose, if that mattered.

"Everybody's inside," promised Sergeant Withers.

If it had been anyone but the trusted sergeant and if she had been less certain of Lyle Curtis' voice on the telephone Susan knew she would have fled, third rails or no. To take courage by coming upon a darkened Pullman in this frightening jungle of converging tracks was comparable to seeking solace in a mysterious cave in darkest Africa. The distant signal towers suddenly looked far outposts of civilization.

Then Lyle Curtis appeared on the rear platform of the lonely Pullman, reached down for her arm and helped her up the steps from the track level.

"Good girl!" he said briefly, but his eyes said several other things.

Pushing open a door, he ushered her around the bend in the aisle and into a brilliantly lighted car thickly populated with

policemen and plain-clothes men. Green curtains were pushed back
on either side of the aisle, displaying berths from which sleepers
seemed only just to have departed. Ahead she saw the burly shoulders and big face of Detective District Commander James J.
McGluggish, known to her from what the newspapers had called
the "Murder on the Face of It" case six months before. He was
standing just outside a drawing-room door. He looked hot and
annoyed.

Eying the confusion, Miss Yates remarked to Mr. Curtis that
she would think he could use more space for doing a jigsaw puzzle.

"And a lot more imagination," muttered Curtis.

Susan looked up at him and saw that his face was tense as it
only was when he was on a man hunt and still without suitable
guideposts. Tersely he explained that a club car was being put on
the siding presently for their convenience. In the meantime, he
was going to ask her to take a look at the body.

Susan shivered inwardly but followed, edging past policemen
in whose eyes the blunt acceptance of a death seemed somehow
of itself unnerving.

A moment or so later Susan stood inside a drawing-room door
realizing, before her eyes fell to the floor, that death was there,
suspended in the heavy, hot air. Then she looked down at the body
and gasped. If on her way downtown she had observed the New
York streets covered with purple snowflakes she knew it would have
been no more astonishing than what met her eyes. With fascinated
horror she stared at the grotesquely dressed body. She wasn't sure
whether a psychopath's nightmare was any more fiendish than a
normal person's, but what she saw seemed to be the work of an
extremely disordered intellect.

The corpse had been a beautiful woman, not more than thirty
years old and now wearing, of all things, a high-necked, long-
sleeved, long-legged suit of underwear under a flaming-red velvet
evening gown. The latter was extremely low cut—the effect fantastic, to say the least. Susan gasped again and decided nothing could
be as unreal as familiar things seen in the wrong combinations.

When she got her breath she noticed the young woman's eyes. They were tightly closed. Lashes, long and extravagant, shadowed the dead white cheeks as if a painter had dabbed them on to embellish death with a final ironic symbol of vanity. Susan began to wonder about the eyes. Shouldn't dead people's eyes be open? She must remember to ask Curtis. It looked as if the beautiful young woman had died quite peacefully in her sleep.

She found the impulse was growing in her to scream. Apparently she simply couldn't learn to face corpses without sheer panic. And it was silly in this case. She didn't know the deceased, had never seen her before—or had she? Suddenly she thought she had. Susan's eyes went back to the closed eyes. Words began to repeat themselves nonsensically in her head:

"Dust to dust. All is vanity. Dust to dust. All is— But," she thought desperately, "I must take this with professional calm. After all, I haven't stumbled over *this* corpse. I've been called in. I'm supposed to give expert fashion testimony." The very idea of this made her laugh a little hysterically. The D.D.C. flung her a rebuking look, and Curtis steadied her elbow. Fiercely Susan wished he had not telephoned her, that they had found out for themselves why the corpse was dressed that way. After all, what did she know about it, except that no one in her right senses could conceive of such an extraordinary combination of garments.

Susan heard Curtis' words as if he were talking on another plane of life. He was saying that they had found no lethal instrument but that there was one not entirely satisfactory possibility that the deceased had managed to give herself a knockout blow by hitting her head on a hook in the private lavatory adjoining the drawing room. Ending her life this way would, he explained, have required the co-operation of a sudden lurch of the train. If it had happened this way it could have been either suicidal or, of course, accidental. Susan judged that Curtis was far from satisfied with either theory, McGluggish optimistically more so. She glanced quickly at Curtis and saw that his expression was not only grimly thoughtful but something else less easily defined. She had seen it before. It was the look to be found on the face of an extremely fine architect inspecting a faulty piece of designing. Next to murderers, she knew, Curtis disliked more than anything joints that didn't quite join, angles which couldn't be made to complement one another, lines which could be made to prove neither their right to stand together nor alone. She also knew it was this point of view, plus his natural mental and physical capacity for adventure, which made Curtis the coming man in the district attorney's office, its best man hunter.

One of the policemen called the D.D.C. outside for a moment, and Curtis said to her quickly in no more than a murmur: "I'm afraid it's not a timely moment for a murder that might attract a good deal of attention, things being the way they are downtown. The department doesn't want one. If there's a reasonable way out along the suicide line they'll take it. The president of the railroad doesn't want a murder. You can't blame him. He called the D. A. Thus my presence. Nobody wants a murder. I don't. But I don't want a murderer to go scot free either."

Susan's nerves tightened. Even if they had been covered with wood she had hated the seemingly perilous passage across third rails in the cavern of tracks outside. After all, she might have tripped and been a corpse by now. Also, she hated the unkempt Pullman and the sight of the fantastically garbed corpse. The stubborn shoulders and quick eyes of the policemen were not pleasant. But she no longer wanted to scream or to run away. She looked down again at the body. The woman *was* beautiful. There was no doubt of that. Brown hair fell almost to her shoulders in an expensively contrived wave. Head in drawing room, feet in the tiny lavatory, there was, even so, grace in her posture. Not even death had deprived her of this. The evening gown with its extremely low décolletage was starkly simple, beautifully cut and unadorned. It suavely outlined a sinuous figure despite the bulk and incongruity of the underwear. The latter was purest lamb's wool, creamy, thick and body-clinging. Its sleeves reached well over the woman's wrists. One part of the gown's skirt had been caught up and displayed a leg covered with the same woolen protection to below the ankle bone.

"It's like seeing a spirited horse carrying a donkey's pack," said Susan. "Lyle, she must have been one hundred per cent whacky. There's no fashion precedent for such a combination of clothes. None whatever. The whole picture is out of a grim world of lost minds. She simply must have been insane." Susan looked up quickly. "But that's an excuse for suicide, isn't it?"

"Not necessarily. Some psychopaths have a greater sense of self-preservation than the so-called sane, I believe."

Susan nodded, and at this moment the detective district commander came back with the train conductor who evidently had been previously interviewed by McGluggish. He seemed to be explaining for a second time that he, himself, had had no dealings with the deceased. A man named Stratfield, in whose private party everyone in this Pullman car had been, had given him everybody's tickets. He knew Stratfield's name because that gentleman had traveled up and down on his train for several years, both winter and summer. He lived near a hamlet called Swiss Village, New Hampshire. Susan gathered that Stratfield also lived in New York, had been located and sent for. He was apparently expected any moment.

Lyle had said nothing yet about the deceased's name. This fact brought Susan back to the thought which in and around all her other trepidations had been worrying her ever since it had occurred to her. Had she seen the dead woman somewhere before? She certainly looked vaguely familiar.

The conductor went on reaffirming what he and the Pullman porter had evidently already told the police, explaining that although he had neither taken the deceased's ticket from her nor spoken to her he had seen the young woman when she got on the train. She had looked to him very sure of herself, a little haughty, you might say—not in the least confused or "crazy." He selected this latter word carefully. McGluggish looked doubtful. She had been dressed in ski clothes, but there had been a blizzard raging around Swiss Village. All the party had been covered with snow. They had come to the train steps directly from sleighs which had driven off while the train was still stopped on signal for Stratfield's party to board it. The conductor had seen all this but he knew none of the names of other members of the party. Further, his information consisted alone of the fact that there had been eight people, three women, all of whom had been provided with drawing rooms, and five men, who had had sections.

Susan glanced again at the corpse. She saw now that though the face looked at peace there were lines of arrogance and conceit in its conformation. Except for the astonishing attire the deceased might have been a queenly Borgia.

Curtis turned to Susan. "You haven't given me much fashion news yet. Please describe the costume in professional terms."

Susan grinned feebly. "The conductor has given you your tip about the underwear. The girl came aboard in a blizzard, wearing skiing clothes. That is skiing underwear. The best quality. The same kind I sell in my winter-sports department. It isn't custom made but it's a special output of a Scottish house and very expensive. But, Lyle, she *must* have been mad to put that extremely formal evening gown on over it."

The D.D.C. interrupted. "Cuckoo as hell."

"Yet there might be another explanation," said Curtis.

"What?" demanded McGluggish.

Curtis confessed that he hadn't the faintest idea yet.

"I wouldn't stop eatin' until you do have," advised the other stolidly. Looking at his wrist watch, he added: "I wish this guy Stratfield would step on it." He then looked down at the body. "The way I figure it is, this dame was despondent over something. Love. Maybe money. We'll find out. Anyway, she was cracked and must have gone clean off her nut when she got alone in this drawing room. Why else would she dress herself all up in this crackpot way?"

Susan turned her attention to counting the five shiny brass buttons on the conductor's coat. It and the tag on his cap held somewhat reverently in one hand were sparkling in the brightly lighted little room. His eyes, too, were bright with curiosity, but it was evident that he didn't fancy corpses on a train under his command. Then Susan remembered another thing she had wanted to ask. She wanted to see the girl's skiing clothes.

Five bags, lying on the floor, were open. A negligee and a neatly folded nightgown were on the couch opposite the made-up berth. The berth showed signs of having been slept in.

"The ski clothes are another angle," said Curtis, as if replying to Susan's unspoken question. "The conductor tells us she was wearing them when she came aboard. They aren't here."

The conductor nodded. "That's right. They was white. Pants and a jacket. A little red cap."

Susan murmured that the woman's having had the skiing underwear already on made the present costume a little more logical.

The D.D.C. glared at her. "How do you figure that? It's nuts to put a dress like that on over underwear like that, isn't it?"

She had to admit that it was distinctly unfashionable.

Curtis began quizzing the conductor on what, in his opinion, could have happened to the outer skiing apparel. Apparently McGluggish had been all over this with him before. The conductor seemed to have no fresh opinions. The young woman couldn't have thrown them out the window, because it was tightly fastened. They would have been too bulky to go down the toilet. The platform doors outside had been locked.

McGluggish looked harassed, then brightened. "But you were carrying one day coach ahead, weren't you?" The conductor nodded again.

"Well, what was to keep her from walking through to that, opening a vestibule door there, or a window, and pitching them off the train? See?" He turned to Curtis. "Not normal, I admit, but this here deceased was nuts, I tell you." Despite his asperity Susan felt that the detective commander was a little sheepish about this neat disposal of the outer apparel.

Curtis said lightly: "I don't believe it either."

Stealing another glance at the corpse, Susan made a sudden mewing sound. All three men turned questioning eyes upon her. "It just dawns on me that I *do* know her," she explained. "That is, she isn't anyone I know personally, but I've seen her lots of times. It's her name I'm not sure of."

"She could be a movie star," suggested the conductor ingenuously.

"No, no," said Susan, trying to think. "No, she's somebody connected some way or other with the fashion business. Might be a
department-store executive. Might have been in advertising. Wait
a minute, I've almost got it. Not her last name, though—the first.
Prunella!"

Curtis spoke encouragingly. "Don't struggle with it. The man
who made the reservations for everybody should be here soon. This
person called Stratfield. He'll be able to tell us, it is to be presumed,
who his guests were."

Another disturbance in the aisle outside accompanied his last
words, and a uniformed policeman stuck part of his head and body
around the drawing-room door to say that a Lawrence Stratfield
had arrived.

When Stratfield made his appearance in the aisle just outside
the compartment a moment later Susan thought he was one of those
men so many women find irresistible. As to face, they look like the
public's idea of a top sergeant of the Marines. They have strong,
quick bodies. No good looks, but personality and force.

Stratfield's expression was grave. His eyes went quickly from
the D.D.C. to Curtis, taking in Susan in passing. He looked as if,
like Susan, he had dressed with some haste. Unlike her, he had
evidently not bothered to complete his toilet en route. His tie was
askew, and his vest inadequately buttoned.

"Always sleep badly on trains," he muttered after saying who
he was and that he had got a call from the police to come right
back to Grand Central. "So I went home after breakfast and was
nearly undressed, with the idea of having a nap. I dashed back as
soon as I could. What's up?"

Curtis introduced himself and McGluggish. "This isn't going to
be pleasant, Mr. Stratfield. We want you to step inside here and
identify a member of the party of people for whom you made reservations from Swiss Village, New Hampshire, to New York last
night."

Stratfield came briskly on into the drawing room, his expression still mystified. Then his eyes fell on the body. He stared in-
credulously at it for a long moment before saying in a high voice:

"My God! Prunella!"

"What can you tell us about it?" barked the D.D.C. Susan decided he did not like Stratfield on some general principle of his own and was accordingly willing to abandon, temporarily at least, his suicide theory.

"I can't tell you anything," gasped the newcomer, "except that the last time I saw Prunella Parton, which was when we came aboard the train yesterday evening, she was the most completely alive person I'd ever known." He looked deeply shocked and took a step nearer the body. "There's—there's no chance that she's just fainted or—or had some kind of attack—?" He looked around at Curtis and the D.D.C. for encouragement he obviously did not really hope to receive.

"She's dead," said Curtis briefly, and Susan found herself saying hysterically to herself:

"The most completely dead person you ever saw." She was beginning to feel giddy again. The close compartment, the body, the men standing about outside like contemplative butchers—it was all so unreal for ordinary living.

McGluggish was prodding again. "You don't know anything about how she died or got into that cuckoo getup?"

For answer Stratfield merely shook his head. He looked dazed.

At this moment the Pullman gave a sharp lurch, and a second later they heard the clash of couplings.

"The club car," said Curtis, looking at the D.D.C.

"Then we'll go in there," the latter barked, and led the way. A plain-clothes man with a notebook brought up the rear.

The club car was brightly lighted but empty. At a signal from Curtis Susan sank down onto a chair near the door, and McGluggish directed Stratfield to sit opposite him. Curtis and the young man with the notebook sat beside the detective commander on a wicker divan.

"Your full name and address," the latter demanded of Stratfield who still appeared shaken but entirely willing to co-operate.

"Lawrence Stratfield." He gave an address on East End Avenue which Susan recognized as expensive. "I have a country place—a studio, really—at Swiss Village, New Hampshire. I'm a painter by profession. Had a party of people, including Miss Parton, up there for a week end of skiing."

"Parton? Prunella Parton? That's her full name, eh? Who was she?"

Stratfield's voice took on a more somber tone. "Charming, a career woman, considered one of the outstanding advertising-copy writers in the country, I believe. She was employed in the advertising agency of two other of my week-end guests, Peter Sutton and David Barron. Their firm's name is Sutton and Barron, Incorporated. They're in the Lincoln Building across from the station here, I believe."

He was then asked who his other guests had been, and, except for some indefiniteness about exact addresses, reeled them off: Miss Joan Sutton, Peter Sutton's daughter, Miss Hazel Manchester, employed by *Inter-Allied News* as a beauty-and-charm columnist and Oliver Penbroke, head of the advertising agency of that name.

The D.D.C. was still dissatisfied. "You made eight Pullman-car reservations including three drawing rooms for ladies and five sections for the men in your party and yourself. You've named six guests: Miss Parton, Miss Sutton, Miss Manchester, Sutton, Barron and Penbroke. You make seven. Who was eighth?"

Stratfield seemed for a moment genuinely at a loss. Then he clapped a hand on a knee. "Young Conway, of course! Miss Joan Sutton asked me to include him. He works for her father at the agency. A copy writer."

Curtis and the detective commander exchanged looks, and Curtis got up and left the club car, disappearing in the direction of the Pullman. During the few minutes he was gone Stratfield explained in a somewhat high-pitched, rambling fashion that they had all driven through the blizzard to the Swiss Village junction where the New York express had stopped on signal. Miss Parton, he said, had not been in the same sleigh with him, but they had all come aboard together.

"Everybody was weary," Stratfield went on, "and it was generally agreed to turn in early. We said good night to the ladies right there, almost at Miss Parton's drawing-room door." He nodded in the direction of the Pullman.

Curtis returned to the club car at this moment and asked casually: "So you didn't see the deceased again—last night or this morning?"

Stratfield shook his head. "No, I didn't. After we said good night we men went into the smoke room—except for young Conway, who, I think, went off somewhere, probably ahead to the club car attached to the train. Miss Sutton was with him, I think. They're in love, you understand."

McGluggish looked as if love were a subject he did not in the least understand, and Susan admitted to herself that it was difficult to imagine him suffering even minute pangs of heartsickness. Though, no doubt, he had.

"You didn't see her this morning before you left the train?" McGluggish barked.

"No. You see, we had more or less said final adieus to the ladies last night, fancying they would take advantage of the thirty minutes' leeway allowed by the railroad for last-minute toilettes after the train is in the station. The only people I actually saw this morning were Mr. Sutton and Mr. Barron. We left together and breakfasted in the station." Seeing every word he uttered was apparently being taken down by the stenographer, Stratfield added: "If you are interested in my exact movements, I stopped at a florist's, Gilchrist's, on Lexington Avenue, and took some flowers from there to Miss Manchester's office. Just a week-end host's gesture. As soon as I got home I started to undress and go to bed. Then one of your men called me—I've told you that, of course—and— Look here! Miss Parton died of something normal, didn't she? I mean, you aren't suspecting foul play?" Stratfield's face was anxious, a combination of incredulity and curiosity.

"She's either killed herself or been murdered," spat out the detective. "Now, you say you didn't sleep very well. Did you happen to hear anything peculiar during the night?"

"Peculiar? Not a thing—unless you call the rocky roadbed they have up in the hills peculiar. If you mean did I hear anyone cry out, any shots or noises other than the noise of the train—no. Do you actually mean that Miss Parton has been dead for some hours with all of us sleeping around her, dressing and leaving the train without knowing it? My God!"

The D.D.C. made a muttering sound, neither confirmation nor denial. Curtis said something in a low voice to him behind a hand. Susan didn't think it very polite, especially since she would very much have liked to hear. But she had seen this public whispering business happen before in police investigations. After a couple of seconds McGluggish asked:

"What did you mean about the only people you 'actually' saw this morning being Sutton and Barron?"

Stratfield pondered a moment. "I'm wrong about that. I saw Penbroke, too, and I think I saw young Conway ducking into the men's room just as I was leaving the train with Mr. Barron and Mr. Sutton."

As Stratfield finished this sentence a policeman appeared at the club-car door where he conveyed a sign-language message to the detective commander. The latter nodded.

"Have each one identify the deceased, then bring 'em in here."

In a few moments the policeman held back the door once more, and a small parade filed into the club car.

CHAPTER SIX

FIRST IN THE SMALL PARADE which then appeared was a snowy-haired, rather small man, probably, Susan thought, in his early sixties. Rimless glasses sparkled before his eyes. His thin mouth was drawn into a line of deep concern. She suddenly remembered having seen him at an Advertising Club banquet and recalled his name, Peter Sutton. He was the distinguished advertising savant and president of Sutton & Barron, Inc.

Following Sutton came a tall, dark man whose age Susan mentally placed at an even forty. There was something sharply aware in his expression. His nose and eyes suggested a ferret. Behind the awareness was a look of shock—or fright—as if he had just seen a ghost and could not escape believing in its existence. The blond boy who brought up the rear looked as if he, too, had seen a phantom and feared either to believe or disbelieve it. His healthy tan, snow tan, Susan diagnosed it, alone saved his face from a pallor she suspected would have been more natural under the circumstances.

"A lean and hungry look," she murmured to herself, and made another diagnosis. "Young man with too many troubles."

McGluggish was not overwhelmed by the prominence of the older men. He motioned to seats and demanded to be told names. The white-haired man said majestically:

"I am Peter Sutton. This is very bad business. Very bad."

The "ferret" said merely: "Barron's the name."

The young man half stammered the name Hinkle Conway and sat down so quickly that the wicker chair creaked miserably beneath him.

"Sit down," barked the D.D.C. unnecessarily, as all three were seated by then.

A moment later Susan discovered that despite his just-having-seen-a-ghost look the dark man was inspecting her silkily. So David Barron was a congenital flirt! Even under the present rather adverse conditions he was evidently following a life pattern. His eyes had gone automatically about the business of sizing her up. No doubt they were cataloging her face, figure, coloring and probable disposition.

"Uugh," she said under her breath.

There followed a routine repetition of the questions already put to Stratfield. When the D.D.C. reached the point of demanding when each of them had last seen the deceased alive Sutton and Barron each confirmed Stratfield's story of the older men having left her at her drawing-room door the night before after bidding all three of the ladies good night there. Conway called minor attention to himself by saying sulkily that he hadn't noticed where Prunella Parton had gone after they boarded the train.

"You didn't tell her good night?" demanded McGluggish in an elephantine tone of social reprimand.

Conway shook his head. "I don't think I told Miss Manchester good night, either, for that matter."

Curtis seemed to lose interest in the trend of both questions and answers. He stood up and moved quietly toward the rear door, giving Susan a quick signal to follow him.

Closing the door behind them, he came to a standstill on the rear platform, hunched a shoulder in the direction of the club car and said: "You and I can spend the next five minutes more profitably, I think. I'm waiting for Medical Examiner Dugan's report, of course, but his assistant guessed death at something less than an hour at eight-fifteen this morning. All this run-around of statements as to what those people were doing last night is probably beside the point. Tell me what else you have remembered about the deceased. You dug up her first name without any leads awhile ago."

Susan said thoughtfully that about all she could recall was that Prunella Parton had been one of the more generally and heartily disliked career women in New York. She had seen her now and again at guest meetings of the fashion careerists' exclusive Tomorrow Club when subjects under discussion had had to do with fashion-ad writing. She had got the impression Miss Parton was brilliant, ruthless and rather a gay bird.

"I didn't know her personally, mind you," Susan went on, "but you know how the girls drop hints. A word here, a mew there. As months whizz by you get curiously complete mental pictures of some people without wanting to, without ever meeting them. It's amazing, Lyle, how many strangers in the fashion business you know all about. Of course, you actually don't, but you know probably as much as anyone does about them. I venture there's no more well-equipped grapevine system in the world than the unofficial 'special-agent reporting' which goes on in the fashion business. And don't think it's only the girl! You should see, and hear, some of the men at work!"

Curtis grinned and said that one day Miss Yates was going to find herself at an altar, and then what good would brittleness do her?

"This sort of talk isn't taking care of your business day," Susan pointed out, looking a little pink. "Anyway, from tidbits of conversation I've picked up here and there, it's quaint Prunella Parton survived as long as she did. It seems to me I've been hearing outraged femininity at work on her for years, sarcastic references to her way with men and general system of ethics. I've been trying to think what the last badge of dishonor being pinned to her was. Something about robbing the cradle. That must have been all of a year ago."

"Remember who was supposed to occupy the cradle?"

"Wasn't interested. Don't think I listened that far. May have heard, but doubt it. Haven't a prayer of a notion now at least. But—oh yes, I do remember something else: hearing two of the girls talking some time later and one of them confiding to the other that Prunella had given up cradle snatching and was busy feathering her own nest—something about some higher-up in her organization, I gathered. Lyle! It couldn't have been the venerable Sutton, but it might have been that dark ferret you've got in there. David Barron, I'd say, has an eye for the ladies?"

Rather dryly Mr. Curtis said: "So I noticed. Yes, it could have been Barton all right. Born wolf."

"Loose modern talk, but I must remember to use the word. It seems singularly appropriate in Barron's case at least."

Curtis said: "Susan, you know you could be a great deal of help to me if you'd do a little ex-officio scouting around among some of your catty grapevine acquaintances. Be an angel, darling, and round up a few choice human felines. Get them together over a luncheon table this noon and *listen*. The girls you can get the hottest dope from won't be your most cherished friends. By the way, we've induced the railroad to have a telephone line brought out here. Regular Twentieth-Century Limited service. All we need is the red carpet and a porter who isn't scared white. This one is, the one who found the very dead Prunella. Will you get on the wire and line up some first-class talkers? The story of our deceased's passing won't have broken for the first editions of the afternoon papers. We've seen to that. Tell you what you do: just hint. Say you've heard Prunella Parton died this morning. Just say 'died' as if she had done it in bed. That will set their tongues wagging sufficiently, or I don't know women—"

"Oh, but you do, Lyle!" Susan remonstrated with mock severity. "I should be the last to deny it."

Accepting this with an equally mock, imperial gesture, Curtis went on to explain that what he wanted her to dig up was all the personal dope about the dear departed she could, including scandal. Even if she got half-truths or downright bias it would help bring out Prunella Parton's personality and probably the names of persons who hadn't cared too much for her.

"Will you do it?" he repeated.

"My shop will go bankrupt if this means I'm starting unofficially on another case with you, Mr. Assistant D. A. I'm just clambering up out of the red ink in which your Peters' case last spring drenched my salon and workrooms." But, despite her bantering tone, Susan's eyes had become serious, her mouth determined. Without another word she permitted herself to be led to the telephone at the rear of the adjoining Pullman.

At the phone Curtis left her and turned to give Sergeant Withers a list of instructions. By the time she had finished rounding up three women well equipped for unedited talk Curtis was again at her elbow. He began asking her at once as they walked back to the club car what she knew about Peter Sutton's daughter Joan.

"Nothing," said Susan, "except that she was a debutante last year and had the bad taste to go to another designer for her battle clothes. That's absolutely all I know about her."

WHEN THEY REACHED the club car the D.D.C. was still asking questions and getting answers of a sort. Another man had swollen the group. He was big, with broad, fat shoulders, big ears and a sharply jolly look. Susan supposed he would be Oliver Penbroke, important competitor of the firm of Sutton & Barron. There were also two women in the assemblage now: one blonde, pretty and very young who wore a rather too adult mink coat and a small hat bearing, like a flag of welcome, an eighteen-inch feather, the other probably thirty and classically garbed for business in a well-tailored coat and a chic felt hat. Both girls' accessories, Susan noted, were carefully assembled. They wore excellent handmade shoes and gloves and carried large sleek handbags of the general dimensions of a dispatch case. With these details their similarity ceased.

Of the older girl Susan said to herself: "Feels a lady spy on tour disguised as busy businesswoman!" Of the younger she remarked mentally: "Gets what she wants and expects to."

Miss Manchester, as McGluggish presently addressed her, was dissembling very well any fears or doubts she might be feeling. Her face, like her clothes, was perfectly made up both as to cosmetics and expression. The younger woman, not yet addressed, would be, of course, Peter Sutton's daughter. In addition to looking acquisitive she looked efficient. No doubt she had a line which stopped them in her young world. But surely such a child couldn't be a murderess! It was unthinkable.

"So, Miss Manchester," the D.D.C. said, eying the tailored girl, "you left the train alone, had breakfast alone at the Ritz, then went to your office? You didn't know anything about Miss Parton being dead until we asked you to come back here and you were shown the body?"

There were edges to Miss Manchester's cultivated tone composed of mingled bravura and wariness.

"There's a girl," Susan told herself, "who thinks before she speaks. She's efficient too. I wouldn't hesitate to employ either one of them as salesladies."

"That's all perfectly correct," Miss Manchester replied to McGluggish. Then, as if on an unguarded impulse, she added two quickly spoken sentences. "But if you're thinking Prunella Parton committed suicide you're bound to be dead wrong. I can't imagine anyone less likely to."

"Why not?" barked her interrogator.

Miss Manchester's guards went up again. Susan saw them going up, automatically composing the oval face with its rather medieval-lady-with-a-falcon features. She said coolly: "I shouldn't have taken her for the type, that's all. I write a beauty column. It is my business to study types. Prunella Parton always appeared to me to be very pleased with life."

"Anything in particular you have in mind?" McGluggish obviously wasn't liking a nonsuicide angle.

"Shall we call it a hunch? I'm afraid I can't be more specific."

He grunted his distaste for hunches and turned his attention abruptly to the younger girl. "Miss Sutton, I understand you and Mr. Conway were next to the last of the party to leave the train this morning. Didn't it occur to you to go and see if the deceased was still aboard?"

Joan Sutton widened her blue eyes. "Why in the world should that have occurred to me?" Her tone was one of sweet bewilderment.

Her inquisitor spluttered. "Why—why, the most natural thing in the world—another girl—a member of your party—a friend—"

With apparently naïve frankness Joan widened her eyes a degree further. "But you see, she wasn't a friend of mine."

"Why not?"

Joan shook her blond head as if she were a pony. "Is everybody you know a friend of yours?" she asked wonderingly. Her eyes, Susan thought, were far wiser than either her tone or her expression.

For a second the D.D.C. looked as if someone had pushed him against an electrically charged fence. He recovered and blustered: "It would have been a natural thing to do. Just natural."

Miss Sutton became confidential. "I must be awfully unnatural. To tell you the absolute truth, it never even occurred to me. Prunella Parton was such a messy person."

"Messy?" McGluggish spluttered again, and Susan saw Curtis concealing a grim smile. "What's that mean? Messy!"

"Just messy."

"Joan!" It was Peter Sutton's voice sounding extremely parental. "Miss Parton was nothing at all in your life. You scarcely knew her. But please remember that she was an excellent copy writer and a brilliant member of your father's staff."

Then Miss Sutton exploded. Her fresh young body quivered with the self-willedness she had apparently been leashing. "She was a two-timing, scheming, lecherous female, Father, and everyone in the world but you knew it," she cried.

CHAPTER SEVEN

PETER SUTTON'S HAIR had seemed to grow a degree whiter as his daughter's words fixed themselves stridently in the listening ears. A gray pallor spread unhealthily over his face. Even the once more composed Miss Manchester and the genial-looking Oliver Penbroke appeared shocked at the bitterness of Joan's invective. The D.D.C. looked at her soft childlike lips and, from his expression, appeared for a moment to be about to have an attack of paternalism himself. If he had such a passing inclination he coped with it successfully, for he asked sharply:

"So you're not sorry she's dead?"

Amazingly, Miss Sutton was a sweet child again, naive and youthfully confused, trying to be oh-so-frank. "I—I shouldn't talk this way but, honestly, I couldn't bear her. Father's right, of course. I hardly knew her. I—I guess she just wasn't my type."

Before McGluggish could say anything to this Hinkle Conway broke into the conversation.

"Look here, since you're so interested in what we all thought of Prunella Parton, I'll tell you what I thought of her. I thought she stood right in the middle of my advancement at Sutton and Barron's. Right in the middle." His words were choppy, nerve gnashed. "Everybody knows," he went on, "I couldn't move ahead until she moved out. And she wasn't moving. We played a silly game over the week end, at Mr. Stratfield's, confessing what would bring each of us to murdering somebody. I looked straight at Prunella and said I could kill a competitive copy writer."

Rendered at an astoundingly impulsive pace, his reckless words brought every pair of eyes in the club car to his snow-tanned face. Under this battery of attention he stilled their flow.

"Well, anyway," he amended uncomfortably, "I thought I might as well tell you."

Curtis, Susan saw, was regarding this big blond young man with great interest. Of them all Oliver Penbroke seemed the only one to find the outburst in the least amusing. Peter Sutton looked shocked beyond words, and David Barron said hastily:

"For God's sake, Conway, don't be a complete ass. We aren't being inquisitioned here. All you are supposed to do is to give any side lights you can on why Prunella killed herself. You needn't act like a damn fool."

Looking as if he now thoroughly agreed, Conway fumbled with his hat. Casting a quick look at Joan Sutton, he muttered: "Lost my head, I guess. Upsetting, seeing her dead and that man keeping at Joan so." This was said directly to David Barron who turned his sharp eyes to the D.D.C. and said:

"We all understood Conway was joking Saturday night. That confessing business was just a lot of horseplay."

Curtis casually interrupted. "You thought, Conway, that someone would remember to quote you?"

"Yes," answered the young man sulkily. "It seemed a good idea to get it out instead of waiting for somebody to spring it against me."

Peter Sutton's clipped words greeted them like an editorial addenda. "This is all ridiculous. There were and are no hard feelings among the members of my staff. I should say there is no more happy business family in the United States."

It sounded to Susan like an institutional slogan or a dignified pep talk for the boys and girls on Monday morning, calculated to start them off inspired for a week of "doing their best for the company's sake."

Curtis said something in an aside to the police official and took the floor once more, addressing his first remark directly to Lawrence Stratfield. "There were no other guests at your house party?"

"No other guests," confirmed the painter evenly. He hesitated a moment, then added: "Miss Parton's sister dropped in on us out of the blizzard late Saturday night with two newspapermen, but they were merely trying to get through to North Conway to a skiing event there. They were covering it for the New York *Globe*. We persuaded them to spend the night and got them off bright and early Sunday morning. They were in the house, at most, five hours."

The D.D.C. had picked up his ears. "What's the sister's name?" he demanded.

Stratfield looked questioningly around at the others. "Dear me," he said, "what is the other Miss Parton's name? This will be a dreadful shock for her," he added.

Joan and her father, Miss Manchester and young Conway all shook their heads with various degrees of vagueness. Oliver Penbroke looked as if no answer were expected of him, but David Barron said crisply:

"Her name is Carol. Carol Parton. She's a young newspaperwoman."

"But," persisted Curtis, turning back to Stratfield, "she wasn't with you on the train last night?"

A trifle wearily, Stratfield said: "She went on with her newspaper companions early Sunday morning, as I said."

Peter Sutton stirred. "I do not see," he remarked, eying through his shiny glasses first the detective commander and then Curtis, "that we can offer you any further information, gentlemen. It would appear we have conveyed to you all we know." His tone suggested rather than insisted that he really might be recognized as a busy man whose minutes were customarily calculated in dollars.

Curtis spoke again with polite reasonableness. "That may be. But so often in cases like this no one thinks to describe some simple episode which afterward turns out to have been of great importance. Now, which of you was best acquainted with Miss Prunella Parton?"

The D.D.C.'s expression indicated that he considered he, himself, had covered with entire adequacy this point. No one answered Curtis. Peter Sutton looked at his watch as if he intended to leave shortly whether the police and district attorney's office liked it or not. On both Barron's and young Conway's faces Susan discovered almost exactly the same expression. For a moment she could not define it. Then, with what she congratulated herself on as practically clairvoyance, she decided it was embarrassment. And there could surely be only one answer to why the blond and impetuous youngster and the world-wise vice-president should both look embarrassed over Curtis' question. They must be, respectively, the "infant conquest" with which Prunella had been associated and "the man higher-up" through whom she had been "feathering her own nest"!

Joan Sutton also said nothing. She sat studying the tip of one of her expensive shoes. Peter Sutton put his watch away.

A voice finally answered Curtis. It was Hazel Manchester's, sounding polite and impersonal. Twice as she spoke she shot David Barron a flickering glance from her thick, shiny lashes.

"I don't suppose you could say that I was an intimate friend of Prunella's. Of course, we had seen something of each other in business through the years. She handled one or two cosmetic accounts for Sutton and Barron. One of them was the face-cream division of the Kork-Petulla Oil Company. Mr. Penbroke's agency has the oil end. I've given Prunella a publicity break in my columns several times lately and as a result had seen a bit more of her than usual. We'd lunch, you know. That sort of thing. What I mean to say is that if there is anything special I could tell you—" Her statement ended in an unexpectedly vague question mark.

"But *you* don't think she was a suicide type?" spat out McGluggish, interrupting Curtis' holding of the floor and sounding as if he felt further word from Miss Manchester immaterial and incompetent.

Susan had been watching David Barron's face. She had the queer impression that he had caught Hazel Manchester's glances and that they had made him doubly uncomfortable. She also suspected before he spoke that he was going to, that being formulated behind his sharply acquisitive face was an irresistible impulse to make a statement.

Barron's tone was businesslike. "I probably knew Miss Parton better than Mr. Sutton or any of our other officers," he explained. "I am the account executive of a majority of the clients whose copy she wrote. My interests lie, moreover, in the copy end of our business. Mr. Sutton has built our art department to its present nationally celebrated stature."

Completely denying the cagey look conveyed by his sparkling eyeglasses, Peter Sutton interrupted with an almost whimsical comment. "Barron," he reprimanded lightly, "I scarcely think the police and the district attorney's office are interested in our opinions regarding the professional reputation of Sutton and Barron, Incorporated, accurate as your remarks may be."

Barron laughed briefly and thinly. "Of course. Of course. I was only trying to clarify. I may say that I worked very happily with Miss Parton. Her death is not only a personal shock but a grave loss to our firm. She was a genius with words. Most capable." His eyes fell on young Conway. "Oh, and, of course, Conway knew Miss Parton as a fellow worker in the same department, but I assure you we can thoroughly discount his, shall we say, youthfully exaggerated statements of a few moments ago. Miss Parton did not stand in his way of advancement. All members of our staff advance on their individual merits. We think very well indeed of you, Conway."

The recipient of this public compliment looked to the contrary of overjoyed. It was evident he would have preferred no publicity at all at the moment. Curtis studied his face, then, as Conway made no reply to his vice-president's benediction, the assistant D. A. turned back to that gentleman.

"Tell me," he asked, "was there any special reason for this week-end party?" For a moment he permitted his eyes to leave Barron and to rest lightly on Oliver Penbroke's bulk, but immediately they returned to Barron.

"Reason?" Barron raised his black eyebrows minutely. "Skiing, of course. We all skied—or tried to. Mr. Sutton is an expert, and young Conway is excellent. And Mr. Stratfield has extraordinarily fine slopes."

Again Conway looked restive under verbal limelight. Glancing at Peter Sutton, Susan thought that Barron's reference to skiing had also unaccountably annoyed him. Almost sarcastically Sutton said:

"Yes, yes, Barron. You're being repetitious. Surely these gentlemen understand Mr. Stratfield's house party was purely social. Purely."

Curtis glanced again at Penbroke who caught his eye this time and rumbled:

"Purely. Ah, excuse another repetition, Sutton."

Peter Sutton blinked noncommittally behind his two glass barriers while the assistant D. A. waited.

Lawrence Stratfield filled the gap. Almost playfully and certainly with the utmost in amiability he complained: "Surely there's nothing illegal about my having week-end guests? After all"—and his high voice dropped a note to a worried tenor—"there were no casualties up at Swiss Village, tragic as a subsequent event has been."

Curtis moved in on his period. "Nothing happened which would have prepared any of you for the sudden death of a member of the party?" The bluntness of the question, his tones and overtones seemed to set every nervous system in the club car ajar, including McGluggish's who, Susan was sure, wanted more than ever for his suicide theory to receive no vital blow.

Mr. Sutton took upon himself the role of spokesman. "Ridiculous," he ejaculated, glasses flashing. "It was an exceedingly pleasant party." He seemed about to say something else, but young Conway straightened his slumped body and remarked laconically:

"Except for the explosion."

"The explosion?" requested Mr. Curtis, and the detective commander sat forward with obvious resentment.

"What explosion?" he barked. "Nobody's said anything about any explosion."

Stratfield explained. Something had gone wrong with an oilstove in the kitchen directly under Miss Parton's bedroom. He stopped short and exclaimed more in a question than a statement, "But surely that wasn't an—an omen or anything to do with her death? Oh, I'm being ridiculous. It was entirely an accident, a most unfortunate but, happily, not serious accident. No one was hurt. And Miss Parton merely fainted from the nerve strain of finding herself barricaded behind a door beyond which the world seemed at the time to be coming to an end. That's exactly the way she described her reaction to me yesterday morning. You see, she was taking a bath and was dozing in the tub when the first blast came. She jumped out, as anyone would, astonished and not quite knowing what to do, she ran toward her bedroom door, down a short corridor from the bath, tried the door, heard another blast, felt the doorknob tremble in her hand and a loud thump on the other side as a heavy chest toppled over against the door. The door opened out, and the chest made her a veritable captive. She was dreadfully frightened, poor girl, and she fainted. But my cook and Miss Carol Parton, who had arrived by then, revived her, and she assured me several times yesterday—I felt, naturally, extremely concerned—that she was none the worse for the episode that is, of course, except for the remnants of shock. It was an extremely trying experience for all my guests, I'm afraid. And damn foolishness. A guaranteed oilstove should not behave that way."

Curtis asked: "What made the stove explode?"

Stratfield said he didn't know. The stove itself and everything in its immediate vicinity in the kitchen, including the ceiling, the floor above and the bed in Miss Parton's room had been too completely destroyed for them to get anywhere with an amateur diagnosis. He had left his butler in the country to receive someone from the oil-burner company today, having finally sent them a wire yesterday when he could not reach them by phone.

"What," asked Curtis pleasantly, "is your butler's name?"

Stratfield looked mildly astonished but said at once that his name was Simon Baggs but that he had been in no way responsible for the explosion. There was every reason to believe he had told the truth in saying he had as usual checked the oilstove before retiring for the night.

"He's an old and trusted employee of mine," Stratfield added. "I'm afraid I rather lost my temper with him in the middle of the excitement Saturday night, but, actually, he's the very essence of reliability and honesty. A dear old fellow, as a matter of fact."

"It did not," inquired Curtis, glancing from face to face, "occur to any of you that the explosion could have been a planned attack on Miss Parton's life, her bedroom and bed being immediately over it?"

CHAPTER EIGHT

THERE WAS AN IMMEDIATE murmur of astonishment and denial. Such an interpretation of the episode seemed not to have entered anyone's mind.

Reflecting the pony-head tossing of his daughter, Mr. Sutton shook his own. "Ridiculous," he reproved Curtis, "utter nonsense. The explosion could just as well have killed everyone in the house. No one could have foreseen it would affect only Miss Parton's room."

Stratfield said: "Quite right, Sutton, but, just the same, it shouldn't have happened. I intend to hold the stove company responsible. A nice thing, inviting guests for the week end and having them blown to bits under my own roof."

There followed, Susan thought, some rather dull repetitions of what each member of the party had said and done on Saturday night. Little conflict in memories resulted. Then Curtis leaned over for another one of his maddening conversations behind a hand.

Susan wished devoutly that there were some sort of auditory periscopic device she could carry around with her on occasions like this.

After listening a moment McGluggish nodded glumly and spat out another question: "We know what Miss Manchester thinks of the suicide angle, but what do the rest of you think of it? What do you, Mr. Sutton?"

"I was not well enough acquainted with the young woman. I know she did brilliant work for us at the agency. But as to her er—

ah, emotional balance—" His words dwindled to silence. Then, with more definiteness, he said: "Suicide is surely not usual among career women."

The detective commander seemed to consider this inadequate. "We don't gauge suicides by professions," he said. "They're not many where they're typically a result of careers, as far as I know." He looked somewhat belligerent. "Of course, among young doctors there's nine cases out of ten the same reason. Trouble with a nurse or some girl and temptations to take an illegal way out, with the result of being refused a license if they're found out. There are a few other 'typical' suicides that we can take a good chance at labeling. But I've never heard of there being any typical careerwomen ones."

Mr. Sutton looked reproving. He glanced at his daughter as if he considered the D.D.C.'s digression both untimely and unsuitable. Joan was looking intensely interested. McGluggish abandoned abruptly his verbal essay and turned to Barron.

"Can you give us a reason as to why she might have taken her own life?"

"Absolutely none," said Barron. "She was brilliant, successful, attractive and popular."

Miss Manchester's words struck the club car like a small bombshell. "Popular with men perhaps, but scarcely with women," she murmured, and smiled serenely. "Of course that was only my impression, you understand."

"Do you know any women who might have murdered her?" demanded McGluggish.

Miss Manchester paused before replying. She might almost have been running over a mental list of women who might suit his purposes but finally she said lightly, "No. No, of course, I don't. Couldn't it have been an accident?"

Without replying, the D.D.C. kept his eyes sharply fixed on hers for a moment, then, turning abruptly to Joan Sutton, he asked: "What do you say?"

"I wouldn't have the faintest notion." Susan thought Joan had been going to say something else, but the girl left it at that.

"What about you?" The question was put to Penbroke who said amiably that he was in the unhelpful position of not even having an opinion. He stirred his big, fat shoulders and smiled blandly.

"And you?" The D.D.C.'s eyes were on Conway. The young man shook his head sullenly and refrained from opening his lips.

Stratfield spoke without being asked. "I thought Miss Parton had an exceptionally optimistic disposition, but, of course, though I have known her for quite a number of years I wouldn't be able to swear to it that, like many high-spirited persons, she didn't have moments of depression. It's not infrequent, I suppose, to find people, seemingly very gay in the presence of others, who have hideous moments of pessimism when they are alone. Many a laugh actually does conceal a broken heart, despite the triteness of the saying. I've often thought the really fortunate people in this world are those who are never 'in high,' dispositionally speaking, and thus never 'in low,' those who trudge along a fairly colorless middle of the road, the plodders, the people without much imagination—"

Evidently foreseeing a capacity on Stratfield's part to continue indefinitely this philosophical debate with himself, McGluggish cut it short. "O.K. Maybe she was the kind who was up one moment, down the next. Any of you ever see any signs of that?"

Barron said: "Well, now that you speak of it, it showed a bit in her work. She wasn't always in the top flights of brilliance. Then again, she would be your true genius."

Conway said, still glumly: "If you'd worked with her you'd have seen that she had moments in both 'high' and 'low,' as Mr. Stratfield put it." The memories inspiring this statement evidently were not of the most comforting caliber.

"You see," the D.D.C. said somewhat accusingly to Curtis, "this doesn't get us anywhere."

Curtis looked thoughtful, then astonished Susan by asking that they go over again exactly what had happened when the party had come aboard the train the night before at Swiss Village. Awhile ago, she recalled, he had told her privately that information about this was an unimportant run-around because the young woman had not died until shortly before reaching Grand Central. She was puzzled by his change of interest.

Curtis had turned to Peter Sutton who answered him by saying he had gone directly to the men's room where he had disrobed for the night. Their berths had already been made up, he explained. When he came out through the smoking compartment adjacent to the men's room Stratfield, Barron and Penbroke had been there chatting. He had bid them a second good night, gone to his berth and immediately to sleep.

"Where," asked Curtis, "were you, Conway?"

"I?" repeated the young man uncomfortably. "Why, I guess I was in the club car ahead."

"Alone?"

Conway looked, if possible, more uncomfortable than at any point in the inquiry. "Miss Sutton and I were having a glass of milk." From both their expressions, this did not appear to be an exact description of the nature of their libations, but Curtis, Susan thought, had not intended to press the point until his glance fell on Peter Sutton's face. Joan's father had quite obviously not received this intelligence with parental enthusiasm. Curtis asked:

"What happened in the club car?"

"Happened, sir?" Conway looked even more unhappy.

"Yes, did Miss Parton come in? Did you hear or see anything which would have had the least bearing on her subsequent death?"

"W-why, no sir. Not a thing. I can't think of anything anyhow. That is—"

"Yes?" prodded Curtis.

"That is, unless it was the fact that Miss Sutton and I thought we saw her sister, Carol Parton, leaving as we came in and we thought it was funny because Saturday night she hadn't said anything about coming back on the same train with us. Of course, she might have got one of the photographers to take the car back to Mr. Stratfield's place and boarded our train further up on the line at North Conway. Driving was awfully bad. If it was she she must have been in a Pullman up ahead and didn't know we were on the same train."

"You got the idea she left the club car *because* you and Miss Sutton came into it?"

"No. No, not exactly. She just sort of hurried out. She might not have seen us at all."

"But you or Miss Sutton or both of you thought she had?"

"Oh no." Joan spoke up. "I simply said to Hinkle, 'Why, that girl rushing off looks like Prunella's sister.' He said, 'Uh-hunh,' and then I said, 'Well, if she saw us I don't blame her for beating it. It didn't strike me that she and Prunella got along any too well.'"

Joan paused, and Curtis asked what Conway had said to that. "Oh, I don't know what he said. We just agreed that when they were looking for Prunella after the explosion Prunella's sister didn't seem terribly upset or anything."

Curtis absorbed this, then asked if anything else had happened in the club car. Joan Sutton and Hinkle Conway shook their heads.

"You didn't see," persisted Curtis, "Miss Carol Parton again? And Miss Prunella Parton did not come in and join you?"

With considerable spirit Joan exclaimed: "I should hope not! No, of course she didn't. Why should she?"

The assistant district attorney said mildly that she might have been thirsty.

With severity Peter Sutton remarked that he hoped it was not going to be necessary for them to remain much longer. He looked at his watch once more and frowned very pointedly.

"I appreciate the setting is not very cheerful," admitted Curtis. "Just one more question—or, rather, two. What time did you three gentlemen turn in?" His eyes moved over Stratfield, Penbroke and Barron. "And did anything occur last evening or during the night which, in view of there being a corpse on the train this morning, might seem important?"

Susan suspected he was deliberately concealing the presumed time of death.

All three men shook their beads. Barron said: "We talked for perhaps fifteen minutes, then Penbroke threw away his cigarette and said good night. You undressed in your berth, didn't you, Penbroke?"

The other nodded.

"Anyway, you were snoring when I turned in, perhaps ten minutes later."

"An old habit," remarked Penbroke in a tone of self-reprimand.

"And," continued Barron, "after Penbroke left the smoke room I went into the men's room. When I came out Mr. Stratfield was having another cigarette. I had one with him, and then we went out to our sections."

"And that was all?"

"That was all."

Curtis seemed satisfied. He said to McGluggish: "That's all I want to ask." He rose, and the detective commander rose.

"You people stay in town where we can reach you if we need any more information. That's all for now, thanks," said the latter.

CHAPTER NINE

SUSAN GLANCED at her watch. It was nearly twelve o'clock. The interrogations had taken far longer than she had thought. The others were filing out of the club car. After a word or so with the detective commander Curtis fell in step with her.

"I," he said, "am going to lead you over those blasted third rails this time."

Curtis clutched her arm and led her firmly in the direction of the vestibule. As they reached it Susan stopped and said:

"The more I think about it the more unlikely it seems that Prunella Parton went mad. But if she didn't she never dressed herself up that way. The murderer must have. Maybe the murderer was the whacky one."

Curtis shook his head.

"There's only one sane explanation: that the murderer wanted to make her look off her head to increase the suicide suggestion. But he, or she, forgot that suicides have to have a *modus operandi*. That hook above the toilet is about as thin as anything I ever heard the police department put forward. The commissioner will never stand for it even though he doesn't want a murder any more than anybody else does."

"Is the bump on her head very bad?"

"Concussion. Bad enough to cause death, the assistant medical examiner thought. Of course, I'm waiting for Dugan's autopsy. He's a thorough man."

Susan asked if it was possible, leaving the toilet hook out of it, for Miss Parton to have stumbled and given her head the fatal blow in falling.

"People so very rarely fall down on flat surfaces and kill themselves. It *could* have happened in this case. The head, you probably noticed, is in a very awkward position. As a matter of fact, it's resting exactly on the center of the concussion area. But that means she had to fall backwards with terrific violence. Most unlikely during the last hour's run on the excellent roadbed into New York. No curves. And this morning there were no sudden lurches of train. I've checked that."

Susan asked if the murderer couldn't have counted on a presumption that the deceased had died during the night in the mountainous New Hampshire district where the train was running over a rocky roadbed.

Again Curtis shook his head. "I have a hunch he or she counted on personal protection through something subtler, such as no apparent motive or too many motives for it to have been sensible to be obviously present when it happened. Of course, the scene was set: insane costuming of corpse, no weapon, most everybody in the vicinity disapproving of victim one way or another. It's not one of those cases you can hope to clear up while you shave or drink a cocktail."

"That young Conway and Joan Sutton showed the greatest personal dislike of Prunella Parton," mused Susan. "I admit they went to some lengths to stress the point. Oh, and certainly the beauty columnist wasn't full of praise and prayers for her."

"They all hated her, in my opinion. I couldn't prove it in court, but I think so. Stratfield, to date, is the least full of animosity, which should make him guilty as hell, but even he held a few unpleasant reservations about the lady, or I miss my guess."

"Maybe," suggested Susan, "the murderer has a passion for charades."

"And maybe not," said Curtis gloomily. Susan shot him a quick glance, but he said nothing more, and they started down the club-car steps.

At the bottom Susan remarked that Prunella Parton had looked very peaceful. "As if she never knew what hit her. Do you suppose she was actually asleep when she died?"

Curtis stopped abruptly, grasping her arm. "By George, you've got something there," he exclaimed. "Wait a minute, I want to talk to that porter again."

Susan turned back with him, and they remounted the car steps. Curtis stuck his head in the Pullman door and snapped an order. "Bring him into the club car," he added, and led Susan back to the still brightly lighted car.

One of the men attached to the district attorney's office presently brought the colored porter.

Curtis sprang his question in a conventional tone: "You closed the dead woman's eyelids?"

The Negro's own eyes looked as if they were about to pop out of his head.

"Ah closed—*Ah closed her eyelids?* Gawd in Heaven, no suh, no. Ah ain't been near that young lady. Ah just looked and called the conductor as fast as Ah could. That is Heaven's truth."

The very idea of having touched the corpse was quite obviously more than he could contemplate with equanimity. Both Susan and Curtis believed him in the glance of commiseration they exchanged. Yet Curtis persisted.

"Her eyes weren't open, then, when you looked into the compartment?"

"No suh, they's not open. They's shut. Tight shut. That's why Ah spoke twice, maybe three times to her. 'Cose, while's it was a peculiar place to sleep, she's lookin' jus' asleep, and sometimes them ladies they's a-takin' a drop. Excuse me, ma'am." He turned apologetically to Susan with a courtliness which nearly undid her sober expression.

Curtis was studying the Negro with satisfaction. He turned to Susan and said in a low tone, "That fixes the D.D.C.'s suicide theory. Eyes open automatically after death and stay open until a living being closes them. Oh, there can be exceptions due to certain rare conditions. There was no excuse, according to the assistant medical examiner, for Prunella Parton's eyes to have closed themselves again."

Susan shuddered as Curtis turned back to the porter.

"I understand you made no stops last night after Swiss Village until five o'clock this morning."

"That's correct, suh."

"And the only passengers in your Pullman were the members of Mr. Stratfield's party, so after they turned in you had no one to look after? No one rang for you?"

"A body could not ask for a no mo' quiet night. They all sleeps right sound and goes to sleep early for city folks. Those winter spo'ts do conduce to that." He scratched his head. "First Ah checks mah linen, unused, for the commissionaire this mornin' at the ya'ds."

"Where did you do that?"

"At mah cupb'a'd right opposite to the compartment where that young lady is." He looked owlishly in the direction of the Pullman.

"But you heard nothing? Nothing to make you believe she had not undressed and gone to bed? She wasn't talking to anyone?"

The porter could not remember having heard any sounds from Miss Parton's compartment.

"And after you checked your linen?" persisted Curtis.

Then the Negro explained he had come and sat in an unreserved section over the wheels, the nearest section to the compartment occupied by the dead woman. He had left the car only once during the night, and then not for more than two minutes. Maybe he had dozed but he was a light sleeper, always had been since he first began railroading twenty-nine years ago. Even somebody snoring could wake him. He had a reputation for being a punctual bell answerer, he modestly assured them.

Curtis nodded. "Then nothing unusual happened at all—all night long?"

"Well, it weren't 'zactly unusualness. It were a nightmare, Ah guesses."

"What was that?"

"The ole gen'leman with the white hair. He's in section nine. The gen'lemen all has sections—uppers not made up, Ah means.

An' long 'bout two-thirty o'clock he begins moanin' to hisself, then he calls out 'Mary! Mary!' twice, right loud. Musta waked hisself up, fo' right after Ah hears him turning over. And that was all. He don't have no mo' nightmares. Ah co'se that dark man, Mista Barron, is kinda restless, tossing around in his berth. Only other sound is that other presiden' man, the big man they says is also a adve'tisement gen'leman. He's snoring right smart."

"You mean the man called Penbroke?"

"That is the gen'leman, Ah guesses. Least, the other gen'lemen when they gets off th' train this morning asks me if that gen'leman way down the platform with a red cap is Mister Penbroke, and Ah says it is the big man, and they says something about maybe they can catch up with him and they'll all have breakfast together. Ah tolds them he has already breakfasted in the club car." For the first time the porter came near to beaming. "That Penbroken presiden' man is certainly a right lavish spender. Five dollars he gives me."

Curtis looked thoughtful. "Who was up first this morning?"

"That gen'leman, Mister Penbroke. Fo' a big man he sure do move like a cat. Out of his berth afore I heard him turning over."

"Where were you?"

"Still sittin' in section one waitin' for ma folks to start wakin' up. They don't none of them asks to be called 'cept the lady what is daid, and she only says to tell her when it's the las' moment to get off."

Curtis asked if the Negro remembered what time Penbroke had arisen and was told that it had been at exactly seven o'clock. He had gone directly to the men's room and had been followed a few moments later by the dark-haired man they had called Barron.

"What happened then?"

"Well, that older presiden' man, the gen'leman with white hair, he trumpeted in his berth."

"He what?"

"He sneeze and blows his nose."

Curtis said he saw what he meant. What had happened next? The Negro said that after a few moments Mr. Sutton had made his appearance in the aisle. At this point Barron had rung from the smoking compartment. He had wanted a split of soda and wanted it in a hurry. Susan judged he hadn't been very pleasant about it. The porter had followed Mr. Sutton down the aisle to answer this call. On his way the porter had not heard any sounds of wakefulness in the other berths. The host of the party, Mr. Stratfield, and its youngest male member, young Conway, had apparently still been sleeping. The youngest lady in the party had not been visible to him, but as he passed her drawing-room door he had noticed it was unlatched and open two or three inches. He had merely wondered if she was up and dressed in case the old man, who seemed to be her father, asked him. He hadn't observed anything about Miss Manchester or the deceased because neither of them had been in evidence. He had fetched Barron's seltzer from the club car ahead and had just returned with it when Mr. Stratfield emerged from behind his green curtains, dressed but sleepy eyed and complaining about the rough roadbed over which they had passed during the night. Stratfield had stumbled down to the washroom, passing the "big presiden' man" as he was leaving it, bound for the club car. The two had exchanged brief good mornings. Then traffic had cleared for a bit. Nothing else had happened until just before the train had come to a standstill at Grand Central.

"And then?" asked Curtis quietly.

The porter scratched his head again. "The big presiden' man, he's told me he wants to get off soon's we stop. Ah was gettin' his luggage to the vestibule when Ah happens to look back. There's a young lady outside the drawin' room where's the lady's daid later. Ah thinks at the time it's the lady herself but Ah been thinkin' it over and don't see, nohow, how it could have been."

"What was she wearing?" asked Curtis.

The porter said that was what made him think it couldn't have been the dead girl, because this one had been wearing a tweed suit and hat. He hadn't seen her face. Only her back.

"What became of her?"

"That Ah don't know. When Ah comes back for the big presiden' man's other bag she's nowhere around. Ah's still thinkin' then it was the lady herself from that drawing room. It ain't so peculiar seein' folks in the aisle of a Pullman a' course."

"Exactly. And then what happened next?"

"The big presiden' man comes back from the club car when the train stops. We was 'zactly on time—seven-thirty. He gets off and leaves with a redcap. About two minutes later the other three gen'lemen comes out of the smoking compar'ment and off they goes."

"Where," asked Curtis, "was the young man, the blond young man, all this time?"

The porter said he guessed he'd been sleeping but that he thought he had gone to the washroom just as the other three "gen'lemen" were leaving the train. So far as he knew, they hadn't spoken or even seen each other. The porter had returned immediately to the car to see if any of his other passengers' luggage was ready. In a few minutes the blond young man had come out of the washroom, still in his dressing gown. He had dressed behind the green curtains of his section. It was some minutes later, seven forty-five, before he reappeared. Now that the Negro thought of it, the blond young man had thrown back his curtains, and the pretty young girl had come out of her drawing room at the same moment. They had said hello and left the train together. Again time had passed. About five minutes later the dark young woman from the other drawing room had appeared and departed. Then silence until eight o'clock when the Negro had knocked on Miss Parton's door. Meantime, after Miss Manchester's departure the porter had been undressing berths but he had kept his attention in the direction of the Parton drawing room, awaiting a signal from its occupant. He could swear that no one had entered or left the Pullman car after Miss Manchester's departure.

When this recital had been completed, prodded as to details by Curtis and distinguished by the porter's railroader concept of time and its passage, Susan suddenly became obsessed by the awful thought that the only person who seemed to have had the best opportunity to dispose of Miss Parton was the Negro himself. She cast him a covert glance. His honest black face was reassuring, and at no time during the interview had he shown any conceivably unnatural agitation, except over Curtis' question as to whether he had shut the dead woman's eyes. And this was really, she knew, not very unnatural. Few people, unaccustomed to dealing with corpses, would have approached the subject with serenity, much less a corpse itself.

Curtis sat studying the Negro's face. "So nothing that seemed to you in the least strange happened all night and up to the time that you entered Miss Parton's drawing room?"

"Only the young lady standing outside her door at 'proximately seven twenty-nine—that is, jus' 'fore we stops."

"Yes," Curtis assured him, "that is something we shall want to go into further. I'll want you at the district attorney's office at four o'clock sharp this afternoon. In the meantime, don't talk—except, of course, to the police if they ask you to."

Curtis rose. "Come along," he said to Susan. But again he paused, turning back to the porter. "Look here," he remarked, taking a pad of paper and a pencil from his pocket. "I want you to draw me a picture of where everybody slept last night. Just a rough sketch." They waited while the Negro complied.

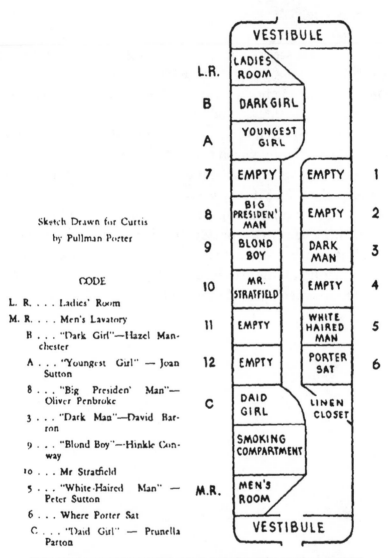

THE NEW HAMPSHIRE-NEW YORK EXPRESS PULLMAN IN WHICH
STRATFIELD'S PARTY TRAVELED

CHAPTER TEN

As SUSAN, in the firm clutch of Lyle Curtis' steel fingers, stepped gingerly over the last roughly boarded third rail and climbed up onto the long platform leading back to the station she explained that she had got three of the best talkers in the fashion business to assemble for luncheon with her.

"I started at that phone with quite an expansive list of possibilities but boiled it down under the headings: 'Wouldn't Know Enough Despite Interest in Gossip,' 'Not Quite Talkative Enough, Too Cautious' and 'Daughters of Loquacity Who Knew Deceased Well.'"

Mr. Curtis admitted in an approving tone that this sounded efficient and clearly to the point. He asked what time Susan was lunching.

"Quarter of one at Hoggarth's. By the way, all three of the girls I asked, Crystine Kurter, who's a copy writer at Fogwit and Putkin, Florence Stonebridge, who does publicity for a string of manufacturers, and Alice Bomm, fashion editor of the New York *Globe*, used to be at Sutton and Barron. I had a hunch that would help, because before they graduated to their present jobs they were co-workers with Prunella Parton. If Prunella's sister Carol was on the train I suppose I'm in special luck to have asked Alice Bomm. They are colleagues now."

Curtis whistled. "Splendid. You couldn't have done better. Why don't you give up the fashion business and come into the department?"

Miss Yates cast him a withering look. "Because I like to keep my job, come administrations and go administrations."

"Just cautious and penurious," admonished Curtis. Then his face turned grave. "Look here, Susan, there's something I want to say to you that I don't want you to forget. I telephoned you this morning against my better judgment."

"I like that!" Susan exclaimed. "Then I've wasted my morning."

"You'll not like it if I find you going off on any private sleuthing ideas in this case. There are times when you are just downright unpredictable."

"Surely you don't mean impetuous?"

"I mean that telling me there isn't any fashion precedent for long underwear worn with a red evening gown is one thing and not, so far as I can see, dangerous to you. But I've noticed a tendency on your part to dig up burial grounds of your own. It may interest you to know that I have other plans for you. An early funeral forms no part of them."

With faint success Susan pretended to look mystified. "What extremely loose talk. You make me sound like an ambulance chaser."

"Hearse would be a better noun. You have no self-solicitude. Do you know what they call you in the police department?"

"Good heavens, have they got me labeled? This *is* embarrassing."

Curtis said severely: "The chief has referred to you in my presence as 'your friend, the corpse tripper.' And—"

"Just because I went to a luncheon a year or so ago and a girl had the bad judgment to drop dead and just because another time I opened a closet door and a corpse fell out and just because—"

"There," scoffed Curtis heatedly, "you see what I mean! You get the point. But this time we have called you in as a fashion expert. Just as a fashion expert. Understand?"

"What," demanded Susan, "about this grilling I'm asked to do this noon?"

Curtis said that if it meant putting her in the slightest danger he would call the whole business off that moment.

"And leave me with three ladies on my hands and nothing to talk about?"

"My heart doesn't exactly bleed over the likelihood of that happening, but I really think there's no reason for anyone to suspect you're helping the D. A.'s office."

"Only just all of those lovely people you had assembled in the club car, one of whom must be the murderer."

"We can't be entirely sure of that. And, besides, the D.D.C., who, you may have noticed, does not approve of ladies having brains, fixed you up with a thoroughly dignified excuse for being present. While you were telephoning he mentioned that you represented the undertaker."

"The old dear! How simply charming of him. You know, Lyle, I think he's been worried about me ever since the Alma Peters case."

"And with good reason. I've never known anybody less able than you to avoid getting unexpectedly mixed up with the wrong people."

Susan sniffed politely and remarked that this was pure libel but that she supposed it was futile to see her lawyer about suing. And, inasmuch as Curtis was so worried about her sleuthing propensities, she would promise to go into no cellars or submarines not specifically recommended by the forces of law and order. "That is," she ended ominously, "I'll promise if you'll agree to keep me apprised of your progress toward apprehending the murderer or murderess of Prunella Parton. I always say that even in a world engaged in mass murders there's nothing like a single one."

"All right. All right. You can sit in my office until this case is finished, but no galloping about on privately conceived inspirations. If necessary I'll have you locked up as a vagrant."

"Of course," murmured Miss Yates, "I have got a fashion-designing salon, a workroom with forty girls in it and a sales staff to keep an eye on. To hear you talk, anybody would think I haven't a thing to do when there isn't a murderer romping about town. By the way, weren't there any fingerprints in Miss Parton's drawing room or in her lavatory?"

Curtis said there had been: Miss Parton's and the porter's. The car, of course, had been pretty thoroughly wiped down and polished before it started south on its New York run. In any case, no other prints had come to light, not even smudges.

They had reached the station rotunda at this point, and Curtis guided Miss Yates toward the taxi exit. A few moments later, safely stowed in a cab, Susan rolled down the window, leaned out and, putting her lips close to Mr. Curtis' left ear, whispered: "If you want a prediction from that soothsayer, Miss Susan Yates, bear this in mind; the murderer or murderess was a sadist. The fashion angle definitely points to it." With this Susan demurely returned her head to the interior of the taxi.

"Come down to my office right after luncheon," called Curtis as the cab moved off.

Immediately Susan felt a prickle along her spine. Without Curtis' bantering presence the memory of the body on the drawing-room floor seemed twice as horrible. Prunella Parton hadn't perhaps been an altogether nice person, but murder was no way for someone to have attempted to adjust his or her differences with the advertising-copy writer. Murder was frightening business. And Lyle needn't have been so emphatic about her staying out of private sleuthing in connection with this one. If she didn't check her tendency to sudden impulses she knew perfectly well she might come to an end highly unfitting a fashion designer.

On this sobering thought, Miss Yates stepped out of the cab in front of Hoggarth's restaurant and turned to pay the driver. As she did so a long black car which had slowed up in the center lane of Madison Avenue traffic picked up speed and disappeared before she had time to see the face of the driver. With a shudder she felt that whoever the man had been, he had also been more than a little interested in her. Was it, she asked herself as she walked toward Hoggarth's expensive façade, because undertakers' assistants might not be likely to lunch there?

Once inside Hoggarth's, Susan felt better. Its discretion of decoration and service had a soothing effect. She sought the phone booths and put in a call for her salon. Miss Button, her secretary, sounded worried. She did hope Miss Yates wasn't going to get herself involved again in one of Mr. Curtis' cases. Miss Button could, on occasion, assume a combination bodyguard and governess role despite the fact that she was a year Susan's junior. Susan knew that Miss Button admired her but suspected that her secretary was also of the opinion that there were times when she was inclined to send her wits away on a holiday. And Miss Button had never entirely favored the district attorney's office since one of Curtis' myrmidons had taught himself to typewrite on her machine.

"Don't be trying, Button," Miss Yates recommended energetically. "I'm not getting involved. I'd just as soon involve you."

"It would be much more sensible," came Miss Button's voice. "Nobody would know me. Everybody in New York knows you. That silly old detective district commander might just as well have said you were a visiting White Wing or a female plumber."

Susan said that it was to be hoped she could be present while depositions were being taken without becoming a menace to a murderer she'd never seen in her life before. "It's not as if I meant anything to those people, Button."

Miss Button used asperity of tone. "You will before you get through," she prophesied.

"Oh, for the love of Pete, don't take it so hard. If you're a good girl I'll let you help if Mr. Curtis needs any feminine assistance other than this luncheon I'm staging."

Miss Button said stonily that she would not forget this promise.

Miss Crystine Kurter and Miss Florence Stonebridge arrived under the Hoggarth street canopy on one another's heels and promptly at the appointed time. Miss Bomm had told Susan she would have to be a little late.

After calming Miss Button over the phone, Miss Yates had managed to direct the activities of Susan Yates, Inc., in a general way, to repair her complexion and to acquire an orchid, the latter as a note least likely to associate her with crime.

Seeing Miss Kurter and Miss Stonebridge following each other in the revolving door, Susan made a brief bow to the Hoggarth foyer mirror and murmured to herself: "Lady investigator now goes to work!"

Miss Kurter and Miss Stonebridge came up briskly. Their perfectly made-up faces were embellished with the kind of smiles reserved for important people. Miss Yates was important as well as charming. She was known on two continents—or had been before the European cataclysm—and she had never found that efficiency need be nurtured in a hard-boiled or even brittle bosom. She was, indeed, a young woman of gentle breeding whose family's financial judgment had become somewhat shattered in 1929 and who, not the least deflated by the results, had set to work and become wealthy and distinguished in her own rights within the span of eleven years.

"Alice Bomm is lunching with us, too," Susan explained to Miss Kurter and Miss Stonebridge, "but she's going to have to join us a bit later. Shall we go on in and order?"

Miss Kurter and Miss Stonebridge made appropriate murmurs, indicating that Miss Yates's wishes were their wishes and where her feet trod theirs would follow.

Ordering finished, Susan plunged with what she hoped was well-staged impetuosity into her news. Had they heard that Prunella Parton had died that morning?

"Died!" exclaimed both young women in astonished unison.

Miss Kurter restrained herself sufficiently to convey the impression that she was shocked beyond speaking. Miss Stonebridge was franker.

"It's a wonder it wasn't murder," she averred emphatically. "You know, at no time in some years would I have been at all surprised to hear someone had murdered Prunella. But fancy her just up and dying!"

Susan said nothing, and Miss Stonebridge continued energetically: "I bet there won't be many noncrocodile tears at her funeral. She's helled around messing up other people's lives too long. That poor Conway kid, for instance." Susan picked up her ears, nodded interestedly and listened. "Prunella," explained Miss Stonebridge, "practically grabbed Hinkle Conway out of the infant class. He had only just come up from Princeton and started work at Sutton and Barron when Prunella, shrewdly sensing he was a kid with talent, began laying her nets. She made a great play for him all right. It would have taken a youngster with ice water in his veins to have resisted her, and no one's ever suggested Conway isn't emotional. You don't know him?" Susan shook her head. "Well, he's young and blond and handsome but all nerves and impetuosity." The latter term having been all too recently applied to herself by Lyle Curtis, Susan winced slightly. Miss Stonebridge bubbled on. "I was in Sutton and Barron's publicity department at the time. Just a glass partition between me and the Parton conquest. Believe me, I saw plenty." Miss Kurter nodded in a way which conveyed better than words that she could well imagine what Miss Stonebridge meant by that. "The way that woman could stage a campaign was sometimes embarrassing," confessed Miss Stonebridge.

"Really?" cooed Miss Kurter, now looking doubtful that anything could carry Miss Stonebridge that far.

Florence Stonebridge ignored the interruption. "In a week, not a day more, certainly, she had young Conway absolutely starry eyed. Of course, it was all put on the up-and-up basis that she had a heart of gold—and just as hard, between the three of us—and was only anxious to help him learn the ropes. Jump the rope, I could have told him, the poor fish. But, of course, it really wasn't any of *my* business, and the point was that Prunella was out to tolerate no competition in the copy department, and a blind man could see that Conway was potentially that. Talent, that youngster! A natural fountain with words. A little youthfully pompous, of course, but that wouldn't have held him back if Prunella hadn't given him all the bum steers in the book. And sweetly! Girls, you really should have seen the technique. From the first day she fixed it. She agreed to edit everything he wrote. Of course, his early stuff needed some pulling together and sharpening but it was good. I used to pop in and help myself to a look. However, there's more than one good way to say most things, and Prunella always thought of the other way. Conway mistook that oblique look in her eyes for passionate and altruistic interest. Prunella always managed, of course, to let the powers higher up, the copy chief and Black Adonis, know that the kid had come to her for help and that she had helped him out."

"The Black Adonis?" queried Miss Yates, apparently enchanted with the conversation.

"That's David Barron, the vice-president. Tell you more about him later. But the net of it is, Prunella won't be missed by Hinkle Conway. She's made him pay her dividends right on the line for months and months. Of course, lately he's been catching on. They tell me he has at least been writing his copy forward instead of backward. I wouldn't know, but I should think the old man's daughter's interest hasn't exactly hindered him either."

"Who?" It was Susan's question.

"Joan Sutton. The president's daughter. They met at some debutante shindig, and Joan fell for Conway, found he worked for Papa, and, being naturally managerial, the little witch probably discovered how the land lay with Prunella. I guess by that time 'The Pruned,' which is what Conway's been privately dubbed at Sutton and Barron, was sort of half in love with Joan and half mad at himself. Anyway, somebody was telling me that Joan tried to get Prunella fired. No soap. Prunella was getting protection from higher up. Barron, I suppose. And, besides, they really have depended on Prunella for sheer brilliance over there. She had what it takes: ability and a capacity for selling herself, plus a few darker arts. But I dare say little Joan won't pine away, either, over Prunella's death. By the way, what did she die of?" Both young women looked brightly at Susan.

"Heart," breathed Susan noncommittally. "Heart went back on her—or so I heard."

But Miss Kurter and Miss Stonebridge had already lost interest in this minor point. "It's funny," averred Miss Stonebridge, "what a lot of scandalous things she got away with without Papa Sutton rising up in wrath. He's completely intolerant of scandal, one is led to believe. Has always been the perfect Puritan, I hear, since his wife ran away and left him, or something, fifteen years ago. Everybody's been waiting for five years for Prunella to get the gate on the basis of immodest behavior, to put it mildly. But she has led a charmed life. Of course, Barron gets away with murder too. Regular wolf. He and Prunella were certainly two birds of the same color. But he'd always stayed shy of office affairs before. Too smart. Too smart, that is, until Prunella decided he was booked as Conquest 98. They tell me it was an adroitly handled campaign, if ever there was one. Barron was supposed to be involved in a very big affair with some friend of his wife's when Prunella stepped in and took charge of his heart. She might as well have married him, the way she's made him toe the line. He used to intersperse affairs with a continuous and, I have a hunch, platonic friendship with Hazel Manchester over at *Inter-Allied News*. They grew up together, and she's been absolutely mad about him for years. But when Prunella stepped in Barron even stopped answering friendly telephone calls from Hazel. I had that straight from his secretary, not, I suppose, that she expected me to repeat it."

"And has this been going on right up to now?" Susan inquired.

"And how!" exclaimed Miss Stonebridge.

Miss Kurter agreed. "Right up to his neck in Parton glue. It's been funny, too, for he's a wily one."

"But some of the wiliest get lost on the subject of dear old sex," pointed out Miss Stonebridge sagely. "I'd say, however, that Barron's been running in luck not to get Papa Sutton down on both of them. Certainly nobody else over at S. and B. was in any dark about what was going on—including young Conway, which must have meant including Joan Sutton."

"Is she nice?" chirped Susan, feeling an abomination to posterity.

"A lamb," agreed Miss Kurter and Miss Stonebridge.

"Blonde, you know," went on the former, "and simply darling. Best schools, and smart. I'm sure if she wants to marry young Conway she will." She looked at Miss Stonebridge as if daring her to deny it.

"But, darling," beamed Miss Stonebridge, "I'd be the last person in the world to deny it. You are absolutely right. She's a deb with vision. Looks sweet, acts sweet but has a well-developed will of her own. My young sister was at a summer camp with her when they were both fourteen. She says Joan simply ran the place with a sugar-coated spoon."

"You say Barron has a wife?" inquired Susan, trying very hard to sound gossipy and casual.

"Oh yes, tucked away somewhere. California, I think. But I believe he's been shrewd enough to avoid giving her justification for a divorce involving big alimony. I mean, I believe she walked out first and then wasn't able to get anything on him. You'd think Prunella would have provided reason enough if all she wanted was important provision for herself. Everybody's been expecting hourly to hear Barron's got socked to pay on the line."

"You would think Prunella would have been a little cautious about running the risk of being named correspondent," observed Miss Yates thoughtfully.

Both girls laughed, and Miss Kurter explained that to the contrary, a nice touch of alienation of affections or correspondence would merely have provided added luster for Prunella's battle-ax.

"Nothing short of murder bothered Prunella Parton," observed Miss Stonebridge in the tone of an oracle.

Susan winced again, wondering if, as some people believed, an idea could be planted in another person's head just by having it in your own. What was it they called it? "Extra perception," or something like that. But it was terribly difficult for her not to go on thinking behind a confusion of thoughts: "Prunella Parton was murdered. Murdered in cold blood. Cliché. Murdered in her sleep. Well, anyway, murdered."

Miss Kurter was giggling, a rather lofty giggle, to be sure. "I do suppose murder would rather have stopped even Prunella."

"When you consider everything," observed Miss Stonebridge, "it's really extraordinary no one did murder her. She's been such a priceless mark for it."

CHAPTER ELEVEN

As MISS STONEBRIDGE finished speaking Susan thought: "Good heavens, Lyle is going to have to sift the alibis and motives of half New York. This is awful."

It was at this moment that Miss Alice Bomm, fashion editor of the New York *Globe*, arrived, smartly turned out and displaying yet another Important Person smile for Susan. General greetings ultimately reaching a degree of muddiness at which they could be happily abandoned, Susan's other two guests pounced on the newcomer with the news of Prunella Parton having passed from their midst.

Miss Bomm characterized herself as stunned, thoroughly stunned. She didn't know when she had heard anything so astonishing. Prunella Parton, of all people, when half New York had been wanting to kill her for years, and then to have her go and just quietly pass out. Incredible. And what were Sutton & Barron, especially the Barron division, going to do without the dear girl?

Susan was a little taken back by discovering Miss Bomm as well acquainted as the other two girls with Miss Parton's most recent amorous attachment. Alice Bomm had, after all, been away from Sutton & Barron much longer than the other two.

Presently Susan shoved in a question. Wouldn't Prunella's death be awfully upsetting to her sister?

Miss Bomm was scarcely reticent on the point. "Carol?" she cried. "Good lord, no. She'll probably throw an 'I-told-you-so' party. She's been convinced for ages that Prunella would kill

herself with cuckoo reducing baths, too much champagne and cyni-
cism. When they lived together they simply couldn't bear each
other."

"Oh," warbled Susan. "Did they used to live together?"

"Until Prunella started her Barron campaign and evidently
plucked herself off a very superior raise. That was about eight
months ago. Carol had been dying to split up, poor youngster, but
you know what newspapers pay girl reporters. She couldn't quite
swing it."

"How," requested Miss Stonebridge, to whom this angle was
evidently as much news as it was to Susan, "did Prunella's getting
a raise make it financially sound for Carol to go off on her own?"

Miss Bomm looked momentarily blank. "That hadn't occurred
to me," she admitted.

"Prunella must have underwritten both apartments," proposed
Miss Stonebridge. "I'm sure she didn't fancy the joint ménage any
more than Carol did. Carol has a sweetly, if youthfully, sharp
tongue, you know. She also had a way of making Prunella's cattiness
and grand airs look merely silly. I think Carol was the one person
in the world who could make Prunella feel as if she were wearing
false teeth and a wig."

"Then why on earth did they live together?" It was again Susan's
question.

The three girls exchanged glances of speculation. Miss Bomm
brought hers into verbal focus. "It's funny, but I always had a hunch
that Prunella used Carol as window dressing, some form of respect-
ability. Two sisters living together somehow sounds more moral
than two sisters living separately, though I can't possibly tell you
why. But it was funny, because, while Prunella has despised as inferior beings most people, I think she positively hated Carol. They
used to have simply fiendish rows. I dropped by their apartment
one night before Prunella moved to Park Avenue. They were going
at it hammer and tongs."

"Coining phrases again, darling?" inquired Miss Kurter, and
was effectively ignored.

"They dropped it, of course, when I rang the bell. Before that I hadn't known what to do. I'd been standing outside the door wondering if it wouldn't be more discreet to go away."

"I know," agreed Miss Stonebridge. "It's so frightfully embarrassing being put in a position of seeming to eavesdrop."

"What was it all about?" prodded Miss Kurter, brushing eavesdropping neatly to one side.

"Something about an operation. I couldn't make out who was supposed to have it or not to have it, but it definitely involved disagreement. They were simply shrieking at each other. Just before I rang the bell Carol yelled something about supposing Prunella thought dollars were better than death, or some such fine alliteration. I probably got that all wrong. They were both talking at once. Of course, I was curious, but though I stayed for three drinks they didn't bring the matter up again—actually pretended to be on the best of terms. Naturally, I couldn't ask what all the death-and-dollars business—if that was it—had been about, inasmuch I had heard it through a closed door."

"Exactly, darling," agreed Miss Stonebridge.

"I did tell Prunella," went on Miss Bomm, "that she was looking a bit under the weather, but she only said: 'Well, my lamb, I don't know that they'd choose you as the "Healthiest Girl in Manhattan."'"

Inspecting Miss Bomm's rather muddy complexion and the deep circles under her eyes, Susan suspected that Miss Parton had evidently hit a sore point with that bit of repartee.

"Then," continued Miss Bomm, "after a while I tried Carol out, telling her she didn't look quite well, but she can be so absent-minded. She was off on some private thought and didn't even hear what I said. I couldn't go on and on telling them both they looked seedy."

"No, of course you couldn't," said Susan, and Miss Kurter remarked that, at least, she'd never heard of either of the Parton sisters undergoing an operation. She turned to Miss Bomm. "Perhaps they were talking about someone else. Everybody knows Carol's terribly energetic in her philanthropic point of view. Maybe she was trying to get Prunella to pay for some unfortunate's honor or something.

Miss Stonebridge looked mildly shocked, then remarked cheerfully that possibly Prunella had been suffering from something malignant, something which had finally killed her, and that Carol had been trying to persuade her to have an operation. "You know," she added in a rather pious tone, "it would have taken a great deal of persuasion to have induced Prunella to have had one inch of her body disfigured by a surgeon's knife. She was enormously vain."

"Enormously," echoed Miss Bomm.

Feeling this angle rather more than adequately covered, Susan attempted to return their thoughts to recent interruptions in the "Pas de scandale" theme song of Sutton & Barron. Miss Bomm confirmed the other two girls' remarks regarding Peter Sutton's distaste for all improprieties and confessed that when she had worked at the agency she had invariably felt exactly like an upset wastepaper basket when she had had to confront the president.

"The way he looked at me, with his fishy eyes magnified by those shiny glasses, always made me feel as if I were various scraps of paper crumpled up and thrown away days before, a slatternly disgrace because I was female instead of male."

"He can't stand women," agreed Miss Stonebridge, drawing in her diminutive stomach and arching her shoulders minutely.

Miss Bomm and Miss Kurter exchanged fleeting glances of speculation, and Miss Kurter inquired sweetly: "Don't tell me, darling, you ever tried to vamp him?"

Miss Stonebridge looked shocked. "What a fantastic idea! I'd be just as likely to go around rolling my eyes at Mayor LaGuardia's 'Fat Boy.'"

Susan interposed another question before rapier play could develop into a time-costly detour. "But you all think the wayward David Barron had settled down to a steady diet of Prunella Parton recently?"

"Oh, for eight months at least," Miss Stonebridge estimated.

Miss Bomm thought it had begun just before Prunella had moved into her own apartment on Park Avenue.

"Just about the time Joan Sutton had successfully rescued the Conway infant," was Miss Kurter's recollection.

Susan turned this time arrangement over in her mind, then asked innocently if Prunella had had a nice apartment. She was informed that it had consisted of an enormous living room, two bedrooms and two baths with a dining alcove and the handiwork of an interior decorator.

"She had Mason Interiors do it, and you know what Lucinda Mason charges," observed Miss Stonebridge, who turned out to be the only one of them ever actually to have been inside the more recent abode of the late Miss Parton. Without being pressed, Miss Stonebridge entered upon an ample description of its elegance.

"Any other men in her life?" asked Susan in, she hoped, a sufficiently gossipy tone.

All three women trilled in horror at her innocence.

"Men?" shrieked Miss Bomm. "Good lord, she strung them like pearls on an anniversary necklace. Prunella was a born collector. When I first knew her, five years ago, she was running around with a very arty crowd. Had on the string a sculptor, an etcher and a modernist painter—the latter rather an exciting gent. Lawrence Stratfield. It's a wonder she didn't try to nab him permanently. They say he wallows in money. Inherited it from a great aunt, or someone, I believe. Certainly he couldn't have made it painting the psychic sunsets and triangular human beings he turns out. Lately he's been doing psychoanalytical souls or something of the sort. But when he paints your soul, I understand, it's more expensive than if he merely dabbles around with your body. Anyway, though I personally think his work is completely aboriginal, he does know simply volumes about art. Really awfully informed. The Kork-Petulla people, you know, have him on their advertising Plan Board. Oh, by the way, did you know, Crystine"—and Miss Bomm turned excited eyes upon Miss Kurter—"and do you people over at Fogwit and Putkin know, that Penbroke's lion's share of the Kork-Petulla advertising appropriation has been wobbling lately?"

Miss Kurter shook a shocked head. "Not really? Oliver Penbroke is probably tearing his hair. He must clean up close to $150,000 a year on Kork-Petulla. Who's after it?"

The fashion editor toyed with her bomb for a moment, then dropped it neatly in the exact center of the luncheon table. "Sutton and Barron, ably assisted by Prunella Parton! Or they were." She paused for the full effect of the explosion. "Our advertising-news columnist was telling me last Saturday that Prunella had brought Lawrence Stratfield into the picture, got him wined and dined by Messieurs Sutton and Barron and got them all invited up to his place—Stratfield's, I mean—in New Hampshire for this past week end. It must have been quite a week end to cause Prunella to come home and fall dead. By the way, when *did* she die?"

Everyone's eyes sought Susan who shook her head. This at least she did not know.

"What a story!" bubbled Miss Kurter, evidently referring to the Kork-Petulla business. "And what a devilish scheme. I've always heard that Lawrence Stratfield has no end of influence with Kork-Petulla. We used to think he was a big stockholder. But Mr. Fogwit told me last winter that he doesn't own a gram of K.-P. stock. They evidently just like him, or, at least, Mr. Petulla does. He's a gay old bird, by the way. Prunella should have gone straight after *him* without bothering about Lawrence Stratfield and his influence. My lord, Oliver Penbroke will have a hemorrhage if Sutton and Barron pull that one off."

"Maybe they won't now that Prunella's passed out," suggested Miss Stonebridge. "I can't imagine a dilettante like Lawrence Stratfield being made to first-aid Peter Sutton and David Barron. Peter Sutton especially. He's the soul of business, while I always thought Larry Stratfield was the soul of arty-arty business and affairs of the heart. Not that I've ever been able to see what women see in him. He's ugly as a mud fence."

"Don't fool yourself," advised Miss Bomm. "He's got what it takes. Haven't you ever noticed, darling, how seducing some ugly men are?"

There was a general murmur of reminiscent agreement in which Susan pretended to join, but for a moment her mind was rather filled with a picture of an extremely good-looking young man provided with an excellent profile, a chin that was a chin, a pair of

extremely efficient-looking shoulders and just a touch of soft
Southern drawl except for the times when she had heard him barking Gatling-gun instructions. What a story she was going to have
to pour into Lyle Curtis' ears! And what her luncheon guests
wouldn't give to know that not only members of the firm of Sutton
& Barron but Oliver Penbroke had been present over the late week
end! Aloud she said discreetly to Miss Bomm:

"You were telling about the days when Prunella was running
around with Lawrence Stratfield's arty crowd. She must have had
rather a full program, dangling a sculptor, an etcher and a modernist painter all at once."

Once more all three girls chirped horror over her innocence of
mind. She was assured that three simultaneous claimants to her
heart had been nothing at all to Prunella Parton.

"Sounds a bit messy," admitted Susan, and Miss Bomm said
that her Sunday editor called it willful acquiescence.

"We mustn't forget she's dead, the hussy," Miss Stonebridge
reminded them sweetly.

At this point Miss Kurter inspected her watch, assured them
all it was horribly late—nearly three. There ensued a general
exodus garlanded with a plethora of thanks to Susan for a simply
darling luncheon.

CHAPTER TWELVE

Susan had had her car sent around while she was at luncheon. She found it parked under the attentive eye of the doorman and headed down the avenue through sparse midafternoon traffic. By twenty past three she was in Curtis' office. He was behind his desk, looking all but snowed under an inharmoniously composed bed of pink, red and yellow memorandum slips surrounding a phalanx of extremely active telephones. He punctuated his remarks into the transmitter of one to say to Susan:

"Do you mind running down to the street to see if you can locate a three-eared guy? I could use him." He returned to the individual at the other end of the wire while the other phones maintained a nervous clamor.

Smiling at Lieutenant Burk who stood waiting by Lyle's side, Susan perched on the edge of an extremely official-feeling chair. Its unrelenting hardness presented her with the thought that those who usually sat on it were probably hopeful of evading the law rather than co-operating with its forces of justice. Moreover, Curtis' sharply disconnected words scarcely created an atmosphere of sociability in the sternly furnished room. Susan looked around her. It had been months since she had been here, and on that occasion she had seen its official occupant weary and betrayed by hope. Then her doodling at this very desk had provided the final segment needed to complete a circle of evidence around a skillful and pitiless murderer.

Curtis, Susan observed, had made no changes in the stark simplicity of the office's decorative scheme. There was still no bronze Napoleon, no mysterious commode containing weird lethal weapons, no skulls or infamous fingerprints, no documents of espionage, no phials of poison. But there were Curtis' broad shoulders and his quick, handsome features excused from perfection by unruly hair and the chin that was almost too much of a chin, deficiencies which had not saved him from being the goal of many a lady in search of a male providing full specifications. But Curtis was quite as well posted on feminine psychology as on criminal, Susan had observed. He was, moreover, capable of exhibiting the skill of a pursued sailfish, the diplomacy of an ambassador and the advantages of a flourishing sense of humor.

"Damn cloying females," he said, slamming down a receiver. "That was our friend Hazel Manchester trying to be helpful." He cupped another instrument around his cheek and spoke into it.

The ensuing conversation from Curtis' end was maddeningly uninformative. "Yes . . . Good . . . No . . . Tailed . . . ? Yes . . . Yes. . . ." At its termination Curtis shot at Susan the hope that she didn't mind waiting and turned to Lieutenant Burk.

"All right, Burk. Go on. You were telling me that Sutton and Barron left the train accompanied by Lawrence Stratfield at just after seven-thirty. They breakfasted together as they said in their deposition?"

"Yes sir. In the Grand Central Oyster Bar. I checked with their redcaps and the waiter in the restaurant. Also the hat-check girl and headwaiter. They left there at eight o'clock. Two other redcaps took them to the Forty-second Street exit of the station where Stratfield grabbed a cab and Sutton and Barron called a street porter to carry their baggage across to their office in the Lincoln Building. They got there a few minutes after eight, according to the porter and an office boy. No stops on the way. And they didn't leave their desks or go unobserved by secretaries until the police call came for them to come to the Pullman siding."

"All of this, unfortunately, doesn't prove much of anything," muttered Curtis, studying the exact top of Susan's hat. "Medical

Examiner Dugan's complete report, which I now have, indicates that at eight-fifteen this morning the body had been dead somewhere around an hour. The train reached Grand Central at seven-thirty sharp. The body wasn't examined by Dugan's assistant for forty-five minutes after that, the porter not having discovered it until eight o'clock. But this puts death probably within fifteen minutes of Grand Central. It might have been just about the time the train was pulling in. It conceivably was half an hour earlier, taking into account a fifteen-minute leeway the other direction over Dugan's 'about an hour.'"

Curtis dropped his eyes from Susan's hat to her face.

"I went back and had a third talk with that porter after I left you this noon," he said. "I'm convinced he would have known it if any stranger had come aboard after the train stopped. And he says no one did. The only stranger was the girl in tweeds he saw standing outside the deceased's drawing room a minute before the train came to a standstill. That porter is an old railroader. He has one of the most accurate time memories I recall encountering. I gave him half a dozen tests. Difficult ones. He knows the difference between one minute, half a minute and three minutes. Most people don't. What I'm getting at is that Prunella Parton was killed by someone on that train and that someone had to have been on it at least from South Norwalk, Connecticut, which was the last stop before Grand Central. There wasn't a stop at One Hundred and Twenty-fifth Street even. And, since Dugan can't be any more definite about the time of death, we can't prove it wasn't a New York county job. Dugan claims he did his best to place it in Connecticut for us."

Susan smiled, knowing Lyle Curtis would have been a very aggrieved assistant district attorney if the medical examiner had.

"Why," she asked, "are you interested in where Sutton and Barron and Stratfield had breakfast and what they did until they were called back to the Pullman siding?"

"The ski clothes. I want to find out who carried them off the train. There's nothing to discount the thought that whoever did is our murderer."

"Couldn't the murderer have planted them on someone else?"

"Not time enough. The murderer evidently had plenty to do as it was. The more I think about it the more my guess is that he must have done the job while the porter was fetching Barron's split of seltzer. That means inside three minutes. The rest of the time the porter was in constant attendance, and various of the men in Stratfield's party were appearing and reappearing in the aisle. I want to get your angle on something, Susan. Actually everything which seems to have been done *couldn't* have been in three minutes. It was only a matter of seconds, of course, to inflict the concussion with whatever variety of blunt instrument the murderer used. And if the victim was sleeping the murder would have been all the more quickly accomplished, no moment lost accounting innocently for his or her presence in the drawing room—just a question of walking in and bashing her. But, then, if she was asleep it's to be presumed she was sleeping in the berth. It certainly had been slept in. It must have taken the better part of a minute, in that case, to drag the body from the berth and plant it in the lavatory doorway. How long do you figure it would have taken an able-bodied person to get that underwear on the corpse, to say nothing of the dress?"

Miss Yates wrinkled her brow. "Heavens, several minutes at least."

"Exactly. So, for working guidance, I'm assuming the underwear was already on the body when attacked. How long would it have taken to add the evening gown?"

"That could have been done pretty quickly. It was all in one piece, of course, and very low necked. There was a side placket with a zipper too."

"Is that what you call the thing over her left hip running up past the waistline? I know it included a zipper. Indulge in them myself. But do you call what it opened a placket, I mean?"

"Yes. A placket is the opening in a skirt or dress or gown—or slip or petticoat, for that matter. Its purpose is to make the garment bigger when open at its narrowest point. This is for convenience in pulling it over the shoulders which are naturally wider than human waists."

"Very ably explained. Did you notice anything peculiar about the zipper placket in the deceased's crimson velvet gown?"

"I don't know that it was peculiar, taking the picture as a whole, but it was open, if that's what you mean."

"That's what I mean. The zipper placket was open, which seems to indicate that the person who put the dress on the body was in a very big hurry. Certainly the murderer didn't dress a live Prunella Parton up that way or induce her to. But the time element is important, I'm sure."

Susan pondered again, then said she thought the evening gown could have been dragged on in a minute despite the inertness of the body and the fact that it wouldn't have pulled on as easily over woolen underwear as over bare skin or a silk slip.

"All right," said Curtis. "We've accounted for two minutes, then, of the three allowed the murderer. In the remaining minute he or she couldn't have come out in the aisle and done much pawing about in someone else's luggage, planting the ski clothes. He had to be out of sight and safe when the porter returned—or in sight but minus ski clothes, as both Lawrence Stratfield and David Barron were. I've checked the porter very carefully on that point. When he came back with David Barton's seltzer Stratfield was just emerging from behind his green curtains. He was fully dressed, so he hadn't time, if he was the murderer, to put on the dead woman's ski pants and jacket under his own clothes. And that's ridiculous and impossible anyway. He couldn't have got them on under his business suit even if they had fitted him, and Burk has been telling me they weren't in his luggage when inspected. That's all ditto for Barron also, but he was nearer the deceased's door, looking urgent—or, as the porter puts it, 'crazy in his head' for his seltzer. Peter Sutton was presumably in the men's lavatory at this point and during the preceding three minutes, but the men's lavatory on this particular Pullman has an entrance both from the train aisle and the smoking compartment. Oliver Penbroke says Sutton didn't come out through the latter where, he says, he was shaving while

Barron was bouncing in and out damning the porter for slowness. Penbroke came out of the smoking compartment, which is also the washroom, just as the porter reappeared with Barron's soda. Penbroke saw their host coming down the aisle. He didn't see Peter Sutton who, presumably, was still in the lavatory. Penbroke thinks it was about four minutes that the porter took to fetch Barron's soda. Barron claims it was ten. I'm taking the porter's estimate of three. In my opinion he's got a nonstop watch inside his head. The young man named Conway says he was asleep all this time, and neither Stratfield nor Sutton appears to have been privy to the scene. They respectively claim to have been dressing and using the facilities of the lavatory."

"And where does all of this get you?" inquired Miss Yates.

"Apparently nowhere. Of course, if either Miss Sutton or Miss Manchester had been away from her drawing room—but they each insist they weren't—then the other one could have achieved all we've outlined and chucked the clothes in the other's luggage, because she could have been out of sight while doing it and could have made her exit later while the porter was carrying luggage to the vestibule."

Susan wanted to know if either of the women could have been strong enough to move the body from the bed to the floor, and Curtis said it was dubious. On the other hand, neither of them looked exactly a frail flower.

"Do you think," asked Susan, "that the murderer parked the ski clothes in his or her own luggage?"

Curtis said he did.

Susan pondered again, then asked if it wasn't odd that Barron had been in such an apparent dither over a split of soda.

Curtis nodded. "Penbroke says Barron was suffering from a hang-over, and Barron says it isn't any of Penbroke's damn business whether he was or not and that, besides, Penbroke was in the same condition on Saturday when he reached Stratfield's place. Barron does admit, however, that he had a bottle of scotch in his berth and took a nip or two during the night. Penbroke would seem to be providing him with a very neat alibi by saying he popped in and out of the washroom during the porter's absence. But Penbroke might have some reason of his own for being so apparently helpful. Why, God alone knows at this point. I can't figure a prayer of a way that Penbroke could have got out of the washroom without being seen by Barron—if Barron is telling the truth that he was just outside or inside the door all the time. And Penbroke certainly couldn't have piled through the lavatory and remained invisible to Peter Sutton unless that gentleman cannot see without his glasses which he might have taken off and also can't feel or hear the presence of another mortal in a cubicle the size of a train lavatory. Even a two-door lavatory of the type used on this particular Pullman is no Madison Square Garden."

"Joan Sutton and Hazel Manchester had their own washrooms and toilets inside their drawing rooms, of course," mused Susan.

Curtis agreed. There had been no reason for them to be muddling about in the aisle until they were ready to get off the train unless they had done so in order to visit other members of the party. This they did not seem to have done or, at least, would not admit having done. The ladies composing Stratfield's house party had not, indeed, seemed essentially fond of one another.

"But you're thinking one of them may have been downright murderously inclined toward Prunella Parton?"

"Somebody was," Curtis snapped, glaring at Lieutenant Burk's unoffending face.

A moment later the telephone again interrupted. When Curtis turned from it Susan said slowly: "But, after all, why did anybody *want* to steal Prunella Parton's skiing outfit? It doesn't make sense."

"Neither does the way she was dressed."

"But what do *you* think the reason was?"

"Theft perhaps. Miss Manchester has called to inform me confidentially that she thinks Miss Parton was wearing a valuable emerald pin when they got on the train at Swiss Village. She noticed it, she says, because 'it looked so odd'—her words—with a ski outfit. There's no emerald pin in Prunella Parton's luggage."

CHAPTER THIRTEEN

As Curtis paused his secretary, Jack Copely, came in with a sheaf of memoranda, whispered something and retired. When he had gone Susan dropped her eyes and remarked with a pointed lack of irony in her tone that she supposed Miss Manchester meant to be awfully helpful, but was it really likely that Miss Parton had secreted her emerald pin in her ski clothes?

"I don't know what Miss Manchester suspects, but unless she's the murderess she doesn't know the ski clothes are missing. We haven't made that public yet. She says she felt it her duty as a citizen to tell me about the emerald pin, having not seen it on the body when the police insisted she identify it. I must say I got the impression that Miss Manchester, as the English say, had got the wind up about something. The admitted purpose of her call smelled distinctly fishy. And Copely just informed me that Miss Joan Sutton doesn't remember the deceased wearing an emerald pin. Besides, if Miss Parton hid her valuables in her skiing garments the murderer was pretty dumb to carry off the whole outfit, pants, sweater, jacket, ski shoes, socks and gloves, in order to gain possession of them."

Susan admitted that it did seem a little cumbersome as a method.

"Or a very sweet red herring."

"Fish laureate of the D. A.'s office!"

Curtis honored Miss Yates with a sour grin. "Anyway, someone did take those ski clothes away from the deceased's drawing room.

They didn't walk out under their own power. What have you got on this angle, Burk?" he demanded, turning to the waiting detective.

Looking optimistic, Lieutenant Burk became immediately articulate. While Susan and Curtis had been talking he had been standing alternately on one foot and the other like a small boy refused a recess hour. Now he took a step nearer the assistant D. A.'s desk. "I know," he began, "whose baggage the clothes weren't packed in. They weren't in Stratfield's. As he said in his deposition, he went from the station to a florist's on Lexington Avenue, Gilchrist's. He went, as I guess he said, in a taxi, and the driver's sure he didn't throw any clothes out the window on account of they were talking and he, the cab driver, was looking back and forth at his fare. They were talking baseball. Stratfield told him he was a painter and would like to paint a modern picture of players in a ball park but he said he guessed the players wouldn't like the way they would look on account of the way he'd do it. Realistic artist, he said he was—or something like that."

Curtis interrupted: "So Stratfield's story was O.K. about going to the florist's?"

"Yes sir. Four dozen American Beauty roses he bought. Fussy, too, he was about them being packed just right. Didn't seem in a hurry or agitated or anything. Took his time. When the box was ready he went back to the cab and said he wanted to go to *Inter-Allied News*. That's where Miss Manchester works. When they got there Stratfield sent the driver to see if she was in. The answer was no. Stratfield then sent the driver back with his box of flowers but called to him at the door and said he guessed he'd take it in and get somebody to put the flowers in water. Of course, Miss M. wasn't there. She hadn't left the train until ten minutes of eight and then she'd gone to the Ritz for breakfast. She had corned-beef hash."

"We are not," expostulated Mr. Curtis, "concerned with her diet."

Lieutenant Burk retained undiminished zeal. "I mentioned it on account of how it was what they call a 'to order'—had to be made up special and took longer to deliver than a reg'lar breakfast. She didn't finish eating until eight thirty-five."

"And then?" demanded Curtis, but he took time out to give Susan the solemn look of a parent dealing with a valuable but, nevertheless, problem child.

"Half a dozen different people, including, of course, the reception-desk girl, remember seeing her come into the news agency about twenty of nine."

Curtis wanted to know if Stratfield had still been there arranging his precious roses. Burk shook his head.

"Oh no. He was only there a few minutes. Got a copy boy to scout around and find a pitcher for the roses. He put them in it and left an unsealed note on Miss Manchester's desk."

"Unsealed?"

"Yeah. I dug it outa the kid that he kind of read it the minute Stratfield left."

"Was its content material or immaterial to our interests, Burk? Kindly restrain yourself if the latter."

"It don't seem important. Just something about Miss Manchester being the perfect guest. Oh"—the lieutenant looked ashamed of himself—"I forgot, I made a copy of it. Verbatim, you might say."

Curtis reached for the note, read it and put it on the desk where Susan could see it. It was brief and, as Curtis remarked, tenderly touching.

>   *Monday morning*
> Dear Perfect Week-End Guest,
> For your diplomacy and poise midst explosions, blizzards and temperaments a conservatory, full and fragrant with the choicest blossoms of a maharajah, would be fitting. Please accept this feeble substitute.
>   From a deeply grateful
>   *Larry Stratfield*

Curtis' eyes were on the lieutenant. "What about Miss Manchester's luggage? You were assigned to inspect it, weren't you, Burk?"

"Yes sir. She went straight from the train to a Grand Central checkroom. Left her baggage there before she went to the Ritz. She picked it up on her way home this noon. She took home some of her roses too. We went through her stuff at the checkroom before she came back for it, and she couldn't have taken nothing out of it between the train and the checkroom because the porter was carrying it and hanging around while she got her check on account of how she had to get change to tip him. The checkroom boys says, also, that she didn't come back or nothing—before we got there, that is."

"Very good," prodded Curtis, "and what did you find?"

"There was a ski suit all right, but only one. It was green. Tyrolean stuff, they call it. Embroidered."

Curtis remarked that he was glad to observe Burk was bearing in mind Miss Parton's suit had been white.

Finding herself possessed of a half-creepy notion that the exact nature of Miss Parton's ski apparel was important, Susan started to say something, but Lieutenant Burk beat her to speech, and she decided to let it pass. Perhaps she could invent some way of obtaining a fuller description from another member of Stratfield's party. But which of the survivors of the trip down from New Hampshire could be expected to give unbiased information? They had all seemed to her very much on their guards. Pretty young Joan Sutton had impressed her as also shrewd and quick witted. Certainly Hazel Manchester was much too self-contained and wary to give away anything inimical to her own interests—in case the nature of the dead woman's ski clothes was. One of the men then? Oliver Penbroke had looked hearty, affable, but very careful behind his outward geniality. Peter Sutton was surely not the person to display his true face to the world. He looked as if he tinctured his soul with a moral germicide each morning. David Barron seemed least likely of them all to come out in the open with anything he could conceal. There remained the young man with yellow hair, Hinkle Conway, who had thought Miss Parton stood in the way of his progress, also the host of the party, the rich and arty Stratfield. His gabby voice might denote a native gossipiness. And Conway seemed to have a temperament capable of becoming his verbal undoing. Both of these men would also probably possess a better-than-average knowledge of the quality and general work-manship of a woman's apparel. As a painter Stratfield must have an eye for line and decoration, and Conway looked as if he might see a woman's clothes before he got around to sizing up her character, a male failing perhaps less rare than generally conceded by men, she thought. Then with an effort Susan brought her attention back to what Lieutenant Burk was saying.

What he was saying was a further description of the inspection he had made of Lawrence Stratfield's baggage in which there had been nothing in the nature of female skiing attire.

"You see, Mr. Curtis," the lieutenant went on, "Stratfield got the call from the police before he had any more than just started to unpack. His Filipino had carried his bag up from the cab and was with him every minute till he left for Grand Central again. Being as he and me—the Filipino, I mean—was both in the navy, we got along fine."

Mr. Curtis muttered something which sounded like "remarkable," but Burk, grinning tolerantly, continued:

"I pulled the telephone angle at Stratfield's apartment. Told the Filo I'd come to check on the phones. There was an extension in the boss's bedroom. His traveling bag was lying open there on one of those suitcase benches, a solid-mahogany one. Nothing cheap about his place. Elegant, you might say. I took a squint at the suitcase and said to the Filo:

"'Your boss been away?'

"'Yeah,' he says. 'He wasn't in the house long enough to more than unpack his shaving kit when he gets called out again. Always on the jump, that guy.'

"I says: 'Is that so?' and he grouses some more and goes on unpacking the bag while I tinker with the phone. Well, sir, there wasn't any lady's ski suit in it. There wasn't any ski suit in it at all. I asked the boy did his boss travel for a living, and he laughs and says:

"'No, for pleasure.'

"He told me Stratfield has a place up in New Hampshire where he goes for winter sports—skiing and such. I asked him what they wore for skiing, and he told me but explained that the boss didn't carry his ski stuff back and forth to New York on account of how he goes up to New Hampshire nearly every week end while the snow is good. To tell you the truth, Mr. Curtis, there wasn't anything feminine in Stratfield's bag except one thing." Burk paused impressively, and Susan held her breath, hoping for a revelation at last.

"Don't feel the need for dramatic suspense, Burk," advised Curtis tartly.

Burk grinned. "It was a lady's handkerchief. An embroidered one."

"Initialed?"

"Yes sir."

"Well," exploded Curtis, "for the love of God, tell us the initials."

"H. M.!"

"Hazel Manchester," murmured Susan, and Curtis cast her a baleful look.

"Thank you, Watson," he said, and turned back to Burk. "A souvenir of the week end, the Filipino thought?"

"That's what he thought, and it isn't the first time it's happened. This Stratfield has a whole drawer full of female stuff. Those Filos like to giggle, even the serious ones. Well, this one of Stratfield's gets himself a full house of snorts out of that drawer. It's got a label on it. He showed me. It says, 'Initial Experiences.' Did you ever hear of anything nuttier, Mr. Curtis?"

Curtis' expression was a picture of enforced composure.

Susan observed: "Ah, a wolf! Your word, Lyle." This Mr. Curtis ignored.

"Look here, Burk," he said in a strenuously even tone, "your sentimental discoveries are all very well, but in this instance I would have more interest in your tale if the souvenir handkerchief had borne the initials of the deceased. I think we may very well leave that angle. Do you think Stratfield's Filipino was on the level that nothing had been taken out of the bag and disposed of?"

"Absolutely. He doesn't like Stratfield. Has what you might call socialistic ideas about it not being right for a guy not to have to work. Inheriting fortunes from distant relatives, he was telling me, is 'socially unsound.' It's my guess that if he thought Stratfield was mixed up in a murder he'd give him away in a minute."

Burk showed every sign of continuing his speculations about this, but Curtis remarked that, much as he disliked interrupting his research into social economy, he would very much appreciate hearing about the contents of the luggage belonging to the other members of Stratfield's party.

Burk obligingly explained that Sergeants Howland and McGuire had visited the offices of Sutton & Barron. He had their reports. They had entered the Lincoln Building, posing as window washers, official arrangements having been made with the building superintendent. In the advertising-agency offices they had managed to scatter secretaries by means of carefully selected profanity and had inspected both luggage and possible hiding places in the offices of the president and vice-president. Young Conway had left his bag in a sort of locker room provided for less important members of the organization. Inspection of it had been easily managed. It had contained no feminine costumes, trophies or souvenirs, nor had Barron's Gladstone bag. Its contents had been masculine in the extreme save for one single item, a letter addressed to David Barron, signed "Prunella" and mailed from San Francisco in early November. Burk admitted happily that this epistle had kinda stuck to Sergeant Howland's pocket.

"In fact, I have it here, Mr. Curtis"—and he produced a hotel envelope carefully protected by a handkerchief.

Raising an eyebrow minutely at his lieutenant but handling the envelope with equal care, Curtis drew forth the enclosed letter and read aloud with a wry expression:

> "Hotel St. Francis
> San Francisco, Calif.
> November 6, 1939.
>
> Dear Davey,
> You were simply sweet to have the flowers waiting for me at the St. Francis. They dispelled the fog through which I drove here from the station.

I think I shall find this city fascinating. Did I mention to you that I'd never been here before?

Are you being true to me, darling, in all ways? You bad boy. Prunella won't like it if you aren't. She'll be very, very cross and may exact punishment. Does one exact punishment or inflict it? A copy writer shouldn't play fast and loose with words to her executive vice-president?

Dream of me, Davey.

Devotedly,

Prunella

"What a romantic day my staff have had," sighed Curtis, winking at Susan. "Have we any more notes for the 'Sentimental Discoveries of a Dick'?" he inquired of Burk.

"To tell you the truth, Mr. Curtis, you haven't heard nothing yet. Mr. Sutton's bag contained the prize item."

"Peter Sutton's?" exclaimed Susan and Curtis together. The sergeant produced from his pocket another exhibit. It was a small leather fold-over photograph case.

Burk flipped it open like a string of picture post cards, displaying six photographs of a woman.

"Same dame in all of them," he commented, placing the case on the desk, "and she looks kinda familiar."

Curtis picked up the case.

"Of course," continued the detective, "unless those are fancy-dress clothes it couldn't be the corpse. I don't guess women have dressed that way for maybe twenty years."

Susan had risen and was leaning over Curtis' desk. He said: "I wouldn't have dreamed it possible for the district attorney's office to need the professional advice of a stylist so many times in one day." Susan flashed him a look, then silently studied the photographs for several long moments. Dejectedly Curtis said he supposed the dress in the pictures was too old-fashioned to come within the span of her professional experience as a designer.

Susan chuckled. "It's part of one's job in my business to have a working knowledge of all basic styles and the recurrent cycles of fashions. Without wishing to brag, those clothes are as familiar to me as if we were making them this season. They are very chic but not unique enough to be fancy dress, so, unless they were bought secondhand, incredible from their look of newness, they were purchased in the fall of 1925. My guess is they were custom-made for the wearer. Beautiful fit, and the last cry that autumn in smartness."

Curtis' face was a brown study. After a moment he said: "Prunella Parton was twenty-nine years old last May. In 1925 she was fourteen years old. The woman in those pictures was certainly more than fourteen."

Susan said she wouldn't say a day under thirty.

"Can you bring any further light to bear?"

Susan shook her head, then nodded it vigorously. "Perhaps I can, at that!" she cried. "This noon I was told by one of those girls that Peter Sutton hasn't looked at a woman for fifteen years, at which time his wife presumably ran away from him, or something of the sort. Could that add up to anything?"

CHAPTER FOURTEEN

"COULD THAT ADD UP to anything!" whistled Curtis, and jabbed one of the phalanx of buzzers on his desk. Jack Copely appeared with practically stratoplane speed, and the assistant D. A. shot out a series of instructions. A detective named Du Bois was to start at once tracing the matrimonial history of Peter Sutton and his former wife and to bring in all tangents thereof. At the same time he was to delve into the parentage of both Prunella and Carol Parton.

When Copely had hurried away Curtis turned back to Burk. "Sorry," he said kindly, "to take that angle away from you, but I've other mountains for you to climb. By the way, Burk. You have a good eye. You only saw the corpse for a moment this morning, didn't you?"

"Yes sir, but the similarity, as you might say, between her and the pictures did kinda strike me."

Curtis nodded approvingly and did not refer to the budding signs of kleptomania suggested by the photograph case and letter lying on his desk. Instead he suggested that Burk continue his report. "What about Peter Sutton's daughter's luggage—? Wait a minute! There's something screwy here. How old, I wonder, is the self-expressive Joan?"

Susan was about to guess twenty-two when Lieutenant Burk informed them that he had checked on her age. "She's twenty-one years old. And," he remarked, "I guess that means she was around seven when those pictures were taken." He eyed the photograph folder darkly.

For a full minute Curtis said nothing, his eyes speculatively straight ahead, then he jabbed Copely's buzzer again. When the secretary reappeared on mercurial feet he added to the instructions for Detective Du Bois. In ascertaining whether Peter Sutton's wife had left him around 1915 he was also to investigate thoroughly Miss Joan Sutton's parentage and to obtain proof of whether Sutton's abandoning wife had been her mother.

Jack Copely dashed off. Casting Burk another quick glance, Curtis dropped his eyes to the photographs once more and asked: "How did you happen to check on Joan Sutton's age?"

"I kinda thought the woman in the picture looked like her, too, as you might say."

"Look here, Susan," exclaimed Curtis. She leaned over his desk and studied it. "What do you think?"

"Un-hunh. Faint. But I think so."

Curtis gave Burk another sharp glance. "You, my boy, are a regular anthropologist."

Burk looked embarrassed.

"Skip it," said Curtis. "Go on about the winsome Joan and her young man. She and Conway are supposed to have left the train together."

"Yes sir, and they did about five minutes before Miss Manchester, according to the Pullman porter, and you are sure right, Mr. Curtis—that black bird has a head for time. Reg'lar clock, like you said. Well, one redcap carried both their bags—their big ones, that is. Miss Sutton carried a little thing about a foot square. The redcap said it was what ladies put their jewels in—and sometimes make-up stuff. They told him first they wanted to go to the Oyster Bar but as soon as they started in there they whirled around and came right out again saying they'd changed their minds and wanted to go to Forty-second Street instead. At the Forty-second Street exit Conway took over both the big bags, and the redcap says they went off west on Forty-second." Burk looked remorseful. "Haven't been able to pick up a thing on them until a lot later. At nine-fifteen Miss Sutton showed up at her father's house in Eighty-ninth Street, telling the butler she'd already had breakfast. Conway

checked in at Sutton and Barron at nine sharp, not telling anybody anything. According to the telephone girl there, he didn't look
in too fancy a humor."

Curtis asked what check had been made on Miss Sutton's luggage. "She arrived home with it, I suppose?"

Burk said she had. The butler had brought both her suitcase
and beauty kit into the house from her taxi. This Burk had learned
from a fellow detective's young sister who had turned out to be
one of the Sutton maids and who had phoned him that there was
nothing in Miss Sutton's bags she had not taken away with her.

Curtis asked: "How soon after the police called did Miss Sutton
leave her father's house? Did she have time to be alone with her
luggage?"

"No sir, she'd only just gotten inside the front door when the
phone rang. She never even went upstairs—turned right around
and took the same taxi again. The butler carried her baggage upstairs after she'd left."

Curtis sighed and observed that there would be no value in
searching ash bins at the Suttons' then. "Where in hell those two
were between the time the redcap left them at the Forty-second
Street exit of the station and the time they showed up respectively
at home and office we perhaps shall never know. Unless your god
of luck, Burk, is really feeling energetic today. By the way, what
did Sutton, Barron and Stratfield do with their luggage while they
breakfasted at the Grand Central Oyster Bar?"

"Checked their bags with their hats."

"All right. What about Penbroke?"

Burk explained that Sergeant Potts and an assistant had worked
on Penbroke's luggage, and Sergeant Potts, buzzed for, appeared.
He was a man of medium height, of indiscriminate age and possessed a pair of ferretlike eyes which reminded Susan vaguely of
David Barron's. There was, she however decided, something definitely more unpleasant about the vice-president of Sutton &
Barron. Sergeant Potts looked merely quick, shrewd and not likely
to be easily fooled. With fewer verbal excursions than Lieutenant

Burk he explained what had happened at the affable Oliver
Penbroke's business establishment.

"We did the window-washing act, Mr. Curtis, and had a good break
with the president's suitcases. There were two of them in his office,
and the train porter said he had two aboard. Nothing in them except
masculine stuff. No female ski suits. But we've run up against a blind
alley, sir, on Penbroke's movements between the Vanderbilt Avenue
Grand Central exit and his office. He was the first of the party off
the train, but the redcap who carried his baggage is a slow-witted
guy. He can't remember what kind of a cab he took. All he can remember is that he took the same one a dame had just stepped out of."

Pushing his buzzer once more, Curtis said: "I want to know
more about that," and when Copely appeared he instructed him to
obtain from the Advertising Club a photograph of Oliver Penbroke,
also a photograph from the society files of a newspaper of the recent debutante, Joan Sutton. Reproductions were to be sent to all
the taxicab-company offices and the drivers' union headquarters.
The cab drivers who had hauled either Penbroke or Miss Sutton
that morning were to report to the D. A.'s office.

As Copely started to leave Curtis called for him to wait a minute
and asked Potts what Penbroke's luggage had looked like.

"Cowhide," replied the sergeant. "Same size. Big ones."

Lieutenant Burk amplified "He was the only one in the party
who had more than one bag except the girls, Mr. Curtis. Of course
the deceased had five."

"Yes," agreed Curtis unhappily, "and not a scrap of ski clothing
except long underwear. All right, Copely, add the luggage descrip-
tions to the photographs of Penbroke and Miss Sutton. She had a
suitcase and a jewel case or beauty kit. She traveled by cab to her
father's house in Eighty-ninth Street and then took the same cab
back to Grand Central. Penbroke went by cab from the Vanderbilt
Avenue exit of Grand Central presumably directly to the Hardmike
Building, Forty-seventh and Madison."

As Copely started away a second time Curtis once more recalled
him, then turned to Lieutenant Burk. "Did it strike you as odd that

though the deceased had five bags and a lot of ski clothes to put in them there wasn't much space empty in any single one of them?"

"Looked as if she would have had to pack her sport clothes in all five bags."

"Exactly," said Curtis, "and people don't pack that way. Ninety-nine people out of a hundred would leave sufficient room in one suitcase for any garments they were going to wear to a train but not when they left it. Too much reassembling otherwise." Curtis turned back to Copely. "Has Withers left for Swiss Village to investigate the Stratfield oil explosion?"

"Yes sir. Noon train."

"Wire the train then. Tell Withers to find out from the servants up there at Stratfield's place whether Miss Parton packed her own luggage. Explain to him what I've got in mind."

Miss Yates leaned across the desk and murmured: "You know, I wouldn't trust that conductor's eye for feminine apparel. When he said she had on ski clothes maybe he only meant he'd seen, say, that she was wearing ski pants and a jacket on account of the blizzardy weather. In a sleigh with robes and things Prunella wouldn't have needed ski shoes and socks necessarily. The porter, who probably has a better knowledge of women's clothes than a conductor, could give you a better description. They might have been terribly warm but soft and supple. Then they could have been packed in less space than one would think offhand."

Curtis had listened attentively. But again he shook his head. "Just the same, if she didn't have *on her person* what I believe you designers call accessories she would have had to have room for them in her suitcases. There wasn't enough empty space in any one bag for all that stuff."

"Perhaps," suggested Susan, "the murderer repacked her bags. No, that won't work. There wasn't time for him or her to do it, was there?"

Curtis shook his head gloomily. "And she certainly hadn't intended to wear that long-armed, long-legged skiing underwear on New York streets. Yet the bag with enough space left in it for that was the one containing another evening gown and a lot of silk undergarments. Most women wouldn't pack used sports underwear in with things like that, would they?"

Susan said she wouldn't. Cloying at the back of her mind persisted an acute interest in the exact nature of Prunella Parton's ski attire. When they were alone she would ask Curtis which of the persons on the train he would feel it safe to quiz on this point. Her choice remained the women for accuracy, but she still thought both Stratfield and Conway would probably prove informative if inclined to tell the truth. She began trying to visualize dependably the exact nature of the ski clothes sold in her salon. Was it conceivable that either Miss Manchester or Miss Sutton could have worn Prunella Parton's garments off the train under her own clothes? "You know it isn't possible," she finally told herself disgustedly, but she wasn't satisfied.

Curtis was asking Potts what chance Oliver Penbroke had had to take anything out of his luggage and dispose of it after he reached his office.

"Unless his secretary is lying he didn't have any chance, Mr. Curtis. She says she was there early on his orders given her Friday before he left. She was waiting in his private office for him when he got in at twenty minutes to eight.

"Wait a minute, Potts. Penbroke was the first off the train, and it came to a standstill at exactly seven-thirty. Ten minutes to his office doesn't mean he exactly dawdled. He had to walk up the platform, cross the rotunda, mount the Vanderbilt Avenue steps, and perhaps, with two heavy cowhide bags and a vague disposition, the redcap was slow coming along. Well—go on."

Potts went on: "I was just going to say that Penbroke's secretary is kinda chatty. We had a time getting her out of his office long enough to go through his bags. She was feeling sorry for herself, having to be down to work so early. She was willing to talk about it. I suppose she thought we wouldn't go quoting her to nobody. What she said was that there she was down at work at seventhirty, the president shows up at seven-forty and starts dictating.

Then he gets a phone call and has to go right out again and he hasn't even finished one letter. Probably she'd find herself still working at eight o'clock tonight, she said."

"Very chatty for a president's private secretary," commented Curtis. "What else did she have to say?"

"Nothing else. I gave Ike Spumoni, who was with me, the signal to pull a nosebleed act and got her to take him off for first aid. Then I went through Penbroke's bags while they were gone. When she brought Ike back her telephone rang and, as it was a girl friend and not business, she didn't bother with us any more. We finished up the windows and beat it."

"All right." Curtis nodded. "We'll have to wait for a report from the taxi driver to see if Penbroke threw one white ski suit and accessories out into Vanderbilt or Madison avenues. If he did, it wasn't picked up by a white-wing. We've checked the street-cleaning department." He looked at Susan, gave a sour grin and suggested that she compose a "Lost and Found" ad.

"Make it sound upset and offer twenty-five dollars' reward."

"What for?" demanded Miss Yates.

"For a lost white ski suit. We'll put it in all the New York newspapers."

"Not with my name on it!"

Curtis admitted that that would be unthinkable. They would call the distressed lady Corea Berea and use one of the D. A.'s private inquiry wires as her telephone number.

Susan picked up a pencil and one of the pink memorandum pads, but her attention to the composition of a want ad was immediately shattered by Curtis' further remarks to Lieutenant Burk. He was pointing out that if young Conway and Joan Sutton had actually seen Carol Parton in the club car the night before then she had been on the train and could have had access to her sister's drawing room. After all, a young woman who hadn't belonged in the Pullman with Stratfield's party had been seen by the porter at the drawing-room door that morning. The question was had that young woman been Carol Parton? And where had Carol Parton spent the morning? He had sent a detective to her apartment after the investigation had been begun on the sided Pullman. Conway, of course, had mentioned thinking he and Miss Sutton had seen the dead woman's sister the night before. But at ten o'clock that morning Miss Parton had not put in an appearance at home. Her part-time maid had been on the premises since eight-thirty. Miss Parton's bed had not been slept in, and the suitcase she had taken with her on Saturday was still missing. The part-time maid had been of the opinion that Miss Parton was still out of town. Otherwise she would have come back to her apartment because, the maid thought, she didn't have to report at her newspaper until noon. At the paper they had also said that Miss Parton wasn't due until twelve-thirty. Moreover, at that hour she had made her appearance at the *Globe*, wearing a tweed coat and hat and carrying a small suitcase which a department man had managed to go through as soon as she had gone out on her first afternoon assignment. It had been remarkable alone for its emptiness, containing as it had one nightgown and one toilet kit.

At this point Susan abandoned the want ad completely and said: "When somebody during the depositions this morning brought up the matter of that explosion didn't they say that Carol Parton had arrived in the middle of the night accompanied by two newspapermen?"

"Yes," Curtis replied, "but the newspapermen left North Conway Sunday noon after the skiing event they were covering and came back to town. They say Carol suggested they get back with the story and pictures, leaving the return of Stratfield's car to her. They think Stratfield had invited her back to the house party and that she didn't want to make them think they'd been left out of the invitation. I've checked that with Stratfield. He did ask her to rejoin the party."

"But she didn't go. Wonder why she didn't?"

"She telephoned Stratfield Sunday noon that they had been delayed on their assignment at North Conway. They had to stay over Sunday night there, she said. On Monday morning they would either bring or send his car back, she promised."

Susan wanted to know if Lyle didn't think all that pretty funny inasmuch as the newspapermen had left with their story and pictures on Sunday noon.

"Extremely queer. Especially so inasmuch as she sent a garageman back with Stratfield's car. I'm expecting Miss Carol Parton here at four o'clock to offer explanations. Whether they will be the truth is something else again." He turned to Burk. "This is where you come in. I want you to tail the deceased's young sister when she leaves here. I'm borrowing a policewoman to go with you and I want to know about Miss Parton's every movement. Put her to bed and get her up. Find out if you can what she was doing from seven-thirty this morning until she showed up at her paper. I've heard from the North Conway police. She checked in alone at an inn there at twelve noon on Sunday, put through two long-distance calls to Swiss Village, Stratfield's number. Stratfield says she only phoned once. According to what the police found out from people at the inn, she sat around all afternoon looking gloomy then checked out again at six o'clock carrying her own bag and not say-ing where she was going. She went to a local garage at five after six and arranged for the return of Stratfield's car. She could have walked to the station and hopped on that express. The conductor says she may have been a girl he remembers. But he doesn't seem positive. He just vaguely recalls a young woman with a tweed out-fit. Stratfield gave me that description. The Pullman porter is due in here any moment. Perhaps we'll get an identification through him." Curtis twisted his wrist to look at his watch. "It's a quarter to four now. Oh, by the way, Potts, you relieve Lieutenant Burk on tailing Carol Parton tomorrow and stick outside to look her over when she comes in this afternoon. O.K., Burk." He turned back to Miss Yates as the two detectives left the office. "Now what did those hellcats have to say this noon?"

Their eyes met, Curtis' quick and determined. He was not see-ing her at this moment, Susan knew, as the young woman he had shown frequent evidence of hoping one day to convince he would make a thoroughly satisfactory husband. He was seeing her as an ally in solving a murder case. She knew in this moment also that

Curtis had no doubt he was up against a shrewd and ruthless murderer, someone who would stop at very little and whose motives might be far from obvious. And Susan was suddenly and very femininely frightened. She wanted to get up and drag Lyle Curtis bodily away from the Parton case. She wanted to so much that the thought seemed to wash up and down like surf in her brain, leaving even the shore line of common sense a suddenly stormy place. But after a few moments of this mental turmoil it occurred to her that if she were going to consider marrying a lawyer who insisted upon being a detective and a number of other dangerous things there was very little virtue in starting to welsh before she was even properly engaged to the man. If only it were primarily for herself that she was afraid! She could then simply tell about the luncheon and go back to her salon, to her familiar world of fashions, fastidious clients, charming friends, gay restaurants, theaters and nothing more murderous than the look in the eye of a size-forty-six customer expecting to be made to look size sixteen. Of course, it was physically possible to do that, but suddenly she knew that if Lyle Curtis was going on leading a dangerous life she wanted to lead it too. Someway, it made everything easier.

CHAPTER FIFTEEN

WHILE THE FANTASTICALLY garbed body of her sister lay across the threshold of a drawing room on the New Hampshire express which arrived at Grand Central at seven-thirty that morning Miss Carol Parton was hastening forward through the club car to her own Pullman five cars ahead. She did not see Oliver Penbroke gulping coffee behind his paper. A moment after the train stopped she was hurrying from it carrying her own suitcase. She walked rapidly up the platform and into the station. Halfway across the rotunda her feet began to lag.

"But where shall I go?" she asked herself.

Walking slowly on through the waiting room, she went into the ladies' room. Inside its doors, she saw dressing cubicles were available for ten cents. She put a dime in the slot of the first door showing an unoccupied signal, went in and closed it behind her.

For a while she sat on her suitcase, a fist pressed into each of her eyes. She was trembling, and her feet felt icy. Presently she stood up and stamped them cautiously. It wouldn't do to attract the attention of the attendant. When she had got the blood running down to her feet again Carol felt better. She opened her suitcase and stared at its contents. She had never known fright like this. It was as if an animal were gnawing at the pit of her stomach. She wished, as she had wished for few things in her life, that she had remained in her Pullman this morning. It had been a useless, an insane, impulse suicidally timed. Someone would be sure to have seen her. Oh, she was a fool, a ridiculous fool. Also, she should never have driven the car into that snowdrift at Swiss Village. If they hadn't borrowed one from Lawrence Stratfield no one at the house party would have known she was in the state of New Hampshire. She hadn't thought Joan Sutton and that blond young man had actually seen her in the club car last evening. They had seemed busy making eyes at each other, but people were usually only too busy to see you when by seeing you they couldn't make trouble. That was the kind of world it was.

Carol shut the suitcase and sat on it again.

She remembered suddenly that her aunt in Georgia had said some people just couldn't make their foresight work—only their hindsight. That was the way she was. She needn't have told Prunella about Oliver Penbroke. If she hadn't a great many things might have been different.

Carol wanted to cry. Her eyes were aching to cry, but no tears came. The tension made them hurt way back behind the balls. She felt hot now but she was still trembling. It was like a fever shiver. She couldn't stop it. Prunella had looked so awful dead. So awful and so beautiful and so alive with her eyes staring up at her. She had been beautiful and she had always been able to make Carol feel guilty of something, of immaturity and awkwardness if nothing more. It was crazy for some of the girls to say she had made Prunella look affected. Nothing had ever defrosted Prunella's glamour. Prunella had been wicked, of course, guilty of all kinds of meanness herself. A lot of people would be glad she was dead.

Struggling to her feet once more, Carol went to the washbowl, ran hot water into it and slowly unwrapped a towel from the shelf. It felt rough to her face even after she had soaked it in hot water, but the heat felt good. It was funny how it seemed to cool her face instead of making it hotter. If only her eyes wouldn't feel as if they were going to burst. If only she could cry. But she couldn't cry over Prunella. You couldn't cry over someone who had hated you for no reason at all and who had hated your mother and told you so nearly every day. Their mother *must* have been good. She had always sent money. It had just been that she couldn't have them in New York, Prunella and her. Suddenly Carol remembered how exciting it had seemed to come to New York after dreaming about it for so many years. She had hardly been able to wait to meet her sister. She hadn't, naturally, guessed what it would be like to live with her, to be treated as if you were the hind leg of a puny, miserable dog.

Carol pushed the drain and let the hot water run out of the bowl. She let the cold water run for a minute, holding the faucet with one hand, the rough little towel in the other under it. Cold water would freshen her face. She studied her face in the mirror over the bowl. The hot water had kind of relaxed her. She mustn't say "kind of." It wasn't in the rule book at the *Globe*. It was difficult, talking one way and having to write another. Maybe she ought to write stories about colored people. After all, she talked like them. But this was a silly way to start thinking. It was maudlin. She'd been awfully lucky to get a job on a New York newspaper. Any other girl from Gretina, Georgia, would have been tickled to death! If she hadn't gotten a job in New York she would never have met Oliver. Sometimes she couldn't believe she had met him. It was like a dream. Any moment she'd wake up. She sat down again on her suitcase. Just sat.

After an hour or more Carol decided the attendant might notice if she stayed in the little cubbyhole any longer. The woman might come and want to know if she was sick—ask questions anyway. People weren't supposed to spend the day in these places. But she couldn't go to her apartment. The part-time maid would be there. She'd know then that she'd gotten in on an earlier train. The police might question the girl. They wouldn't expect her at the paper until twelve-thirty as usual. The thing to do would be to walk somewhere. No, that wouldn't do. She knew a lot of people in New York now. Someone might see her. The thing to do was to find out if there wasn't a noon train, to pretend she'd been on that.

Not daring to go back through the highly trafficked rotunda to the information desk, she decided to find a telephone booth where she could phone Grand Central Information.

Standing up, she dabbed powder on her nose and scrutinized her face again in the mirror. Some people thought she was interesting looking. Nobody, she guessed, thought she was pretty. It was funny, she having to make intensity her mainstay and Prunella being so beautiful she could act languid anywhere and get away with it. Only Prunella hadn't been languid. She had been after something every minute, after anything anybody else had, especially a man somebody else had. Prunella had been really bad. Carol shuddered. Then she remembered why, for one reason, she had opened her suitcase. She hadn't brushed her teeth this morning. It was odd, but she liked to brush her teeth. It seemed to wake her face up.

She opened her suitcase again, fumbled around and found her toothbrush and the paste in her toilet kit. She brushed her teeth very hard, letting the brush go round in semicircles over her gums, the way the dentist had told her to do it. Then she rinsed her mouth with water from a paper cup.

She felt better now, and it occurred to her that it would be a good idea to go to the newsreel theater in the station. She'd have to go out through the rotunda again to do it, but if she hurried and kept her head down probably nobody would notice her—nobody who mattered. She might even stop at the information booth. No, better not do that.

She opened the door and saw there were telephone booths a few feet away. She went into one and then realized she didn't know the number. She came out, lugging her suitcase, and went over to the phone books spiked with chains to a high, narrow table. After finding the number she went back to the booth. Grand Central Information said there would be a train in from North Conway, New Hampshire, at twelve-fifteen. Carol looked at her watch. It was nearly nine o'clock now. Nearly! Dear heaven, three hours and fifteen minutes before twelve-fifteen! Would the newsreel theater be open yet?

On one of her sudden impulses Carol dialed Oliver Penbroke's number. She suddenly felt unaccountably disturbed about him. The police would have no trouble finding out what Prunella had been trying to do to him. The girl with the silky voice who ran his switchboard answered. No, Mr. Penbroke was not in. Who was calling? Carol tried to make her voice sound deep and husky. She said she was Mr. Havemeyer's secretary. They would call Mr. Penbroke back later. No, no message. She hung up the receiver and was filled with dread all over again that the girl might have recognized her voice. Well, she could have gotten off the train in some station and called New York. The girl didn't have to know whether it was long distance or not. What if the police demanded to know where she had phoned from? She might say she couldn't remember what station, that she hadn't noticed. What if they wanted to know why she had called Oliver Penbroke? If they did that she could give a good-enough answer. She wished now that she had said it was long distance calling. Wouldn't that have constituted an alibi? She was clever enough at the paper. They didn't pay her much but they liked her. She knew that. Why couldn't she be clever about this?

On another impulse Carol put a second nickel into the telephone and dialed the Penbroke Agency again. When the girl answered she raised her voice to a sharp staccato, repeated the number crisply, said: "I have a call for you. Long distance." Having said that much, she was terror-stricken that that wasn't what long-distance operators said. Didn't they name the city or town? Well, she couldn't name a city or town. She had no idea where the North Conway train would be three hours and fifteen minutes out of Grand Central. Maybe it wouldn't be stopping at a station at all. The chances were it wouldn't be. But it was too late now. She'd have to come on the wire with her own voice. Oliver's operator was waiting.

"Hello," she said in her rolling Georgia voice, "this is Miss Carol Parton calling. I'd like to speak to Mr. Penbroke, please—and will you please hurry? I'm calling from a railroad station—just while the train stops. I've only got a minute."

The silky voice said: "Mr. Penbroke isn't in, Miss Parton. He was called out suddenly just after he got in this morning. Any message for him?"

"Just say I called on my way down from New Hampshire. I'll call again when I get to New York. Thank you." She hung up. It was pretty dubious whether she had put it over with that silky-voiced girl. These New York operators were so smart!

AT TWELVE-FIFTEEN Carol came out of the newsreel theater and telephoned the Penbroke Agency again. The operator said she was sorry, but Mr. Penbroke had telephoned in from outside that he wouldn't be back until after lunch. Carol hung up without giving her name.

At two-thirty Carol tried once more to reach Oliver Penbroke, but he still wasn't in. At three o'clock she had to go back to the paper to write the story which had been her early-afternoon assignment. They told her the district attorney's office had called. She was to be in Lyle Curtis' office at four o'clock—about her sister's death. The city editor expressed his condolences. Carol supposed she could have learned about Prunella's death while she was out and so admitted her knowledge. She thanked the city editor, wrote her story and went down to the lobby where she tried Oliver Penbroke again. She said this time who she was, and the operator explained that Mr. Penbroke had just tried to reach her at the *Globe*. He'd gone out now. Any message?

"No, thank you. Just say I called, please."

CHAPTER SIXTEEN

GIVING LYLE CURTIS back his own look of determination, Susan began her story of the luncheon-table conversations. She told it with speed and precision. Curtis alternately watched her lovely, expressive face and made notes on a memorandum pad. When she had finished he said:

"So it boils down to this"—and began reading what he had written.

> "According to Acquaintances of Deceased
> Prunella Parton generally disliked by women. Quite
> a she-wolf. Had affair with Hinkle Conway. He's con-
> sidered impetuous. She stood in his professional
> path. Their affair apparently terminated some
> months ago.
>
> Rescuer—Joan Sutton, a deb with vision and ex-
> ecutive ability. Joan probably tried but failed to get
> Prunella dismissed from her father's agency. Why
> did she fail?
>
> Prunella's affair with David Barron probably
> brewing when she broke off with Conway. Did this
> alliance bring deceased into higher-salary bracket,
> permitting move to Park Avenue? According to Fash-
> ion Editor Alice Bomm, two sisters had furious ar-
> gument about eight months ago. Subject: dangerous
> operation. (Check with medical examiner on
> deceased's organic condition.)

Query: Could ill health have brought Prunella to suicide? (Then where are the ski clothes? And how did she kill herself?)

Was Prunella restricting David Barron's amorous activities and/or proving a financial nuisance? (Where is Barron's wife?)

Peter Sutton has reputation of rigorously disapproving of scandal and of "not having looked at a woman in fifteen years," yet he continued to employ the practically notorious Prunella Parton (who mysteriously resembles pictures carried in his luggage). Wait for reports on Sutton's estrangement from his wife and identity of Prunella Parton and Joan Sutton's mother. (What's this all about anyway?)

Sister Carol frequently heard to predict that Prunella would "kill herself with cuckoo reducing baths" (one of which probably saved her life during Stratfield house-party explosion). Carol not supposed to have been able to afford an apartment of her own. (Was Carol on the train?)

About five years ago "in an arty crowd" Prunella knew Lawrence Stratfield. He is said to have been one of her attachments at the time. (Was he still jealous of her?)

"To which we must add," said Curtis, looking up at Susan, "a question about who had the best opportunity to carry the ski clothes from the train and to dispose of them before his or her luggage was inspected. That adds up to Joan Sutton, Hinkle Conway, Carol Parton—if she was on the train—and Oliver Penbroke—until we can find his taxi driver."

Susan nodded, tapping a pencil on the memorandum pad upon which she had started to compose the want ad. Curtis asked if she had finished it.

"Got diverted. How's this?

Lost: probably mid-town Monday lady's white ski
outfit size 16 specially for owner very anxious to have
returned $25 reward."

Curtis considered it a moment, then said "Better make the reward a hundred bucks. Would that cover the price of the outfit?"

"Just about, if she had bought her stuff from me, which she
didn't."

"I don't suppose anyone would charge her any more," remarked
Curtis obliquely.

"Certainly not. Our prices bear no peers."

At this moment Copely came in to say that the Pullman porter
had arrived. Curtis gave Copely the want ad and said to send the
porter in at once. As Susan made no move to go, he grinned at her.
"There is, of course, that high-priced business of yours, but you
are more than welcome to stay."

"I want to hear more about that ski suit."

"Professional jealousy?"

"Nitwit. A sleuthing contagion I've caught from certain people
I know."

The porter arrived, still looking rather shaken. Curtis attempted
to put him at ease, explaining that he wanted to know more about
the young woman who had been standing outside the drawing room
as the train pulled into Grand Central.

"Did she seem in a hurry?"

"Ah thought she was rushin' to get breakfast before leaving the
train. She must have went towa'd the club cah."

Curtis asked if she had been carrying anything, anything white,
anything which might have been the ski suit the dead girl had worn
the night before.

"No suh, she weren't carryin' nothin'."

"If you saw her again from the same position you saw her this
morning would you recognize her?"

"Ah do thinks as how Ah would."

"We'll give you a chance. I'm going to take you into another
office. After a bit several ladies will walk down a hall. If you see
the girl you saw this morning hold up your hand. Understand?"

"Yass suh."

"Wait here for a moment," instructed Curtis, and loped out of the office into his secretary's. In a moment he was back and led the way through another door into a room which afforded a view of the public corridor and elevator rack. Within the next few moments half a dozen young women, all wearing hats and coats, several in tweeds, emerged from elevators. Each walked away from them toward Copely's office. Susan could see them filing out again presently, entering elevators farther down the rack. As one young woman followed another the Pullman porter shook his head forlornly. Once more an elevator door rolled open. Quick feet sounded on the corridor floor. A young woman in a tweed suit and tweed hat moved swiftly toward Copely's hideaway. The Negro waved his hand excitedly in the air. Curtis rose, closed the door into the corridor and came back to the porter.

"You think that was the same young woman?"

"Yass suh. She even walk the same, and it is the very same coat and hat."

Copely came to the door. "The sister is waiting," he announced.

"Coming," said Curtis, but turned back to the Negro. "This young lady here"—and he indicated Susan—"would like to have you give her a description of how the young woman who died looked when she came aboard the train last night."

"Yes," said Susan quickly, "did her white suit look awfully heavy and bulky?"

"It look pow'ful warm, like best blankets. Not so bulky, Ah don't say."

"Like an expensive blanket," mused Susan. "The kind you can double up into relatively little space?"

"Yass ma'am, like the ladies in the big houses in the South used to have. Homespun, they called them."

Susan asked if the deceased had been wearing ski shoes, but the porter shook his head doubtfully. This he didn't remember. Gloves? Again he did not recall. The white ski pants and jacket and the bright red cap were, however, sharp in his memory, also the fact that "everybody had been laughing like as if they'd had a right smart pleasant drive through the blizzard."

Susan said to Curtis: "In the sleigh with rugs she wouldn't have needed heavy shoes or even gloves."

"You've pointed that out before. But what became of them? She skied at Swiss Village. There were not even ski shoes in her luggage."

Susan shook her head disconsolately. "I don't know. Only I still keep thinking the bulk of her suit has an important bearing."

"What you are thinking is that someone wore those clothes off the train under his or her own clothes?"

Susan did not know, she admitted, exactly what she was thinking.

"All right," said Curtis to the Negro, "you have been very helpful. Just keep yourself available until further notice."

When he had gone after bidding her the most courtly of goodbys Susan asked: "Lyle, he couldn't have done it surely?"

Curtis explained that the department had made a very thorough search of any possible direct or indirect relationship with Prunella Parton, finding none. They had painstakingly checked the porter's general reputation. It was above reproach. He had been with the Pullman Company for twenty-nine years, and not only had he never been in any trouble or even suspicion of trouble but there did not seem to be a case on record of an attack on a woman by a Pullman porter. Besides, what about the missing ski clothes? If the porter had stolen them after someone else had murdered Prunella where had he concealed them? A thorough search had been made of his own personal effects aboard the train, of the club car and Pullman closets, even of the baggage car. There wouldn't have been much point in his stealing them and hiding them in someone else's luggage. How would he have gotten them back?

Curtis paused, frowned, then smiled down at Susan. "Want to join McGluggish's undertaking crew again? I'm going in to talk to Carol Parton. You tag along and take an inappropriately inconspicuous chair."

"I'm coming!" said Susan, and followed him.

CHAPTER SEVENTEEN

Miss Carol Parton sat in Curtis' office, chaperoned by Jack Copely's alert eyes.

Curtis greeted her with formality, expressing his condolences and explaining that the district attorney's office was engaged in investigating the cause of her sister's death.

Carol straightened quick shoulders under inexpensive but becoming tweeds and thrust a hand into each of her jacket pockets.

Watching her, Susan thought: "An interesting face. She looks both clever and intelligent. They can be such different qualities—" Then she stopped surmising in order to listen to what Miss Parton was saying.

At the moment at least she sounded far from gay but she seemed strung on high-tension wires. It gave her a supervelocity reaction to everything. Even her lips moved with rapid expressiveness despite her Georgia drawl. After a preliminary skirmish of polite remarks Carol said: "I might as well confess, Mr. Curtis, that Prunella and I didn't get on awfully well." Curtis waited, saying nothing, and Carol hurried on. "When I came to New York more than two years ago Prunella had already been here for three years. She'd gotten a swell job at Sutton and Barron and was making good in a big way. When we met she said I could come and live with her."

"When you met? What, exactly, do you mean, Miss Parton?" requested Curtis. "You sound as if you hadn't met before then."

"We hadn't. Prunella knew a lot more than I did about why but she always acted mad at our mother. She wouldn't talk much. About all I know is that Mother couldn't keep us together. I was brought up by an aunt in Atlanta. Mother's mother in California took Prunella. My aunt May always said Mother felt it more suitable for us not to grow up in a place like New York. Of course, I was always crazy to get up here. But, anyway, I'd never seen my half sister until I finally made the grade and arrived in New York. So, you see, I'm not suffering now the way I would if we had been kids together."

"Your half sister?"

"Oh yes, we had different fathers. From as much as Prunella would ever say, her father died. I don't even know his name. She took *my* father's name—Parton."

"What is your father's full name?"

"Was. He's dead. His name was John Parton, and he died of pneumonia, Aunt May told me. It was back in 1918. That was the year Mother shipped me off to Atlanta. Prunella was already in California. She always said Mother abandoned us. But she was hard about everything."

"And your mother?"

"She's dead, too, if that's what you mean. She died in 1925 in Paris."

"What," asked Curtis, "is your aunt May's address?"

"Heaven, I guess." Despite the seeming bitterness of her words Carol sounded like a small forlorn child.

Curtis changed back to Prunella. "So your half sister asked you to come and live with her when you came to New York? I suppose you felt that was very kind of her?"

"At first I did. Then I found out she only wanted me as a kind of morality clause."

Curtis waited attentively.

"She always had a lot of men, you see, and two sisters living together sounded like a household. It cut out the 'woman-alone' angle. She was trying to lure Lawrence Stratfield to the altar about that time—I think he was the only man she ever wanted to marry—and he's a stickler for the right people. He *might* have married 'one of those charming Parton sisters,' you know. He could have told people: 'Their parents are dead, but they are so brave and have made such a charming home for themselves despite fate.' Marrying that wild Prunella Parton who lives alone' was something else again. Nobody can ever say Prunella didn't figure things out to the last detail. Still, my being there didn't catch him and, feeling differently about Mother's memory, got Prunella and me off to a bad start. Our 'charming household' was never much of a success." Carol Parton subsided abruptly.

"So you finally decided not to try it any longer?"

"We agreed it wasn't such a hot idea when Prune got a big raise. That was nine months ago. She was making ten times as much as I ever will, I guess. Anyway, she offered to put up something toward my having an apartment of my own, a cheap one, of course. I'm Grove Street and like it. She went Park Avenue. If it hadn't suited her plans to make sure I cleared out she wouldn't have done it. No one could say Prunella was generous."

Curtis interrupted to ask casually if her half sister had no longer been seeking a matrimonial alliance with Lawrence Stratfield.

"Oh no, all that had blown over ages ago. Larry Stratfield turned out not to be the marrying sort. He strung Prunella along worse than she strung him."

"And her heart interest changed?" Susan shuddered over the deceptive fatherly tone in Curtis' voice.

"Well, if you can call it that, *de mortuis*, as Aunt May used to say, and everything, but Prune's heart never guided her much, I guess. Anyhow, the man of the hour was David Barron. I think he has a wife. In any case, he didn't require Prune to have an established household. Preferred the contrary, I think."

Carol Parton's tone and general manner had made several shifts in the course of this conversation. When speaking of her mother, Susan thought, she had seemed soft, childlike, sentimental. But her references to her half sister had been bluntly, even bitterly put.

Now Carol studied Curtis' desk for a moment before remarking:

"I don't know why, for the love of Mike, I'm telling you all this, Mr. Curtis, except that you expected me, I suppose, to come in here crying my eyes out over Prune and—and I just can't! Besides, lots of people would tell you how mean she was to me."

Again Curtis said nothing for a few moments, then, like a cat pouncing, he asked why she had gone to her sister's drawing room on the train that morning.

For a long second Carol kept her eyes fastened to the desk. As she spoke she moved them to the inexpensive little handbag lying in her lap and exclaimed: "I don't know what you're talking about, I guess."

"I think you do."

She looked up then, attempting wide-eyed astonishment. "Why, I wasn't on that train, Mr. Curtis."

"You were in North Conway yesterday?"

"Y-yes."

"And arrived in New York this morning on a seven-thirty train?"

Carol's eyes dropped once more to her lap. "No sir. No, I got in at twelve-fifteen."

Curtis shot Susan a quick glance. "Really," he said icily to Carol, "that's curious. You've been identified as being on the seven-thirty train. Hadn't you better reconsider your statement?"

"Why—why, how could I have been when I was on the twelve-fifteen?"

Curtis explained sharply that a man with an excellent memory had just left his office and that he had identified her positively as the girl he had seen outside Prunella Parton's drawing room.

Watching Carol's face, Susan saw her courage ebbing. She was beginning to crumble but was still hanging on to bravura. Her head shot up proudly, and her eyes flashed. "All right. Suppose I was? I have a right to travel on trains. I went into their Pullman to tell Mr. Stratfield I was sorry not to have gotten back to his house party. He asked me to come back. I wanted to be polite."

"You took the train at North Conway?"

"Y-yes."

"If you knew Mr. Stratfield's party was getting on at Swiss Village why didn't you go to their Pullman last night and speak to Stratfield?"

Carol's defiance held although her fright was obvious now. She made her next statement pugnaciously. "If I had gone then Prunella would have bawled me out about something. Anything. She always managed to. I thought if I went at the last minute I could just say my piece and get away. I certainly wish now, of course, I had waited and telephoned Mr. Stratfield."

"Well, why didn't you?"

"I was afraid Joan Sutton and that blond boy—that they might have seen me in the club car last night. If they had I thought it would look funny if I didn't go into their Pullman this morning."

As Curtis said "I see. What, exactly, happened when you reached your half sister's drawing room?" Carol Parton's eyes grew more frightened. Her shoulders wilted, and she said fervently: "Even though I hated her it was awful."

"What was awful?"

I tapped on the door and when there wasn't an answer I opened it and looked in. She was lying there half in the bathroom and half in the drawing room. Someway I knew she was dead, though I've never seen a dead person before."

"What did you do?"

"I just ran away. I don't know whether the porter saw me or not. Oh," she added gloomily, "but he must have. How else would you know?"

"You were seen," Curtis agreed noncommittally. "You know that wasn't very proper behavior, Miss Parton. You should have raised an alarm. Called the porter. The conductor. Had a doctor summoned. It was very odd not to, don't you think?"

"Odd?" Carol used the word as if its meaning were vague to her. "Not feeling the way I did about Prunella, it wasn't."

Curtis said: "Come now, Miss Parton. You know you went into the drawing room, that you did various things in there and then left, taking away your half sister's ski clothes."

Carol Parton was on her feet in one bound. She grasped her gloves as if they were a weapon and grabbed up her handbag from one corner of Curtis' desk. "I know my way around a little!" she cried. "After all, I've worked on a New York newspaper for two years—nearly three. If you're trying to trick me into confessing I murdered Prune it just won't work. I didn't and I'm not going to say I did."

"Please sit down."

Carol collapsed on the chair, and Curtis continued:

"If your own hands are clean, and even though you didn't like your half sister, you must be interested in having a murderer apprehended."

Leaning back in the chair she had so hastily abandoned and resumed, the girl looked as if all defiance had left her. If Curtis had struck her a physical blow she could not have looked more nervously and emotionally defeated.

"All right," she half screamed, "but I don't see how I can help. I don't know anything about it. I had the idea something just killed her. *Something*, you know."

Curtis said he was afraid he didn't quite know.

"Well, that she fell on her head or something."

"You think suicide unlikely?"

Straightening her shoulders, Carol shook her head mutely. Then she said: "You didn't know Prunella. She had the world too much by the tail. She even hated to go to bed at night for fear something of interest would happen before morning."

Watching, Susan saw the girl's eyes go curious. Staring at Curtis, she asked with apparent bewilderment: "Say, how *was* she killed?"

Curtis studied her thoughtfully. After a moment he said: "A blow on the head."

"But women don't kill that way, do they?"

"Women?"

Carol made a quick gesture with her gloves. "If somebody killed her it must have been a woman. Women hated her. Men didn't. She got too much into their blood. I can't imagine a man actually wanting to kill her."

"Why," Curtis inquired, as if he had no idea, "did women hate her?"

Miss Parton relaxed and sounded as if he were really too ridiculous. "Don't tell me you haven't caught on to that yet? They hated her because it never occurred to her they had any right to their possessions. Everything everywhere belonged to Prunella Parton. Everything that was hers was hers and everything that was yours was hers. I couldn't keep a beau two minutes once I let her get her eyes on him. And it wasn't that any of my men friends interested her particularly. It was just her nature."

Curtis' next question came like a rattle of shrapnel. "How did you spend yesterday, Sunday, Miss Parton?"

The girl's answer came as rapidly as his question, but Susan was sure her body had tensed once more beneath the tweed suit. "I've told you. Covering a ski event at North Conway, New Hampshire. It's no secret."

"But the newspapermen with you left North Conway at noon. Why didn't you?"

"Larry Stratfield asked me Sunday morning to bring the borrowed car back myself and to join the house party, as I said. At first I thought I'd go, but the roads were so bad and I was tired. Being on the same party with Prune was no treat, so I phoned that the job was taking longer than I had anticipated and that I'd have a North Conway garage get the car back. I knew the *Globe* would pay for that. Afterward I thought I hadn't exactly been what Aunt May would have called gracious. That's why—honestly, it is—I went in their Pullman this morning."

"How did you know which was your sister's drawing room? How did you know she had a drawing room?"

Carol looked astonished. "Oh, Prunella would have a drawing room. But I didn't know which was hers. I just tried the first one I came to, and—and there she was. Oh, it was awful!"

"There's nothing else you want to tell me?"

"Not a thing." Defiance was beginning to return.

"Very well. We may have to talk again, of course. Don't leave town. Keep yourself available."

Carol, taking this as dismissal, got up and flung herself out of the room without so much as a glance around it.

Copely and Susan said "Whew!" in concert. Curtis threw up his hands.

"What do you make of her?" he demanded disgustedly.

"She tells a lot and nothing, Mr. Curtis," said the secretary.

"I don't think she likes being suspected of murder," remarked Susan, and Curtis cast her a baleful glance.

"They so often don't," he said. "But, just the same, I'm not convinced she did it. The porter didn't think she was carrying anything. And whoever committed the murder must have carried off the ski clothes."

Susan puckered her brow and asked if it were possible Carol could have held the garments right in front of her so the porter wouldn't have seen them.

Curtis said yes, possible, but unlikely; after all, Pullman cars weren't a block long, and there was nothing wrong with the porter's eyesight. He'd been able to identify Carol Parton in the D. A.'s corridor from a much greater distance than the length of his Pullman car.

Susan glanced at her watch. "Well, your Lieutenant Burk is tailing her anyway. Maybe if she did it she'll give herself away. It's twenty-five to five. I've simply got to beat it back to Susan Yates, Incorporated. Oh, Lyle!" Susan stopped halfway to the door. "That Penbroke person must have seen Carol and whether she was carrying anything if she went through the club car coming from and going back again to her own Pullman. He was supposed to have been having breakfast right up to the moment before the train came to a standstill at Grand Central. According to your porter, the strange girl was at Prunella's door just a minute or so before then. The porter was carrying Penbroke's bags to the vestibule when he saw her, wasn't he? Then she must have passed the bland president of the Penbroke Advertising Agency."

Curtis said: "Would you believe it? I thought of that myself."

From the door Susan made a face at him and disappeared.

CHAPTER EIGHTEEN

AT HALF-PAST ELEVEN on this same Monday morning Mrs. David Barron picked up her mail at the hotel desk in Los Angeles. She was on her way to the beauty shop for her every-other-day facial-improvement session. She might, she maintained, be a slack person about some things, but no one could say she lacked the moral fortitude necessary for keeping intact a youthful skin. In her expensive suite where the California morning sun revealed ruthlessly what was reflected in the mirrors she had only an hour before told herself that it would probably be years before she would have to have her face actually lifted. It had survived a marriage which pleased her only financially. It had survived a persistent diet of cocktails, champagne and too many cigarettes. Running idly through her pile of mail, Mrs. Barron sauntered toward the private car exit of the hotel. Halfway across the lobby, her thoughts unexpectedly removed themselves from their customary adhesion to herself and the immediate aspects of life, bringing to the surface a subject she had trained her not-too-busy mind to taboo. This subject was David Barron, her husband. As a source of income David was all right. In fact, Lucretia Barron found him extremely convenient. But when one wanted to marry a poor though attractive man a monetary settlement was infinitely preferable to alimony which would cease upon remarriage. If only she could successfully nail David with a provable case of infidelity!

The last envelope upon which her eyes had fallen was pale mauve. It bore her name and address in a flourishing hand, an air-mail stamp and a New York City postmark. Instinctively Lucretia knew the writer was a woman. This in itself was unique. She possessed few women friends.

Quickly she ran a long carmine fingernail under the flap. Along her nerves ran a tingling sensation. She was suddenly extremely anxious to know what lay inside this tasteful envelope.

A moment later a double sheet of heavy note paper was in her hand. She sank into one of the lobby chairs and read what the writer had to say.

> R.F.D. 2
> Westover, Conn.
>
> Dear Mrs. Barron,
> It has been brought to my attention that you would find interest in adequate proof of a situation which might provide you with a divorce and permanent settlements from your husband. It may be possible to be of assistance. A personal conference would, of course, be necessary. I feel I could convey certain information out of a spirit of co-operation. As I am coming to California within the next few weeks, a conference might be arranged if you so desire.
>
> Cordially,
> Eloise Abelard

Lucretia Barron read this epistle over three times before it occurred to her what there was about it which disturbed some inner recess of that sector she customarily referred to as her brain. The trouble lay in the way the note was written. The bold and dominating handwriting of the envelope had not penned the enclosure. It was typewritten, even to the signature. Lucretia Barron, though lacking a studious nature, distrusted typewritten signatures, if for rather vague reasons. However, the hints contained in the note in her hand were of such a pleasing nature that she put aside this passing concern and leveled her attention upon the suggestion proposed. Had it come at last? Had David, for all his canny philandering, finally tripped himself? She had thought he would one day! Of course, she had had plenty of proof of his "going about" with women but not once, to date, had she been able to uncover anything which her lawyer would say constituted "indisputable proof."

It was at this point that Lucretia turned over in her mind who Eloise Abelard might be. Vaguely, the name seemed to ring a familiar note. She wasn't much of a reader, aside from the newspapers and one or two fiction magazines of the lightest types, but someway the name reminded her of a book or a character, of something, indeed, of which David himself had once spoken. Of course, David had been at one time frightfully well read. However, it really scarcely mattered who Eloise Abelard was. What mattered was her willingness to stand up for another woman, to come forward with proof of the thing Lucretia craved more than maintaining her beauty. She would send a reply off before evening. Of course she must meet this person! It would be absurd not to, even if the woman was cagey enough not to write by hand.

As Mrs. Barron was settling down under a dusky-brown mud pack and a pink silk coverlet at the beauty salon an awful possibility occurred to her. The word hovered on her lips a little sickeningly: "Blackmail!"

The writer might expect her to *pay* for information! That was very awkward indeed. The last thing in the world Lucretia ever wanted to do was to pay for anything. Perhaps it would be as well to show the typewritten letter to her attorney. He was wily. If there were a mouse to smell he would smell it. Yes, she must do that. She wouldn't answer the note until she had.

But this decision Lucretia Barron did not abide by. Cheered with three cocktails and a Chicago telephone call (charges reversed) from the very attractive and very poor young man she thought of marrying, she went to her desk at five-thirty that afternoon and wrote out a night-letter telegram to Eloise Abelard, R. F. D. 2, Westover, Conn. Lest she should change her mind when the effect of self-reliance engendered at the moment should wear off she then went at once and filed it. Cheered by more cocktails and a late party that evening, she gave the matter only passing thought until two representatives of the Los Angeles police department were announced to her on Tuesday morning.

CHAPTER NINETEEN

ON HER WAY UPTOWN from the D. A.'s office late Monday afternoon, Susan drove her smart open coupé against a biting February wind. It sent blood rushing to her cheeks and made her look anything but a young woman with thoughts turned to murder. She was thinking Curtis had forgotten to ask Carol Parton about the operation Alice Bomm had heard discussed by the Parton sisters. She must not forget to remind him. It might be important.

Bringing her car to a standstill at the curb in front of her Fifty-seventh Street salon, Susan got out and dove into the maelstrom which was the end of a busy day at Susan Yates, Inc., when the head and genius of the establishment had been absent.

Not again until she was dressing hurriedly for a theater and supper engagement did Susan have time to turn her thoughts uninterruptedly to the Parton case.

"I wonder who Prunella's doctor was?" she asked herself, pinning on one of the orchids Stanley Van Groesbeck had sent in advance of his arrival to escort her that evening. "If Prunella had to have a serious operation eight or nine months ago and didn't on her sister's advice, or for other reasons, perhaps she was still in bad health. Perhaps she did fall in the Pullman drawing room, give her head a frightful crack and pass out. Perhaps she fell when the train was rocking around the curves in the New Hampshire mountains. No, that won't do. She had been dead at most an hour and a quarter when the assistant medical examiner viewed her body this morning."

Susan snapped shut the clasp on her corsage pin. "Wait a minute!" she cried aloud to her quiet bedroom. "Couldn't she have cracked her head in New Hampshire, gone into a coma, never come out of it and died before the train reached Grand Central? Perhaps they can't estimate the time of a wound but only approximate times of death!"

At this moment she heard her front doorbell ringing. Then her maid, Lillian, came to say Mr. Van Groesbeck had arrived. Pushing the Parton case from her thoughts, Susan hurried out, anxious not to be late for the theater curtain. It was a revival of *Men in White*—which she had missed a few seasons earlier.

Concerned with the play and conversation with her escort between acts, Susan successfully eluded concentration on the death of Prunella Parton until it was brought abruptly back to mind during the second-act intermission. She stood smoking with Van Groesbeck in the lobby when a sprightly and self-assured voice just behind her cried:

"I knew it! I knew you weren't an undertaker. You're Susan Yates, the designer!"

Susan turned quickly and faced Joan Sutton accompanied, not at all omnipresently, by young Conway.

Susan grinned and introduced Stanley Van Groesbeck whom Joan cooed over as the socially prominent aviator before she turned back to Susan.

"Isn't it awful? As the English say, too thrill making! The murder, I mean. I've never been so excited in my life."

Susan thought that Joan might be merely excited but that behind an exquisitely ecstatic veneer the girl looked unnerved. There were lines around her eyes certainly not usually present in a twenty-one-year-old face, and she had seen Joan's hand trembling when she had given it to Van Groesbeck. Joan Sutton was frightened, if not for herself for someone else. But she was putting up a beautiful front.

"How'd I do during the inquisition?" she asked Susan chattily.

"I rather got the idea you don't intend to spend the rest of your life in mourning for the deceased."

"The rest of my life! Hinky, did you hear what Miss Yates said? I'm not spending even two minutes. Imagine that man—that policeman, not Mr. Curtis, because I thought he was cute—I mean, really too exciting looking—asking me why I didn't go and bang on Prunella Parton's door and accompany her from the train this morning. You'd think he thought I was her nurse or her most admiring chum."

During this expansive diatribe Hinkle Conway had been looking vaguely uncomfortable. Susan thought that, alive or dead, Prunella was probably a difficult subject even if Joan Sutton had rescued him from her clutches. He looked, however, as if he were accustomed to Joan brandishing Prunella's name about. But Susan decided, with a further sidewise glance at Conway, that he had certainly once been utterly fascinated by Prunella and was trying very hard to pretend it had all been a long, long time ago and now quite finished. He looked unhappy and prematurely hard, all done up in the same facial package. Susan felt a little sorry for him as Joan's words pattered on, tidily consigning Prunella to what she made clear she considered an altogether appropriate fate.

"If," thought Susan rapidly, "Joan Sutton murdered Prunella Parton she'll not stop there. She'll keep on murdering people when it suits her fancy until she's caught and electrocuted. She's wise beyond her years and brittle. She's competent and fearless. She can hate. One shouldn't be able to hate that much at twenty-one. She's not saying a word she doesn't want to say. She only pretends to have no control over her tongue. I believe she means me to report every word. Is she trying to prove that no one talking so ruthlessly and with such abandon could possibly have done murder? It's her idea of an alibi, I believe, and she's managing to make it appear that Conway is agreeing and co-operating with her every step of the way. Maybe she thinks he murdered Prunella. Maybe she knows he did!"

"And," Joan was saying, "Hinky could tell you the havoc Prunella Parton made at Daddy's office. Of course, Daddy's such a lamb. He never sees anything but the work accomplished. He doesn't humanize much in business, I guess. He's absolutely an idealist—thinks everyone working for him loves everyone else, the duck! But Prunella put it over on David Barron too. David even let her get away with the credit of introducing Mr. Stratfield to the agency as her own precious contact. David knew him all the time. Hinky knows he did. He saw a very chatty letter from Mr. Stratfield on David's desk months ago, didn't you, Hinky?"

The color in Conway's snow-tanned face deepened. "Oh, I say, Joan, you make me sound as if I were a blasted snooper. I just happened to see it. I don't know what it said, really."

"Well," expanded Joan, "anyway, Hinky saw that it said 'Dear Barron,' which means they must have known each other past the 'Dear Mr. Barron' stage, you know. But Prunella got away with making a big impression on Dad just the same. That's the kind of a female she was. Can you blame me for utterly loathing her? Anybody behaving that way in my set would be definitely blackballed. You see what I mean?"

Van Groesbeck was looking startled, having no idea what Miss Sutton was talking about. Joan appeared oblivious of deficient diplomacy in revealing her innermost thoughts before him or anyone else who might be overhearing them in the crowded lobby. Tossing her long blond hair, she continued to emphasize her venom until the curtain bell rang. They threw away their cigarettes then and filed back into the theater. As they were about to part Joan whispered quite audibly to Susan:

"There are lots of things I could tell you about that female. I mean lots!"

"Come to my shop and tell me," Susan whispered back. "We'll sneak off and have tea or something."

"Tomorrow or the next day," promised Miss Sutton, and disappeared as the lights began to lower. A man whose back looked vaguely familiar to Susan had stopped a moment before on the other side of Joan. Now he, too, disappeared into the darkened theater.

CHAPTER TWENTY

As THE THIRD ACT of the revival of *Men in White* began persons connected with the Parton case were variously engaged. Three rows behind Susan, although unknown to her, Oliver Penbroke's bulk more than filled an aisle seat. In Los Angeles Mrs. David Barron, having filed her night letter to Eloise Abelard, was dressing to dine with friends. In her apartment in New York Hazel Manchester was spending the evening alone.

Miss Manchester intended to go to bed early. To pass the early evening, because her mind was too preoccupied for reading, she strolled about her living room rearranging a dozen of the roses Lawrence Stratfield had left at her office that morning. She had brought two dozen of them home because the others were more than adequate for a business desk and because the deeply vivid color of American Beauties especially suited her small but exquisite living room, a room which had been planned for years with David Barron's dark, quick face in her mind.

Standing before the mirrored mantel, Hazel arranged some of the roses there in a square frosted bowl. Then she moved to a low table by the couch and put the remainder in a wide-necked antique crystal bottle. Yes, they did suit the room. She regretted she had not had them quite so effectively arranged when David had dropped in after their cocktails that afternoon. After his telephone call at her office, half an hour after their inquisition on the train, she had come all the way uptown to bring them. Well, never mind, he had at least seen roses in profusion, a dozen at her office, two dozen at home. He must be convinced she possessed admirers.

On the whole Miss Manchester was quite pleased with her conquest of Lawrence Stratfield over the week end—not that she had the slightest intention it should outlive her immediate needs, but, meantime, it was an extremely timely piece of luck.

Curling up on the couch where she could catch in a corner of each eye both vases of flowers, Miss Manchester permitted her thoughts to travel over a bit of time, space and memory. For one thing, Lucretia Barron had always been entirely unsuited to David. Lucretia was an essentially selfish, silly woman. Moreover, doing a seemingly ruthless thing often produced an entirely felicitous result. With Prunella out of the way, Lucretia was the only problem. David's call on her at *Inter-Allied News* late that afternoon, his suggestion of cocktails and his visit to her apartment surely suggested that Stratfield's attentions over the week end had focused her in his eyes as she had not been since childhood. David's family would be pleased, too—as would hers. She knew that when she had been no more than thirteen or fourteen her mother and Mrs. Robert Barron, David's mother, had secretly discussed and cherished the hope that little Hazel and little David would one day marry! However, when David was nineteen he had come home to Princeton late one Monday afternoon from a rather precocious week end in New York, bringing with him a luscious bit of femininity called Lucretia. Hazel could see his mother now, her face tearstained and swollen, coming across the lawn between their houses, falling into her mother's arms and crying hysterically:

"David—David was married last night to a dreadful—simply dreadful girl. What *am* I going to do? Poor, poor David. My baby. My baby!"

There had been quite a bit of that. Mrs. Manchester had consoled Mrs. Barron as best she could, her own private hopes having been equally shattered by David's sudden and unseemly adventure into matrimony. Ultimately, of course, Lucretia Barron had taken her place—at least a place of sorts—in the family and the Princeton community. But she had never fitted. She had always been a little common, a little too openly grasping. Mrs. Manchester had once or twice neatly summed up the whole matter with a brief:

"If Lucretia were only clever enough at least to pretend being a lady—!"

But that Lucretia had not accomplished. The "nice families" of Princeton had never quite accepted David's frothy wife. With even more finality Lucretia had never accepted them. It could not be said, however, that she had held David back in his career. The very thought of more and more money within her reach had been sufficient for Lucretia to make every proper gesture calculated to spur her husband to bigger and bigger commercial achievements. She had behaved herself, too, while he was on the way up in the firm of Peter Sutton. Only when the firm's name ultimately had become Sutton & Barron and Barron's income was an established and fairly corpulent matter had she begun to spread her wings, to engage in a few open indiscretions. The separation had come about when David Barron was amply able to support two affluently maintained domiciles. It was all a bit sordid, Hazel thought, her eyes on the roses in the frosted bowl.

With the departure of Lucretia to the West Coast, she had hoped David might turn to her, his childhood chum, for consolation. Disappointingly, David had immediately stepped further out of her life. She saw him now perhaps three or four times a year. He would ring up, rather as a family duty, it seemed, and ask her for dinner or the theater. Of course, at family reunions they saw each other. The Manchester and Barron families still celebrated Thanksgiving and Christmas together. But it had remained horribly true that David still thought of her—or had until the past week end—as "the little girl next door." And, meantime, she had been growing up so concentrated on developing beauty and charm with which to attract her childhood love that she had actually become a beauty-and-charm columnist. She was an expert who told other people how to do it, who guided other women's affairs of the heart while waiting, year after year, until now she was close to thirty, for her own hopes to bud.

For some time the interference had not been primarily the vain and futile Lucretia but the brittle, seductive Prunella Parton.

What luck it had been meeting Lawrence Stratfield at a dinner party the week before and getting herself invited to his week-end house party. Fate had played very efficiently into her eager hands. David had looked really conscious of her when he had walked into her office late that afternoon. He definitely hadn't missed noticing the roses either. In the taxi he had said:

"Look here, Hazel, despite all the years we've known each other I'll be damned if I've known how lovely you are until this past week end at Stratfield's. I suppose men have been telling you that for years while I, like a damn jackass, have been bumming all over the place, unconscious of what the home town had to offer."

Hazel hoped she had handled this scene with all the poise and distinction she recommended to readers of her column. She had sighed with just the proper amount of wistfulness but had tried very hard to keep her expression faintly amused. Obviously, David liked brittle women, from the examples he had fallen for. She couldn't expect him to go for anything much short of that. He liked surface effects. The thing to do, of course, was to induce him to like surface effects but to want to have them overlay character and brains, not the silliness of a Lucretia, not the viciousness of a Prunella. Anyway, the decks were cleared now for action. Only Lucretia remained to be disposed of, and the divorce courts could certainly take care of that angle. Hazel sighed again, a very happy, satisfied sigh of expectancy.

MEANWHILE, AS THE THIRD ACT of *Men in White* progressed four people around a bridge table in Lawrence Stratfield's apartment paused to discuss Prunella Parton's death. In addition to Stratfield, they were Mr. and Mrs. Cadwalader and a Mrs. Petulla, the latter the majority stockholder in the Kork-Petulla Oil Company.

"The police," said Stratfield, "are, I find, without much imagination. They think Prunella killed herself. And, you know, I find myself possessed of the most curious conviction that it was murder."

"Murder!" shrieked Mrs. Cadwalader and Mrs. Petulla in excited unison. "Lawrence, *you don't!*"

"Yes, I do," insisted Stratfield, pleased with the effect he was creating. "I can't tell you why. It sounds fantastic, of course, but some sixth sense keeps telling me that someone managed to pop her off. She was quite a girl, you know. God knows what the current phrase for it is. 'Glamour girl' isn't strong enough. We used to say 'vampire.' I dare say she had a fairly adequate list of enemies. You know anybody could have been on the train. We wouldn't have known it. Simply anybody could have slipped into her drawing room during the night. I've often thought it's just like sleeping in a tent on Broadway to sleep in a train anyway. A green flap between you and any passing murderer!"

The women screamed prettily again, and Percy Cadwalader remarked that, from the reports he'd read in the afternoon papers, it was his opinion that Lawrence was letting his artistic imagination run away with him. The police had practically satisfied themselves of suicide resulting from a morbid state of mind and ill health.

"It seems to me," he said, "that the autopsy didn't show she had undergone some mysterious sort of operation which the earlier afternoon editions hinted she had, but still the police say the way she was dressed should be proof enough for anybody! By God, I agree. Long underwear and an evening gown!"

"Fantastic," cooed Mrs. Petulla.

"She must have been mad," agreed Mrs. Cadwalader.

"Well," said Stratfield, "I suppose the police must be right—morbid state of mind, suicide. But I can't quite shake off my little private theory of murder. Besides, suicide is so dull. Anybody can commit it. You have to be somebody or other to get murdered."

"Lawrence, you're incorrigible," moaned Mrs. Petulla, and added more decisively, "Well, I bid three hearts, opening."

Thus Prunella Parton was raised and buried under an evening of shrewdly contracted bridge.

PETER SUTTON SPENT his Monday evening at home. He bid his daughter good night when she left for the theater with Hinkle Conway and not for the first time in the past few days told himself that the young man of her acquaintance least likely to cope with Joan's self-centered fieriness was this blond fledgling. After that he sat thinking concentratedly about Joan for a long time. At half-past ten he had arrived at a definite decision.

"And there's no time like the present," he muttered to the silence of his library. Then he glanced at his watch, adjusted the reading light to his liking and opened the Aldington translation of Boccaccio's *Decameron.*

Lieutenant Burk's policeman friend's sister, the Sutton parlormaid, was thus rewarded for her trouble when she came into the room a few moments later, presumably to empty ash trays. She had agreed to report to Lieutenant Burk what happened in the household that evening. In picking up the ash tray at her employer's side, her eyes fell on a full-page Jean De Bosschère illustration. This happenstance had the immediate and decisive effect of convincing her that a man sitting alone at home gazing at however effectively unclothed females was probably capable of anything, including murder.

This opinion was reported to Curtis about eleven o'clock that evening. The assistant D. A. said to himself: "In an era of psychology-mad wishful thinkers, escapists and sublimators Sutton's evening entertainment did not seem essentially unique." He thought no more about it and began making a series of notes on the pad before him.

> 1. Cross off further investigation of Mrs. David Barron as possible murder suspect. (Los Angeles police report she was at Clement Stanes's studio party in Hollywood from ten o'clock Sunday night until 5 A.M.)
>
> 2. Remember to tell Susan autopsy showed no signs of Prunella having had an operation.
>
> 3. Quiz Hazel Manchester further as to why the emerald pin interested her. Check with Prunella's maid.

4. Bear in mind that increase in salary Prunella got at Sutton & Barron late last summer seems inadequate to have maintained her in style she immediately afterward accustomed herself to.

5. What is meaning of driver's license found in Prunella's apartment this afternoon, name of Eloise Abelard, Westover, Conn.? (Send Sergeant Jones up there to investigate first thing Tues. A.M. Have him take house keys found, same drawer, in deceased's desk.)

6. Ask Susan to manage private chat with Joan Sutton. (Our self-expressive postdeb knows or thinks she knows something: a. detrimental to herself; b. detrimental to her father; c. detrimental to young Conway.)

7. Why the hell is Susan out tonight with that jackass Van Groesbeck? (Report of tails put on Joan Sutton and Hinkle Conway.)

Having absent-mindedly written down the latter notations, Mr. Curtis hastily struck them from the record. Then he found himself wondering if Susan had read the afternoon papers with their reports that the police were convinced Prunella Parton had committed suicide. Probably Susan hadn't. After leaving his office at five o'clock she had stuck her head back through the doorway and remarked: "Even if the police are right I shan't read any optimistic reports of theirs. It's so much more entertaining being pessimistic with you!"

Without writing it down, Mr. Curtis again thought: "What the hell is Van Groesbeck to her? Daredevil flyer and nitwit." On this pleasant conviction, he went home for a few short hours of sleep.

CHAPTER TWENTY-ONE

JOAN SUTTON and Hinkle Conway went from the revival of *Men in White* to El Morocco. Under its star-splattered ceiling they sat and talked with such drawn faces that a woman at the next table informed her companion that the new trend in babies was the elderly type.

"Look at those children!" she hissed with elegant detachment. "Not a wrinkle in their faces but plenty in their brains, I'll venture."

This remark was not made inaudibly. Joan heard every word of it. "Come on, Hinky," she muttered, "let's get out of here. There's a giraffe peering over the fence."

Conway paid the bill, and they made their way to the street.

"Don't let a ruminant mammal get you down," he advised as they waited for a taxi.

"That woman!" scoffed Joan. "It's not what she said. It's the way I feel. She complimented us by saying we don't show our wrinkles. I'm going home to bed. Maybe tomorrow—"

The taxi drew up at this moment, and they were solicitously ushered into it by the doorman. "I don't follow you, Joan," began Conway.

"Oh, for goodness' sake, don't start that again," the girl begged. "Really, darling, you're being trying. Anybody would think I was three years old and you didn't dare tell me the difference between hot and cold water. I'm not going to say any more tonight. We're both jittery."

Wearily her companion remarked that she was crazy and lapsed into a vast silence.

In this manner they reached the Sutton residence. Conway paid off the cab and escorted Joan across the sidewalk.

"Are you planning to walk all the way home?" she inquired.

Conway said yes in the briefest way possible, and Joan said nothing more until they had mounted the stone steps. Then: "All right, darling. Ring me tomorrow and don't worry about anything. I don't care what, there's a way out of everything."

Again Conway said he hadn't the faintest idea what she meant. In answer Joan energetically planted a stark strip of lipstick, like a postal cancellation, across his lips. "I can love as hard as I can hate," she said a little hoarsely, and disappeared behind her father's expensive front door.

The blond young man stood staring at the closed portal. After a while he went down the steps, turned east and strode off, a Bronze Age horseman come to life.

Conway's tail from Curtis' office had some difficulty in keeping up with his hasty and violent pace but managed to see him, twenty minutes later, turn in at his own apartment house.

"They ought to provide us with roller skates," observed the detective to the 2 A.M. quiet. He lit a cigarette and entered the building opposite Conway's. It was too cold a night to keep standing around outside. He'd had enough of that El Morocco. There was no doorman in the building he had chosen. He leaned against the door and stared out into the quiet street.

Ten minutes passed, and the detective was suddenly galvanized into attentiveness. Across the street, appearing on the run, was the young fellow with blond hair. He didn't look so neat now. There was a wisp of white showing at the bottom of his dark trousers. The street light illuminated a negligently turned-down collar where ten minutes before stiff wings and a black bow tie had supported Conway's neck.

"That's pajamas he got underneath," the detective told himself, and turned hastily out into the night.

Conway was going east, walking at the general pace of a lynx. A white fog was hanging over upper Manhattan, and the detective had almost to run to keep the young man in sight. He prayed that he shouldn't be left out on a limb by the other picking up a late-cruising taxi. Scarcely had this thought crossed his mind than that was precisely what happened. A cab screeched to a standstill ahead, and Conway got into it. But the tail's luck held for the time being. A cruising radio car was coming down the street. He hailed it, presented his credentials and hastily explained his mission. The radio men allowed him to wedge in beside them and sped on after the taxi.

"Just keep it in sight but stay behind. He may look out back, recognize your buggy and change his plans," advised the detective. They fell back as far as the fog would permit.

The cab was making for East End Avenue. Expensive apartment houses and remodeled private houses began to appear on their left, the river, white canopied by the fog, on their right.

"What's he done?" asked one of the radio men.

"Search me," said the detective. "Suspect in that Parton case. Girl that died on the train this morning. I hear you people say it was suicide."

Both the policemen grunted. Then one of them asked: "You been tailing him all evening?"

"Sure. Theater, El Morocco. Best joints."

"He's getting out of the cab."

They slowed down. Conway seemed to be paying his fare. He had left the cab just south of the Gracie Mansion.

The detective said: "I'll hoof it from here. But maybe you guys better cruise along behind. I don't like this setup. I'd put the kid to bed, you see. Then out he comes, all ginned up over something."

"O.K.," said the man at the wheel.

The detective got out and walked north, the radio car cruising casually behind him. Then he saw that everything ahead wasn't as it should be. A figure had appeared through the obscuring fog from the opposite direction. It seemed to have sprung up from nowhere. Another man.

The two figures melted for a moment into one, then became two men scuffling. The now panting detective couldn't make out who had attacked whom. One of them let out a short, sharp yell. He couldn't tell which.

"Damn this fog," yelped the detective. He was putting all he had into catching up. Somebody else was running—the person who had come from the other direction, he guessed. He could make out a strip of white at the bottom of the black trousers standing still on the pavement. The owner of these trousers seemed to be doubled over. It looked as if he was hurt.

The detective yelled: "What's goin' on?"

There was no answer, but immediately the owner of the white-edged trousers starting running north, hotfooting it. It looked as if he was going after the other figures which had been swallowed up in the fog. The detective, was reducing the intervening distance, but not enough, and, looking over his shoulder, he couldn't see the radio car any more. The men in it, he figured, hadn't seen what had been happening. Past the Gracie Mansion the fog was deeper. Then he spotted eerie lights ahead. The same cab coming back from a brief optimistic cruise to the north probably. In its headlights he could make out Conway's figure, hazy but recognizable. Conway was hailing the taxi, getting into it. The cab spun around in a U turn and disappeared.

The detective yelled back for the radio boys. They came up, and he climbed in with them, not bothering to explain until he had. They took up speed. At first the taxi was still nowhere in sight. After two blocks they spotted it. It was turning west, going fast. They followed and opened up on the siren. The detective was explaining what he had seen happen.

"Maybe," offered one of the radio-car men, "he's making for the precinct station."

After several blocks of fog-disturbed progress this proved an accurate prediction. Conway's cab was coming to a standstill in front of a building with green lights outside. Conway was getting out, one arm hanging limp. The radio car screeched to a standstill behind the taxi. All three men spilled out.

CHAPTER TWENTY-TWO

SERGEANT WITHERS, ENSCONCED in the back seat of a sleigh, came down the long hill from Swiss Village Lodge into the hamlet. He was studying the terrain with a moody and unseeing eye. Apparent facts were defeating him. At the lodge he had met Stratfield's insurance adjuster and the oilstove company's representative. Their ultimate verdict had been an accidental explosion.

Sergeant Withers wasn't satisfied. The complete demolition of the kitchen and the floor under the bed Prunella Parton was to have slept in still seemed to him excessive. It had removed too effectively all causal evidence. He didn't like it.

Withers had checked with the old butler very carefully as to which members of the party knew Miss Parton was occupying the room she had. The old fellow thought no one had known, not even his employer. The butler himself had put Miss Parton in there because she was an old friend of Mr. Stratfield's, a particular young lady and thus due the best room.

The rosy-cheeked maid had at first seemed to know nothing at all of value, having been sent off by sleigh the previous Saturday night after dinner. She had been suffering from hysterics which the cook's talk of "smelling death" had inspired. During the course of his interview, however, Sergeant Withers had pried one piece of information out of the maid. David Barron had known Miss Parton was in the east suite. While the maid had been with Miss Parton helping her unpack Saturday noon Mr. Barron had tapped at the door and had started to enter. Then he had seen the maid and, according to her opinion, decided it wasn't a nice thing to do—entering a lady's private bedroom that way. In any case, he had only come as far as just inside the door. She couldn't recall exactly what he had said—something about did she, Miss Parton, know whether you could get drinks served in your room at Mr. Stratfield's. The maid had thought it fresh of him, a gentleman expecting to get liquored up at noontime. Miss Parton had told him he'd probably find something to drink in the lounge downstairs. The maid thought Miss Parton hadn't liked her seeing a man in her room, even only a foot into it. That had been the entirety of the episode.

Stratfield's cook, Mrs. Bumpet, had been the least reticent of the servants. She had told Withers flatly and determinedly that there had been death in the air on Saturday night. Naturally Sergeant Withers, one of Curtis' brightest young men, had not been satisfied with her contention that she had known this through the resources of her nose. He had excavated in his most persuasive tone for more convincing evidence. But Mrs. Bumpet had stuck by her olfactory sentinels although she had admitted that even her alarm clock which she customarily brought from her bedroom each night and set by the kitchen clock before retiring had not sounded as usual. Every sound and odor in the house had, according to her weepy version, been in cahoots with the powers of darkness. Pressed further about the clock, she had said she had heard it ticking all the way from her room on the third floor before ever she had brought it down to the kitchen to set. That wasn't normal and just went to show that nothing had been normal that night. Sergeant Withers had inquired if it couldn't have been another ticking she had heard. Mrs. Bumpet had resisted this notion. It had been her alarm clock. She guessed she knew how it ticked! She had heard it in the hall and on the stairs, too, when she had been on her way to fetch it. And death had smelled plain as anything. She'd smelled it long before dinner. It was a precious wonder she'd been able to get dinner at all.

Sergeant Withers was convinced that an X ray of the cook's memory would have given him his answers. She had evidently observed certain entirely material facts, not in the phenomenon category, which had brought about what Mr. Curtis would term psychic unrest. What these facts were he could not drag from her.

Now, in the sleigh which he had hired in the hamlet, the sergeant was trying to recapitulate all that he had been told, almost told, and several things he had not been told at Swiss Village Lodge. The not-tolds, of course, included who, other than the vice-president of Sutton & Barron, had known where Prunella Parton was to sleep. Had there been a time bomb ticking in the kitchen, and if so, placed there by whose hand? Also, why had Miss Parton left behind part of her skiing clothes? This latter fact had been conveyed to him not by the rosy-cheeked maid who was supposed to do upstairs work but by the cook who had taken it into her head, she had explained, to see to it that they have a regular good house cleaning on Monday morning.

"That east soot where the explosion was worst was something for eyes to see," she had explained. I took my pail and my mop and dustcloths and the vacuum up there bright and early. I cleaned up the mess best I could. Plaster dust clean all over the place, there was. I decided I better do up the closet, too, while I was there. To get at the top shelf I had to get myself a chair to stand on and when I got up on it what did I see but that the poor young lady had left a whole pack of her clothes, skiing shoes and socks, a muffler and a wool blouse, all tucked up neat and tight and shoved back in the very corner of the shelf. I thought to myself: 'Bless me, that's a funny kind of place to put them.' Then I decided somebody must have stuffed them up there after the explosion—to get them off the floor maybe. Miss Parton hadn't used the soot after they got her out of the bathroom hall. Mr. Stratfield had her put in a spare bedroom across the hall."

"Did the maid pack her bags on Sunday?" Withers had asked, mindful of Curtis' telegram about that point.

Mrs. Bumpet had been emphatic. The young lady had done her own packing, shame that it was. She had been all tuckered out, she had. Mrs. Bumpet had gone up herself after dinner to see if there wasn't something she could do, the maid being that harum-scarum.

Sergeant Withers had gleaned that Mrs. Bumpet had also gone to Prunella's bedroom with the idea that her first-aid administrations of the night before might be rewarded by their recipient inasmuch as she went on to explain at some length how she personally had brought Miss Parton to consciousness on Saturday night, how she had fetched her tea and been what might be called generally useful. From the satisfaction in her tone the sergeant had also judged that Miss Parton had not been entirely unmindful of the services rendered.

Recalling Mrs. Bumpet to her original theme, Withers had next asked why Miss Parton had packed her own bags.

"Why indeed? This country girl we've got helping out is too lightheaded to come in out of the rain. It didn't come to her to go up during the afternoon and ask to be of help like she had on Saturday. And such a nice young lady Miss Parton was, coming down to my kitchen with me and asking just how I make my Duke of York salad dressing." Mrs. Bumpet had mopped a large tear.

Hopeful of bringing to the surface something else materially helpful, Sergeant Withers had prodded further. He had asked Mrs. Bumpet to describe the other members of the week-end party. This she had claimed she couldn't be expected to do, seeing as how she hadn't seen any others of them, excepting the young man with yellow hair. That was, she hadn't seen the others except in the upper hall while the men were looking for Miss Parton's body, and there wasn't any lights on.

"When," Withers had persisted, "did you see the young man with yellow hair?"

"When he comes to the butler's pantry while I'm telling Simon Baggs as how I smell death. I'd seen him before that, too, in the lounge while Baggs was valeting upstairs. I was looking for him— Baggs, I mean—and I stuck me head in the studio. The young man was standing over by the big window talking to himself. I wasn't surprised, what with the feelings I was having."

"What was he saying?"

"I'm not one to be getting him in trouble. A real nice young man, he seemed. Refreshment to the eyes."

"Better tell me."

"Oh, it wasn't nothing." Then Mrs. Bumpet had paused, suddenly goggle eyed and looking doubtful. Evidently the exact nature of what Conway had said had only just occurred to her. "Well now, it was kind of odd, as you might say."

"What?"

"Wishing somebody didn't exist."

"Who?"

"Oh, he didn't say—not that I heard."

"You didn't speak to him?"

"Me? I guess I know eticut better than that. The idea!"

"You saw him next in the butler's pantry?"

"I did."

"What did he come in there for?"

Mrs. Bumpet had explained: "Him and another gentleman was wanting a drink, the way gentlemen will."

Coming to this point in the meager facts he had reaped at Swiss Village Lodge, Sergeant Withers found the sleigh had reached the village. It was stopping in front of the post office. The boy driving turned around from the front seat and asked:

"Want I should take you to the station? Train ain't due for an hour yet."

Sergeant Withers said he wished to telephone. Where could he?

The boy cast a heavily gloved thumb in the direction of the post office. "In there's one."

Withers got out and entered the one-story building. Inside was a wall phone with a crank. On a rough shelf nailed to the window sill was a dubious-looking bottle of ink and a pen suggesting it had been placed there during the postmastership of John Wanamaker. Opposite the door was a small battery of glass-faced mail boxes and a caged window behind which stood an ancient man, a relic if Withers had ever seen one. He didn't look as if he'd be able to hear thunder, but, going to the phone, Withers nevertheless lowered his voice, taking no chances. When he got through to Curtis in New York he gave his report in extremely restrained terms. This duty completed, he walked over to the postmaster whose interested expression indicated better than words that he had missed not a syllable of the sergeant's conversation.

"Good and cold this morning," remarked Withers.

The postmaster pulled in his chin. "Not so bad as yisterday. You from the insurance company?"

Withers shook his head. "You know Mr. Stratfield?" he countered.

In immediate retaliation for being given a question in answer to one the ancient also merely nodded.

Withers decided he had better amend his approach. "I'm not from the insurance company but I have been looking over the explosion up at the Stratfield place."

The postmaster nodded again as if he knew all about that; no use wasting time with obvious village-wide information.

"Big house party up there over the week end," added Withers. Once more the relic nodded.

"Did you know any of the guests?"

"Might have. You from the police?"

"What makes you ask that?"

"Couple newspapers called up this morning asking did I know anything local about the young lady that died on the train. Just thought you might be police."

Withers further revised his nonconfessional attack. He pushed his credentials under the iron bars and waited for the postmaster to put on his spectacles and read them. Over this matter the worthy took his time. "District attorney's office, eh? Was she done in?"

"We aren't assuming she was or wasn't. Did you know anything local about her?"

"Wasn't never up to Swiss Village before, if that's what you mean. Her name was Parton, the newspapers said. We ain't got no Partons in these parts. Old New York family, maybe, town being named after her folks."

"What town?"

"Where she lived, I figured."

"She lived in New York City."

"Did she? Well, she mailed a letter to some relative then. A Miss Prunella Parton, it was, on the envelope, addressed to Parton, New York."

Withers' ears stood rigidly upright. "She mailed a letter to Prunella Parton, Parton, New York?"

"There was one in the post-office door box Monday morning—yesterday."

"You didn't see her mail it personally?"

The relic looked faintly outraged. "This post office and other gover'rnent buildings is closed Sundays and nights."

Withers asked where Parton, New York, was.

"Don't know. Can't know all the towns in the United States. I put it in the southbound mailbag because New York State is south of here."

"Any return address on the envelope?"

"There was not."

"Huumm. Lady's writing?"

"Don't know. Some men write like women, some women like men, 'n my experience. You know how to tell the difference?"

Withers had to admit that he did not. He chatted aimlessly a few moments more, then made for the wall phone and put through a second call to the district attorney's office.

At the other end Curtis said they would get Washington onto it at once.

After this Withers vainly attempted to extract further shocks or revelations from the withered lips of the postmaster and ultimately took his departure.

Outside in the icy wind of the street, another thought struck him. He pushed open once more the creaking door, and, bringing with him a blast of air which seemed straight off polar regions, shut it behind him hastily.

"I was thinking of that envelope you were telling me about," he said. "Did it look as if it had been written in kind of a hurry?"

"Yes and no."

"How do you mean?" This with infinite patience.

"The name was neat as a pin. The address was kinda hasty. Downhill, you might say."

"Could two different people have written it? I mean, one person the name, another the address?"

"Nope. Same person feeling different. Plenty of time with the name. Then in a hurry. Young man, let me tell you something. I've

been postmaster here for nigh on to forty years. Writin' on enve-
lopes can be right interesting. Gives insight into folks. Yep. Right
interesting sometimes."

Withers concluded he had extracted all of the postmaster's fac-
tual data and made his departure final this time.

CHAPTER TWENTY-THREE

AN HOUR OR TWO before Sergeant Withers had been making discoveries at Swiss Village Lodge and in the hamlet post office Susan Yates had been waking up in her New York apartment. One glance at her dressing-table clock informed her that she might steal fifteen minutes more, but sleep eluded her now. Her brain had taken up the Parton case as if electrically set to go to work on it immediately upon awaking. She tried to recapture drowsiness but presently gave it up as futile, rang for her breakfast tray and had her bath while it was being prepared. She found she was more anxious than she had suspected to hear what Lyle's myrmidons had accomplished with the tasks he had set them the day before. At eight o'clock she rang the district attorney's office and found Curtis already at his desk. He had been home for five hours' sleep, he said. Business was hustling this morning.

"Among other things," he explained, "we need your fashion advice again. Something odd happened on the island of Manhattan last night."

"Oh, Lyle, what?"

"Not on the phone. Could you pop in here—?" He left the sentence attractively unfinished.

"You beast," moaned Susan, "you know I'll come after such a fiendish invitation to my natural curiosity."

Curtis chuckled. "What time may we expect your delectable presence?"

"Oh, I'll come right away and hope to be in my shop by nine o'clock. Even for the D. A.'s staff it doesn't seem practical for me to go into bankruptcy."

"I'm not so sure about that, if you would care to be a little less general. It would scarcely seem worthwhile for the entire D. A. staff. Personalize the proposition a little, and it will be a pleasure to assist you in the legal aspects."

Susan said: "That's pure impertinence, but I'm on my way," and banged down the phone. As she dressed she remarked to herself: "Apparently the only way I can keep out of that young man's life will be to marry him. But I don't know. Or do I?"

CURTIS' OFFICE, as usual, resembled a kaleidoscopic combination of a factory working at top pitch and an exhibition of colored memorandum pads. In the middle of the room the assistant D. A. sat, looking as if he were attempting interplanetary communication. He was once more balancing a telephone receiver in each hand and carrying on alternate conversations into two transmitters. Finally he recradled both instruments and said:

"Good morning, fair one. Why would a gentleman be walking along East End Avenue at 2 A.M. clad in a pair of pajamas over which were worn impeccable dinner clothes?"

"I'm a designer of women's clothes. Did you drag me down here to ask me *that?* What gentleman?"

"A blond and somewhat excitable young man called Hinkle Conway. He claims to have suffered from assault and battery, assailant unknown to him, or, at least, obscuring identification by wearing a mask. And at an early hour this morning one of our men found a domino mask lying on the exact top of an ash can in the service areaway entrance to Lawrence Stratfield's apartment house."

"Lawrence Stratfield's? Good heaven, a plant?"

"It wouldn't seem too bright for him to have hidden it himself so openly."

"Did the attack on Conway presumably take place in Stratfield's neighborhood?"

"Half a block away, in front of the Gracie Mansion, one of New York's historic spots."

"What has Stratfield got to say about it?"

"He seems to think it's a good joke on him. He was playing bridge all evening with three of our richer citizens. They all swear he wasn't absent from the table for any but the most trivial recesses. Stratfield is, no doubt, busy at this very moment ringing up everybody he knows to tell them somebody's trying to plant an assault-and-battery charge at his door."

"Won't Conway tell you what he was doing parading around in pajamas?"

"He says somebody telephoned him, saying it was Assistant District Attorney Curtis and for him to come right up to the Gracie Mansion in connection with the Parton case. He says I said not to bother to dress. Having a nice sense of the proprieties, he claims he did stop to throw on the nearest things at hand, the dinner clothes he had just removed."

"A compromise at least for general street wear. What was he trying to do—emulate Prunella?"

"There's a certain similarity. Only Conway didn't get killed. It seems he knows how to use his fists. He only got his shoulder thrown out."

"Ski-underwear and dinner gown. Pajamas and dinner clothes," mused Susan. "I must say either somebody with a peculiar sense of humor or a slight case of insanity is involved in all this."

Curtis went on to explain that Conway had taken Joan Sutton to the theater and supper. Susan interrupted to vouch for the former.

"Oh, I forgot for the moment. That's right, you *were* there. I had a very complete report from Joan and Conway's tails. Wearing black velvet, weren't you? And orchids?"

Susan asked if he had obtained a satisfactory list of her jewels and, making a face at him, asked if anybody had seen the holdup.

"Conway's tail was nearly present. Not quite. There was a fog. Conway claims a man ran out of the mist, wearing a mask, tried to mash him on the head with something hard in the toe of what looked like a sock. He defended himself, attempted to follow his assailant and, finding no sign of the man, took a taxi to the nearest precinct police station. Moreover, that's all the tail can say he did and didn't do."

Susan widened her eyes. "You think there's something funny about it?"

"It's possible to throw one's own shoulder out of place without anybody's help. But the tail did see another man. If he merely used the other man as a foil then perhaps we have a—"

"Wait!" cried Susan. "I warn you, if you say red herring I shall scream."

"All right. Flaming sardine then."

"What about Stratfield? Did you have a detective watching him?"

"Yes, and he neither heard nor saw anything all evening except Stratfield's three richly endowed guests going into the building at five to eight and leaving at 3 A.M. When they left they were chatting about what 'a lamb' Lawrence was and what 'rotten luck' he had at bridge. His Filipino says he lost one hundred and twenty-five dollars. But, as I said, he's not grumpy this morning and takes the finding of the mask practically on his doorstep as an amusing, if grim, joke."

"You think the attack on Conway is bound to have something to do with the Parton case?" asked Susan.

Curtis looked noncommittal and thoughtful. "It could," he remarked, "have been a retake photograph of how Prunella came to her end: something hard in the end of a sock. A sock, mind you, would have looked natural in any of the men's luggage. Damn natural. And the women were carrying short ski stockings. As a matter of fact, I've gone over Burk's and the other detective's reports again, checking what everybody had in his and her luggage. As long as they weren't carrying Prunella's ski suit or obvious weapons what else they carried didn't seem particularly important yesterday. Today it does. Well, Stratfield had a box, unopened and still sealed, of expensive golf balls. Of course, he could have had a single one on his person. He could have disposed of that later. Peter Sutton was carrying one of these fashionable heavy wooden bowls of shaving soap, small, hard, neat and capable of being shoved down into the toe of a sock. Medical Examiner Dugan says it could have done the trick and he says a golf ball possibly could have, but there's another angle to that: in Hinkle Conway's suitcase was a heavy gold-plated golf ball. He somewhat hysterically now claims that he doesn't know how he came to be possessed of it and was intending to return it to Stratfield when he saw him."

"To Stratfield?"

"Yes, it belonged to Stratfield. A golf trophy. Stratfield had it in an open-faced cabinet at his New Hampshire place. He showed it to David Barron and one or two others. Conway says he saw it but that he certainly didn't steal it. Stratfield, of course, admits that it is his. He seemed somewhat put to it deciding whether it would let Conway down easier if he claimed he had given it to him or said that he didn't know how he came to have it in his luggage. In any case, he didn't seem to want to get the boy in bad."

Susan asked what he finally had said. Curtis explained that Stratfield had finally insisted that they just forget the whole matter; maybe he had given it to Conway and maybe he hadn't; lots of times, with the greatest innocence, guests pack things that don't belong to them and send them back later.

"But, just the same," added Curtis, "Stratfield gives me the impression that he thinks Conway either stole the ball or someone else did and planted it on the young man. I don't think Stratfield is quite as amused by everything which happened at his country house, on the train and in his street last night as he would have us believe."

"I shouldn't think he'd be jumping up and down with gaiety. But please go on and tell me what potential lethal weapons the others were carrying," begged Susan.

"David Barron had an electric razor sufficiently rounded at one end to have been the weapon. Joan Sutton carried, of all things, a hard darning ball. Made of ebony. Lieutenant Burk's handmaiden in the Sutton ménage says she always carries a darning kit when accompanying her father on trips. The elder Sutton, it appears, is subject to holes in his socks, can't risk carrying an adequate number to make certain of not being caught short. Darning appears to be Joan's one domestic accomplishment."

"Did Hazel Manchester have a possible weapon?"

"The round object she had isn't so hot, according to Medical Examiner Dugan. In fact, it leaves him cold. A gold watch, size of a walnut, to be worn suspended from her shoulder, as I understand it."

Susan nodded. "And Carol Parton?"

"Nothing round, rounded or essentially hard in her luggage when we finally saw it. That wasn't, you remember, until noon yesterday. She had all morning to herself to dispose of anything, presumably. Dugan was kidding, of course, but he suggested maybe she visited the day-coach vestibule on the train, made herself a snowball, left it there to ice and used it when she was ready."

"It would have had the advantage of melting afterward," agreed Susan thoughtfully.

Then Susan remembered to check with Lyle on the thought she'd had the night before. Could Prunella have fallen some hours before her death, fractured her skull, gone into a coma but not died until just before the train reached Grand Central?

Curtis listened attentively. He inspected the ceiling for a long moment when she had finished, then shook his head. "How did her eyes get closed? You, my fair one, brought that point up yesterday morning."

Susan sighed, frowned and remarked that there had been something else which the night before she had meant to remember to ask him. "I suppose it was ridiculous, too," she amended when the thought would not come to her.

Curtis said it might be far from ridiculous and to be sure to tell him when she remembered, then he said abruptly, "Look here, my good woman, will you marry me when this damn case is over?"

Susan pretended to shudder. "Nine hundred years from now, you mean? This puts me in a very embarrassing position. I had set my mind on doing something to help you solve it in as few years as possible."

Curtis ejaculated gleefully that it was an honor to live in an era when a man could expect such co-operation from a woman.

As a rich, successful and talented career woman, Miss Yates came remarkably close to giggling. "The really humiliating part is that this morning when I was tossing around in bed, having heebie-jeebies over your fiendish old case, I thought of something which maybe will be useful."

"Splendid. This brings you one step nearer the altar if, as I am cheerfully assuming, that abandoned giggle was acknowledgment of consent."

With severity Miss Yates said that he would have to wait and see. As chief assistant stool pigeon for the district attorney's office she really couldn't have her mind taken off her work.

"What did you think of, tossing in bed this morning?"

"That one night at college I had the sniffles, a pain in my stomach and couldn't sleep because I felt like a cake of ice. I couldn't seem to get warm no matter how many blankets I dragged onto the bed. So finally I decided to get up and put on my ski underwear, it being the warmest thing I possessed. It was soft and clinging wool just like Prunella Parton's was. There's something about woolly, clinging things when you're having a chill. Perhaps Prunella Parton had a chill Sunday night. After all, she'd been submitted to a lot of cold weather in New Hampshire. Perhaps she wasn't used to outdoor winter sports. Then there had been the shock of the explosion at Stratfield's on Saturday night. In short, it isn't too farfetched to believe she might have put on her ski underwear to sleep in on the train, is it?"

Curtis inquired: "And the murderer, having a modest turn of mind, added the crimson dinner gown as a tasteful touch?"

"Perhaps there wasn't an open-front robe handy."

"Or perhaps," said Curtis with a new tight look around his lips and eyes, "our murderer sought the happy plan of confusing the apparent circumstances."

Susan suddenly became conscious of the whirlwind going on around them. So concentrated had she been on their talk that she had forgotten the two men in the corner answering phones and making stenographic notes of what came over the wires. She had scarcely seen Jack Copely arriving intermittently to lay memoranda on Curtis' desk. At least, Lyle's phones had given them a few moments for uninterrupted conversation. Now he gave her a long look before saying:

"But I'm inclined to think you've hit the nail on the head with that other notion of yours—that she had been sleeping in the underwear. I've thought so all along, because of the time element, but I couldn't think why. Why the murderer added the evening gown may turn out not to have been essential. To make Prunella look insane is possibly as good a theory as any. Am I going to get drunk when this case is over!"

Susan grinned. "I don't see how anyone could very well blame you. By the way, you don't really tie up Conway's attack and Prunella's death because of the way they were dressed, do you?"

Curtis said it only suggested a thought pattern on someone's part. Certainly it didn't prove anything. "No trace of Conway's alleged assailant, I suppose?"

"None whatever." Curtis was interrupted by the simultaneous ringing of two of his phones.

Susan sighed. "Now *that's* started again!"

Curtis answered one phone, said: "Wait a minute, please," put the receiver down on his desk, turned to the other, listened a few moments, then said: "Good work, Du Bois. Excellent. In Paris? *He* got it? Well I'll be damned. She had been sent to California before that? I see. Yes. Yes. Also in Paris?"

As he talked and listened Curtis was making hasty notes on one of the snowfall of colored pads banked on his desk. Finally he said: "A very nice piece of work. Make a personal report to me when you get to the office. Tell Copely I want to see you right away."

He replaced this receiver and turned to pick up the other one awaiting attention. Susan's eyes were pinned to this other instrument. The person at the other end might conceivably have heard the retorts Lyle had been making to Du Bois. Fear that this could somehow prove a boomerang suddenly assailed her. She instantly tried to put it aside as an indication of the kind of jitters she could develop by involving herself in murder cases. For the tenth time since rising she told herself that sleuthing was definitely not her line. It was bad for her nervous system and, after all, as remote and ridiculously foreign a corollary to fashion designing as anything imaginable. Perhaps if she did marry Lyle she could solace what psychologists would no doubt call her sleuthing drive by a program of being merely the "home influence" of a man hunter. There was something about marriage which made some men ill content to have their wives personally involved in their professions. Perhaps Lyle was one of these men. But in a department of her brain labeled "logic" she knew this to be a shoddy piece of reasoning. Lyle Curtis was the sort of man who had sufficient inner balance, self-respect and working tolerance to take advice from anyone—man, woman or child—without losing self-esteem in the process. If she married him he'd probably induce her to sit at a desk right in the D. A.'s office and expect her to run her Fifty-seventh Street salon from it. Perhaps she ought to encourage him to join a nice quiet, respectably solid corporation law firm with a good dull name like Grogwit, Storehope, Dillbang and Curtis.

Into the telephone transmitter Curtis was saying: "Oh yes, Mr. Penbroke. Very kind of you. Yes. Yes, that's right. Indeed? Oh yes, I see. With you, eh? Oh, you are quite certain? Well, well. Yes, I quite see that. Impossible, as you say. Nothing at all? Yes." There was a bit more of this, and then Curtis said good-by.

Looking across at Susan, he said: "That was Penbroke. We were too late reaching him, I'm afraid. There's one chance in a hundred we weren't." He picked up a phone and asked for Carol Parton to be tried at her apartment and at her newspaper.

A few moments later the bell rang. "Yes?" said Curtis. "Oh yes, Miss Parton. In my office yesterday afternoon you told me about going to your half sister's drawing-room door on the train yesterday morning. What did you do immediately after that? Oh, you met Mr. Penbroke and had coffee with him? How does it happen you did not think to tell me that yesterday? I see. Thank you, Miss Parton. Yes, that's all." He turned from the phone. "She 'didn't think

I'd be interested!' Well, we were too late on that one. They've checked with each other. But they hadn't when she was here or she would have produced this jewel of a thought as proof that she didn't carry off her sister's ski clothes."

"Isn't," asked Susan, "Penbroke rather stupid to try to alibi her with a story the club-car porter can refute?"

Curtis' eyes were narrowed in thought. He came out of it and nodded. "Most quickly hatched alibis have weak spots the perpetrators don't think of at the time. They probably got this story together over the telephone in a hurry."

"This case," observed Miss Yates, "is nutty."

"Wait," promised Curtis, "until you hear what Sergeant Du Bois has found out. His news is news indeed."

CHAPTER TWENTY-FOUR

"Is Du Bois," Susan asked Curtis, "the man you sent on a genealogical expedition to turn up the parentage of the Misses Joan Sutton, Prunella and Carol Parton and the matrimonial experiences of Peter Sutton?"

"Right. And Du Bois is a sound man." At this instant Jack Copely stuck his head in the door and said Sergeant Du Bois had come in.

The middle-aged man who made his appearance on Copely's heels was not Susan's idea of a "sound man" attached to the district attorney's office. He was a picture of morning elegance, bearing every earmark of the kind of rich and idle citizen who would be devoted to his club chair by the window and probably concentrated on the more illustrious branches of his family tree. It was only when he grinned at Curtis that his own personality emerged from beneath the externals of face and clothes.

Curtis said; "This is Sergeant Du Bois, Susan. Miss Yates, Du Bois. We find it convenient for Sergeant Du Bois to possess a passion for apparently nonessential information. He's one of my best men."

The sergeant bowed and then grinned again like a small boy caught wearing his father's dress clothes. His report was crisply given and well organized. The lady wearing the 1925 fashions in the photographs purloined from Peter Sutton's luggage had been born Mary Torrington, daughter of a Mr. and Mrs. Lee Torrington. Her parents, though Americans, had resided largely in Europe. Her father, deceased in 1910, had been an attaché of the American

Embassy in Paris at the time. After his death the mother and daughter, then nineteen, continued residence in Paris for a few months, then disappeared. They re-entered the United States in December 1910 and remained for a few months in New York City. Early in 1911 they took up residence in San Francisco. There was then a baby granddaughter named Prunella, and the child's mother was calling herself Mrs. Marchande. Her husband, a George Marchande, the few friends they made in San Francisco were told, had died just after the birth of the baby in New York a few months before. (No record of George Marchande or this marriage.) In 1917 Mrs. Marchande left San Francisco. Friends there were told that she had been married again in New York to a John Parton. Simultaneously they were told that young Prunella had been legally adopted by her stepfather. The child, subsequently known as Prunella Parton, again came to live with her grandmother in San Francisco after a few months. A baby girl, Carol Parton, was born to Mary and John Parton, November 1917, in New York City. John Parton died in January 1918 of pneumonia. Baby Carol was ultimately sent to live with her father's sister in Atlanta. This had been early in February 1918. Mary Torrington "Marchande" Parton married Peter Sutton in March 1919. Their daughter Joan was born December 1919. Peter Sutton divorced Mary Sutton in Paris in 1925. (Charges not matter of record.) Mary Sutton died in Paris four months later. Prunella Parton went on living with grandmother in San Francisco until 1935 when the grandmother died and she came to New York and was immediately employed by the firm of Sutton & Barron as an advertising-copy writer. Her half sister, Carol Parton, came to New York from Atlanta in the early part of 1938. The two sisters had lived together until nine months ago. Prunella then moved to an apartment of her own on Park Avenue, Carol into a small apartment in Greenwich Village. Du Bois had unearthed no social connections between Peter Sutton, his daughter Joan and the other daughters of his former wife. But Prunella had continued to prosper as a copy writer in the firm of Sutton & Barron.

"My goodness," said Susan interestedly. "So Joan, Prunella and Carol were all half sisters with the same mother?"

Sergeant Du Bois nodded, and Susan commented ironically that that didn't help too much. "Couldn't you, Lyle, have a couple of these people really fond of each other?"

Lyle wanted to know if she didn't think Joan Sutton and young Conway were? And what about Sutton, Barron and Stratfield? They seemed to be dealing amiably over the Kork-Petulla account. Carol Parton, moreover, evidently had Oliver Penbroke as an ally. Both Stratfield and Barron seem to have been fond of Prunella—except that she hadn't been able to get Stratfield to marry her. And what about Peter Sutton? Prunella, the possibly fatherless daughter of the woman he had divorced, had no sooner arrived in New York five years ago than he had given her a job in his advertising agency.

"Well," insisted Susan, "you will admit that Prunella and Carol Parton do not seem to have been overly fond of one another. And isn't it funny that Penbroke pulls a long-whiskered lie like that about Carol Parton? Any love affair between them seems to have escaped my ladies at luncheon yesterday. By the way, have you located the taxi drivers you sent for?"

Curtis nodded and explained Joan had been picked up by a cab at Forty-third and Fifth Avenue at eight forty-five Monday morning. She had not acted queer, had given her home address and remained quietly in the back seat "doing her face" in a mirror provided by the taxi company. The same driver had driven her back to Grand Central, having been loitering in the block after depositing her at her doorstep. A privately owned cab had transported Oliver Penbroke. The driver had seen the district attorney's office broadside at his local union headquarters and had come around the night before. His story had been a little more complicated. On getting into the cab Penbroke had instructed that he be driven directly to the Hardmike Building on Madison Avenue but had altered these instructions to include a stop at the Hotel Eden. The driver said he hadn't been inside long. Only ten cents' worth of waiting on the taximeter. But whether his fare had carried anything which might have been a lady's ski outfit into the hotel with him he hadn't noticed. Penbroke had instructed him to keep his eye on his luggage while he was gone, and this he had done. One of the clerks at the

Hotel Eden recalled having seen Penbroke, whom he knew by sight, in the lobby for a moment or so early Monday morning. He said Penbroke had gone to one of the phone booths, dialed a number and come out again immediately. He had not gotten his number, the clerk had thought.

"Perhaps he was trying to reach Carol Parton, do you think?"

Curtis nodded. "That's what we think. We still don't know where she kept herself all yesterday morning, and one of those last telephone calls I got indicates that perhaps Penbroke doesn't know, either, for the club-car porter who served him his coffee yesterday morning reports that a young lady answering Carol Parton's description did pass through the car, going to the Pullman behind and returning from it. But he is sure Penbroke did not see her because he remembers distinctly that the gentleman was busy behind a copy of the *Herald Tribune*. The porter's very definite about one other thing: no lady joined Penbroke for coffee or any other reason."

"So," asked Susan, "you think that indicates that Penbroke perhaps did not know Carol was on the train, that he may have tried to telephone her apartment from the Hotel Eden, not wanting his secretary to hear the conversation when he reached his office, and that they only managed to contact one another and compose the having-coffee-together-in-the-club-car tale after Carol was in your office yesterday afternoon?"

"Looks that way."

Susan pondered while Curtis turned to Sergeant Du Bois and made some inquiries about the sources he had used for checking Peter Sutton's matrimonial history. Then Susan remarked that one person who apparently did not hate anyone connected with the case was Miss Hazel Manchester.

Curtis frowned and said that at any rate Miss Manchester did not seem to have hated Prunella's emerald pin. He had gotten the impression that the beauty-and-charm columnist had possessed a very real admiration for this item.

"And," commented Susan, "Lawrence Stratfield seems to admire Hazel Manchester, galloping around buying her roses first thing in the morning. But that doesn't get us anywhere. I'm all for good hates as nice sound reasons for murder. They seem so much more reasonable."

Curtis looked at Sergeant Du Bois. "There's nothing for it but a sociable chat with the venerable Peter Sutton who divorces his wife—not his wife *him*—then carries pictures of her around in his luggage fifteen years later, employs her perhaps fatherless child and graces the advertising business as its most scandal-proof practitioner."

Du Bois nodded. "Peter Sutton," he agreed, "seems to require some looking into. But he's a tough baby, Chief. Firebrand. Brooks no criticism. Sits on the best boards of directors. Goes to the best church."

Curtis turned to one of his battery of phones. "Get me Peter Sutton, president of Sutton and Barron," he said into the transmitter.

As they waited Susan inspected her nose in her compact mirror. Then Curtis was saying pleasantly:

"Good morning, Mr. Sutton. A point has arisen in connection with the death of your late employee, Miss Prunella Parton, which makes it necessary for us to seek further information from you. I beg pardon? No. No. I'm afraid Mr. Barron wouldn't have just the information we want. Would eleven this morning suit you—at the district attorney's office? Ah, that's very courteous of you. At eleven then."

He replaced the receiver and groaned: "The excellence of Sutton's attitude may be a flaming sardine, an alligator or nine oysters. Maybe it's only a pale goldfish. He's frightfully involved in the marts of trade but generosity itself in co-operative spirit. He's pining to do anything he can as a good citizen, emphasized it."

At this moment Sergeant Withers' first telephone call came through from Swiss Village, putting them, as Curtis pointed out, exactly nowhere. But a few moments later, just as Susan was preparing to leave, Withers called a second time regarding the letter bearing no return address and mailed to Prunella Parton at Parton, New York. Curtis immediately put through a call to the chief

assistant of the postmaster general in Washington, and Susan presumed that within a few moments the dead-letter office would be
engaged in what sounded to her a perfect example of the needle-
in-the-haystack experiment.

CHAPTER TWENTY-FIVE

WHILE CURTIS CAME DOWN with another siege of telephone calls Susan waited, and he pushed across the desk to her the notations he had jotted down late the night before. His remarks relative to the disposition she had made of her own evening had been carefully blocked out, but additional penciled notes of a less personal variety sprawled in the margins. One indicated that an appointment had been made for Miss Manchester to appear at the district attorney's office at twelve that noon, another that Prunella Parton's salary had been fifteen thousand dollars a year, beginning the previous July, an increase of one thousand dollars over the preceding year.

"Not enough of an increase," thought Susan, "to be the inspiration for moving from an apartment shared with her sister to single occupancy of a two-bedrooms, two-baths, dining-and-drawing-room one on Park Avenue, plus partial payments on a separate apartment for Carol."

In the paragraph regarding a proposed chat between Susan and Joan Sutton Curtis had made some marginal notes while talking to Sergeant Withers at Swiss Village. These said:

"Stratfield's butler at Swiss Village says Miss Sutton told young Conway that Mr. Barron had received a letter she wanted Conway to allow her to tell her father about. Try to pry more about this out of her. Had to do with Prunella Parton or somebody 'getting away with something,' according to butler who says Mr. Stratfield could 'make nothing of it' when he told him about it. Miss Sutton alleged to have sounded 'extremely angry.'"

Below this was another hastily jotted pencil notation:

"Ask Conway whom he had in mind when Stratfield's cook heard him say to himself: 'If only she didn't exist at all.'"

At this moment Curtis hung up the receiver on his latest call, and Susan asked: "What is this illegible scrawl about not, after all, crossing Mrs. David Barron off the suspect list?"

"That angle has been reopened a bit since I wrote that. Because of the Eloise Abelard driver's license we found in Prunella Parton's apartment I sent Sergeant Jones out to Westover, Connecticut, with some of the boys early this morning. They knew Eloise Abelard, all right, at Westover, Jones reports. The postmaster knew her because she cashed ten one-hundred-dollar money orders there last August and paid the rent on a small unattractive farmhouse in the neighborhood for a year in advance. In December she cashed ten more money orders. Again one-hundred-dollar ones."

"Who on earth was she, and why was her driver's license in Prunella's apartment?"

"Jones went out to Connecticut armed with a photograph of the deceased. It has been identified by the postmaster, by Miss Abelard's nearest farmer neighbor and by the local real-estate agent as a very excellent likeness of Miss Eloise Abelard herself."

"None of my great aunts would like me to say it," exclaimed Susan, "but I'll be damned!"

"A uniquely appropriate observation."

"But what on earth was Prunella Parton up to, renting an unattractive farmhouse, cashing money orders by the dozen?"

Curtis said he didn't want to engage in overstatements but it looked like a slight case of blackmail.

"Jones," he continued, "got the real-estate man to take him into the farmhouse. It's on an isolated and distinctly dirt back road. So far as the real-estate man knew, Miss Abelard didn't exactly live there but came for week ends—sometimes once a week, sometimes once a month in bad weather. There isn't much housekeeping equipment in the place. Bare necessities. She did not employ a local maid but she did buy a certain amount of food in the town. Enough, evidently, to make the grocer and dairy think of her in terms of city week-ender. The postmaster had the impression that the money orders were from her father—a sort of allowance, he thought. He assumed that maybe she traveled for some company on account of her address being Westover on her driver's license. He did not place her in New York City because the money for the money orders was deposited here by someone signing the name Frank Abelard, care of the Hotel Eden. The Hotel Eden turns out never to have had a guest of that name.

"Cash," continued Curtis, "for the August money orders was deposited at the Grand Central Post Office in New York, in November at the main post office on Eighth Avenue. Money-order applications must be preserved at the post office of issue for three years from date of issue so they have the originals at both, but they are busy offices, and we haven't so far unearthed a clerk who can remember any identifying details of a sender named Frank Abelard. Moreover, Frank Abelard's signature doesn't tally with any suspect's in the Parton case."

"It just doesn't make sense," exclaimed Susan.

Curtis said he hadn't told her the whole story yet. Jones had given the farmhouse a thorough search and, pushed back in a Dutch oven in the fireplace, he'd found an envelope. Inside it, snapped together with an elastic band, was a packet of ten uncashed one-hundred-dollar money orders from Frank Abelard to Eloise Abelard, dated February second, nearly a month ago. The postmaster said "Miss Abelard" had picked up an envelope addressed to her just before noon on the Saturday of that week. She had asked him how much of a money order he had the cash on hand for. He had had to tell her he couldn't go over twenty-five dollars without sending to Bridgeport or South Norwalk—which he couldn't do before Monday on account of the Saturday-afternoon closing hours. She then had said she'd get the cash later. The next time anybody saw her in town was on Washington's Birthday—last week. Perhaps she had forgotten that that was a legal holiday and the post office would be closed. Anyway, the ten orders dated February second were still uncashed.

"That means she left one thousand dollars hanging around in a Dutch oven?"

Curtis nodded.

"Why," asked Susan, "do you suppose her orders were always in one-hundred-dollar amounts?"

"You can't make a single money order out for more. Matter of law. Moreover, 'Frank Abelard's' generosity with his 'daughter' did not consist of simply the orders Jones has found or the two lots she cashed in August and December at the Westover post office. 'Miss Abelard' collected a thousand dollars from the central San Francisco post office in November. Miss Parton, according to David Barron's interesting correspondence, was in San Francisco in November. Incidentally, she said in that letter to him that she had never been in San Francisco before—and, according to Sergeant Du Bois's findings, she had lived there until her maternal grandmother died five years ago."

Susan asked how they had found out in such a short time about the San Francisco money order. Curtis explained they had done that through the office of issue, the main post office in New York City. Also, a thousand dollars had been paid into the Wall Street branch post office by "Frank Abelard" in September and cashed in Chicago by "Eloise Abelard." According to the cashier of Sutton & Barron, Miss Parton had been in Chicago early in September and in San Francisco in November. In January "Frank Abelard" had again used the main post office in New York, and his "daughter" had got her money from an office in the Bronx, identifying herself, as usual, by her driver's license.

Susan commented that a thousand dollars a month, clear, should be adequate to maintain quite a nice Park Avenue apartment.

"Yes, they weren't paying her much more than that at Sutton and Barron. They raised her from fourteen thousand dollars to fifteen thousand dollars last July."

"So I noticed on your memorandum. There's something else I don't understand though. How did Prunella Parton get that driver's license?"

"Very simple. She just walked into a motor-vehicle bureau, I imagine, and made out an application, giving her address as Westover, Connecticut. It was a Connecticut license. The motor-vehicle people don't check addresses unless a driver has an accident. She probably didn't actually use it for driving her car—at least, she probably didn't until she had established her residence at Westover. If she had got into any traffic trouble around there she'd of course have had to use it or divulge the fact that she wasn't Eloise Abelard. But once you have a driver's license and yourself identified with it renewals, et cetera, are pretty much a matter of routine. If you don't get into trouble nobody stops to consider whether you're who you claim you are or not."

Susan said that the original Eloise and Abelard would turn over in their graves at such goings on but that she supposed there were quite a few people in the world who would commit murder to avoid paying blackmail to the tune of twelve thousand dollars a year.

"Or maybe the payee was willing to come across with that much but the lady suddenly demanded more," suggested Curtis.

Susan screwed up her face in concentrated thought. "And the person being blackmailed might have been someone you haven't even heard of in connection with Prunella's death?"

Curtis admitted that that could be true but asked her to recall what the Pullman porter had said. No one other than the one female whom he had seen outside the deceased's drawing-room door had been in the car, except the members of Stratfield's private party.

Susan sighed.

Curtis drew a sizable memorandum pad toward him and began writing, motioning Susan with his left hand to come around the desk and look.

Blackmail Possibilities

If Peter Sutton was the blackmailed person, why didn't Prunella Parton simply demand her spoils in the form of a bigger salary?

Note: Sutton & Barron are incorporated. It might have looked too loose-handed to other stockholders. Could have been started with the $1000 raise in July, and more been demanded by Prunella in August.

Ditto above for David Barron on salary-blackmail angle.

Was it Joan Sutton?

Note: Joan has an income from her paternal grandmother of $12,000 a year, approximately. But what could Prunella have been blackmailing a twenty-one-year-old girl for?

Was it young Conway?

Note: Most unlikely he could have paid it. His salary is $6500 a year, and his Ohio family are in an even lower income bracket.

Was it Oliver Penbroke?

Note: Penbroke could have forked up a thousand a month all right, but what could she have "had" on him?

Ditto for Stratfield. He is supposed to have inherited richly from an aunt, lives well without visible source of income from any work more serious than his bum paintings, but ditto as to what she could have blackmailed him for.

Hazel Manchester?

Note: Income, partly salary, partly royalties on syndicated column, for past two years has not exceeded $8000. Ditto above as to cause for blackmail.

Carol Parton?

Note: She makes $40 a week. Unless she's been robbing banks she could not possibly have paid her half sister $7000 in past seven months. Could "bank robbing" be both cause of blackmail and source of revenue to pay it? Could this be true of Conway?

"Who do you favor?" inquired Mr. Curtis, looking up at Susan's mystified face.

She shook her head. "It's difficult to think of the patriarchal Peter Sutton being her victim, though he doubtless could afford the output, and it is funny he divorced Prunella's mother, then employed her dubiously fathered child. David Barron, I'd say, could have been up to a lot of things he didn't want the world to know about, and so, I suppose, could the big amiable Oliver Penbroke. But I'd say the only thing imaginable Prunella could have had on a girl as young as Joan Sutton was the threat to circulate the report that her mother had once had a child out of wedlock. Would as cocky a youngster as Joan pay through the nose for that? I agree that young Conway and Carol Parton seem completely farfetched possibilities from their income standpoints, and Carol doesn't look to me like a girl who robs banks though she does look neurotic. Oh, by the way, why have you put Mrs. David Barron back on the dubious list?"

Curtis said because Mrs. David Barron had dispatched from Los Angeles the night before a night letter to Miss Eloise Abelard at Westover, Conn., saying she was extremely anxious to have a talk with her. They had picked up this news in a routine way, he explained.

"I tell you," announced Miss Yates, "this case is completely nutty. I'm losing my mind and I haven't the faintest idea what's keeping yours intact."

Curtis ran a quick hand through his hair. "These surface signs of sanity you observe are mere camouflage."

"What are you doing about Mrs. David Barron?"

"We've asked the Los Angeles police to inquire of her why she sent that telegram."

At this moment one of his phones rang, and he cupped the receiver. Replacing it after several minutes of listening and muttering brief comments from his end, he said: "That was Los Angeles. Mrs. Barron has come clean—so she says. She's shown them a letter, typewritten both as to content and signature, purporting to come from Eloise Abelard of Westover, Connecticut. It suggests Miss Abelard could be helpful in providing evidence which would give Mrs. Barron a divorce with permanent monetary settlement."

"Meaning unsavory information about her husband's moral behavior?"

"Evidently."

"Who would have been better able to do that, from all I heard yesterday noon from the girls, than Prunella Parton?"

"Exactly. And yet Mrs. David Barron could have typed that letter to herself. She claims the envelope was handwritten and postmarked New York City but she destroyed it yesterday morning. No proof of her statement about it as a result."

Susan looked a little wild. "But Mrs. Barron could not have been Prunella Parton alias Eloise Abelard?"

"No," admitted Curtis gloomily. "She couldn't have been. Moreover, she was in Los Angeles Sunday night and she did send her wire after Miss Parton was dead. But—"

"I know. Don't tell me. Her letter could be some sort of flaming sardine, daughter of the red herring. I'm getting out of this office. If I stay here a moment longer and let my mind become one ravel more snarled you will have to order a strait jacket to carry me out in. And I absolutely refuse to wear any garments not designed at Susan Yates, Incorporated, a firm of which, however, you may shortly hear no more. It's really possible if I don't spend at least five minutes a day there. Good-by!" And Susan suited action to her words and departed.

CHAPTER TWENTY-SIX

IN THE STREET BEFORE the district attorney's office Susan looked up and down the block trying to remember exactly where she had parked her car. It seemed hours since she had pried herself out of bed to come downtown. When she located her convertible coupé and started toward it another idea popped into her head. She had forgotten to promise Lyle that she would arrange to talk with Joan Sutton. Peter Sutton's daughter had made that relatively easy by suggesting it herself in the theater lobby the evening before. On a sudden inclination to tell Curtis rather than to wait to phone back from her salon, Susan wheeled about sharply. At the same instant a man behind her shouted, tires squealed and a delivery truck whizzed past her right hip. She had turned out of its path with not a second to spare. It careened drunkenly back off the curb. The man on the sidewalk who had shouted began to swear, gesticulating after the driver. He turned to Susan then to see if she was hurt.

"Couldn't even get the license number," he complained.

Susan, feeling thoroughly shaken, looked after the vagrant truck which was making off madly into the traffic lane. Hanging out its back door, successfully shielding the license plate, was a roll of carpet. An accidental circumstance, of course. And yet— She wondered. Certainly the runaway car had behaved very peculiarly. Even in a city like New York where people seemed to be continually knocked down by one form or another of motor vehicle it was rare for anyone to be practically attacked on the pavement. She shuddered and felt more than a little ill. It had been a narrow escape. She could still feel the flying force of the truck shying violently past her hip.

"Good thing you turned just at that moment," the unknown man congratulated her.

Susan smiled weakly. "And now, of course," she confessed, "it's put completely out of my head what I was going back to do."

The man asked sympathetically if she wanted him to hail a taxi for her, but Susan shook her head, explained she had a car of her own in the block, thanked him and made for it. Very carefully she drove uptown, possessed of a ridiculous nightmare kind of premonition that the crazily driven truck might still be stalking her.

AN HOUR BEFORE her appointment at the district attorney's office Miss Hazel Manchester began acting very oddly indeed. She was bent over the bottom drawer of a steel filing cabinet which occupied one corner of her private office. The drawer was halfway open. Miss Manchester peered at something pushed into the very back of it. She continued to do this for some seconds, then rose cautiously and retreated to the door which she carefully and silently locked. After that she went back to the drawer and stared down at it for some more moments, a deep frown corrugating her forehead. Presently she reached for a pair of gloves lying neatly beside the handbag on her desk. She put them on her hands and crouched down before the drawer again. With her gloved hands she drew several articles from it. They included a sheer white wool sweater, a pair of hand-woven white wool ski pants, light as a feather but very warm looking, and a jacket which matched the pants. She rose, laid these articles on her desk and gave them very careful scrutiny, her expression, meantime, tense and extremely cautious. Color was high in her cheeks.

Giving a wary glance at the locked door, Miss Manchester then walked to one of her windows and stood there drumming aimlessly on the pane, staring with apparently unseeing eyes at the mass of skyscrapers beyond. Someone passing the door made her start once violently. Otherwise nothing else happened for several minutes.

Miss Manchester turned, hurried back to her desk. Other footsteps were outside her door. They had stopped there. She hastily dumped the white garments into her wastepaper basket and, grabbing a newspaper from the desk, stuffed it in after them. But the second footsteps also went on past her door, accompanied by a cheerful whistle. That was only Tom, then, one of the office boys who was always whistling and always off key.

At this point Miss Manchester appeared to begin to throw off her mood of indecision. She looked around her office, rather wildly, it was true, but as if any action would be better than none. Her eyes fell on a pasteboard department-store box lying on the proof table in the corner. It bore the name of Ronsell and Bonner, a Fifth Avenue shop. Crossing to the box, she removed the lid and looked at the dark green garment inside. It was neatly folded and decorated with tiny brightly colored wool hearts.

Retreating to the wastepaper basket, she brought the white garments to the table and managed to tuck them neatly under the green one. She gazed a long time at the box, then shook her head. Removing the white pieces, she placed them on the table and stood frowning once more. She went back to the window and stood there quite a while, apparently lost in thought.

At last, with a look of determination, she went to her desk, picked up an ink bottle and returned to the proof table. Very carefully she began to spill ink on various parts of the white garments. She waited a few moments, letting the ink sink into the feathery wool, then took the white pile to the radiator behind her desk and dried each garment carefully.

When they were all thoroughly dry she returned to the suit box, carefully folded the white pants, sweater and jacket and again put them under the green woolen garment. Replacing the box lid, she tied it securely and went to her telephone, asked for an outside wire and dialed a number.

"Ronsell and Bonner?" she inquired after a moment. "Please give me the service department. Service department? This is Miss Hazel Manchester. I am calling you from my office at *Inter-Allied*

News. Last Thursday I had you send over to me two green Bavarian ski suits in two different sizes. I am keeping the size sixteen. The size fourteen was too small. Will you please have your delivery truck call at my office for the smaller one and credit it to my account? Yes, that's right. And one thing more. I'm sending over to you an old ski suit of mine which you can later throw away. Some ink has been spilled on it. I wish you would see if your sports department can supply me with another suit in exactly the same material—only, I want it bright red. Yes, red. Perhaps they could send me samples. And after they've had a look at this old one just tell them to throw it out. You have that straight? Yes, that's right. Thank you."

Miss Manchester rang off, crossed the room silently to the door, as silently unlocked it and returned to her desk where she inspected her wrist watch, made up her face, put on her hat and prepared to depart for the district attorney's office.

MEANWHILE, LYLE CURTIS had received his caller, Peter Sutton, who was looking, as Susan had called him, patriarchal—the picture of dignity and affluence. Glasses shining, Mr. Sutton had seated himself with care opposite Curtis at the desk. Sedately he inquired of what service he could be.

"It's a matter of the parentage of Miss Prunella Parton," replied Curtis, keeping his eyes fastened on his distinguished guest's face. Sutton's facial expression did not alter to the smallest degree that Curtis could determine.

"Her parentage?"

"Yes."

"There's some question of it?"

"Yes. An angle which you are best able to help us with, I think, Mr. Sutton."

"I?"

"Yes, inasmuch as the young lady's mother was once your wife."

Still Sutton's expression of dignified attention did not waver. "Quite so. Quite so. A long time ago. And, curiously, I cannot help you. Her mother told me very little about her first daughter's father."

"You didn't know him, then?"

For the first time since he had entered the room the advertising man's expression underwent a slight alteration. Curtis was conscious that it had occurred but mystified as to the reason. Why had his last question caused it? The older man's self-assurance had certainly lessened. It was as if a thought crossing his mind had left a mark on his countenance as imperceptible as a light breeze touching a wheat field, but also as if, beneath on the ground, seeds not yet germinating had stirred, forming a new pattern, becoming less secure.

"Always," Curtis thought, "however lightly a breeze may blow, its passing is visible to sufficiently alert eyes." He waited for Peter Sutton's reply and realized that from behind his sparkling eyeglasses Sutton was watchfully waiting too. The elder man's gaze was fastened keenly on nothing at all, on an invisible atmospheric spot between himself and Curtis. Had his eyes been an anemometer adjusted to report the most insignificant change in direction of the wind he could have seemed no more mechanically alert.

Sizing up this rigid awareness and the indefinable change he felt had occurred within the other man, Curtis decided the shadings of this interview were very fine indeed. It had not been the statement that Prunella's mother had once been his wife which had affected Peter Sutton. He seemed to have been fully expecting that. It was the question whether he had known Prunella's father which had caused the man's composure to shift. Curtis repeated the question.

"No," said Peter Sutton, "I was not acquainted with him." He might have been speaking of some higher form of mathematics of which he had heard but the intricacies of which he had not studied.

"His name was?" Curtis again waited, his eyes drilling a relentless search of Sutton's face.

Sutton stirred. One of his heavily veined hands reached for the second from the bottom button of his coat, slowly unbuttoned it, slowly rebuttoned it as if he had been testing its securing threads. Then he spoke quite casually. "That, too, is curious. I do not know his name. I may once have known it but I have completely forgotten it." His eyes now met Curtis' through the shining barrier of his glasses.

"Surely you can recall it, Mr. Sutton."

"You seem astonished."

"I am astonished. Men usually know the names of their wives' previous husbands—of the fathers of their stepchildren." Curtis maintained his watchfulness with the competence of a radio-control-room timekeeper.

Sutton moved one of his hands with temperate irritation. "But, inasmuch as I do not, can I be of any further service to the district attorney's office?" He reached for his watch, looked at it and frowned briefly.

"Your wife, Mary Sutton, was divorced by you, Mr. Sutton, in Paris in 1925 on charges not made public. When a man divorces the mother of his child he does not often employ that woman's daughter by a former marriage—her daughter born out of wedlock."

Had Curtis' words been a meteor falling on top of his desk they could have created a no more startled expression on Peter Sutton's face. This, then, was something he definitely had not expected.

"I am afraid I do not understand you," he began, then stopped short as if hoping further reply would suddenly and miraculously become unnecessary. It seemed more that than a refusal to say more.

Curtis turned over a folder on his desk. "Because of European conditions some records are not easily available to us at the moment in France, but our man had a bit of luck with this. The evidence, privately given in the case of Sutton versus Sutton for divorce, was to the effect that Mary Sutton had once, unknown to her husband and before their marriage, had a child out of wedlock." Curtis looked up. "You sought severance of your marital relations on that ground, did you not, Mr. Sutton? And was not Prunella Parton the child in question?"

Without opening his mouth Sutton nodded dully. Even the sparkle of his eyeglasses seemed diminished. He took them off presently and began polishing them slowly with his breast-pocket handkerchief. Without them his eyes looked faded and indecisive. The silence stretched into another long minute.

"Why," asked Curtis softly, "did you take Prunella Parton into your employ ten years after you had divorced her mother?"

Sutton put his glasses back on and, spacing his words carefully, said: "Because she needed work. Because she promised to work hard, to earn her salt."

"No other reason? I better tell you we believe there was."

The other reason came then in a burst of seeming hopelessness. Curtis had the feeling he had created a situation Peter Sutton had been fearing for years, fearing and knowing he would one day have to meet.

"Yes, there was another reason. She threatened to tell my daughter Joan—the whole world perhaps—that her mother had had a bastard daughter—herself. It would have killed me to have Joan know that. Killed me. But Prunella Parton, I'm afraid, didn't care in the least what the world thought of her. She envied my daughter because Joan has a father. She envied Carol Parton, too, for the same reason. Because Carol had a father. I'm convinced of that. In fact, she told me so that day in my office five years ago when I employed her. But she promised to behave herself if I would give her a position in my organization. I did."

"To buy her off?"

Peter Sutton was at once more at ease. "You may put it that way if you wish, Mr. Curtis. I considered it a sound business move. She was intelligent. Ambitious. She proved extremely capable. As long as she had a good position with my firm I assumed, and rightly, I think, she would have no inclination to disgrace its name—the name of Sutton, that is. Many families have had to do similar things, my dear sir. I did nothing essentially rare. I merely stopped, with no disadvantage to my business, a rash young woman from talking indiscreetly and quite unnecessarily. As I arranged matters, there was no point in her ruining Joan's life."

"So for five years you kept her in your employ?"

"Approximately that long, I should say. Perhaps a month more or less. I don't recall the exact date of her employment. And she earned her salary. Every bit of it. She could handle words." He said this not with admiration but with a kind of self-satisfaction, as if it were to be expected that any move Peter Sutton made, even one into which he might be forced, could be expected to turn out advantageously for him or his business.

Curtis scarcely sprang his next question. He asked it as casually as if he had been inquiring about the weather. "And then lately
she threatened you again?"

Sutton looked instantly astonished at this. Astonishment
seemed to cover his face as if he had automatically turned on a
special spigot designed to convey it. "To the utter contrary," he
exclaimed. "I had no trouble at all with the young woman after I
employed her. I even came to believe that her wild chatter in my
office the first day she called on me was more youthful—ah—well,
pressure than anything else. Naturally, I do not applaud such tac-
tics, but there are people in the world who when they want something very much see very little difference between the right and
wrong way of getting it. They suffer a moral lack, of course. But
they are not always vicious, certainly not always criminally
minded." The last sentences were tacked on, Curtis felt, in a spirit
of self-righteous tolerance. "In other words," Sutton added, "following her employment I had no reason to find fault with the girl."

"You approved of her moral behavior?"

"I knew nothing about it. So far as I know, she lived an orderly
enough life. Did she not?"

"We have reason to doubt it."

"Indeed?" Sutton pursed his lips. He was once more the sanc-
timonious Peter Sutton sitting on the best boards of directors, as
Sergeant Du Bois had said. Doubting he could be openly shunted
from this throne of self-protection a second time in one interview,
Curtis shortly terminated it.

HINKLE CONWAY was Curtis' next visitor. He looked less youthfully
truculent than he had during the club-car inquiry and greeted the
assistant district attorney with something approximating a half-
sheepish, half-apologetic grin.

"How's your shoulder?" asked Curtis.

"Sore and lame," answered Conway. "And, by the way, is anything being done about my getting slugged in the street?"

"Don't worry about it. We're working on that. I want to ask you
some questions."

Conway said he'd be glad to answer anything and that he supposed Curtis must think him an awful ass! "Why?"

"Oh, scowling and hissing words yesterday on the train. You
know, I didn't see, and I don't see yet, how anyone could have had
any more reason for wanting to get rid of Prunella Parton than I did.
And yet I didn't even try to kill her. It didn't even occur to me."

"Why did you say at Lawrence Stratfield's place that 'everything
would be all right if she just didn't exist'?" Curtis verbally under-
lined the quotation.

"Because it would have been. You see, Joan and I are—well—
more or less privately engaged, but I don't want to be the kind of
human rat who makes a nest for himself by marrying the boss's
daughter. I want to work my way up decently at Sutton and Barron
and, when I have, marry Joan. But Prunella stood directly in my
way. She was after my scalp—I know it now—from the moment I
went to work there. I—I guess she thought I had a certain amount
of talent, and she didn't want any competition."

"I see," said Curtis. "And yet you say you didn't kill her?" His
eyes were fastened on Conway's face with all the vigilance they had
given Peter Sutton. Somewhat to his surprise, the boy looked faintly
amused.

"You know, Mr. Curtis, I don't actually believe in murder. Oh,
of course, I don't believe in it at all. But I've got an awful feeling
that someway I would have been less of a hunk of Ohio River mud
if I *had* murdered Prunella Parton. At least, I think I should have
thought of it."

Curtis studied him some more and carefully. Presently he
asked: "What was this business I'm informed of that Miss Sutton
wanted you to let her tell her father? Something about Prunella
Parton pulling a fast one in posing as the liaison between your
agency and the Kork-Petulla people through Stratfield? Something
also about a letter."

Instantly Conway looked truculent again. "That's a lot of
kibosh," he said. "I don't know anything about it." And that, although he continued the interview for twenty minutes longer, was
all Curtis could pry out of the young man.

CHAPTER TWENTY-SEVEN

AT TWELVE O'CLOCK SHARP, just as Hazel Manchester, by official bidding, was walking into the district attorney's building, Joan Sutton telephoned Susan. She sounded rather excited; also, she sounded young, natural and devoid of serious worries. It had been her intention until halfway through breakfast, she said, to ask Miss Yates to have cocktails with her that afternoon. Perhaps they still could despite the fact that her father had had a simply incredible attack.

"Attack?" Susan tried to sound more sympathetic than curious.

"Yes. At breakfast. It seems he spent last evening worrying about me. I'm supposed to take sudden deaths too seriously for my years. He's afraid it will make me neurotic or something. Isn't it a scream?"

"Well, of course, having somebody you all knew pass out that way would be upsetting. You feel all right, though, don't you?"

"Simply marvelous. But you know how fathers are! He wants me to start right in this afternoon being psychoanalyzed. Imagine, at my age! I always thought you had to be forty, at least."

Susan murmured that she didn't suppose there was really an age limit.

"Apparently not, because Father has arranged everything. He's lined up New York's outstanding analyst. Of course, Father would do that! I'm to be in the man's torture chamber at four o'clock. He's only supposed to harass me for an hour, but then it would be five, and he's way over on the West Side—too distinguished, apparently, to bother about Park Avenue. Oh, but *could* you meet me in *that* part of town? I think it's too exciting running into you that way at the train inquisition and again at the theater and, of course, I simply adore your clothes. Moreover"—Miss Sutton lowered her voice to a hoarse whisper—"I really could tell you a lot of things about Prunella Parton which you could pass on to that good-looking assistant district attorney—that is, if you want to. I haven't figured out why you were in on things yesterday morning. At least, I'm not sure. It did occur to me that, men being the way they are, maybe Mr. Curtis and that fat police officer called you in to tell them why Prunella had dressed herself up that way. Did you ever see anything so fantastic? I'm certain it must have completely defied the male mind for explanation. I do wish you'd tell me what you think. I've thought and thought, and just nothing occurs to me—I mean, no sane answer."

"I've given it a bit of thought, too," confessed Susan, "and with no better results. Perhaps we can put our heads together and think of something practical."

"Well, if you had ever watched Prunella Parton going through her bag of feminine tricks you would never have guessed she'd let herself be seen even dead in such an outfit. It's too bad Father didn't think to have *her* psychoanalyzed."

"Isn't it?" agreed Susan.

"Look," said Joan, "I promise to buy simply scads of clothes from you in the future if you'll only just come along and let me get Prunella out of my hair by talking to you as an unbiased person."

A little annoyed at Miss Sutton's frank commercialization of her proposal, Susan nevertheless said she'd be delighted. Why couldn't they meet somewhere in the psychoanalyst's immediate neighborhood?

"Oh, good! You'll be simply a lamb to. I don't know the West Side awfully well, but there must be some place over there where they have something decent to drink. Wait! I remember seeing a rather elegant *bistro* on Central Park West. I'll think of the name in a minute. Something silly. I have it! The Wise Owl. Shall we try it? It's somewhere in the sixties."

"Perhaps we'll pick up wisdom in a place named that. I'll look up the address in the telephone book and be there around five. I'll wait for you if the analyst holds you up."

Joan remarked enthusiastically that no doubt she would be a wreck but that she'd be there.

Hazel Manchester's interview with the assistant district attorney did not last very long. She appeared to Curtis to be in a confidential and utterly frank mood, but he soon realized that, while she talked eagerly and with apparently every intention of being extremely helpful, she actually said very little. She had noticed Prunella Parton's emerald pin because it had been such a lovely one and because, she admitted apologetically, it looked so silly worn on a ski sweater. She had seen it when Prunella had opened her jacket after they got on the train at Swiss Village. There hadn't been any special reason for her ringing Curtis up to tell him about it except that, while no one had suggested such a thing, she had had a sort of premonition that Mr. Curtis suspected Prunella hadn't killed herself and, inasmuch as she agreed that Prunella was the last person in the world to have done that, she had simply thought theft might have been a murderer's motive. She hadn't, she insisted, suspected any foul play in connection with the explosion at Lawrence Stratfield's New Hampshire place. To the contrary, she admitted to an inborn suspicion of all oilstoves. In her opinion anything could be expected of them. It was very lucky, of course, that Prunella had been taking a bath. Indeed, it was very lucky they hadn't all been blown up.

Curtis sought in vain to bring out any indication of personal antipathy for the deceased on Miss Manchester's part. Only one conviction was definitely left in his mind at the close of their talk: Hazel Manchester was in love with David Barron.

After the beauty-and-charm columnist had departed Curtis turned to the problem of concocting a means of luring "Frank Abelard" to call for the ten one-hundred-dollar money orders which had been found in the Dutch oven at Westover, Conn. His ultimate decision was to take Elmer Gans, a neighboring farmer, into their confidence, a check on the latter's antecedency and reputation proving thoroughly satisfactory.

Sergeant Jones, who was waiting in Westover, was instructed by long distance to make arrangements with Elmer Gans and to remain in the Gans farmhouse until the plan either developed or failed. Then Curtis rang for Copely.

"Any reports on our ski-suit ads?"

"No sir. Not a single answer at any of the newspaper offices by letter, and the special operator here has only received one call— from a sportswear house offering to supply the bereft lady with another ski suit at a reasonable price."

Curtis pushed a memorandum across his desk toward Copely. "I want this in at least the last editions of the afternoon papers, all editions tomorrow, including the morning papers. Read it back to me, Jack, will you?"

Copely obediently read:

> Found: Near Gate My Place Metal Box Containing Uncashed Money Orders Name Frank Abelard Communicate Elmer Gans Westover Conn. 251 Ring 2."

"How does it sound to you, Copely?"

"Legitimate."

"Sufficiently hopeful of a reward?"

"Well, a dirt farmer wouldn't spend the money to advertise something he'd found if he didn't expect one, Mr. Curtis."

Curtis grinned. "That's what I thought, Copely. O.K. Shoot it through."

AT FOUR O'CLOCK Tuesday afternoon Assistant District Attorney Curtis received a telephone call from Sergeant Batty, stationed at *Inter-Allied News.*

"The Manchester dame's sent a box back to Ronsell and Bonner," he explained, but added that he guessed everything was O.K. "It was in her office yesterday. On account of there not having been nothing in her bag we searched in the Grand Central parcel room. I didn't go through her office with no fine-toothed comb but I did happen to look in that box after she went out with her boy friend in the afternoon. All there was in it was another green ski suit like the one in her suitcase—only this one still had store tags on it. I guess it was the wrong size or something. She's sent it back anyway. The boy called for it five minutes ago. He was from Ronsell and Bonner, all right. Had the store's name on his cap and on his uniform's shoulders. It was their delivery car outside."

"Then that sounds on the up and up," approved Mr. Curtis. "But you were right, Batty, to keep your eyes open. And keep on her tail. Hopkins will relieve you at the usual time."

SUSAN ARRIVED PUNCTUALLY at the Wise Owl. Outside it was pouring rain, but the *bistro* was doing a heavy cocktail-hour business. Its clients seemed to be largely West Siders on their way home from Wall Street, the cotton district and Seventh Avenue. There was an inordinate number of men and several women at a huge round bar. Tables were scattered about in profusion, groups of three and four of them separated from other groups by means of shoulder-high partitions. The walls were black mirrors on which were etched incredible owl-bearing arborvitae. The decorator seemed to have been sorely tried in making a decision between garishness and the suggestion of a sufficiently simple milieu for owls. Although the latter effort fell short of success amid the overlayer of super-elegance there was, atop each partition, a modernistic white glass owl, looking down upon the proceedings with round, beady eyes and more an air of astonishment than wisdom.

Susan settled herself at a table in one of the paddock-like enclosures and occupied the time waiting for Joan Sutton by indulging an old habit of hers. She endeavored to guess the natures, background and general characters of the people around her. When she could not see their faces she made her diagnosis by analyzing their voices and scraps of conversation drifting her way. One man she tabulated as in the coat-and-suit business. He was feeling violent about federal control. He was clever but uneducated, she thought. His grammar wasn't bad, but there was a parrotlike quality about it. He sounded as if, rather later than earlier in life, he had begun to imitate better-educated companions without knowing the rules. A woman, whose profile she could only partially see at a table on her left, was evidently a determined traveler, from the tenor of her conversation. Moreover, she was losing no time in establishing her travels firmly in the mind of her companion with equally determined zeal. The shoulder-high partition at Susan's back formed, she presently found, a somewhat effective sounding board, bringing her more sharply than those behind it probably guessed morsels of their conversation. There seemed to be only two persons in the party she could thus overhear: a man and a woman. She had the impression that they were being pretty cautious about being overheard by their adjacent neighbors. They were probably facing each other and talking close to the partition, she surmised. There was something vaguely familiar about the man's voice. From one or two disconnected phrases, Susan decided he was a physician. The woman with him could be a nurse. There seemed little love lost between the two. The woman seemed definitely angry about something. She kept raising her voice a note or two on the phrase: "What if they do get a hold of them?" Presently she switched to repeating another phrase: "Being seen . . . doesn't make you a doctor. . . ." Then she evidently went back to her former subject: ". . . go out there looking for them . . . maybe walk into a trap. . . ." Susan found these scraps teased her imagination.

The man had evidently been keeping his temper but suddenly he, too, raised his voice momentarily. It was, Susan thought, the cautiously raised voice of a physician giving a nurse sharp instructions in a sickroom. "You're not invisible . . . my dear. . . . Clerk . . . might have a pair of eyes in his head. . . . People can be traced. . . ."

"Just thinking of me . . . ?" snapped the woman irritably.

"Of us. . . ."

It made no sense, of course, and for a while Susan lost interest while watching another party of people assembling around the table opposite her. But the thought persisted in her mind that she knew the man behind her. Presently she began mulling over the various physicians and surgeons of her acquaintance. She had decided the

man behind her was a surgeon, from some word the woman had
used. But she could not place his voice. After a while she abandoned trying and glanced at her wrist watch. Miss Sutton was very
late. It was twenty-five past five. Susan looked down the busy room.
Not a sign of Peter Sutton's decorative daughter. People at the table
next on the right were preparing to leave and making a racket about
it. It wasn't, she thought, a particularly nice place. Voices all over the
restaurant were rising stridently as more drinks were consumed.
The crowd around the round bar was particularly boisterous.

It was then that the voice of the man behind the partition
reached her again. She had the impression that the couple were
standing up and sought to catch a glimpse of their faces in the black
glass wall opposite her. But it was a hazy and fleeting reflection.
The man's words she caught more clearly through some quality in
his voice rather than loudness of tone. He still seemed to be pur-
posefully speaking in a cautious undertone. What she caught was:

"Find out what days . . . due at . . . analyst's and the hours. . . .
Cancel all my appointments for those hours. . . . People under psy-
choanalysis sometimes . . . rush out . . . middle . . . treatment. . . .
Taking no chances . . . running . . . into her. . . ." The rest was lost
in the general clatter of the people leaving the next table.

Susan rose hastily from her table on a sudden half-formulated
conviction that she knew the voice, that she must try to match it to
a name she also knew, that it was of tremendous importance now
to patch together what the man and woman had been saying. She
buried herself in the exodus of people from the adjacent table and
reached the *bistro's* foyer just as a man, accompanying a redheaded
woman, was going out the front door. One more disconnected sentence she caught. The man was saying:

"Wait . . . look for taxi. . . ."

Outside it was raining harder, huge drops straight from a ter-
restrial refrigerator. The Wise Owl entrance was on the side street.
The man with the memory-pricking voice had gone toward the corner, leaving the woman under the wind-swept canopy. Susan stood
still, as if she, too, were waiting for a cab. Her own car was parked
down the block, but if she wanted to see the man's face there would
be no time to go and get it.

The redheaded woman was not four feet away from her. Other people were crowded under the canopy. There was a general hubbub of comments to the effect that nobody could hope to pick up a taxi in such rain. Susan saw that the other woman was pretty common looking. Her hair was more orange than red—touched up, of course. It was the color of carrots. She wasn't young—not a girl, at least. Her skin was her nicest feature. It was milk white. A slash of hard red mouth cut across it ruthlessly, however, and the red-brown eyes which followed the man with a steady stare were small and mean. She wore at a rather rakish angle a large expensively made beret. Her shoes were high heeled and smart, her coat well cut and topped with an ample mink collar which she clutched closely around her throat. Huddled out of the rain, Susan sized up these points, trying fruitlessly to place the carrot-head. As she watched a more violent gust of wind pelted the pavement with today's substitution for yesterday's blizzard. The canopy offered scant protection. The other woman's coat blew open. Before she could grab it and wrap it around herself again Susan had time to catch a swift picture of the starched white skirt of a nurse's uniform. She couldn't think what overheard words had made her believe the woman might be a nurse. It was obvious now that she was also a rather affluent one, from her outer apparel.

At this moment the woman started walking rapidly toward the corner, holding her coat tight against the downpour. Ignoring the rain, Susan rushed after her, determined to get another glimpse of the man. But she was too late. At the corner a cab door was just slamming shut behind the carrot-head. The man was already in it. She could see the back of his head as the cab made a U circle into the northbound traffic of Central Park West. Miraculously, another taxi stopped directly in front of Susan. A man got out of it, slammed the door and ran across the pavement. Susan scrambled into it, crying to the driver:

"See that cab that just pulled out into north traffic? Keep right behind it. I want to go where they're going and I don't know the address."

The driver threw the car into gear and made the light by a hair's breadth. They started crawling north in the center lane. The carrot-head and her companion were two cabs ahead in the inside lane. Traffic was heavy. The downpour continued in unabated icy blasts.

"Get right behind that other cab if you can," said Susan, peering through the rain-washed window to see if she could make out the features of the man in the taxi ahead. She couldn't, but on the next light the cab immediately ahead of hers made a left turn, and, from force of habit, instead of following her instructions to get in the inside lane her driver pulled ahead into the vacant space afforded. For a fleeting second Susan caught a rain-punctuated glimpse into the other taxi. The woman was leaning forward, obscuring the man's face. Susan was sure she had seen her peering at them. "Get behind them, not ahead," protested Susan.

"O.K. When this light changes," promised her driver. "You can't hand-pick your spots in weather like this." Susan supposed he was right. But she wished the carrot-head hadn't been given an equal opportunity to see her.

The up-and-down-avenue lights went green. The other cab pulled ahead, and Susan's driver pulled in behind it. If the couple had suspected she was following them this would surely convince them. Susan crouched back, her heart thumping loudly. She tried to reassure herself. Taxis were always pulling in and out of lanes. There was nothing essentially odd about their maneuver. But the impression persisted that the couple had been warned of her interest in them and that the woman, at least, had seen her face. Another thought was shoving its way into Susan's consciousness. She was sure now that in some crevice of memory she knew the man's voice. His name still eluded her, however.

"If," she presently informed the reflection of her worried face in the cab's mirror, "I keep on being so delightfully psychic I'll land in a nice well-run home for the mentally deficient."

But her psychic impressions were not denied some evidence of practicalness by the forthcoming maneuver of the cab ahead. It might, of course, have been accidental but it was beautifully timed and equally unlawful. A split second before the next up-and-down red traffic light came on the taxi bearing the carrot-head and her companion swung into the center lane and made a hair-raising cross-traffic left turn into a "no turn on red light" street. It disappeared in the flood of cross-town traffic which immediately closed in on it as the light changed.

"Oh well," sighed Susan, "I'm just not cut out for tailing people. I better leave such matters to Lyle's myrmidons." She raised her voice and said to her driver: "Forget that other cab. I'm going home instead," and gave him her street number.

REACHING HER APARTMENT, Susan found that abandoning pursuit of the redheaded woman and her male companion had not been at all the same thing as abandoning a desire to know more about them. The suspicion foremost in her mind was that their talk about avoiding someone and about a psychoanalyst could have had something to do with Joan Sutton. This took her, with belated recollection, to the telephone. She had completely forgotten her engagement with Peter Sutton's daughter. Reaching the Wise Owl over the wire, she asked that Miss Sutton be paged. Some moments later Joan's voice greeted her. "Oh, Miss Yates! Did you give me up and leave? I was horribly late. Or couldn't you make it?"

Susan selected the most suitable white lie she could think of, then proposed that Miss Sutton come along to her apartment where they could have something to drink before a warm fire. The girl appeared to confer with her watch, reported that it was nearly six, then finally, on apparent impulse, said:

"All right, I'll dash in for one drink. I'll be right along."

Susan gave her address and replaced the receiver. Immediately the telephone bell rang. A hard, efficient woman's voice asked:

"Miss Susan Yates?"

"Yes, this is Miss Yates."

"Look—you want to know more about the murder of Prunella Parton?"

Was she imagining this, or was it the same voice which had come to her through the sounding-board quality of the Wise Owl partition?

"I'm afraid I do not quite follow you," Susan lied.

"I guess you do. And if I'm not mistaken you'll be interested in walking past number 27 DeVise Street on the lower East Side at eleven o'clock tonight. If you do you'll see standing in the doorway there the man who murdered Prunella Parton. Just a tip. Good-by." The phone clicked off, leaving Susan with the receiver limp in her hand.

Before calling Curtis, which was her immediate decision, Susan telephoned her garage. They were to pick up her car near the side-street entrance of the Wise Owl and deliver it to her door. After Joan's call and before Curtis' arrival she was determined to visit a certain West Side street. She would get Miss Sutton to give her the address without knowing she had.

There was only one thing to do, of course: tell Curtis. She might be six kinds of nitwits but she wasn't quite foolish enough to visit a lower East Side street alone at eleven o'clock at night. There was something decidedly dubious about the whole business, anyway; but it had sounded like the carrot-head's voice. Then if the woman *had* been with—? But the name still escaped her though it seemed to be hovering directly on her tongue. "In any case," she reasoned, "it's downright unmoral to go around identifying people because of an indefinable quality of voice and sketchily heard conversations." Just the same, she was certain she knew the voice. Also, she found she was trembling in the pit of her stomach.

In a state of indecision, Susan dialed the district attorney's office and asked for Curtis. His voice sounded not entirely lacking in cheerfulness. Susan said:

"From that have been happening, I don't know that I even dare talk on a telephone, much less trust my own nervous system. How about coming up to my apartment for dinner and letting me tell you what has been happening to me? I assure you, I'm a nervous wreck but I'll give you a cocktail and a comfortable chair to sit in."

"Coming," affirmed Curtis quite heartily. "I think we're on the last lap of the trail, and there's not much more to be done until the morning papers are out. An evening with you, my girl, will be the exact tonic I need. I suppose that chap Van Groesbeck isn't going to be hanging around?"

"Oh," replied Susan, regaining a sense of reality, "he's only coming for dinner and the evening but he won't mind in the least your being here."

Curtis sounded severe. "I was bringing a white orchid. You get a dandelion now if I can find one"—and he rang off.

SUSAN'S DRAWING ROOM had been turned into a miniature district attorney's office at various times during the course of the evening. Her colored Lillian was half beside herself from answering the telephone. Plans and counterplans had been hatched before her fire. One thing Curtis had absolutely forbidden was that Susan should go within ten miles of 27 DeVise Street at eleven o'clock or any other hour. She was to stay put in her apartment. Men previously dissociated with the Parton case were to take care of the lower East Side rendezvous.

Though Susan had been taking mental dives for it all evening the name of the man with the carrot-haired woman had remained tantalizingly buried.

At a minute before eleven quiet at last settled in Miss Yates's apartment. It was not reflected in the beating of Susan's pulses, however, nor in the general atmosphere of tension. Lillian had got some sort of hang of what was going on and lingered in the hall, her black face lined with concern. Susan was sitting before the fire. Curtis stood by the windows staring out at the sky line, a hand within easy reach of the telephone. Eleven tinkles came from Susan's chime clock in the hall. A second ticked by, then sixty of them. Susan was counting. Another minute began and passed. No one said anything. Then a log in the fireplace softly crumpled, hissing faintly. Sixty more seconds passed. Susan was intent on her wrist watch. Another tick from the clock in the hall. Another and another. Thirty of them. The phone rang blatantly. Curtis had the receiver in his hand. "Yes," he snapped. "Who? Well I'll be damned. What has he got to say for himself? Typewritten? Yes. Oh, make it loitering. Anything to hold him. Wait a minute—make it held for questioning. That'll be better. I'm on my way downtown."

He turned from the phone. "There are seven ripe suspects in this case, Susan. You and I guessed wrong. The man they found standing in the doorway of 27 DeVise Street was David Barron. He was carrying a thirty-eight automatic and a license to carry it, also a typewritten note which he claims he received at his apartment at seven o'clock this evening telling him to wait in the doorway of 27 DeVise Street at eleven o'clock tonight if he wanted to know who killed Prunella Parton."

"Barron!" breathed Susan. "But that man's voice in the *bistro!* I don't think it was Barron's."

"Voices can be misleading, my sweet. Well, I'm off for the inquisition." From the doorway Curtis turned. "And if you stick your head outside this apartment before tomorrow morning at a reasonable hour I'll have you locked up as a vagrant. Understand?" He turned to Lillian. "Lock the door and see Miss Yates doesn't disobey the instructions of the law. I'm appointing you a deputy to carry out my orders."

Lillian fervently insisted that wild horses wouldn't induce her to let Miss Yates loose in the wilderness of Manhattan Island.

After Curtis had gone Lillian proceeded to cajole Susan into her bed. She brought her hot milk and left the room. To Susan's amazement and quickly dispensed anger, she heard a key turn in the outside of her bedroom door. Her sense of humor coming to her rescue, she put down the milk and giggled into her pillow. "Dear old Lillian! Locking me in! Perhaps it's just as well."

But Miss Yates was only momentarily thwarted. If a deputized Lillian was going to keep her secure in her bedroom she could still manage a few matters over the telephone. She dialed her secretary's home number.

Miss Button's mother answered and called her daughter.

"I've got something definitely odd to ask you, Button," explained Miss Yates. "Haven't you at one point told me you have a mole on your left shoulder that you'd like to get taken off? Oh, good. Now, don't sound shocked. I'm not tight or mentally unbalanced—at the moment. Look here, my girl, would you mind hopping in a cab and spending the night with me? I've got a matter of the utmost importance to discuss with you. I've just thought of a name! No, I'm quite sober. You'll come then? Splendid. And, oh, by the way, you'll have to get Lillian to unlock my bedroom and let you in. She's got me a prisoner. Lyle Curtis made her a deputy something or other. Yes, it's very troublesome. Come right over, will you?"

Twenty minutes later a severely official-looking Lillian admitted Miss Button to Miss Yates's bedroom and promptly locked the door again with a jailer's zeal.

It was twenty minutes of two before Susan and Miss Button finished their conference.

SUSAN DRIFTED into sleep, with the various factors which the day had brought stirring restlessly in the hands of her unconscious mind. The district attorney's office, she began to dream, was located in the outskirts of Berlin, and Curtis was forced by law to wear a long red wig. To her horror, she suddenly knew that she was having a nightmare about a nightmare. It was a different dream and yet the same one she had had the night before. There was the same river, but it was a river in China and not Berlin, and the people standing along the banks were rioting because their leader, a beautiful woman, had died and her enemies had carried her through the streets dressed in long-sleeved, long-legged ski underwear and a flame-colored velvet evening gown. Curtis was there. He had arrived miraculously from Berlin but he still had on the red wig.

Susan woke with a jerk. Both her hands were asleep, and she felt a sudden hysterical conviction that she was not alone in the room. Lying perfectly quiet except for a cautious attempt to massage her tingling hands, she listened. There was no sound in the room. The wind through her eighteenth-floor bedroom windows was stirring the sheer curtains, but silently, with a breathless quietness. It was a moonlight night, and a streak of moonlight lay on the carpet by the windows. Convinced that she was not alone, Susan put out her hand to the phone by her bed. And then she remembered Miss Button was spending the night in the other twin bed.

"BARRON WON'T," explained Curtis over the phone the first thing Wednesday morning, "admit to anything but having received his typewritten note and followed its tip. He claims the note was left in his mailbox. He lived in a walk-up. Expensive one, but no doorman.

So no one saw the note delivered. That's his story, and he sticks to it. We had to let him go. Can't hold him. But what David Barron does every minute of the time from now on will be known to the district attorney's office. Not that we didn't know before. His tail followed him down to DeVise Street last night but didn't have a chance to phone in until my other men had picked him up. By the way, tell me again what Joan Sutton told you last evening about Barron letting Prunella pose as the liaison between Sutton and Barron and the Kork-Petulla million-dollar oil account."

Susan explained: "When Joan stopped in here for a drink after I missed her at the *bistro* she said Barron knew Stratfield long before Prunella introduced them. Conway saw a letter or something Barron had from Stratfield months ago. Yet Barron pretended not to know the advertising-art adviser to Kork-Petulla. He let Prunella introduce Mr. Stratfield to the firm, let her take full credit for negotiating the 'friendly relations' designed to get all the Kork-Petulla business away from Oliver Penbroke's agency and on the books of Sutton and Barron."

"Well," said Curtis, "Barron claims he didn't know Stratfield and 'what the hell difference does it make to anybody?' There's something screwy in Denmark and several other places I could name."

Susan fervently agreed.

CHAPTER TWENTY-EIGHT

SERGEANT JONES HAD greatly enjoyed his breakfast at Mrs. Elmer Gans's kitchen table. He had not, in fact, breakfasted so elaborately in many years. Pork chops, there had been, and sausages, an enormous pot of fragrant coffee and hot biscuits. The meal had been topped off, to his amazement, being a city-bred man, with large pieces of homemade apple pie. While he was wondering how long it would take him to digest this feast the telephone on the Ganses' kitchen wall rang twice.

"That's ours, Elmer," said Mrs. Gans.

Sergeant Jones was immediately alert. "May be what we're waiting for," he warned as Elmer lumbered to the phone, a shrewd look on his weather-wrinkled face.

"Hello," said Elmer. "Yes ma'am, my name is Elmer Gans. Yes ma'am, I did." Elmer turned and gave Sergeant Jones a broad wink, hunching one husky shoulder in a manner which was, Jones judged, supposed to indicate the person at the other end of the wire was the one they were expecting. "You say your pa ain't able to come out here and wants to send you?" Gans looked back at Jones for confirmation or denial on this point. Jones wrote hastily on a piece of paper:

"Tell her she must bring signed instructions from her father. Also, speak about expecting a reward."

Gans nodded and put his mouth back against the transmitter. "I had to check with Ma. She says she guesses we could give up the box to you if your pa wrote us a letter and the signature the same's on the money order. Only if your pa don't come hisself I might not be wanting to give up the whole box on account of how I was kinda expecting maybe he'd give me a little something. One thousand dollars is a pile of money to find for a body."

Sergeant Jones pressed an ear against the receiver held in Elmer Gans's gnarled hand. The voice at the other end sounded hard and expedient. It was saying:

"Listen, we're going to fix you up all right. Don't worry about that. When I get out there I'll have a nice present for you. I can be there by eleven o'clock."

Sergeant Jones nodded at Elmer Gans.

"All right," Elmer announced into the phone. "I won't say I won't take nothing on account of how I will. You're sure these money orders 're your pa's? If somebody else calls, claimin' 'em, I mean?"

The voice on the other end said: "Certainly they're ours. I'll bring you a letter from my father, and you can match the signatures. They'll be O.K., all right." The phone snapped off.

"Well, I never," commented Mrs. Gans. "That come quick enough to suit anybody. Imagine!"

AT ELEVEN O'CLOCK Sergeant Jones, wearing overalls and an old khaki hunting coat minus most of its buttons, was ready with the Gans family to receive their guest. He had noted and conveyed the news to Curtis by phone that "Frank Abelard's daughter" had not asked for special directions about how to reach the isolated Gans farm. That was an impressive point.

At five minutes after eleven an automobile stopped in the road in front of the farmhouse. Its occupant inspected the mailbox, then drove through the open gates. A woman wearing a red-fox coat which coarsely accentuated her carrot-colored hair came across the snowy yard to the front door.

Sergeant Jones said to Elmer: "I'll take charge from now on. Mrs. Gans, let her in."

"I'm May Abelard," the woman on the doorstep curtly introduced herself. "My father sent me for the money orders you found. I brought a letter from him so you can see the signatures are O.K."

Sergeant Jones came forward with the metal box which the district attorney's office had supplied for the occasion. He opened it and put it on the sitting-room table. Miss Abelard handed Elmer the letter she had taken from her handbag. She looked, to Jones, anxious to get her hands on the money orders and get away—not exactly nervous but not relaxed. She also looked hard as steel rivets.

Among other work for the district attorney's office, Sergeant Jones had studied in its handwriting-identification department. Curtis considered him one of his abler men. If he could have seen him now he would have appreciated his talent as an actor. Sergeant Jones did not at the moment need a straw behind his ear to pose as Elmer Gans's son. Miss Abelard displayed not the slightest doubt of his connection with the household.

The signature on the very brief letter in his hand, instructing Elmer Gans to turn over to his daughter the money orders found near his farmhouse, matched with precision the Frank Abelard signatures on the money orders. The sergeant, looking over Elmer's shoulder, said: "It's O.K., Pa."

Elmer stepped into his role. "How much is your pa thinking getting all these things back to him is worth?"

Miss Abelard was efficient and quick. "Fifty dollars," she said promptly, and took a bill from her purse.

Elmer looked deeply disappointed. "'Tain't what I'd call enough for gittin' a thousand dollars back," he remonstrated.

Miss Abelard was again prompt. "All right, we'll make it one hundred dollars, but not a cent more. If you won't take that we'll inform the Post Office Department, and you'll have government men down here to find out what you're trying to get away with."

Elmer shook his head. "'Tain't enough. To tell you the truth, I was expectin' at least five hundred dollars."

"Five hundred!" Miss Abelard laughed rudely. "Listen, mister, do you want the hundred dollars or post-office men asking you questions?"

Stubbornly Elmer continued his mulish expression. "I'm thinkin' they'd say I deserved more, findin' all that. I ain't fixin' to hand that whole box over to you for no pikey hundred dollars."

It was clear that Miss Abelard's hands felt very itchy. It seemed to be all she could do to keep them off the tin box. She looked at Mrs. Gans. "You don't want your old man pulled in by the post-office people, do you?"

Mrs. Gans looked effectively blank. Sergeant Jones had done a good theatrical director's job with both the Ganses.

Elmer took his cue. "I don't want to hold nobody's money up. For all I know, you folks may be needin' it, but I ain't goin' to give you the whole lot of them orders. Son, you give the young lady five of them."

He turned to Miss Abelard. "That'll mean I'm handin' over five hundred dollars to you. I think your paw ought to give me five hundred dollars cash for the rest. You go back home and tell him that when you folks is willin' to make me a decent reward in cash I'll turn the whole caboodle of orders over to you—but not afore."

Miss Abelard's face looked angry. She made several remarks to Elmer which were not in the best school of taste. He remained magnificently adamant. After fruitlessly working the reward offers up to two hundred dollars, which Sergeant Jones shrewdly estimated was the sum total she had with her, she accepted with poor grace five of the money orders, handed over the cash and departed, her color about as high as the tone of her carroty hair.

From the car she again hotly expressed herself, promising to come back with post-office detectives. She then drove off, knocking off a piece of Elmer's gate in the process.

"We ain't goin' to get in no trouble, are we, young man?" Mrs. Gans asked Sergeant Jones.

The sergeant was hustling out of the hunting coat and overalls. An official car had appeared miraculously from the direction of Elmer's barns. Jones was halfway out the door before he finished his reply: "You and Mr. Gans are working for the district attorney's office now. The post-office department knows all about the whole thing. You sit tight and you'll have Mr. Curtis and the D. A. himself out here yet to thank you in person before you get through." Leaping for the official car, the tin box under his arm, he called out the window: "And if that dame or anybody else shows up demanding the rest of the money orders before I get back you tell 'em you decided there was something funny up and you turned the whole lot in at the New York Post Office. Tell them you got your son to drive you to town with 'em, that you didn't want any trouble. I've left a couple of men in the barn to give you protection. Be seeing you folks soon." The long car shot through the gate, neatly avoided further damaging it and disappeared down the road in the direction the carroty-headed girl had taken.

"Think of it, Ma," observed Elmer Gans, "we're workin' for the New York district attorney's office now, and that's a right smart young chap, that Sergeant Jones."

"He's a good eater too." Mrs. Gans smiled proudly.

AT HALF-PAST TWELVE that noon Miss Button, dressed in street clothes, came into Miss Yates's private office. "I went around there, and you're right—Miss Sutton's psychoanalyst and a Doctor Victor Prudence do share the private house. It's just off Central Park West, as you said. Very neat and orderly. The analyst is on the first floor, Doctor Prudence on the second, with a private entrance for each of them. The analyst keeps his shades drawn on the street side. Doctor Prudence has aluminum Venetian blinds. I went up the stairs. A sign on his door notes office hours two to five. Nobody answered when I rang. Evidently signs mean what they say in Doctor Prudence's official life."

"He means them to, at least," commented Miss Yates. She looked thoughtful. "All right, Button, I hate to let you do this—but, as you say, I'd be recognized. I don't see how having a mole taken off can possibly do you any harm."

Miss Button's eyes held a gleam of suppressed excitement. "I wouldn't miss finally having a hand in one of your insanities, Miss Yates, for anything in the world. It's dreadful," she added, "working for someone who never lets you take any chances when she's always going out of her way to get into trouble herself."

"I don't," said Susan, "know what I should do without you, Button." They grinned at each other with one of those looks of mutual respect which Susan suspected men believe women never feel for one another. "All right, heaven knows, I hope nothing goes wrong. You appear there at a few minutes after two. Say Mrs. Petulla sent you. It's a weighty name, in any case. If the receptionist presses you say Mrs. Howard Petulla. There isn't such a person, to the best of my knowledge." Susan paused and said a little dubiously: "I don't very well see how Doctor Prudence can refuse to remove a mole. It would look odd. It would be the same thing as if you went into a presumably bona fide drugstore, asked for aspirin and were refused. It would cast suspicion on the establishment. Say you've finally got up your courage to have the mole off and that you'd like very much to have it done before your courage lapses again; you know, act jittery, afraid of operating tables for even unimportant operations. Oh dear, are you sure you want to do it?"

Miss Button nodded her head emphatically. "Besides, I can do without my mole very nicely."

CHAPTER TWENTY-NINE

CLUTCHING THE TIN BOX, Sergeant Jones said: "She's a good driver, that orange blossom."

"Yeah," muttered the official chauffeur. "She can drive like hell. It's a drive-it-yourself buggy."

"Yeah," agreed Sergeant Jones.

The man in the back seat said: "It's from Hepstein's Garage. I can see their tag."

Both men in the front seat said: "Yeah."

They were nearing the end of the Merritt Parkway. The car ahead turned right into the Cross-County Parkway and sped on. Sergeant Jones and his companion kept it in sight but hugged an intervening automobile.

At the beginning of the Henry Hudson Parkway Jones instructed his driver to pull up directly behind the redhead's car. Traffic was thicker now and bore signs of continuing so into the city. The woman ahead kept her car at an even forty-five miles an hour, considerably over the speed limit, but she drove smoothly and did not cut in and out. She seemed determined to make the best time possible without too much likelihood of getting a ticket for her efforts.

At the Seventy-ninth Street parkway exit she turned off. Jones and his companions followed. Jones had put on dark glasses and pulled his hat low. He didn't in the least resemble Elmer Gans's overalled son.

They let another car come between them and the one they followed at the Riverside Drive light. Behind the Museum of Natural
History they turned north and followed uptown traffic to the first
eastbound street. The car ahead turned there. They turned. Passing the Planetarium, they waited again for a light on Central Park
West, then crossed into the Central Park transfer. Coming out on
Fifth Avenue, they followed the drive-it-yourself car downtown for
a few blocks, then east. Finally it stopped before a rental garage.
The carrot-head got out, went inside for a moment, came out and
hailed a taxi. Jones had instructed the man in the back seat to hop
out and make inquiries inside. He and the driver followed the taxi.
It went down Lexington Avenue to Thirty-fifth Street, turned right
to Park and up Park north again to the Grand Central ramp, up
that and to a standstill at the upper entrance of the Hotel Commo-
dore. The carrot-head popped out of the taxi and disappeared
through the revolving doors. Sergeant Jones fleetly followed at an
apparent amble.

He was inside the doors in time to see the carrot-head disappear into a ladies' room. With instructions of a sepulchral nature
Sergeant Jones had left the tin box with the official driver. He took
a newspaper from his pocket and began loitering, first making certain there was only one exit to the ladies' room. Carrot-head did
not reappear for some twenty minutes. She hurried away then down
into the lobby, across it, down the Forty-second Street steps and
was into and gone in a taxi before Sergeant Jones could slam the
door of another. But luck was with him. Within a quarter of a block
his driver had the taxi ahead well tailed.

The carrot-head made three more stops, each one in hotels with
exits on different streets. Sergeant Jones, seeming to lumber along
sleepily, was not out of view of her for more than split seconds
here and there. As he followed in a third change of cab he sensed
that the woman was at last feeling free of possible pursuit. Through
the rear window he could see her hands arranging the back of her
violent-toned hair.

After fifteen minutes' more driving Carrot-head permitted herself to be deposited at Sixtieth Street and Central Park West. She

looked around carefully after her cab had driven off. Sergeant Jones's driver had come to a complete standstill without a second to spare. The sergeant figured that, from her position at the curb, this had been accomplished in time for them to look like a cab which had been parked there before she came up. He waited inside, paying the driver, meanwhile, and instructing him to follow along behind slowly in case he should be needed again.

After a few moments the woman began walking north. Ultimately she turned into a side street and walked down it a few doors. The house before which she stopped was on the north side, a two-story red brick one, spick-and-span, with neat orchid shutters and a look of well-kept gentility. As she disappeared into one of its two orchid-doors Sergeant Jones strolled up and observed that it was the entrance to the second floor. He strolled back to the cab, leaned on the front window sill and gave some terse instructions. The driver was to get out, leaving his ignition switch open. He was to go back to the corner and call the D. A.'s office where he was to ask for Curtis or his secretary. He was to explain where Sergeant Jones was and that the sergeant wanted at least three men to surround the red brick house with orchid shutters. If Jones needed the cab while the driver was away it was understood he would take it. This accomplished, Jones waited. Nothing at all happened in the street. It was a quiet one, and it was still the lunch hour. Presently the driver came back, and ten minutes later a car stopped at the foot of the street, disgorging three ordinary-looking men who spotted Sergeant Jones and the red brick orchid-shuttered house. Jones strolled past them. Without looking at them, he said in a singsong voice:

"Two of you find the rear areaway. Stop anybody who tries to get out the back. Gilbert, you lounge up the block, keeping me in sight. I may have to go inside. Don't follow unless I signal you to. We're after a dame who had hair the color of oranges when she went inside. She might change that. The cabbie up there is with us. O.K." He lumbered on, then came slowly back.

Miss Button appeared in front of the red brick house at precisely two-five. The redhead had been inside for twenty-five minutes.

Sergeant Jones looked Miss Button over and emitted a low whistle. He had a good memory. He knew Miss Button, and it took a good memory to do that, for he had only seen her twice in his life during one of Curtis' cases six months before.

With considerable amazement, some suspicion and a dash of worry the sergeant watched Miss Button open the stairway door of the brick house and disappear behind it. He was on the point of following when footsteps down the quiet block held back his own. The man who was approaching came on and turned in at the house next door to the one he was watching.

Sergeant Jones looked precisely like a cat at a rathole. It had occurred to him that he not only knew the man but that it might be possible to enter one house from the other.

To say that Miss Button climbed the thickly carpeted stairs without trepidation would have been a faulty speculation. From all that she and Susan had discussed into the early hours of that morning, she had her own opinion of Dr. Prudence's character and habits. Still, he certainly had never seen *her* before. There was no earthly reason to believe anything would go wrong. All she had to do was to get a good look at his face. Miss Yates's idea that Curtis could arrest him first on the charge of practicing without a license and go on from there seemed sound. It also seemed simple enough. But she must play her part with poise—or, rather, with just the right degree of jitters. As a matter of hard fact, she *didn't* care much about operating tables. She hadn't told Susan just how frightened she could be of surgeons and knives, nor had she told Miss Yates that, in her own mind, she had determined it wouldn't be necessary to go through with the whole operation. Ever since leaving Susan's salon she had been developing a theory of her own. Just as the surgeon was about to begin to remove the mole she would go all fluttery and feminine and beg him to allow her to come back the next day. She would have seen his face by then. People often went to dentists and backed out of having their teeth pulled at the last moment. The more she thought about it the more certain she was that this stratagem wouldn't be letting down Miss Yates or the other citizens of New York City. If she followed their original plan only that far she could still give evidence that Dr. Prudence had proposed to operate on her.

Reaching the upper floor, Miss Button rang the doctor's bell and waited. The door was opened by a carrot-headed woman in a nurse's uniform. She had, Miss Button thought, a pretty hard mouth but she managed to make her smile pleasant enough as she said a professionally cheerful:

"Good afternoon."

"Oh, good afternoon," fluttered Miss Button. "You know, I'm an awful fool. Mrs. Petulla recommended a doctor to me in this block. I guess I've got the right one? Prudence *sounds* like it because I know I thought of being *perfectly safe* when she said it. You see, I've got a mole. My right shoulder. It's driving me frantic, but I'm a perfect goose about having things taken off. Would you— could you get Doctor Prudence just to get it off quickly before I change my mind?"

"Doctor doesn't usually take cases of that nature," said the carrot-head, first inspecting Miss Button and then turning to an appointment book. "I could ask him, of course, though he's hardly a moment this afternoon. Just be seated, and I'll see." She disappeared through a swinging door. Miss Button sank down onto a chair and waited. She heard a door slam. There were footsteps in the hall outside. Another door was opened and shut with precision. Several minutes passed, and nothing more happened. Miss Button began to feel more and more uneasy.

Then the nurse-receptionist reappeared. She gave Miss Button a hard look, seemed reassured and said:

"Doctor says he'll take you right away. Any friend of Mrs. Petulla. Don't be frightened, Miss—"

"Hollister," said Miss Button.

"Miss Hollister," repeated the woman in the nurse's uniform, and added encouragingly, "It's really nothing at all. Doctor's so expert. Oh yes, and you pay now. Twenty-five dollars."

Miss Button struggled to keep her fingers from shaking as she extracted the money from her handbag. But, after all, her strategy was being feminine and having the jitters about an unimportant operation. If this flame-haired woman only knew how really scared she was!

"I even behave this way at dentists'," said Miss Button.

The nurse put the money into a drawer. Her expression was bored now. "Come this way," she directed, and went ahead past the swinging door and down a brief hall. She opened another door, held it for Miss Button, shut it behind her.

They had entered an apparently fully equipped surgical room. It smelled of disinfectant and heaven knew what. Miss Button's heart missed a beat.

"I expect you won't have to undress much," the nurse said. "Just slip your dress off whichever shoulder the mole is on. Right shoulder, is it? O.K. That'll give Doctor enough area. Now lie down on your face."

Trembling, Miss Button stretched out on the operating table.

"Humm," murmured the nurse, touching the mole with energetic fingers. Miss Button wanted to scream. "But it's really nothing," the woman repeated. "By the way, Doctor wanted me to ask you if your health is generally good. I'll take down details later—while you are resting."

"Oh yes," cried Miss Button hastily, "my health is usually excellent."

It was then that she felt the brief sharp prick in her upper arm, just below the shoulder. A moment later she began to feel drowsy. It was like a cover coming up and up, submerging her in a vast unconsciousness. Miss Button lay very still indeed.

SERGEANT JONES FELT HIMSELF in rather a predicament. Coincidences did happen, of course, in life. Not all connected New York houses communicated with one another from their interiors, but still— Also, he could be mistaken about the identity of the man who had entered the old-fashioned residence next the house with orchid shutters. After all, he had only seen him once on the sided Pullman, Monday morning, and he hadn't seen him any too well—just a glimpse as the gentleman had taken his turn at identifying the body in the drawing room.

Sergeant Jones gave the problem serious thought. Ultimately he turned and walked up the steps of the old-fashioned brownstone house into which the man had disappeared He rang the doorbell and waited. There was a sign above the bell which said "Furnished Rooms" and under it, in smaller letters: "Vacancy."

A slattern maid opened the door and asked what he wanted.

"Have you got a room for rent?" inquired Sergeant Jones, not taking off either his hat or the dark glasses.

"Third floor, rear. D'you want to see it?"

Sergeant Jones was inspecting the hall behind the girl. There was a broad stairway which had once been beautiful. Surprisingly, at the right of it was a glass-enclosed elevator. The disrepair of the house scarcely suggested such elegance.

"I'm not much for walking," said Sergeant Jones. "Bum knee." He hunched a shoulder at the elevator. "Does that run up to the third floor?"

The slattern maid screwed her face up into a sneer. "Deary me," she sniffed, "you have got ideas. That there's a private el-e-vator for the apartment on the second floor. It ain't for the use of no boarders."

"I might be interested in a whole apartment if it's for rent," mused Sergeant Jones aloud.

The maid looked at him suspiciously and terminated his speculation by announcing that it wasn't. "Let to a gentleman."

"Oh well, then, I'll look at the room. But I don't like the idea of that climb."

The girl sniffed again and led the way. Sergeant Jones, limping ably, followed. When they reached the second floor the sergeant saw that it was in better repair than the rest of the house. Looking at the closed door, he asked, "Is the third floor all fixed up like this?"

"No," said the maid, not very expansively, and climbed on up the second flight of stairs. At the top she turned to the left, threw open a creaking door and displayed a downtrodden and barely furnished room, a close kin in decorative degradation to the first-floor hall.

The sergeant went and sat on the bed, testing its springs. He got up and looked out both the windows, finding he was a floor above the top of the adjacent house, as he had assumed he would be. Then he asked: "How much?"

"Five a week."

"All right, I'll take it until I can find something better. I'm really looking for an apartment."

The maid said: "The missus is out, but I kin sign a receipt. She dragged a dirty "Payment Received" pad from the confines of her apron, filled in the space allotted to cash and inquired the name of the new roomer.

"R. J. Swift," said Sergeant Jones.

The maid filled that in, added a scrawl, presumably her signature, and held out her hand for the five-dollar bill the sergeant had produced.

"Where's your stuff?" the girl asked.

"Got to send for it," explained Mr. Swift, and edged her determinedly out the door.

When her footsteps had retreated down the stairs he crept out and descended to the second floor where he tapped cautiously but audibly on its door. He waited. Nothing happened. He looked over the stair well. There did not seem to be anyone down in the hall. He rapped more forcibly. Still no sound of movement or life from within or below.

Out of a pocket Sergeant Jones drew a key ring, selected a key and inserted it in the lock. The knob turned smoothly in his hand. He went inside and softly closed the door. The apartment had brightly tinted walls. It was furnished richly and with a degree of taste, it seemed to him. On the left of the entrance was another closed door. He tried it and met with resistance. Again he drew out his keys and unlocked it. In front of him was a brief drop to the top of the small elevator resting at the main floor. He closed and locked the elevator shaft and began searching the apartment, concentrating on the side which abutted the orchid-shuttered house.

After, some little time he found the door. It was in a closet in the bedroom, hidden by a row of clothes on a rack and a large mothproof bag. All the clothes were women's. By experimentation he found that the whole rack was capable of swinging outward, giving access to the door behind it.

Sergeant Jones put his ear to the door and listened attentively. He could hear voices faintly. Two women were talking. One voice was louder than the other. He made out the words:

"It isn't much of an operation. Really nothing at all."

The other voice seemed to be saying something about dentists and surgery. It sounded scared.

Then the first voice said: "Come this way," and silence followed. He could hear nothing more though he strained his ear with all the ardor of a lifelong eavesdropper.

CHAPTER THIRTY

SUSAN SAT AT HER DESK feeling as if she would jump out of her skin at any moment. She should never have let Miss Button do it! She couldn't think why she had allowed the girl to prevail upon her. Of course, it would have been more dangerous for her to go herself, but she was used to taking chances. She had taken one chance or another every day of her life since she had put a pair of shears into a fifty-dollar-a-yard material to cut her first custom-made gown. She took a chance by being a businesswoman. She had certainly taken chances by sticking her nose before into Lyle Curtis' cases. But Miss Button was different. Miss Button wasn't accustomed to climbing out on ice-covered limbs and managing not to slip off. Miss Button lived an orderly life. Susan had only told her of her plan in order that there would be someone to ring Curtis if she didn't show up again after going to the other doctor's office in the building where Joan Sutton's psychoanalyst practiced.

Her midnight conversation with Miss Button came flooding back. It had been a mistake to tell her that perhaps the man and the woman in the other taxicab had seen and possibly recognized her. That had been really what had most worried Button, that and the fact that the man had seen her on the sided Pullman.

Just the same, it was absurd to have allowed Button to take the chance. There might be a special system through which Dr. Prudence received his patients. Perhaps they had to have a code word, a recommendation from some one of a few persons. Perhaps using Mrs. Petulla's name had been more stupid than wise. They might suspect Button from the moment she opened her mouth. Susan was becoming momentarily more certain that the whole plan had been a horrible mistake.

She glanced at her desk clock. Two-fifteen. Well, Button wouldn't be much more than in the office by now.

An inner warning kept going up and fluttering violently in her head. She glanced at the telephone. Wouldn't it be better to tell Curtis everything and let him surround the house? Wouldn't it be better to let him take a chance on the doctor being on the premises? But what if the doctor wasn't? What if he were warned off by such a maneuver and, being warned, escaped Curtis completely? If he never showed up again at the house where Joan's psychoanalyst practiced how would it be possible to prove anything? From what she had heard of men—and women—engaged in this type of practice, their patients never saw them. Their patients were anesthetized before the doctor came into the operating room and then were sent home before they were completely in their right wits again. They definitely never saw the surgeon at all, were incapable of going into court and bearing witness against him.

Suddenly one word from these thoughts leaped into cold relief in Susan's brain: "Anesthetized!"

Her heart seemed to be engaged in standing teetering on the edge of a plunge. If they suspected Button in the least wouldn't that be just what they would do to her? And would they stop at just an ordinary anesthetic?

Susan reached so violently for her telephone that she upset a vase of flowers.

A LOW-SLUNG, SLEEK convertible coupé appeared at the end of the block where Joan Sutton's psychoanalyst and Dr. Victor Prudence practiced. Out of it hopped a very smart-looking but equally frightened-appearing Susan Yates. A second later a dark closed car drew up behind the coupé, and Assistant District Attorney Curtis emerged from it followed by four men. He said to Susan:

"Can't stop to punish you now but when I have more time I'm going to do it right over my knee."

Susan followed meekly. Her high fur hat seemed suddenly something a child had put on to make it feel grown up. From under it she scanned the street and saw a man coming up to them.

The man said: "Sergeant Jones gave me a signal to stand by and keep a lookout. He's gone into that brownstone."

"'What's happened in the other place?" snapped Curtis.

"A girl went in," said Gilbert, "about twenty minutes ago. That's all."

"You know why Jones went into the brownstone?"

Gilbert shook his head.

"Anything suspicious about the brownstone?"

"Not that I know of. A man went in there right after the girl went in the other place."

Curtis demanded a description of the man, but Gilbert hadn't been near enough and had been watching the orchid-shuttered house anyway. Curtis looked at Susan, then back at Gilbert. Hastily he painted a brief verbal portrait.

Gilbert said: "It could have been him, Mr. Curtis. I'm sorry I didn't notice more particular."

Curtis asked: "Where are the other men who came with you, Gilbert?"

"Jones sent them behind the house. There's an areaway there on the left."

"All right." Curtis nodded. "Get around there and stay with them. Tell them to stop anybody who tries to leave either the house with the purple shutters or the brownstone."

Gilbert hurried away, and Curtis motioned to two of the men who had followed him out of the car. "You heard what I told Gilbert? Same thing applies out front here." To the other pair he said: "Come on," and led the way down the street. Susan trudged along, feeling more than ever like a frightened child. She was certain now something awful had happened to Miss Button. On the other hand, perhaps the man in the Wise Owl hadn't been who she thought. Perhaps he wasn't "Dr. Prudence." Perhaps the whole thing was a figment of her imagination. Perhaps Dr. Prudence was a nice thoroughly legal old gentleman with white hair and surgical skill in removing tonsils. What if her interference was leading Curtis into professional embarrassment and needless delay in his own solution of the Parton case? Still, he had had men watching the house with orchid shutters, it appeared.

Curtis pulled open the door, and they all filed in and up the stairs, Susan bringing up the rear. Curtis, she decided, had forgotten all about her. In the foyer at the top a pungent odor met them. Susan stared at the two closed doors. Curtis motioned the other men to take the second one. He softly pushed open the first. Susan followed. He had drawn a gun, she saw, and it sent a fresh quivering along her nerves.

They were in what was obviously a professional waiting room, a high-class one. There was the inevitable desk effecting a compromise between a lady's one for social notes and a practical office desk. The chairs were comfortable and expensively upholstered. Ahead was a swinging door. No one was in sight.

Curtis moved on through the swinging door. Susan crept forward on his heels. Beyond the swinging door, still walking like cats, they encountered the other two men. Evidently the door they had come through from the foyer gave on the same hall in which they all four now stood. On the left was another door. When Curtis cautiously opened it they saw that it looked like a consultation room, empty of human beings. Curtis stepped inside and quickly inspected it. From the desk he picked up a package of small slips of paper held together with a rubber band. He put it into his pocket. A man's voice reached them, coming through the door on the right of the hall. He was saying:

"But if you're sure you weren't followed, then how did *she* get here? How would they know where to send her?" He sounded angry.

So did the woman. "I changed cabs four times," her voice insisted stridently. "A mosquito couldn't have followed me."

"You were a damn fool to telephone me to come here unless you were positive you weren't followed," snarled the man.

"But I *was* positive. I *am* positive."

"What about *her* then?"

Curtis came out into the hall and moved softly nearer the door through which these heated words were coming. He put a hand carefully on the knob. The pungent odor was stronger in the little hall than it had been in the foyer. Susan thought it would be awful if she were to sneeze. She wanted to terribly. But she didn't. She pressed the bridge of her nose until she almost heard it cracking.

Slowly, a quarter of an inch at a time, Curtis was opening the door. Susan forgot about wanting to sneeze. Her eyes were glued on the widening crack. And then she saw Miss Button lying face down on an operating table, her eyes bandaged, her body horribly quiet. She looked dead!

The man in a surgeon's coat and the woman in a nurse's uniform, storming at each other, were paying no attention to the girl on the operating table and they had their backs to the door. Tossed out on a clear part of the table between them were a number of articles comprising the recent contents of Miss Button's handbag. The woman in the nurse's uniform held the empty bag in her hand. Susan recognized it—and, on the table, keys to her salon, a compact she had given Miss Button for Christmas, a book of small swatches of silk. In the surgeon's hand was an envelope. He still hadn't seen the deputation in the hall although Curtis had the door open several inches now. Shaking the envelope in the nurse's face, he demanded in a high, angry tone:

"If you weren't followed, why is it we have a patient come to us with a letter in her handbag addressed care of Susan Yates, Incorporated? Susan Yates is hand in glove with the assistant D. A., isn't she?"

Susan's heart seemed to turn over. She and Button had forgotten about removing marks of identification but, of course, they had not projected their imaginations to the point of anticipating Dr. Prudence and his nurse would go through Miss Button's handbag.

"I tell you," screamed the woman, "I wasn't followed!"

"Shut up," commanded the man. "Somebody will hear you." He gestured toward the door and, in so doing, turned a degree further toward it and suddenly saw his callers.

Then a number of things began to happen very rapidly. Curtis and the other men had the pair at the operating table covered with their guns. The man in the surgeon's coat, amazingly, had a gun in his hand too. He seemed to have produced it from nowhere.

"Drop it!" Susan heard Curtis snap. Then everything became rather much of a dream to her. The detectives were between her and the operating room. She couldn't see anything but their husky shoulders. She heard one of them cry:

"He's going through that door!"

A banging sound like a door slammed shut followed. Then the report of a gun. The wall of shoulders between her and what was happening in the room suddenly broke. She could see one of the men snapping handcuffs on the redheaded woman. Curtis and the other man were pulling at a door behind the operating table, to the right of it in the direction of the front foyer. After that there was a conglomerate sound of scuffling, another revolver report, and four men were suddenly back in the room. Susan blinked. The fourth man was Sergeant Jones who certainly hadn't been in the raiding party. He was holding a gun between Dr. Prudence's shoulder blades.

So they hadn't shot the doctor. He still seemed capable of walking and scowling. Also, he looked like a man doing the fastest thinking of a lifetime. After a moment, while they began snapping handcuffs on him—someone had taken his gun away from him—he began to compose his sensual face, to control its fury, to coat it with a carefully arranged expression.

Curtis was speaking rapidly and with no sympathy whatever. He looked and sounded a man hunter at the end of a trail. Susan suddenly thought how awful it must be to be in the other man's shoes.

"All right, Doctor Prudence," Curtis snapped. "Miss Yates very thoughtfully supplied me with your name before I left my office, so the warrant is correctly made out, everything in order, and I picked up the uncashed money orders from your desk awhile ago. It is also fortunate that Sergeant Jones happened to fancy a stroll through your hideaway next door. We might have had to shoot to kill otherwise. Of course, it wasn't awfully gallant of you to try to walk out on this woman here." He nodded toward the infuriated redhead. "But, then, the first law of man is self-preservation and all that. Still, not gallant."

The handcuffed man opened his sensual lips. "I may ask, I suppose," he requested in a rather high voice that somehow did not reflect the ugly acquisitiveness of his face, "what the meaning of this intrusion is and what charge there can possibly be against me?"

Curtis laughed coldly. "By all means, Lawrence Stratfield, you may ask. It's thoroughly legal to ask. We want you for the murder of Prunella Parton last Monday. We also want you on the charge of blackmail and for practicing medicine without a license."

CHAPTER THIRTY-ONE

LYLE CURTIS STRETCHED out his legs before Miss Yates's fireplace and looked reflectively at the glass in his hand. "I think," he said, "it will be nicer to live in your apartment. You seem to know how to combine comfort with elegance."

Severely, Susan said: "You are the kind of man who teases innocent women and children. I shall scream if you don't go on and clear up the Parton case."

Curtis complained that that would be a nice thing for his reputation. "'Miss Yates screamed when proposed to'—it doesn't sound well," he pointed out.

"'I'll paste you one,' as Sergeant Jones said chummily to that carrot-head yesterday afternoon. *Will* you get on with your revelations? You were telling me the story of how, fifteen years ago, a young and not so nice medical student performed an operation which he shouldn't have, was caught out on an ethical limb and denied a doctor's license, how he disappeared, murdered a recluse—a medico named Doctor Prudence—borrowed his name and license to practice medicine, studied art, for which he had no talent as a painter but plenty as a conversationalist, and in private life began calling himself Lawrence Stratfield. As 'Doctor Prudence,' I understand, Lawrence Stratfield acquired uncountable dollars. His fees were exorbitant, and he made it his practice to blackmail each and every one of his patients. How did he get away with that?"

Curtis said: "They were never able to identify him. Nurse Carrot-head always gave them knockout drops, as she did Miss Button, before he made his appearance in the operating room. Afterward they were sent away in a semi-dazed state, very bleary about the whole business except that they had parted in advance with sizable fees. Afterward they found themselves under the commands of a voice on the telephone—or else! They couldn't prove the voice belonged to 'Doctor Prudence' whom they'd never laid eyes on or heard speak. You can't identify people you've never seen, heard or received handwriting or fingerprints from."

"Just the same," put in Susan, "isn't it amazing he was able to get away with everything for fifteen years?"

Curtis admitted it but pointed out that Stratfield had developed carefulness to an art. "He was careful about everything until Prunella Parton worked her wiles sufficiently to uncover a hint. A hint was as good as an army of occupation to Prunella."

Susan said it must have been a feat, however, even for Miss Parton's seductive talents.

"She went about it as methodically as a scientist with his test tubes. Ultimately she discovered his professional alias. I think she must have contrived a bit of housebreaking at that point, because she got possession of a complete list of his blackmail victims. Armed with that, she selected a victim and induced her to send her to 'Doctor Prudence' as a patient under, of course, an assumed name. In other words, she pulled the same stunt that you and Miss Button planned, except that she showed more foresight."

"How?"

"She took an *anti*anesthetic before she went. Stratfield must have been pretty astonished when he walked into his operating room and found a wide-awake Prunella Parton waiting for him. However, Prunella made one mistake. She was afraid to go without someone knowing—in case he turned really nasty. She took her half sister partially into her confidence. Carol says she didn't tell her who she suspected 'Doctor Prudence' was. All she said was that she intended to pretend to have an operation in order to find out the truth about a certain man and that it would be worth good money to know. She and Carol had an argument about it. One of your career girls overheard that, you remember. Of course, not understanding that Prunella was planning actually to blackmail a blackmailer, Carol thought she was insane to take such a chance out of curiosity. She didn't think Prunella really meant what she had said about 'good money.' When Prunella died Carol wondered if the doctor could have killed her, of course. Unfortunately, she had forgotten his name. She was afraid to come to me with such a farfetched story and nothing more tangible to go on."

Susan asked if Stratfield had broken down and confessed to everything.

"Not that bird." Curtis laughed. "Not at first, at least. He hasn't amassed a fortune in fifteen years of duel and unlawful living without a devil of a lot of shrewdness as well as carefulness. He wouldn't admit a damn thing until late last evening when the dead-letter office came through with Prunella's letter to herself. Up to then, for all we could get out of him, he had been playing charades with Carrot-head in the house with orchid shutters. By the way, I've often wondered why persons suspecting someone is harboring unholy designs upon them don't always write their suspicions down— just in case. It would save us such a lot of effort. It was very thoughtful of Prunella. If she hadn't been interrupted while putting her name and address on the envelope she wouldn't have repeated her last name instead of writing New York City, and Stratfield would have been locked up within twenty-four hours."

"Who interrupted her? Stratfield?"

"No, Oliver Penbroke. He called on her in her bedroom at Swiss Village Lodge. Being something of an amateur psychologist, he had suspected for a long time that Prunella had not had a proper father. He thought that was the reason she hated Carol so much. You see, Penbroke knew that the girl's mother had become Mrs. Peter Sutton. He also knew about the divorce and charges kept quiet. Incidentally, it's to Penbroke's credit that he apparently didn't even toy with the idea of using his knowledge to induce Peter Sutton to lay off trying to steal the Kork-Petulla account from him. He thought Sutton and Barron were playing a ruthless but ethical game. He thought Prunella was playing a ruthless and unethical one. He went to her bedroom to warn her he wasn't going to take her maneuvers lying down."

"And Prunella wrote herself a letter which gave everything away? Aren't you surprised she'd do that?"

"Why not? If nothing happened to her the letter would have come back into her hands, according to her plan of mailing it to herself. If Stratfield made a second and successful effort to murder her, then, she assumed, the police would find the letter in her mailbox. Stratfield would be fittingly punished. She intended to have the letter available indefinitely, not knowing when Stratfield might strike again."

"Did she provide you with a list of Stratfield's blackmail victims?"

"Indirectly. She explained that she had put the list in a lockbox under an assumed name in a Philadelphia bank. The Philadelphia police brought it up to us early this morning. But to go back a bit, it was last August that Prunella got hold of the list and began demanding a thousand dollars a month from Stratfield to keep quiet. About Christmas time, he admits, she began demanding more. Then suddenly she proposed a temporary compromise concerned with Kork-Petulla as an account for Sutton and Barron. Stratfield couldn't figure it out. He suspected that Prunella had expanded her blackmailing to include David Barron. He knew Barron had successfully deprived his wife, Lucretia, of moral evidence she longed for. Lucretia wanted a money settlement from Barron and a divorce. Prunella could provide the evidence, and he thought she proposed to do so if Barron didn't pay her to keep still. Of course, Prunella was playing a safe game there because she knew, no matter what she did to Barron, Peter Sutton would be afraid to fire her. Until last week Barron was still holding out. He didn't think she'd actually offer her own affair with him as evidence to his wife. He was stalling.

"Meantime," continued Curtis, "Stratfield was scouting around trying to nail Prunella with something he could hold over her head without playing the goat himself. He had decided months ago that

Barron was a victim. It was a hunch, he says. She may have let something drop. Anyway, he had written Barron a friendly letter, hoping to induce him to talk. Stratfield, of course, didn't intend to admit that Prunella had any hold on him, the distinguished Lawrence Stratfield. He merely intended to work around to being of assistance if Barron was in a jam, to get evidence that way. Barron never got his letter. Conway saw it and read enough to be convinced that Barron and Stratfield were friends. Then Prunella happened into Barron's office before he reached his desk that morning. She saw the letter, destroyed it and warned Stratfield not to try any more tricks like that. She pointed out that he had a great deal more at stake than she had, a large and lucrative list of victims, an expensive surgeon's office and probably a criminal record in connection with his acquisition of Doctor Prudence's name and license to practice medicine. As a matter of fact, she was right. When Stratfield, who was born to the name of Clement Sochens and who was in the United States under a forged passport, met the real Doctor Prudence the doctor was suffering from amnesia. He was living alone in an isolated part of Arizona. Sochens had just been denied a doctor's license. He intended to acquire one by hook or crook. He traced Doctor Prudence's real identity, stole his papers and murdered him. The police never had the case on their dockets. We traced all of this angle through the doctor's license. We've been in touch by telephone today with the real Doctor Prudence's university and his home town. He and Stratfield did not in the least resemble each other even fifteen years ago. But Stratfield, or Sochens, rather, hadn't run any special risk that way. No one ever saw the fake Doctor Prudence. Besides, New York is a long way from Arizona, and the real Doctor Prudence was a queer egg with only distant relatives and practically no friends. Apparently, no one went to the trouble of investigating what had become of him."

"Did Stratfield attack young Conway in front of the Gracie Mansion?" asked Susan.

Curtis nodded. "He was afraid Conway might put two and two together about the letter he had written Barron when he heard Joan was so excited about it. He thought, moreover, that Conway, with his wild talk and plenty of reasons for disliking Prunella, was a very good proposition as the presumed murderer. He figured nobody would suspect him of attacking Conway practically on his own doorstep and that it would be thought even less likely he would discard a mask openly in the ash bin of his own building. Also, he had the bridge players as his alibi. He knew they'd say he hadn't been absent from the table long enough to have gone down to the street. He had left the table while he was dummy and he had set the stage for a vigorous bridge post-mortem to follow, inevitably, the playing of the hand. He shrewdly guessed they never would believe any perceptible amount of time had passed before his return. He used a short cut, too, out the back of the building. If worst came to worst his trump card was a means he had of making one of his guests go all the way in protecting him."

"I think," said Susan, "I can guess which guest that was! But first tell me when Stratfield admits he planned to dispose of Prunella."

"He didn't struggle particularly to bare his soul about that, not even when he knew his goose was baked on all sides by the arrival of Prunella's letter. But he was rather apologetic that it took him so long to execute his plan. He arranged the week end, naturally, with utmost care. Each guest was invited for a very specific reason. Hazel Manchester, because she's in love with Barron; Joan and young Conway, because they are infatuated and because Prunella had not exactly prospered Conway's career. In any case, Prunella was at least a psychological irritant in all three of their lives. Then he wanted Peter Sutton because Prunella had once bragged to him that the president of Sutton and Barron would never dare dismiss her. He wanted Barron for obvious reasons and Penbroke because he might find murder preferable to losing one hundred and fifty thousand dollars a year in Kork-Petulla commissions. By chance Stratfield had shown the gold golf ball to Barron and one or two others on Saturday evening. He kept it in an open cabinet where anyone might have stolen it. Later, when the explosion failed, he remembered that. It was his intention, by the way, to plant the ball in Penbroke's bag on the train. He mistook Conway's for Penbroke's. Penbroke played golf and seemed to him from the beginning the leading potential suspect. Stratfield estimated everything basically in financial terms, and Penbroke had the most dollars and cents to lose."

Susan asked how Stratfield had managed the explosion. Curtis said that had been relatively easy. Stratfield had used a time fuse. After the explosion, when he went down to the cellar to see if he could get his electric system working again, he stopped by the kitchen to make sure no incriminating evidence remained. Penbroke had followed closely on his heels, claiming to have a decent knowledge of electricity, but Stratfield managed to interest Penbroke in a couple of false clues.

"Knowing how his butler would react, he had merely told him that Miss Parton was an old friend and fastidious, resting assured that Baggs would put her in the guest suite without more specific instructions.

"That the explosion failed to dispose of Prunella was disappointing. During the early hours of the morning Stratfield decided that while another attack could not wisely be made on her under his own roof, she must be killed over the week end. It would be too troublesome to gather together again such an ideal group of potential suspects. He decided then to use the gold golf ball in the toe of a sock as the weapon and one of the rocky curves the train would take in New Hampshire as the moment. The alertly wakeful Pullman porter spoiled his plan to commit the murder during the night. He waited in vain for an opportunity. However, when Barron sent the porter for a split of seltzer in the morning the stage became suddenly set. Conway was still asleep. The ladies were behind closed drawing-room doors. Penbroke, Sutton and Barron were in the smoking compartment and the adjacent lavatory."

Curtis paused, then said: "Imagine, Susan, Stratfield waiting his moment behind the green curtains of his section all night long. He remained fully dressed in order to be ready at a second's notice."

"Dressed to kill." Susan sighed.

"Exactly. And after committing his murder he dressed the corpse fantastically as pure hokum. First, when the moment came, he darted from his section and made Prunella's drawing room in a second or so. She was asleep, he tells me. Meantime, Barron had gone back into the smoking compartment, leaving the aisle free of traffic. Stratfield suspected that Barron was the boy he'd have to keep his eye on. Barron was tight and having the jitters. He had heard him moving about in his section during the night. He suspected Barron had been hitting the bottle. But, as a result, he believed the vice-president of Sutton and Barron would be primarily concentrated on his hang-over and ways and means of thawing out his nervous system. This proved to be the case."

Again Curtis paused. For a long moment he studied Susan's attentive expression. "You were right, my girl," he said, "about Prunella sleeping in her ski underwear. The shock of the explosion and the conviction that Stratfield might try a second time to kill her had evidently unnerved her. Small wonder. She wouldn't, I assume, have written herself a letter otherwise. It's more than possible she had a chill during the night. In any case, Stratfield, or Sochens, admits she was sleeping in her underwear. She must have missed the absence from her luggage of certain items she had packed. That had probably not added to her serenity."

"Had Stratfield hidden the things the cook found?"

"Yes. He was prowling about, laying plans, and saw Penbroke go into Prunella's room. Then he saw Mrs. Bumpet, the cook, go in. He assumed Mrs. Bumpet must have seen Penbroke, so when Prunella and the cook came out and went down to the kitchen together he waited until Penbroke also emerged, then he went in and tried to make it look as if Penbroke had gone through Prunella's luggage. He mixed up the content of all her five bags and took some of her ski clothes to the bedroom she had had the night before. He hid them where Mrs. Bumpet found them the next morning. He was certain his cook would give evidence that Penbroke had done it. For what reason didn't matter. It would look queer and add materially, he thought, to a case against the head of Penbroke and Company."

Susan said: "Stratfield must have worked pretty fast in Prunella's drawing room."

"He did. He'd had all night to plan every step. He didn't waste a motion. First, while she slept, he whanged her on the head with the gold golf ball in a sock. Then he dragged her off the berth and laid her on the floor, being very careful to have her head rest exactly on the point of the concussion. As a trained, if unlicensed, surgeon he knew all about that. And, as a matter of fact, one possibility he counted on was another idea you had: that it might be decided she had fallen during the night, suffered concussion, lain in a coma and died later. He added the red evening gown, as I said, for purposes of confusion and general hokum.

"All in all, the whole job, including returning to his own section and planting the golf ball in Conway's suitcase en route, took him just shy of three minutes. He dumped the ski pants, sweater and jacket in his bag, locked it and emerged from behind his curtain fully dressed and making for the smoking compartment just as the porter returned. He tells me he had backed out of Prunella's drawing room. If anybody had appeared he intended to pretend to be walking forward to the smoking compartment then."

Curtis looked at Susan. "I wonder what made you think of that delayed-coma angle?"

"Pure matter of association," responded Miss Yates, looking arch.

"Association of ideas?"

"No. Association with an assistant district attorney. One begins to doubt everybody and everything, palling around with you. I'm afraid I couldn't think of making the experience a daily one."

"That," said Mr. Curtis, "is a matter we shall go into more thoroughly in a few minutes. You asked for details of the Parton case and you are going to get them."

Susan smiled enigmatically. "It's a pleasure. You're a born raconteur. From that standpoint, it wouldn't be bad seeing you every day."

"Before we go any further," remarked Curtis, ignoring this digression, "I have another piece of credit to bestow: your identification of Lawrence Stratfield's voice in that Wise Owl joint. It saved a lot of time and trouble. The dead-letter-office people could have taken days more with their job. Of course, I don't say I, in the least, agree with your method of proving it was Stratfield's voice—I mean, Miss Button and her mole, et cetera. It was smart reasoning, but you are both lucky she got nothing more than a shot in the arm. By the way, how did you find out who Joan Sutton's psychoanalyst was?"

"I asked Joan when she came to my apartment for a drink."

"Then what did you do?"

"I drove around and took a look at the office setup. I saw it was a private house shared by two doctors. I decided the other doctor, a Doctor Prudence, was the one I had heard talking, the one whose name and face I couldn't place. I was sure he had a thoroughly unhealthy reason for fearing to be seen by Joan. They must have come near to encountering each other. Otherwise, why should he have been so upset?"

Curtis explained that on Tuesday afternoon Stratfield had seen Joan going into the psychoanalyst's just as he was entering the house next door. He had no desire to be seen anywhere in the immediate neighborhood of "Dr. Prudence's" by anyone connected with the Parton case. The carrot-headed nurse, of course, lived in an apartment on the second floor of the next-door house, but Stratfield was too upset by finding Joan practically on his premises even to remain in the apartment to talk things over. He dragged the nurse out to the Wise Owl. The queer acoustic quality of the partition defeated his caution, of course.

"They had," he went on, "no idea of that. They only got excited about you when they saw you peering out of a taxi window at them on Central Park West. Then they decided it would be a good idea to send you on a wild-goose chase to DeVise Street and to involve Barron in the matter. Stratfield was disappointed we hadn't by then picked on either Penbroke or Conway as the murderer. The carrot-head telephoned you, of course, and Barron. Also, earlier in the afternoon she had telephoned Barron, pretending to be Hazel Manchester and asking him to come and see her late that afternoon at *Inter-Allied News*."

"What on earth was the reason for that?"

"Before I go into that I would like to point out that we have policewomen for the kind of job you let Miss Button do."

Susan said: "We both thought of that but agreed that no police-woman would look sufficiently frivolous to be worrying about a mole on her shoulder."

"Well," admitted Curtis, "Miss Button's presence at the time of the raid brought things to a rapid head. It was a nice little conversation we overheard, including the fact that Miss Susan Yates is known to be hand in glove with the district attorney's office. Could you change that, please, to hand and heart?" Curtis didn't wait for a reply. "Without Button's professional visit Stratfield might, when we raided the place, have been able to pose as a patient waiting to see the doctor. He certainly wouldn't have been caught in his surgeon's getup going through a lady's handbag. And his handwriting wasn't on the money orders. It was the carrot-head's. All we could have proved at that point was that Stratfield was on Doctor Prudence's premises and that Doctor Prudence's nurse had been paying blackmail to a person named Eloise Abelard. There's no law against *paying* blackmail. I hadn't seen the ski clothes then and their thorny decorations."

"Their what? You haven't told me anything about finding the ski clothes!"

Curtis grinned. "Never mind," he promised irritatingly, "I'm coming to that."

"Well, if you must imitate your Lieutenant Burk with delayed suspense, you could at least tell me who the carrot-head really is."

"The nurse Stratfield operated on fifteen years ago on the eve of hoping for a doctor's license. She's played along with him all these years for the sake of the spoils. We're trying to find out if they were ever married. But it doesn't really matter."

Curtis had already told Susan about Stratfield's having spotted their fake "Lost and Found" ad about the money orders and the nurse's visit to the Elmer Gans farm. He had also explained they had held out some of the money orders in case she should destroy those she took away with her. They spoke of this again for a moment. Then Susan said the only important brain storm she considered she had had in the Parton case was the suggestion to Miss Button to say at Dr. Prudence's that a Mrs. Petulla had sent her.

"Was that just a brain storm?" Curtis wanted to know.

"Subconsciously, I suppose, it was a result of wondering about Stratfield, a dilettante painter, having so much influence over Kork-Petulla's advertising account. That business sounded farfetched to me from the beginning. I wonder if one of the Kork-Petulla ladies wasn't involved?"

Curtis grimaced. "You are positively clairvoyant. In the future I shall refer to you as my Delphic friend. That's exactly what Stratfield's hold on the situation was. The chief stockholder of Kork-Petulla is at present a Mrs. Francine Petulla, née Kork, who was unfortunate enough to get herself in trouble last spring. Stratfield recommended 'Doctor Prudence.' Mrs. Petulla went to him and afterward periodically received telephoned demands of one sort or another. Not having been permitted to see 'Doctor Prudence,' she had no vaguest suspicion, naturally, that he and Stratfield were one and the same person, especially as it happens Stratfield was the father of her child. Can you tie that one for crooked dealings in a subcellar? Moreover, Stratfield went on being her very good friend, apparently as fearful as she of their misfortune leaking out. He pretended a terrific concern about her reputation and as each blackmail demand came along he advised Mrs. Petulla to accede to whatever the blackmailer asked. As you may guess, I had a rather extraordinary conversation with Mrs. Petulla last evening. She was so darned delighted that her days of persecution were over that she opened up like a night-blooming cereus." Curtis' expression grew momentarily grave. "Of course—" he began.

Susan leaned forward and put a warm hand on one of his. "Calm your fears, my friend. You've as good as not told me any of that. I may have a lot of gabby acquaintances, but to date I haven't found it a contagious habit."

Curtis nodded with considerable emphasis. "It never occurred to me you'd talk, my dear, unless you thought the lady's full confession was a matter of official record. It isn't. I felt damn sorry for her, as a matter of fact."

"I don't wonder," agreed Susan emphatically. "What a fiendish hell she must have been living in. Stratfield's nothing short of a beast."

"Not a very pleasant member of society."

Presently Susan said that there were still several points she didn't have straight. For one, why had Stratfield been conniving to get the Kork-Petulla business away from Oliver Penbroke's agency?

"You remember I said awhile ago that Prunella increased her demands on Stratfield around Christmas and that she then proposed a compromise involving Kork-Petulla?"

"Yes. It sounded as if she wanted to feather her nest at the agency by bringing in a big account."

"I don't think she precisely wanted to feather her nest. She had Sutton lined up permanently. I think she wanted to command a vice-presidency, a sufficiently distinguished position for people to think twice before they suspected her of any chicanery. But, more than that even, she hated her half sister, Carol, because Carol's legitimate father had legalized her status by giving her the name Parton. Moreover, Prunella hadn't been able to put over a wealthy marriage for herself. She was essentially not the sort of girl men want to marry. Penbroke thinks she couldn't stand it to see Carol engaged to a wealthy, successful man. She wanted to ruin Penbroke. She knew that Mrs. Petulla was on Stratfield's blackmail list. Her compromise proposition was that he instruct Mrs. Petulla to change agencies. Of course, Stratfield didn't mind doing that because it let him out of paying the piper with any more hard cash."

"In that case, why bother to murder her?"

"Because in January, after he had got the Kork-Petulla proposition going, she said a thousand a month cash wasn't enough, that she'd have to have two thousand in the future."

"Just a nice lovable girl, the type you adore having in for a cozy evening."

"But a girl who didn't know how far not to stick her neck out."

Susan said it was a wonder Prunella hadn't gone after Joan Sutton's scalp in a tangible way. Joan, as well as Carol, had had a legal father. Why stop at just hating Carol?

Curtis said he suspected Prunella had been about ready to start on Miss Sutton. Being an obstacle in the path of Joan's infatuation for young Conway was probably only a beginning. "For the moment she had larger fish to fry however."

Innocently Miss Yates inquired if he meant a flaming sardine?

"Don't goad me," instructed Mr. Curtis.

"Well," asked Susan, "speaking of crawling things, have you found out why Peter Sutton was so upset when you asked him if he'd ever known Prunella's father?"

Curtis' expression sobered once more. He explained that he had had a long talk with Peter Sutton the evening before. He had probably not been told the whole story, but Sutton seemed to feel a peculiar responsibility for not having saved Prunella's father from perishing in a snow-bank in the Bavarian Alps thirty years ago. Evidently there had been no scandal or anything of the sort about it, but it still seemed to be preying on Sutton's mind. He had first met his future wife at that time. She had been engaged to the young man who had perished and was the mother of his child, which, of course, Sutton had not then known. Years later, after Sutton had met Mary again and married her, she confessed to being the unmarried mother of Prunella. The baby had been born in New York a few months after the Bavarian tragedy.

"I believe," Curtis went on, "Sutton divorced her because he feared a scandal connected with his name might leak out. And I believe that on one side of his conscience he has been regretting his treatment of her ever since. She died presumably of a broken heart; may have been suicide. Last Monday he was carrying around pictures of her in his luggage. Undoubtedly we'll never know the real story about all that, but I'm ready to confess I felt sorry for a number of people last evening. Only none of them were named Stratfield."

"I should think not. The beast! But what a lot of private anguishes you've had to bring to light, Lyle."

They were both thoughtful for a few moments, staring into the fire. Then Susan asked: "What about the ski clothes? You promised to tell me what became of them."

"A woman in the service department of Ronsell and Bonner telephoned me just before you did yesterday afternoon. She had been busy thinking about a curious collection of merchandise they had received from Miss Manchester. It seems she's an ardent newspaper reader. She had absorbed all the details of the Parton case and had noted that among those present on the New Hampshire Pullman was Miss Hazel Manchester. Miss Hazel Manchester had returned to Ronsell and Bonner a green ski suit. Wrong size. She had also sent in the same box an ink-splattered white ski suit, instructing them by phone to duplicate it as to quality, but in bright red, and to throw the old one away. The Ronsell and Bonner woman was a nosy parker with an active imagination. She thought Miss Manchester had pulled the neatest trick of the week, that she'd covered up blood with ink. I was about to send two sergeants up for Miss Manchester when you telephoned me what your Miss Button was up to. I had decided that someway or other Miss Manchester must be the carrot-head whom Sergeant Jones had been tailing. It didn't seem to fit, but I felt it had to."

Curtis stared ruefully at his highball glass.

"I suppose," remarked Miss Yates, "to make you go on I shall have to bribe you with another drink."

"It would be only common decency."

Susan rose, rang for Lillian and returned to the fire. "Before I ask you to go on and tell me how Stratfield planted the ski clothes I might as well admit that I feel unwashed and all kinds of things," she said. "These aren't very nice people we've been associating with, Lyle. That is, some of them aren't."

"Miss Manchester's rather nice."

"Very handsome."

"And Carol and Penbroke are merely heartily in love."

"And I suppose Conway and Joan are all right. What's been the matter with Joan anyway? Did she think her father was guilty of murdering Prunella?"

Curtis said his guess was she had thought Conway was. She had begun acting so queerly and talking so wildly, trying to cover up for him, that she had got her father beside himself with worry. He was afraid Prunella had gone to Joan with the story about her mother and that Joan in a youthfully headstrong temper had killed her. That was what brought him to the decision of having her psychoanalyzed.

"Which," Susan pointed out, "was pretty lucky all around. I wouldn't have been an atom of service to you if he hadn't. You've thought of that, of course. If Peter Sutton hadn't decided to send Joan to an analyst, and to one particular analyst, Stratfield wouldn't have been whispering against a *bistro* partition. If he hadn't I wouldn't have got my memory stirred by some quality in his voice. I wouldn't have wondered whom, going to what psychoanalyst's office, the owner of the voice was so anxious to avoid. Of course, the peculiar details of all that would never happen in books where, contrary to life, the long arm of circumstance is taboo."

Curtis disagreed. It was perfectly logical, he said, for Peter Sutton to have decided Joan must be psychoanalyzed, and if Susan meant it was stretching the arm of circumstance too long for Sutton to have chosen the particular doctor he had she was mistaken about that.

"Why?"

"Because it wasn't such a long arm. That particular analyst gets the biggest fees in New York, probably twice as much as any of the competition. Now, Peter Sutton had the most expensive ski instructors as a youth. He goes to New York's most costly barber. He's made it a lifelong habit to judge everything by its value in dollars and cents. They tell me he preaches at the agency that not even humor should ever be used for its own sweet sake. Naturally, he would send Joan to the man he did. And I dare say Stratfield chose the office address he did because of the impeccable reputation of his downstairs neighbor who was such a good man he had never felt it necessary to pay Park Avenue rents. Of course, Stratfield wouldn't have been as safe on Park Avenue in a big apartment building. Besides, when you have been the wife of an assistant district attorney for a while, my girl, you will know that all cases are won with a break or two, generally in reverse order on the part of the criminal."

Lillian arrived at this moment and provided Miss Yates and her guest with fresh highballs. They sipped for a few moments in silence, then Curtis said he also believed enough in Fate with a capital "F" to be convinced that if Peter Sutton hadn't decided to have his daughter psychoanalyzed and hadn't sent her to a man sharing "Dr. Prudence's" house and "Dr. Prudence" had not talked against a particularly acoustical partition they would, if they were due a break, have got it from some other quarter. The Swiss Village postmaster and his interest in the daily mail passing through his office had, as a matter of fact, been a beautiful piece of luck.

"Speaking of breaks," asked Susan, "does Stratfield admit having anything to do with that runaway truck which nearly disposed of me in front of your office?"

"No. When his moment of frankness was finally reached I asked him. I don't believe he really knew anything about it. We've got to put that down to an odd-lot Manhattan episode with no planned criminal underpinnings. Just the same, I'd like to lay my hands on the driver of that truck!" Curtis looked so fierce that Susan practically blushed.

"Why," exclaimed Susan, "did Carrot-head lure David Barron to call on Miss Manchester at *Inter-Allied News?*"

"So we would think he planted the ski clothes."

"How could he? They weren't in his luggage. He had no other way of bringing them from the train, did he?"

"No, but Prudence and Carrot, Incorporated, didn't know we knew that. They also hoped we would believe Barron attempted to lure you to DeVise Street in order, as Carrot-head elegantly puts it, to rub you out."

Susan shuddered.

Curtis finished his highball and said: "If, instead of making up a cock-and-bull story about an emerald pin, Hazel Manchester had come to me with the facts as soon as she found herself in possession of Prunella's lost skiing garments we might have closed the case on Monday."

"On Monday!"

"Yes. We knew what Miss Manchester didn't know we knew—that she hadn't brought the stolen ski clothes from the train. If they were later in her office only one person could have put them there. That person was the only suspect who had access both to her office and to a receptacle in which to transport the clothes before his luggage was inspected. Wherever they went after breakfast, Joan Sutton and young Conway didn't go to Hazel Manchester's office. I made sure of that. And Oliver Penbroke didn't go there. Lawrence Stratfield did. There were no ski clothes in his luggage when inspected. His taxi driver said they talked back and forth. The presumption was that Stratfield had had no opportunity to open his luggage and pitch a pair of ski pants, a sweater and a jacket out onto Lexington Avenue."

"I'm dumb, obviously," complained Susan, "and I still don't see how he did it."

"Would it clarify matters any for you to know that there were rose thorns embedded in the spotted ink garments sent by Miss Manchester to Ronsell and Bonner?"

"Rose thorns!" exclaimed Miss Yates.

"Yes. Stratfield didn't pitch away ski clothes. He pitched away roses. There's also a little matter of time involved. It was from Grand Central to the florist's on Lexington Avenue that Stratfield engaged his cab driver in conversation about painting a baseball team in action, a conversation the fellow wouldn't be apt to forget. From the florist's to *Inter-Allied News*, we actually had no record of repartee between Stratfield and the taximan. That was so clear all along that I didn't see the forest for the trees. Stratfield bought four dozen roses but left on Miss Manchester's desk only three dozen. He had been particular about having the flowers packed. When he got in the cab with them he began scattering a dozen of them, one at a time, along Lexington Avenue. We didn't advertise for someone who had seen a dozen roses under the wheels of traffic. If we had, we wouldn't have got an answer. Such things aren't noticed in a city like New York."

"You actually mean he put the ski clothes in the box of roses?"

"You see, you were right in being so interested in their intrinsic bulk."

Susan chuckled. "I kept trying to figure out if someone could have worn them off the train under his or her own clothes. I must say it never occurred to me that Stratfield was running around planting them on poor Miss Manchester out of a box of roses."

"And not unnaturally scaring her to death when she found them. She's a smart girl and has read a lot of detective stories but she lost her head."

Thoughtfully Susan said she still didn't see why Stratfield had gone to so much trouble stealing the ski clothes, and Curtis explained that he had put precisely that question to him. The answer had been that Stratfield had been afraid the time of Prunella's death might end by tripping him someway. He had been determined to pile up as much evidence as possible against as many people as possible, to plant a maze of conflicting trails.

"Well, he succeeded in that," admitted Susan. "Did he lie about the second telephone call Carol Parton was supposed to have made from North Conway to Swiss Village?"

"Yes, he knew she called Penbroke up after she had talked to him, declining his invitation for the remainder of the week end. He was delighted with an opportunity to make her out a liar. So many people knew she and Prunella didn't get along. He was disappointed not to have her on the scene at the time of the murder, and delighted when it turned out she had been on the train, after all."

Susan asked if Curtis thought Stratfield had believed he had committed the perfect crime.

"When his nurse telephoned him yesterday afternoon that everything had been on the up-and-up at the Gans farmhouse, that the farmer merely wanted more of a reward and that she was certain she hadn't been followed I think he breathed his first peaceful breath since Monday morning. He had a lot at stake and he'd taken some pretty big chances."

"Closing Prunella's eyes wasn't very smart for a doctor. In doing that he killed his best bet of making it look like a suicide."

"Oh, but Stratfield did not add that little touch. You remember, in my office, Carol Parton became upset chiefly when I suggested she had gone into the drawing room and done various things—including removing the ski clothes? Well, she did go in. First she stood just inside the door, overcome with shock. Prunella's dead eyes seemed to be looking at her accusingly, as they always had. In sheer panic she went over and closed them before she ran away."

Sipping her highball, Susan bemoaned the fact that she had been so slow putting a name to the voice she had overheard at the Wise Owl. "After all, none of your other suspects talked in any essentially unusual way. Stratfield had a peculiarly high-pitched voice for a man. It didn't match his top-sergeant appearance."

Curtis said there was no reason for her to have connected a surgeon's conversation with a dilettante painter and *bon vivant*. "Even if Stratfield does have surgeon's hands," he added.

Susan laughed. "But I have such a lot of practice listening to disgruntled clients through the fitting-room walls. I should be an expert eavesdropper. By the way, what happens to Sergeant Jones for having tailed the carrot-head so well?"

"Sergeant Jones was recommended to a lieutenancy this morning for having led us to the doctor's office in more ways than one. But, as for me, I'd rather take my cardiac condition to a minister— that is, if you are satisfied, my dear Miss Yates, that the Parton case is finished."

COACHWHIP PUBLICATIONS

COACHWHIPBOOKS.COM

MURDER
IN STYLE

Emma Lou Fetta

ISBN 978-1-61646-232-1

COACHWHIP PUBLICATIONS

NOW AVAILABLE

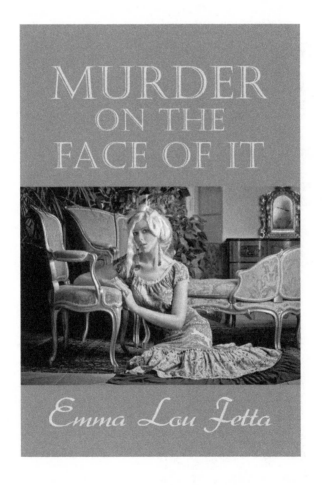

MURDER
ON THE
FACE OF IT

Emma Lou Fetta

ISBN 978-1-61646-233-8

COACHWHIP PUBLICATIONS

COACHWHIPBOOKS.COM

MURDER OF
THE HONEST BROKER

WILLOUGHBY SHARP

ISBN 978-1-61646-211-6

COACHWHIP PUBLICATIONS

NOW AVAILABLE

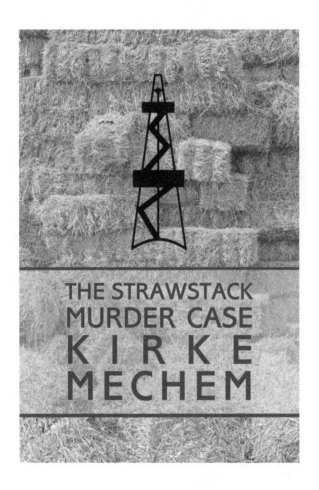

THE STRAWSTACK
MURDER CASE
KIRKE
MECHEM

ISBN 978-1-61646-179-9

COACHWHIP PUBLICATIONS

COACHWHIPBOOKS.COM

THERE IS
NO RETURN
THE ADELAIDE ADAMS MYSTERIES
ANITA BLACKMON

ISBN 978-1-61646-223-9

COACHWHIP PUBLICATIONS

NOW AVAILABLE

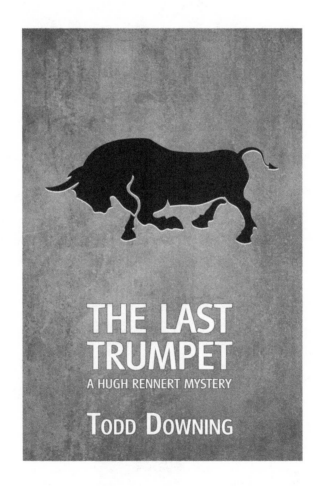

THE LAST
TRUMPET
A HUGH RENNERT MYSTERY

TODD DOWNING

ISBN 978-1-61646-152-2

CPSIA information can be obtained
at www.ICGtesting.com
Printed in the USA
LVHW051923230423
745122LV00003B/483